THE BILLIONAIRE OF CORAL BAY

BY
NIKKI LOGAN

MILLS
BOO

First Published in Great Britain 2017
By Mills & Boon, an imprint of HarperCollins*Publishers*
1 London Bridge Street, London, SE1 9GF

© 2017 Nikki Logan

ISBN: 978-0-263-92273-8

23-0217

Romantic Getaways

Escape to Paradise!

This Valentine's Day escape to four of
the world's most romantic destinations
with these sparkling books from
Mills & Boon Romance!

From the awe-inspiring desert to
vibrant Barcelona, and from the stunning
coral reefs of Australia to heart-stoppingly
romantic Venice—get swept away
by these wonderful romances!

The Sheikh's Convenient Princess
by Liz Fielding

The Unforgettable Spanish Tycoon
by Christy McKellen

The Billionaire of Coral Bay
by Nikki Logan

Her First-Date Honeymoon
by Katrina Cudmore

Nikki Logan lives on the edge of a string of wetlands in Western Australia with her partner and a menagerie of animals. She writes captivating nature-based stories full of romance in descriptive natural environments. She believes the danger and richness of wild places perfectly mirrors the passion and risk of falling in love. Nikki loves to hear from readers via www.nikkilogan.com.au or through social media. Find her on Twitter, @ReadNikkiLogan, and Facebook, NikkiLoganAuthor.

For Pete
Who came when I needed him most.

CHAPTER ONE

THE LUXURY CATAMARAN had first appeared two days ago, bobbing in the sea off Nancy's Point.

Lurking.

Except Mila Nakano couldn't, in all fairness, call it lurking since it stood out like a flashing white beacon against the otherwise empty blue expanse of ocean. Whatever its crew were doing out there, they weren't trying to be secretive about it, which probably meant they had permission to be moored on the outer fringes of the reef. And a vessel with all the appropriate authorisation was no business of a Wildlife Officer with somewhere else to be.

Vessels came and went daily on the edge of the Marine Park off Coral Bay—mostly research boats, often charters and occasionally private yachts there to enjoy the World Heritage reefs. This one had 'private' written all over it. If she had the kind of money that bought luxury catamarans she'd probably spend it visiting places of wonder too.

Mila peeled her wetsuit down to its waist and let her eyes flutter shut as the coastal air against her sweat-damp skin tinkled like tiny, bouncing ball bearings. Most days, she liked to snorkel in just a bikini to revel in the symphony of water against her bare flesh. Some days, though, she just needed to get things done and a wetsuit was as good as noise-cancelling headphones to someone with synaesthesia—or 'superpower' as her brothers had always referred to her cross-sensed condition—because she couldn't *hear* the physical sensation of swimming over the reef when it was muted by thick neoprene. Not that her condition was conveniently limited to just the single jumbled sensation; no, that would be too pedestrian for Mila Nakano. She *felt* colours. She *tasted* emotion. And she attributed random personality traits to things. It might make no sense to anyone else but it made total sense to her.

Of course it did; she'd been born that way.

But today she could do without the distraction. Her tour-for-one was due any minute and she still needed to cross the rest of the bay and clamber up to Nancy's Point to meet him, because she'd drifted further than she meant while snorkelling the reef. A tour-for-one was the perfect number. *One* made it possible for her to do her job without ending up with a thumping headache—complete with harmonic foghorns. With larger groups, she couldn't control how shouty their body spray was, what mood the colours they wore would leave her in, or how exhausting they were just to be around. They would have a fantastic time out on the reef, but the cost to her was sometimes too great. It could take her three days to rebalance after a big group.

But one… That was doable.

Her *one* was a Mr Richard Grundy. Up from Perth, the solitary, sprawling metropolis on Australia's west coast, tucked away in the bottom corner of the state, two days' drive—or a two-hour jet flight—from here. From *anything*, some visitors thought because they couldn't see what was right in front of them. The vast expanses of outback scrub you had to pass through to get here.

The nothing that was always full of something.

Grundy was a businessman, probably, since *ones* tended to arrive in suits with grand plans for the reef and what they could make it into. Anything from clusters of glamping facilities to elite floating casinos. Luxury theme parks. They never got off the ground, of course; between the public protests, the strict land use conditions and the flat-out *no* that the local leaseholder gave on development access through their property, her tour-for-one usually ended up being a tour-*of*-one. She never saw them, their business suit or their fancy development ideas again.

Which was fine; she was happy to play her part in keeping everything around here exactly as it was.

Mila shed the rest of her wetsuit unselfconsciously, stretched to the heavens for a moment as the ball bearings tinkled around her bikini-clad skin and slipped into the khaki shorts and shirt that identified her as official staff of the World Heritage Area. The backpack sitting on the sand bulged first with the folded wetsuit and then with bundled snorkelling gear, and she pulled her dripping hair back into a ponytail. She dropped the backpack into her work-supplied four-wheel drive then jogged past it and up towards the point overlooking the long, brilliant bay.

She didn't rush. *Ones* were almost always late; they underestimated the time it took to drive up from the city or down from the nearest airport, or they let some smartphone app decide how long it would take them when a bit of software could have no idea how much further a kilometre was in Western Australia's north. Besides, she'd parked on the only road into the meeting point and so her *one* would have had to drive past her to get to Nancy's Point. So far, hers was the only vehicle as far as the eye could see.

If you didn't count the bobbing catamaran beyond the reef.

Strong legs pushed her up over the lip of the massive limestone spur named after Nancy Dawson—the matriarch of the family that had grazed livestock on these lands for generations. Coral Bay's first family.

'Long way to come for a strip-show,' a deep voice rumbled as she straightened.

Mila stumbled to a halt, her stomach sinking on a defensive whiff of old shoe that was more back-of-her-throat *taste* than nose-scrunching *smell*. The man standing there was younger than his name suggested and he wasn't in a suit, like most *ones*, but he wore cargo pants and a faded red T-shirt as if they were one. Something about the way he moved towards her... He still screamed 'corporate' even without a tie.

Richard Grundy.

She spun around, hunting for the vehicle that she'd inexplicably missed. Nothing. It only confounded her more. The muted red of his T-shirt was pumping off all kinds of favourite drunk uncle kind of associations, but she fought the instinctive softening that brought. Nothing about his sarcastic greeting deserved congeniality. Besides, this man was anything but uncle-esque. His dark blond hair was windblown but well-cut and his eyes, as he slid his impenetrable sunglasses up onto his head to reveal them, were a rich blue. Rather like the lagoon behind him, in fact.

That got him a reluctant bonus point.

'You were early,' she puffed.

'I was on time,' he said again, apparently amused at her discomfort. 'And I was dropped off. Just in time for the show.'

She retracted that bonus point. This was *her* bay, not his. If she wanted to swim in it before her shift started, what business was it of his?

'I could have greeted you in my wetsuit,' she muttered, 'but I figured my uniform would be more appropriate.'

'You're the guide, I assume?' he said, approaching with an out-thrust hand.

'I'm *a* guide,' she said, still bristling, then extended hers on a deep breath. Taking someone's hand was never straightforward; she never knew quite what she'd get out of it. 'Mila Nakano. Parks Department.'

'Richard Grundy,' he replied, marching straight into her grasp with no further greeting. Or interest. 'What's the plan for today?'

The muscles around her belly button twittered at his warm grip on her water-cool fingers and her ears filled with the gentle brush of a harp. That was new; she usually got anything from a solo trumpet to a whole brass section when she touched people, especially strangers.

A harp thrum was incongruously pleasant.

'Today?' she parroted, her synapses temporarily disconnected.

'Our tour.' His lagoon-coloured eyes narrowed in on hers. '*Are* you my guide?'

She quickly recovered. 'Yes, I am. But no one gave me any information on the purpose of your visit—' except to impress upon her his VIP status '—so we'll be playing it a bit by ear today. It would help me to know what you're here for,' she went on. 'Or what things interest you.'

'It all interests me,' he said, glancing away. 'I'd like to get a better appreciation for the...ecological value of the area.'

Uh-huh. Didn't they all...? Then they went back to the city to work on ways to exploit it.

'Is your interest commercial?'

The twin lagoons narrowed. 'Why so much interest in my interest?'

His censure made her flush. 'I'm just wondering what

filter to put on the tour. Are you a journalist? A scientist? You don't seem like a tourist. So that only leaves Corporate.'

He glanced out at the horizon again, taking some of the intensity from their conversation. 'Let's just say I have a keen interest in the land. And the fringing reef.'

That wasn't much to go on. But those ramrod shoulders told her it was all she was going to get.

'Well, then, I guess we should start at the southernmost tip of the Marine Park,' she said, 'and work our way north. Can you swim?'

One of his eyebrows lifted. Just the one, as if her question wasn't worth the effort of a second. 'Captain of the swim team.'

Of course he had been.

Ordinarily she would have pushed her sunglasses up onto her head too, to meet a client's gaze, to start the arduous climb from *stranger* to *acquaintance*. But there was a sardonic heat coming off Richard Grundy's otherwise cool eyes and it shimmered such a curious tone—like five sounds all at once, harmonising with each other, being five different things at once. It wiggled in under her synaesthesia and tingled there, but she wasn't about to expose herself too fully to his music until she had a better handle on the man. And so her own sunglasses stayed put.

'If you want to hear the reef you'll need to get out onto it.'

'Hear it?' The eyebrow lift was back. 'Is it particularly noisy?'

She smiled. She'd yet to meet anyone else who could perceive the coral's voice but she had to assume that however normal people experienced it, it was as rich and beautiful as the way she did.

'You'll understand when you get there. Your vehicle or mine?'

But he didn't laugh—he didn't even smile—and her flimsy joke fell as flat as she inexplicably felt robbed of the opportunity to see his lips crack the straight line they'd maintained since she got up here.

'Yours, I think,' he said.

'Let's go, then.' She fell into professional mode, making up for a lot of lost time. 'I'll tell you about Nancy's Point as we walk. It's named for Nancy Dawson...'

Rich was pretty sure he knew all there was to know about Nancy Dawson—after all, stories of his great-grandmother had been part of his upbringing. But the tales as they were told to him didn't focus on Nancy's great love for the land and visionary sustainability measures, as the guide's did, they were designed to showcase her endurance and fortitude against adversity. *Those* were the values his father had wanted to foster in his son and heir. The land—except for the profit it might make for WestCorp—was secondary. Barely even that.

But there was no way to head off the lithe young woman's spiel without confessing who his family was. And he wasn't about to discuss his private business with a stranger on two minutes' acquaintance.

'For one hundred and fifty years the Dawsons have been the leaseholders of all the land as far as you can see to the horizon,' she said, turning to put the ocean behind her and looking east. 'You could drive two hours inland and still be on Wardoo Station.'

'Big,' he grunted. Because anyone else would say that. Truth was, he knew exactly how big Wardoo was—to the square kilometre—and he knew how much each of those ten thousand square kilometres yielded. And how much each one cost to operate.

That was kind of his thing.

Rich cast his eyes out to the reef break. Mila apparently knew enough history to speak about his family, but not enough to recognise his surname for what it was. Great-Grandma Dawson had married Wardoo's leading hand, Jack Grundy, but kept the family name since it was such an established and respected name in the region. The world might have known Jack and Nancy's offspring as Dawsons, but the law knew them as Grundys.

'Nancy's descendants still run it today. Well, their minions do…'

That drew his gaze back. 'Minions?'

'The family is based in the city now. We don't see them.'

Wow. There was a whole world of judgement in that simple sentence.

'Running a business remotely is pretty standard procedure these days,' he pointed out.

In his world everything was run at a distance. In a state this big it was both an operational necessity and a survival imperative. If you got attached to any business—or any of the people in it—you couldn't do what he sometimes had to do. Restructure them. Sell them. Close them.

She surveyed all around them and murmured, 'If this was my land I would never ever leave it.'

It was tempting to take offence at her casual judgement of his family—was this how she spoke of the Dawsons to any passing stranger?—but he'd managed too many teams and too many board meetings with voices far more objectionable than hers to let himself be that reactive. Besides, given that his 'family' consisted of exactly one—if you didn't count a bunch of headstones and some distant cousins in Europe—he really had little cause for complaint.

'You were born here?' he asked instead.

'And raised.'

'How long have your family lived in the area?'

'All my life—'

That had to be…what…? All of two decades?

'And thirty thousand years before that.'

He adjusted his assessment of her killer tan. That bronze-brown hue wasn't only about working outdoors. 'You're Bayungu?'

She shot him a look and he realised that he risked outing himself with his too familiar knowledge of Coral Bay's first people. That could reasonably lead to questions about why he'd taken the time to educate himself about the traditional uses of this area. Same reason he was here finding out about the environmental aspects of the region.

He wanted to know exactly what he was up against. Where the speed humps were going to arise.

'My mother's family,' she corrected softly.

Either she didn't understand how genetics worked or Mila didn't identify as indigenous despite her roots.

'But not only Bayungu? Nakano, I think you said?'

'My grandfather was Japanese. On Dad's side.'

He remembered reading that in the feasibility study on this whole coast: how it was a cultural melting pot thanks to the exploding pearling trade.

'That explains the bone structure,' he said, tracing his gaze across her face.

She flushed and seemed to say the first thing that came to her. 'His wife's family was from Dublin, just to complicate things.'

Curious that she saw her diversity as a *complication*. In business, it was a strength. Pretty much the first thing he'd done following his father's death was broaden WestCorp's portfolio base so that their eggs were spread across more baskets. Thirty-eight baskets, to be specific.

'What did Irish Grandma give you?' Rich glanced at her dark locks. 'Not red hair…'

'One of my brothers got that,' she acknowledged, stopping to consider him before sliding her sunglasses up onto her head. 'But I got Nan's eyes.'

Whoa...

A decade ago, he'd abseiled face-first down a cliff for sport—fast. The suck of his unprepared guts had been the same that day as the moment Mila's thick dark lashes lifted just now to reveal what they hid. Classic Celtic green. Not notable on their own, perhaps, but bloody amazing against the richness of her unblemished brown skin. Her respective grandparents had certainly left her a magnetising genetic legacy.

He used the last of his air replying. 'You're a walking billboard for cultural diversity.'

She glanced away, her mocha skin darkening, and he could breathe again. But it wasn't some coy affectation on her part. She looked genuinely distressed—though she was skilled at hiding it.

Fortunately, he was more skilled at reading people.

'The riches of the land and sea up here have always drawn people from around the world,' she murmured. 'I'm the end result.'

They reached her modest four-wheel drive, emblazoned with government logos, halfway down the beach she'd first emerged from, all golden and glittery.

'Is that why you stay?' he asked. 'Because of the riches?'

She looked genuinely horrified at the thought as she unlocked the vehicle and swung her long sandy legs in. 'Not in the sense you mean. My work is here. My family is here. My heart is here.'

And clearly she wore that heart on the sleeve of her Parks Department uniform.

Rich climbed in after her and gave a little inward sigh. Sailing north on the *Portus* had been seven kinds of awesome. All the space and quiet and air he needed wrapped up in black leather and oiled deck timber. He'd even unwound a little. But there was something about driving... Four wheels firm on asphalt. Owning the road.

Literally, in this case.

At least for the next few months. Longer, if he got his way.

'Is that why you're here?' she asked him, though it looked as if she had to summon up a fair bit of courage to do it. 'Drawn by the riches?'

If he was going to spend the day with her he wasn't going to be able to avoid the question for long. Might as well get in front of it.

'I'm here to find out everything I can about the area. I have...business interests up here. I'd like to go in fully informed.'

Her penetrating gaze left him and turned back to the road, leaving only thinned lips in its wake.

He'd disappointed her.

'The others wanted to know a bit about the history of Coral Bay.' She almost sighed. 'Do you?'

It was hard not to smile at her not so subtle angling. He was probably supposed to say *What others?* and she was going to tell him how many people had tried and failed to get developments up in this region. Maybe he was even supposed to be deterred by that.

Despite Mila's amateurish subterfuge, he played along. A few friendly overtures wouldn't go amiss. Even if she didn't look all that disposed to overtures of any kind—friendly or otherwise. Her job meant she kind of had to.

He settled into the well-worn fabric. 'Sure. Take me right back.'

She couldn't possibly maintain her coolness once she got stuck into her favourite topic. As long as Mila was talking, he had every excuse to just watch her lips move and her eyes flash with engagement. If nothing else, he could enjoy that.

She started with the ancient history of the land that they drove through, how this flat coast had been seafloor in the humid time before mammals. Then, a hundred million years later when the oceans were all locked up in a mini ice age and sea levels had retreated lower than they'd ever been, how her mother's ancestors had walked the shores on the edge of the massive continental drop-off that was now five kilometres out to sea. Many of the fantastical creatures of the Saltwater People's creation stories might well have been perfectly literal, hauled out of the deep sea trenches even with primitive tools.

The whole time she talked, Rich watched, entranced. Hiring Mila to be an ambassador for this place was an inspired move on someone's part. She was passionate and vivid. Totally engaged in what was obviously her favourite topic. She sold it in a way history books couldn't possibly.

But the closer she brought him to contemporary times, the more quirks he noticed in her storytelling. At first, he thought it was just the magical language of the tribal stories—evocative, memorable…almost poetic—but then he realised some of the references were too modern to be part of traditional tales.

'Did you just call the inner reef "smug"?' he interrupted.

She glanced at him, mid-sentence. Swallowing. 'Did I?'

'That's what I heard.'

Her knuckles whitened on the steering wheel. 'Are you sure I didn't say warm? That's what I meant. Because it's shallower inside the reef. The sand refracts sunlight and leads to—' she paused for half a heartbeat '—warmer conditions that the coral really thrives in.'

Her gaze darted around for a moment before she continued and he got the distinct feeling he'd just been lied to.

Again, though, amateurish.

This woman could tell one hell of a tale but she would be a sitting duck in one of his boardrooms.

'Ten thousand years from now,' she was continuing, and he forced himself to attend, 'those reef areas out there will emerge from the water and form atolls and, eventually, the certainty of earth.'

He frowned at her augmented storytelling. It didn't diminish her words particularly but the longer it went on the more overshadowing it became until he stopped listening to *what* she was saying and found himself only listening to *how* she said it.

'There are vast gorges at the top of the cape that tourists assume are made purely of cynical rock, but they're not. They were once reef too, tens of millions of years ago, until they got thrust up above the land by tectonic plate action. The enduring limestone is full of marine fossils.'

Cynical rock. *Certain* earth. *Enduring* limestone. The land seemed alive for Mila Nakano—almost a person, with its own traits—but it didn't irritate him because it wasn't an affectation and it didn't diminish the quality of her information at all. When she called the reef *smug* he got the sense that she believed it and, because she believed it, it just sounded...possible. If he got to lie about in warm water all day being nibbled free of parasites by a harem of stunning fish he'd be pretty smug too.

'I'd be interested to see those gorges,' he said, more to spur her on to continue her hyper-descriptive storytelling than anything else. Besides, something like that was just another string in his bow when it came to creating a solid business case for his resort.

She glanced at him. 'No time. We would have had to

set off much earlier. The four-wheel drive access has been under three metres of curi—'

She caught herself and he couldn't help wondering what she'd been about to say.

'Of sea water for weeks. We'd have to go up the eastern side of the cape and come in from the north. It's a long detour.'

His disappointment was entirely disproportionate to her refusal—sixty seconds ago he'd had zero interest in fossils or gorges—but he found himself eager to make it happen.

'What if we had a boat?'

'Well, that would be faster, obviously.' She set her eyes back on the road ahead and then, at this silent expectation, returned them to him. '*Do* you have one?'

He'd never been prouder to have the *Portus* lingering offshore. But he wasn't ready to reveal her just yet. 'I might be able to get access…'

Her green gaze narrowed just slightly. 'Then this afternoon,' she said. 'Right now we have other obligations.'

'We do?'

She hit the indicator even though there were no other road-users for miles around, and turned off the asphalt onto a graded limestone track. Dozens of tyre-tracks marked its dusty white surface.

'About time you got wet, Mr Grundy.'

CHAPTER TWO

BELOW THE SLIGHTLY elevated parking clearing at Five Fingers Bay, the limestone reef stretched out like the splayed digits in the beach's name. They formed a kind of catwalk, pointing out in five directions to the outer reef beyond the lagoon. Mila led her *one* down to it and stood on what might have been the Fingers' exposed rocky wrist.

'I was expecting more *Finding Nemo*,' he said, circling to look all around him and sounding as disappointed as the sag of his shoulders, 'and less *Flintstones*. Where's all the sea life?'

'What you want is just out there, Mr Grundy.'

He followed her finger out beyond the stretch of turquoise lagoon to the place the water darkened off, marking the start of the back reef that kept most predators—and most boats—out, all the way up to those gorges that he wanted to visit.

'Call me Richard,' he volunteered. 'Rich.'

Uh, no. 'Rich' was a bit too like friends and—given what he was up here for—even calling them acquaintances was a stretch. Besides, she wasn't convinced by his sudden attempt at graciousness.

'Richard...' Mila allowed, conscious that she represented her department. She rummaged in the rucksack she'd dragged from the back seat of the SUV. 'I have a spare mask and snorkel for you.'

He stared at them as if they were entirely foreign, but then reached out with a firm hand and took them from her. She took care not to let her fingers brush against his.

It was always awkward, taking your clothes off in front of a stranger; it was particularly uncomfortable in front of a young, handsome stranger, but Mila turned partly away, shrugged out of her work shorts and shirt and stood in her bikini, fiddling with the adjustment straps on her mask while Richard shed his designer T-shirt and cargo pants.

She kept her eyes carefully averted, not out of any prudishness but because she always approached new experiences with a moment's care. She could never tell how something new was going to impact on her and, while she'd hung out with enough divers and surfers to give her some kind of certainty about what senses a half-naked person would trigger—apples for some random guy peeling off his wetsuit, watermelon for a woman pulling hers on—this was a *new* half-naked man. And a client.

She watched his benign shadow on the sand until she was sure he'd removed everything he was going to.

Only then did she turn around.

Instantly, she was back at the only carnival she'd ever visited, tucking into her first—and last—candyfloss. The light, sticky cloud dissolving into pure sugar on her tongue. The smell of it, the taste of it. That sweet, sweet rush. She craved it instantly. It was so much more intense—and so much more humiliating—than a plain old apples association. But apparently that was what her synaesthesia had decided to associate with a half-naked Richard Grundy.

The harmless innocence of that scent was totally incompatible with a man she feared was here to exploit the reef.

But that was how it went; her associations rarely had any logical connection with their trigger.

Richard had come prepared with navy board shorts beneath his expensive but casual clothes. They were laced low and loose on his hips yet still managed to fit snugly all the way down his muscular thighs.

And they weren't even wet yet.

Mila filled her lungs slowly and mastered her gaze. He might not be able to read her dazed thoughts but he might well be able to read her face and so she turned back to her rummaging. Had her snorkelling mask always been this fiddly to adjust?

'I only have one set of fins, sorry,' she said in a rush. 'Five Fingers is good for drift snorkelling, though, so you can let the water do the work.'

She set off up the beach a way so that they could let the current carry them back near to their piled up things by the end of the swim. Her slog through sun-soaked sand was accompanied by the high-pitched single note that came with a warmth so everyday that she barely noticed it anymore. When they reached the old reef, she turned seaward and walked into the water without a backward glance— she didn't need the sugary distraction and she felt certain Richard would follow her in without invitation. They were snorkelling on his dollar, after all.

'So coral's not a plant?' Richard asked once they were waist-deep in the electric-blue water of the lagoon.

She paused and risked another look at him. Prepared this time. 'It's an animal. Thousands of tiny animals, actually, living together in the form of elk horns, branches, plates, cabbages—'

He interrupted her shopping list ramble with the understated impatience of someone whose time really was money. Only the cool water prevented her from blushing. Did she always babble this much with clients? Or did it only feel like babbling in Richard Grundy's presence?

'So how does a little squishy thing end up becoming rock-hard reef?' he asked.

Good. Yes. Focusing on the science kept the candyfloss at bay. Although as soon as he'd said 'rock-hard' she'd become disturbingly fixated on the remembered angles of his chest and had to severely discipline her unruly gaze not to follow suit.

'The calcium carbonate in their skeletons. In life, it provides resilience against the sea currents, and in death—'

She braced on her left leg as she slipped her right into her mono-fin. Then she straightened and tucked her left foot in with it and balanced there on the soft white seafloor. The gentle waves rocked her a little in her rooted spot, just like one of the corals she was describing.

'In death they pile up to form limestone reef,' he guessed.

'Millions upon millions of them forming reef first, then limestone that weathers into sand, and finally scrubland grows on top of it. We owe a lot to coral, really.'

Mila took a breath and turned to face him, steadfastly ignoring the smell of carnival. 'Ready to meet the reef?'

He glanced out towards the reef break and swallowed hard. It was the first time she'd seen him anything other than supremely confident, verging on arrogant.

'How far out are we going?'

'Not very. That's the beauty of Coral Bay; the inside reef is right there, the moment you step offshore. The lagoon is narrow but long. We'll be travelling parallel to the beach, mostly.'

His body lost some of its rigidity and he took a moment to fit his mask and snorkel before stepping off the sandy ridge after her.

* * *

It took no time to get out where the seafloor dropped away enough that they could glide in the cool water two metres above the reef. The moment Mila submerged, the synaesthetic symphony began. It was a mix of the high notes caused by the water rushing over her bare skin and the vast array of sounds and sensations caused by looking down at the natural metropolis below in all its diversity. Far from the flat, gently sloping, sandy sea bottom that people imagined, coral reef towered in places, dropped away in others, just like any urban centre. There were valleys and ridges and little caves from where brightly coloured fish surveyed their personal square metre of territory. Long orange antenna poked out from under a shelf and acted as the early warning system of a perky, pincers-at-the-ready crayfish. Anemones danced smooth and slow on the current, their base firmly tethered to the reef, stinging anything that came close but giving the little fish happily living inside it a free pass in return for its nibbly housekeeping.

Swimming over the top of it all, peering down through the glassy water, it felt like cruising above an alien metropolis in some kind of silent-running airship—just the sound of her own breathing inside the snorkel, and her myriad synaesthetic associations in her mind's ear. The occasional colourful little fellow came up to have a closer look at them but mostly the fish just went about their business, adhering to the strict social rules of reef communities, focusing on their eternal search for food, shelter or a mate.

Life was pretty straightforward under the surface.

And it was insanely abundant.

She glanced at Richard, who didn't seem to know where to look first. His mask darted from left to right, taking in the coral city ahead of them, looking below them at some particular point. He'd tucked his hands into balls by his hips and she wondered if that was to stop him reaching out and touching the strictly forbidden living fossil.

She took a breath and flipped gently in the water, barely flexing her mono-fin to effect the move, swimming backwards ahead of him so that she could see if he was doing okay. His mask came up square onto hers and, even in the electric-blue underworld, his eyes still managed to stand out as they locked on hers.

And he smiled.

The candyfloss returned with a vengeance. It was almost overpowering in the cloistered underwater confines of her mask. Part of her brain knew it wasn't real but as far as the other part was concerned she was sucking her air directly from some carnival tent. That was the first smile she'd seen from Richard and it was a doozy, even working around a mouthful of snorkel. It transformed his already handsome face into something really breath-stealing and, right now, she needed all the air she could get!

She signalled upwards, flicked her fin and was back above the glassy surface within a couple of heartbeats.

'I've spent so much time on the water and I had no idea there was so much going on below!' he said the moment his mouth was free of rubbery snorkel. 'I mean you know but you don't...*know*. You know?'

This level of inarticulateness wasn't uncommon for someone seeing the busy reef for the first time—their minds were almost always blown—but it made her feel just a little bit better about how much of a babbler she'd been with him.

His finless legs had to work much harder than hers to keep him perpendicular to the water and his breath started to grow choppy. 'It's so...structured. Almost city-like.'

Mila smiled. It was so much easier to relate to someone over the reef.

'Coral polyps organise into a stag horn just like a thousand humans organise into a high-rise building. It's a futuristic city…with hovercraft. Ready for more?'

His answer was to bite back down onto his snorkel's mouthpiece and tip himself forward, back under the surface.

They drifted on for another half-hour and she let Richard take the lead, going where interest took him. He got more skilled at the suspension of breath needed to deep snorkel, letting him get closer to the detail of the reef, and the two of them were like mini whales every time they surfaced, except they blew water instead of air from their clumsy plastic blowholes.

There was something intimate in the way they managed to expel the water at the same time on surfacing—relaxed, not urgent—then take another breath and go back for more. Over and over again. It was vaguely like…

Kissing.

Mila's powerful kick pushed her back up to the surface. That was not a thought she was about to entertain. He was a *one*, for a start, and he was here to exploit the very reef he was currently going crazy over. Though if she did her job then maybe he'd change his mind about that after today.

'Seen enough?' she asked when he caught up with her.

His mask couldn't hide the disappointment behind it. 'Is it time to go in?'

'I just want to show you the drop-off, then we'll head back to the beach.'

Just was probably an understatement, and they'd have to swim out of the shallow waters towards the place the continental shelf took its first plunge, but for Richard to understand the reef and how it connected to the oceanic ecosystem he needed to see it for himself.

Seeing was believing.

Unless you were her, in which case, seeing came with a whole bunch of other sensations that no one else experienced. Or necessarily believed.

She'd lost enough friends in the past to recognise that.

Mila slid the mouthpiece back into her snorkel and tooted out of the top.

'Let's go.'

Richard prided himself on being a man of composure. In the boardroom, in the bedroom, in front of a media pack. In fact, it was something he was known for—courage under fire—and it came from always knowing your strengths, and your opponents'. From always doing your homework. From controlling all the variables before they even had time to vary.

This had to be the least composed he'd been in a long, long time.

Mila had swum alongside him, her vigilant eyes sweeping around them so that he could just enjoy the wonders of the reef, monitoring their position to make sure they didn't get caught up in the current. He'd felt the change in the water as the outer reef had started to rise up to meet them, almost shore-like. But it wasn't land; it was the break line one kilometre out from the actual shore where the reef grew most abundant and closest to the surface of anywhere they'd swum yet. So close, the waves from the deeper water on the other side crashed against it relentlessly and things got a little choppier than their earlier efforts. Mila had led him to a channel that allowed them to propel themselves down between the high-rise coral—just like any of the reef's permanent residents—and get some relief from the surging waves as they'd swum out towards a deeper, darker, more distant kind of blue. The water temperature had dropped and the corals started to change—less of the soft, flowy variety interspersed with dancing life and more of the slow-growing, rock-hard variety. Coral mean streets. The ones that could withstand the water pressure coming at them from the open ocean twenty-four-seven.

Rich lifted his eyes and tried to make something out in the deep blue visible beyond the coral valley he presently lurked in. He couldn't—just a graduated, ill-defined shift from blue to deep blue to dark blue looking out and down. No scale. No end point. Impossible to get a grip on how far this drop-off actually went.

It even had the word 'drop' in it.

His pulse kicked up a notch.

Mila swam on ahead, rising briefly to refill her lungs and sinking again to swim out through the opening of the coral valley straight into all that vast blue…nothing.

And that was where his courage flat ran out.

He'd played hard contact sports, he'd battled patronising boardroom jerks, he'd wrangled packs of media wolves hell-bent on getting a story, and he'd climbed steep rock faces for fun. None of those things were for the weak-willed. But could he bring himself to swim past the break and out into the place the reef—and the entire country—dropped off to open, bottomless ocean?

Nope.

He tried—not least because of Mila, back-swimming so easily out into the unknown, her dark hair floating all around her, mermaid tail waving gently at him like a beckoning finger—but even that was not enough to seduce him out there. The vast blue was so impossible to position himself in, he found himself constantly glancing up to the bright surface where the sunlight was, just to keep himself oriented. Or back at the reef edge to have the certainty of it behind him.

Swimming out over the drop-off was as inconceivable

to him as stepping off a mountain. His body simply would not comply.

As if it had some information he didn't.

And Richard Grundy made it his priority always to have the information he needed.

'It's okay,' Mila sputtered gently, surfacing next to him once they'd moved back to the side of the reef protected from the churn of the crest. 'The drop-off's not easy the first time.'

No. What wasn't easy was coming face to face with a limitation you never knew you had, and doing it in front of a slip of a thing who clearly didn't suffer the same disability. Who looked as if she'd been born beneath the surface.

'The current…' he hedged.

As if that had anything to do with it. He knew Mila wouldn't have taken him somewhere unsafe. Not that he knew her at all, and yet somehow…he did. She just didn't seem the type to be intentionally unkind. And her job relied on her getting her customers back to shore in one piece.

'Let's head in,' she said.

There was a thread of charity in her voice that he was not comfortable hearing. He didn't need anyone else's help recognising his deficiencies or to be patronised, no matter how well-meant. This would always be the first thing she thought of when she thought of him, no matter what else he achieved.

The guy that couldn't swim the drop-off.

It only took ten minutes to swim back in when he wasn't distracted by the teeming life beneath them. Thriving, living coral turned to rocky old reef, reef turned to sand and then his feet were finding the seafloor and pushing him upwards. He'd never felt such a weighty slave to gravity—it was as indisputable as the instinct that had stopped him swimming out into all that blue.

Survival.

Mila struggled a little to get her feet out of her single rubber fin and he stepped closer so she could use him as a brace. She glanced at him sideways for a moment with something that looked a lot like discomfort before politely resting her hand on his forearm and using him for balance while she prised first one and then the other foot free. As she did it she even held her breath.

Really? Had he diminished himself that much? She didn't even want to *touch* him?

'That was the start of the edge of Australia's continental shelf,' she said when she was back on two legs. 'The small drop-off slopes down to the much bigger one five kilometres out—'

Small?

'And then some of the most immense deep-sea trenches on the planet.'

'Are you trying to make me feel better?' he said tightly.

And had failing always been this excruciating?

Her pretty face twisted a little. 'No. But your body might have been responding instinctively to that unknown danger.'

'I deal with unknowns every day.'

Dealt with them and redressed them. WestCorp thrived on *knowns*.

'Do you, really?' she asked, tipping her glance towards him, apparently intent on placating him with conversation. 'When was the last time you did something truly new to you?'

Part of the reason he dominated in business was because nothing fazed him. Like a good game of chess, there was a finite number of plays to address any challenge and once you'd perfected them the only contest was knowing which one to apply. The momentary flare of satisfaction as the challenge tumbled was about all he had, these days. The rest was business as usual.

And outside of business…

Well, how long had it been since there was anything outside of business?

'I went snorkelling today,' he said, pulling off his mask.

'That was your first time? You did well, then.'

She probably meant to be kind, but all her condescension did was remind him why he never did anything before learning everything there was to know about it. Controlling his environment.

Open ocean was not a controlled environment.

'How about you?' he deflected as the drag of the water dropped away and they stepped onto toasty warm sand. 'You don't get bored of the same view every day? The same reef?'

She turned back out to the turquoise lagoon and the deeper blue sea beyond it—that same blue that he loved from the comfort and safety of his boat.

'Nope.' She sighed. 'I like a lot of familiarity in my environment because of—' she caught herself, turned back and changed tack '—because I'm at my best when it's just me and the ocean.'

He snorted. 'What's the point of being your best when no one's around to see it?'

He didn't mean to be dismissive, but he saw her reaction in the flash behind her eyes.

'I'm around.' She shrugged, almost embarrassed. 'I'll know.'

'And you reserve the best of yourself *for* yourself?' he asked, knowing any hope of a congenial day with her was probably already sunk.

Her curious gaze suggested he was more alien to her

than some of the creatures they'd just been studying. 'Why would I give it to someone else?'

She crossed to their piled-up belongings and began to shove her snorkelling equipment into the canvas bag.

Rich pressed the beach towel she'd supplied to his chest as he watched her go, and disguised the full-body shiver that followed. But he couldn't blame it on the chilly water alone—there was something else at play here, something more…disquieting.

He patted his face dry with the sun-warmed fabric to buy himself a moment to identify the uncomfortable sensation.

For all his success—for all his professional renown— Rich suddenly had the most unsettling suspicion that he might have missed something fundamental about life.

Why *would* anyone give the best of themselves to someone else?

CHAPTER THREE

MILA NEVER LIKED to see any creature suffer—even one as cocky as Richard Grundy—but, somehow, suffering brought him closer to her level than he'd yet been. More likeable and relatable Clark Kent, less fortress of solitude Superman. He'd taken the drop-off experience hard, and he'd been finding any feasible excuse not to make eye contact with her ever since.

Most people got no phone reception out of town but Richard somehow did and he'd busied himself with a few business calls, including arranging for the boat he knew of to meet them at Bill's Bay marina. It was indisputably the quickest way to get to the gorges he wanted to see. All they had to do was putter out of the State and Federal-protected marine park, then turn north in open, deregulated waters and power up the coast at full speed, before heading back into the marine park again. They could be there in an hour instead of the three it would take by road. And the three back again.

It looked as if Richard would use every moment of that hour to focus on business.

Still, his distraction gave her time to study him. His hair had only needed a few strategic arrangements to get it back to a perfectly barbered shape, whereas hers was a tangled, salt-crusted mess. Side on, she could see behind his expensive sunglasses and knew just how blue those eyes were. The glasses sat comfortably on high cheekbones, which was where the designer stubble also happened to begin. It ran down his defined jaw and met its mirror image at a slightly cleft chin. As nice as all of that was—and it was; just the thought of how that stubble might feel under her fingers was causing a flurry of kettledrums, of all things— clearly its primary role in life was to frame what had to be his best asset. A killer pair of lips. Not too thin, not too full, perfectly symmetrical. Not at their best right now while he was still so tense, but earlier, when they'd broken out that smile…

Ugh…murder.

The car filled with the scent of spun sugar again.

'Something you need?'

He spoke without turning his eyes off the road ahead or prising the phone from his ear, but the twist of the mouth she'd just been admiring told her he was talking to her.

She'd meant to be subtle, glancing sideways, studying him in her periphery, yet apparently those lips were more magnetic than she realised because she was turned almost fully towards him. She snapped her gaze forward.

'No. Just…um…'

Just obsessing on your body parts, Mr Grundy…

Just wondering how I could get you to smile again, sir…

'We're nearly at the boat launch,' she fabricated. 'Just wanted you to know.'

If he believed her, she couldn't tell. He simply nodded, returned to his call and then took his sweet time finishing it.

Mila forced her mind back on the job.

'This is the main road in and out of Coral Bay,' she said as soon as he disconnected his call, turning her four-wheel drive at a cluster of towering solar panels that powered streetlights at the only intersection in the district. 'It's base camp for everyone wanting access to the southern part of the World Heritage area.'

To her, Coral Bay was a sweet, green little oasis existing in the middle of almost nowhere. No other town for two hundred kilometres in any direction. Just boundless, rust-coloured outback on one side and a quarter of a planet of ocean on the other.

Next stop, Africa.

Richard's eyes narrowed as they entered town and he saw all the caravans, RVs, four-by-fours and tour buses parked all along the main street. 'It's thriving.'

His interest reminded her of a cartoon she'd seen once where a rumpled-suited businessman's eyes had spun and rolled and turned into dollar signs. It was as if he was counting the potential.

'It's whale shark season. Come back in forty-degree February and it will be a ghost town. Summer is brutal up here.'

If he wanted to build some ritzy development, he might as well know it wasn't going to be a year-round goldmine.

'I guess that's what air-conditioning is for,' he murmured.

'Until the power station goes down in a cyclone, then you're on your own.'

His lips twisted, just slightly. 'You're not really selling the virtues of the region, you know.'

No. This wasn't her job. This was personal. She forced herself back on a professional footing.

'Did you want to stop in town? For something to eat, maybe? Snorkelling always makes me hungry.'

Plus, Coral Bay had the best bakery in the district, regardless of the fact it also had the only bakery in the district.

'We'll have lunch on the *Portus*,' he said absently.

The *Portus*? Not one of the boats that frequented Coral Bay. She knew them all by sight. It hadn't occurred to her that he might have access to a vessel from outside the region. Especially given he'd only called to make arrangements half an hour ago.

'Okay—' she shrugged, resigning herself to a long wait '—straight to Bill's Bay, then.'

They parked up on arrival at the newly appointed mini-marina and wandered down to where three others launched boats for a midday run. Compared to the elaborate 'tinnies' of the locals, getting their hulls wet on the ramp, the white Zodiac idling at the end of the single pier immediately caught her attention.

'There's Damo.' Rich raised a hand and the Zodiac's skipper acknowledged it as they approached. 'You look disappointed, Mila.'

Her gaze flew to his, not least because it was the first time he'd called her by her name. It eased off his lips like a perfectly cooked salmon folding off a knife.

'I underestimated how long it was going to take us to get north,' she said, flustered. 'It's okay; I'll adjust the schedule.'

'Were you expecting something with a bit more grunt?'

'No.' *Yes.*

'I really didn't know what to expect,' she went on. 'A boat is a boat, right? As long as it floats.'

He almost smiled then, but it was too twisted to truly earn the name. She cursed the missed moment. A tall man in the white version of her own shorts and shirt stood as they approached the end of the pier. He acknowledged Richard with a courteous nod, then offered her his arm aboard.

'Miss?'

She declined his proffered hand—not just because she needed little help managing embarkation onto such a modest vessel, but also because she could do without the associated sounds that generally came with a stranger's skin against hers.

The skipper was too professional to react. Richard, on the other hand, frowned at her dismissal of a man clearly doing him a favour.

Mila sighed. Okay, so he thought her rude. It wouldn't be the first time someone had assumed the worst. And she wouldn't be seeing him again after today, so what did it really matter?

The skipper wasted no time firing up the surprisingly throaty Zodiac and reversing them out of the marina and in between the markers that led bigger boats safely through the reef-riddled sanctuary zone towards more open waters. They ambled along at five knots and only opened up a little once they hit the recreation zone, where boating was less regulated. It took just a few minutes to navigate the passage that put them in open water, but the skipper didn't throttle right up like she expected; instead he kept his speed down as they approached a much larger and infinitely more expensive catamaran idling just beyond the outer reef. The vessel she'd seen earlier, at Nancy's Point. Slowing as they passed such a massive vessel seemed a back-to-front kind of courtesy, given the giant cat would barely feel their wake if they passed it at full speed. It was only as their little Zodiac swung around to reverse up to the catamaran that she saw the letters emblazoned on the big cat's side.

Portus.

'Did you think we were going all the way north in the tender?' a soft voice came to her over the thrum of the slowly reversing motor.

'Is this yours?' she asked, gaping.

'If she's not, we're getting an awfully accommodating reception for a couple of trespassers.'

'So when you said you were "dropped off" at Nancy's Point…?'

'I didn't mean in a car.'

With those simple words, his capacity to get his mystery development proposal through where others had failed increased by half in Mila's mind. A man with the keys to a vessel like this in his pocket had to have at least a couple of politicians there too, right?

The tender's skipper expertly reversed them backwards, right up to the stern of the *Portus,* where a set of steps came down each of the cat's two hulls to the waterline. A dive platform at the bottom of each served as a disembarkation point and she could see where the tender would nest in snugly under its mother vessel when it wasn't in use. Stepping off the back of the tender and onto the *Portus* was as easy as entering her house. Where the upward steps delivered them—to an outdoor area that would comfortably seat twelve—the vessel was trimmed out with timber and black leather against the boat's white fibreglass. Not vinyl… Not hardy canvas like most of the boats she'd been on. This was *leather*—soft and smooth under her fingers as she placed a light hand on the top of one padded seat-back. The sensation was accompanied by a percussion of wind chimes, low and sonorous.

Who knew she found leather so soothing!

The colour scheme was conflicting, emotionally, even as it was perfect visually. The tranquillity of white, the sensuality of black. Brown usually made her feel sad, but this particularly rich, oiled tone struck her more specifically as…isolated.

But it was impossible not to also acknowledge the truth.

'This is so beautiful, Richard.'

To her left, timber stairs spiralled up and out of view to the deck above.

'It does the job,' he said modestly, then pulled open two

glass doors into the vessel's gorgeous interior, revealing an expansive dining area and a galley twice as big as her own kitchen.

She just stared at him until he noticed her silence.

'What?'

'Surely, even in your world this vessel is something special,' she said, standing firm on the threshold, as though she needed to get this resolved before entering. False humility was worse than an absence of it, and she had a blazing desire to have the truth from this man just once.

On principle.

'What do you know about my world?' he cast back easily over his shoulder, seemingly uncaring whether she followed him or not.

She clung to *not* and hugged the doorway.

'You wouldn't have bought the boat if you didn't think it was special.'

He turned to face her. 'It wouldn't be seemly to boast about my own boat, Mila.'

'It would be honest.' And really, what was this whole vessel but big, mobile bragging rights? 'Or is it just saying the words aloud that bothers you?'

He turned to face her, but she barrelled on without really knowing why it affected her so much. Maybe it had something to do with growing up on two small rural incomes. Or maybe it had something to do with starting to think they might be closer to equals, only to be faced with the leather and timber evidence very much to the contrary.

'I'll say it for you,' she said from the doorway. 'The *Portus* is amazing. You must be incredibly relaxed when you're out on her.' She glanced at the massive dining table. 'And you must have some very happy friends.'

'I don't really bring friends out,' he murmured, regarding her across the space between them.

'Colleagues, then. Clients.'

He leaned back on the kitchen island and crossed his ankles. 'Nope. I like silence when I'm out on the water.'

She snorted. 'Good luck with that.' He just stared at her. 'I mean it's never truly silent, is it?'

He frowned at her. 'Isn't it?'

No. Not in her experience.

She glanced around as the *Portus*' massive engines thrummed into life and they began to move, killing any hope of silence for the time being. Although they weren't nearly as loud as she'd expected. How much did a boat have to cost to get muted engines like that?

Richard didn't invite her in again. Or insist. Or cajole. Instead, he leaned there, patience personified until she felt that her refusal to step inside was more than just ridiculous.

It was as unfriendly as people had always thought her to be.

But entering while he waited felt like too much of a concession in this mini battle of wills. She didn't want to see the flare of triumph in his eyes. Her own shifted to the double fridge at the heart of the galley.

'I guess lunch won't be cheese sandwiches out of an Esky, then?'

The moment his regard left her to follow her glance, she stepped inside, crossing more than just a threshold. She stepped wholly into Richard's fancy world.

He pulled the fridge doors wide. 'It's a platter. Crayfish. Tallegio. Salt and pepper squid. Salad Niçoise. Sourdough bread.'

She laughed. 'I guess I was wrong, then. Cheese sandwich it is.' Just fancier.

He turned his curiosity to her. 'You don't eat seafood?'

'I can eat prawns if I have to. And molluscs. They don't have a strong personality.'

That frown just seemed to be permanently fixed on his face. 'But cray and squid do?'

Her heart warmed just thinking about them and it helped to loosen her bones just a little. 'Very much so. Particularly crayfish. They're quite…optimistic.'

He stared—for several bemused moments—clearly deciding between *quirky* and *nuts*. Both of which she'd had before with a lot less subtlety than he was demonstrating.

'Is it going to bother you if I eat them?'

'No. Something tells me I won't be going hungry.' She smiled and it was easier than she expected. 'I have no strong feelings about cheese, either way.'

'Unlucky for the Tallegio then,' he murmured.

He pulled open a cabinet and revealed it as a small climate-controlled wine cellar. Room temperature on the left, frosty on the right. 'Red or white?' he asked.

'Neither,' she said regretfully. Just looking at the beading on the whites made her long for a dose of ocean spray. 'I'm on the clock.'

'Not right now you're not,' he pointed out. 'For the next ninety minutes, we're both in the capable hands of Captain Max Farrow, whose jurisdiction, under international maritime law, overrules your own.'

He lifted out one of the dewy bottles and waved it gently in her direction.

It was tempting to play at all this luxury just for a little while. To take a glass and curl up on one of those leather sofas, enjoy the associated wind chimes and act as if they weren't basically complete strangers. To talk like normal people. To pretend. At all of it.

'One glass, then,' she said. 'Thank you.'

He poured and handed her a glass of white. The silent moments afterwards sang with discomfort.

'Come on, I'll give you a tour,' he eventually offered.

He smiled but it didn't ring true and it certainly didn't set off the five-note harmony or the scent of candyfloss that the flash of perfect teeth previously had. He couldn't be as nervous as she was, surely. Was he also conscious of how make-believe this all was?

Even if, for him, it wasn't.

She stood. 'Thank you, Richard.'

'Rich,' he insisted. 'Please. Only my colleagues call me Richard.'

They were a good deal less than colleagues, but it would be impossible now to call him anything else without causing offence. *More* offence.

'Please, Mila. I think you'll like the *Portus*.' Then, when she still didn't move, he added, 'As much as I do.'

That one admission… That one small truth wiggled right in under her ribs. Disarming her completely.

'I would love to see more, Rich, thank you.'

The name felt awkward on her lips and yet somehow right at the same time. Clunky but…okay, as if it could wear in comfortably with use.

The tour didn't take long, not because there wasn't a lot to look at in every sumptuous space but because, despite its size, the *Portus* was, as it happened, mostly boat. As Rich showed her around she noted a jet ski securely stashed at the back, a sea kayak, water skis—everything a man could need to enjoy some time *on* the water. But she saw nothing to indicate that he enjoyed time *in* it.

'No diving gear?' she commented. 'On a boat with not one but two dive decks?'

His pause was momentary. 'Plenty to keep me busy above the surface,' he said.

Something about that niggled in this new environment of truce between them. That little glimpse of vulnerability coming so close on the heels of some humble truth. But she didn't need super-senses to know not to push it. She carried on the tour in comparative silence.

The *Portus* primarily comprised of three living areas: the aft deck lounge that she'd already seen, the indoor galley and the most incredibly functional bedroom space ever. It took up the whole bow, filling the front of the *Portus* with panoramic, all-seeing windows, below which wrapped fitted black cupboards. She trailed a finger along the spotless black surface, over the part that was set up as a workspace, complete with expensive camouflaged laptop, hip-height bookshelves, a disguised mini-bar and a perfectly made up king-sized bed positioned centrally in the space, complete with black pillow and quilt covers. The whole space screamed sensuality and not just because of all the black.

A steamy kind of heat billowed up from under Mila's work shirt. It was way too easy to imagine Rich in here.

'Where's the widescreen TV?' she asked, hunting for the final touch to the space that she knew had to be here somewhere.

Rich leaned next to the workspace. 'I had it removed. When I'm in here it's not to watch TV.'

She turned to face him. 'Is that because this is an office first, or a bedroom first?'

The moments the words left her lips she tried to recapture them, horrified at her own boldness. It had to be the result of this all-consuming black making her skin tingle, but talking about a client's bedroom habits *with* said client was not just inappropriate, it was utterly mortifying.

'I'm so sorry...' she said hurriedly.

Rich held up a hand and the smile finally returned, lighting up the luxurious space.

'My own fault for having such a rock star bedroom,' he joked. 'I didn't buy the *Portus* for this space, but I have to admit it's pretty functional. Everything I need is close by.

But who needs a TV when you have a wraparound view like this, right?'

She followed his easy wave out of the expansive windows. There was something just too…perfect about the image he created. And she just couldn't see him sitting still long enough to enjoy a view.

'You work when you're on board, don't you?'

Those coral-coloured lips twisted. 'Maybe.'

Mila hunted around for a topic of discussion that would soak up some of the cotton candy suddenly swilling around the room. 'Where do your crew sleep?'

The business of climbing down into one of the hulls, where a small bed space and washing facility were, gave her the time she needed to get her rogue senses back in order.

'…comfortable enough for short trips,' Rich was saying as she tuned back in.

'What about long ones?'

He glanced out of the window. 'WestCorp keeps me pretty much tethered to the city. This is shaping up to be the longest trip I've taken since I got her. Three days.'

Wow. Last of the big spenders.

'Come on.' He straightened, maybe seeing the judgement in that thought on her face. 'Let's finish the tour.'

The rest of the *Portus* consisted of a marble-clad *en suite* bathroom, appointed with the same kind of luxury as everywhere else, and then a trip back out to the aft deck and up a spiral staircase to the helm. Like everything else on the vessel, it was a wonder of compact efficiency. Buttons and LED panels and two screens with high-tech navigation and seafloor mapping and a bunch of other equipment she didn't recognise. The *Portus*' captain introduced himself but Mila stood back just far enough that a handshake would be awkward to ask for. She'd rather not insult a second man today. Maybe a third.

'Two crew?' she murmured. The vessel was large enough for it, but for just one passenger…?

'It's more efficient to run overnight. Tag-teaming the skippering. Get up from the city faster. I left the office at seven two nights ago and woke up here the next morning. Same deal tonight. I'll leave before sunset and be back in Perth just in time for my personal trainer.'

Imagine having a boat like this and then rushing every moment you were on her. This gorgeous vessel suddenly became relegated to a water taxi. Despite the wealth and comfort around her, she found herself feeling particularly sorry for Richard Grundy.

Captain Farrow pressed a finger to his headset and spoke quietly, then he turned to Rich.

'Lunch is served, sir.'

'Thanks, Max.'

They backtracked and found the sumptuous spread and the remainder of the wine set out on the aft deck. The deck-hand known as Damo lowered his head respectfully then jogged on tanned legs up the spiral stairs to the helm and was gone.

Rich indicated for her to sit.

The first thing she noticed was the absence of the promised crayfish. In its place were some pieces of chicken. The little kindness touched her even as she wondered exactly how and when he'd communicated the instruction. Clearly, his crew had a talent for operating invisibly.

'This is amazing,' she said, curling her bare legs under her on the soft leather. The deep strains of wind chimes flew out of the back of the boat and were overwhelmed in the wash, but they endured. Mila loaded her small plate with delicious morsels.

'So how long have you worked for the Department?'

Rich asked, loading a piece of sourdough with pâté and goat's cheese.

It wasn't unusual for one of her tour clients to strike up a personal conversation; what was unusual was the ease with which she approached her answer.

She normally didn't *do* chatty.

'Six years. Until I was eighteen, I instructed snorkelers during the busy season and volunteered on conservation projects in the off-season.'

'While most other teens were bagging groceries or flipping burgers after school?'

'It's different up here. Station work, hospitality or conservation. Those are our options. Or leaving, of course,' she acknowledged. Plenty of young people chose that.

'Waiting on people not your thing?'

She studied her food for a moment. 'People aren't really my thing, to be honest. I much prefer the solitude of the reef system.'

It was the perfect *in* if he wanted to call her on her interpersonal skills. Or lack of.

But he didn't. 'What about working on the Station? Not too many people out there, I wouldn't have thought.'

'I would have worked on Wardoo in a heartbeat,' she admitted. 'But jobs there are very competitive and the size of their crew gets smaller every year as the owners cut back and back.' She looked out towards the vast rust-coloured land on their port side. 'And back.'

He shifted on the comfortable cushions as though he was perched on open reef flat.

'Vast is an understatement,' he murmured, following the direction of her eyes. And her thoughts.

That was not awe in his voice.

'Remote living is not for everyone,' she admitted, refocusing on him. 'But it has its perks.'

He settled back against the plush cushions but his gaze didn't relax with him. If anything, it grew more focused. More intense. 'Like what?'

'You can breathe up here,' she started, remembering how cloistered she'd felt on her one and only visit to the capital when she was a teen. 'The land sets the pace, not someone else's schedule. It's…predictable. Ordered.'

She forked up a piece of chicken and dipped it in a tangy sauce before biting into it and chewing thoughtfully.

'Some people would call that dull…' he started, carefully.

Meaning he would? 'Not me. Life has enough variability in it without giving every day a different purpose.'

'And that's important…why, exactly?'

His gaze grew keen. Too keen, as if he was poking around in a reef cave for something.

Oh…

She should have known he would notice. A man didn't get a boat like this—or the company that paid for it—without being pretty switched on. A deep breath lifted her shoulders before dropping them again. For a moment, Mila was disappointed that he couldn't just…let it lie. She understood the curiosity about her crossed senses, but all her life she'd just wanted someone to *not* be interested in her synaesthesia. So that she could feel normal for a moment.

Apparently, Richard Grundy wasn't going to be that someone.

She sighed. 'You're asking about…'

Funny how she always struggled to broach the subject. He helped her out.

'About crayfish with optimism and the smug reef.' She held her tongue, forcing him to go on. 'You seem very connected to the environment around you. I wondered if it was a cultural thing. Some affinity with your ancestors...?'

Was that what he thought? That it was *cultural*? Of all the things she'd ever thought were going on with her, it had truly never occurred to her that it had anything to do with being raised Bayungu. Probably because no one else on that side of the family had it—or any of the community.

It was just one more way that she was different.

'It's not affinity,' she said simply.

It was *her*.

'If anything, it probably comes from my Irish side. My grandmother ended up marrying a Japanese pearler because other people apparently found her—'

Unrelatable. Uncomfortable. Any of a bunch of other 'un's that Mila lived with too.

'Eccentric.'

But not Grandfather Hiro, with his enormous heart. A Japanese man in outback Australia during the post-war years would have known more than a little something about not fitting in. Pity he wasn't still around to talk to...

Rich laid his fork down and just waited.

'I have synaesthesia,' she blurted. 'So I hear some sensations. I taste and smell some emotions. Certain things have personalities.'

He kept right on staring.

'My synapses are all crossed,' she said in an attempt to clarify. Although even that didn't quite describe it.

'So...' Rich looked utterly confounded. '...the crayfish has an *actual* personality for you?'

'Yes. Kind of...perky.'

'All of them?'

'No. Just the dead one in your fridge.'

It was impossible not to ruin her straight face with a chuckle. Force of habit; she'd been minimising her condition with laughter for years. Trying to lessen the discomfort of others. Even if that meant taking it on herself. 'Yes, all of them, thank goodness. Things are busy enough without giving them *individual* traits.'

He sat forward. 'And the reef is actually—'

'Smug,' she finished for him. 'But not unpleasantly so. Sky, on the other hand, is quite conceited. Clouds are ambitious.' She glanced around at things she could see for inspiration. 'Your stainless steel fridge is pleasantly mysterious.'

He blinked. 'You don't like sky?'

'I don't like conceit. But I don't pick the associations. They just…are.'

He stared, then, so long and so hard she grew physically uncomfortable. In a way that had nothing to do with her synaesthesia and everything to do with the piercing intelligence behind those blue eyes.

Eventually his bottom lip pushed out and he conceded, 'I guess sky is kind of pleased with itself. All that overconfident blue…'

The candyfloss surged back for a half-moment and then dissipated on the air rushing past the boat. She was no less a spectacle but at least he was taking it in his stride, which wasn't always the case when she confessed her unique perception to people.

'What about the boat?' he asked after a moment. 'Or is it just natural features?'

Her lips tightened and she glanced down at the rapidly emptying platter. 'I'm not an amusement ride, Rich.'

'No. Sorry, I'm just trying to get my head around it. I've never met a…'

'Synaesthete.'

He tested the word silently on his lips and frowned. 'Sounds very sci-fi.'

'My brothers did call it my *superpower,* growing up.'

Except that it wasn't terribly super and it didn't make her feel powerful. Quite the opposite, some days. 'I didn't even know that other people didn't experience the world like I did until I was about eleven.'

Before that, she'd just assumed she was flat-out unlikeable.

Rich dropped his eyes away for a moment and he busied himself topping up their glasses. 'So you mentioned sensation? Is that why you tensed up when you shook my hand?'

Heat rushed up Mila's cheeks. He'd noticed that? Had he also noticed every other reaction she'd had to being near him?

That could get awkward fast.

'Someone new might feel okay or they might…not.' She wasn't about to apologise for something that just…was… for her.

Rich studied her. 'Must be lonely.'

Her spine ratcheted straight. The only thing she wanted more than to be treated normally was *not* to be treated with pity. She took her time taking a long sip of wine.

'Are my questions upsetting you?'

'I don't… It's not something I usually talk about with strangers. Until I know someone well. People generally react somewhere on a spectrum from obsessive curiosity to outright incredulity. No one's ever just shrugged and said, *All right, then. More sandwiches?*'

Oh, how she longed for that.

'Thank you for making an exception, then.' His eyes stayed locked on hers and he slid the platter slightly towards her. 'More sandwiches?'

It was so close, it stole her breath.

'Why are you really up here, Rich?' she asked, before thinking better of it. It shouldn't matter why; she was paid to show him the area, end of story. His business was as much his own as hers was. But something pushed her on. And not just the desire to change the subject. 'I'm going to look you up online anyway. Might as well tell me. Are you a developer?'

He shifted in his seat, took his time answering. 'You don't like developers, I take it?'

'I guide a lot of them. They spend the day banging on about their grand plans for the area and then I never see them again. I'm just wondering if you'll be the same.'

Not that she was particularly hoping to see him again. *Was she?*

His body language was easy but there was an intensity in his gaze that she couldn't quite define.

'None of them ever come back?'

'Some underestimate how remote it is. Or how much red tape there will be. Most have no idea of the access restrictions that are in place.'

He tipped his head as he sipped his wine. 'Restrictions? Sounds difficult.'

'Technically,' she went on, 'the land all the way up to the National Park is under the control of three local pastoralists. Lifetime leaseholds. In Coral Bay, if anyone wants to get a serious foothold in this part of the Marine Park, they have to get past the Dawsons. No one ever has.' She shifted forward. 'Honestly, Rich? If you do have development plans, you might as well give up now.'

Why was she giving him a heads-up? Just because he'd been nice to her and given her lunch? And looked good in board shorts?

Blue eyes considered her closely. 'The Dawsons sound like a problem.'

The boiled eggs of loyalty materialised determinedly at the back of her throat. 'They're the reason the land around Coral Bay isn't littered with luxury resorts trying to position themselves on World Heritage coast. They're like a final rampart. Yet to be breached. That makes them heroes in my book.'

Rich studied her for a long time before lifting his glass in salute. And in thanks. 'To the Dawsons, then.'

Had she said too much? Nothing he probably didn't already know, or wouldn't find out soon enough. But still…

She ran her hands up and down arms suddenly bristling with goose pimples.

'Cold?' Rich asked, even though the sun was high.

Mila shook her head. 'Ball bearings.'

CHAPTER FOUR

Rich wanted to believe that 'ball bearings' referred to the breeze presently stirring wisps of long, dark hair around Mila's face, but what if she sensed ball bearings when she was feeling foreboding? Or deception. Or distrust.

What if she had more 'extra-sensory' in her 'super-sensory' than she knew? He *was* keeping secrets and she *should* feel foreboding. But that wasn't how Mila's condition worked. Not that he had much of an idea how it *did* work, and he didn't want to pummel her with curious questions just for his own satisfaction. He'd just have to use the brain his parents had spent a fortune improving to figure Mila out the old-fashioned way—through conversation.

A big part of him wished that the heroic Dawsons *were* an impediment to his plans—a good fight always got his blood up. But Mila would be dismayed to discover just how easy it was going to be for him to build his hotel overlooking the reef. The handful of small businesses running here might have had mixed feelings about the percentage that WestCorp took from their take—the motel, the café, the fuel station, even the hard-working glass-bottom boat tours—but they couldn't honestly expect not to pay for the privilege of running a business on Wardoo's land, just as Wardoo had to pay the government for the privilege of running cattle on leasehold land.

Money flowed like an ebbing tide towards the government. It was all part of the food chain.

Except now that same government was shifting the goalposts, looking to excise the coastal strip from the leasehold boundaries. The only part that made any decent profit. And his analysts agreed with him that the only way to get them to leave the lucrative coastal strip in the lease was to make a reasonable capital investment in the region himself—put something back in.

Governments liked to see potential leveraged and demand met.

And—frankly—he liked to do it.

WestCorp needed the lucrative coastal strip to supplement the Station's meagre profits. Without it, there was nothing holding Wardoo in any half-competent finance holdings and, thanks to his father's move to the big smoke forty years ago, there was nothing holding *him* to Wardoo. His heritage.

That was why he'd hauled himself out of the office—out of the city—and come north, to see for himself the place that had been earmarked for development. Just so he could be as persuasive as possible when he pitched it to the responsible bureaucrat. He'd lucked out with a guide who could also give him a glimpse of community attitudes towards his business—forewarned absolutely was forearmed.

It didn't hurt that Mila was such a puzzle—he'd always liked a challenge. Or that she was so easy on the eye. He'd always liked beautiful things. Now she was just plain intriguing too, courtesy of her synaesthesia. Though he'd have to temper his curiosity, given how touchy she was about it. Had someone made her feel like a freak in the past?

The *Portus'* motor cut out and they slowed to a drift. Mila twisted and stared at the ancient rocky range that stretched up and down the coast, red as far as they could see. She knew where they were immediately.

'We'll have to take the tender in; there's only a slim channel in the reef.'

It was narrow and a little bit turbulent where the contents of the reef lagoon rushed out into open water but they paused long enough to watch a couple of manta rays rolling and scooping just there, clearly taking advantage of the fishy freeway as they puttered over the top of it. Damo dropped them close enough to wade comfortably in, their shoes in one hand and sharing the load of the single kayak they'd towed in behind the tender in the other. They hauled it up to the sandbar that stretched across the mouth of Yardi Creek. Or once had.

'This is why we couldn't just drive up here,' she said, indicating the mostly submerged ridge. 'Thanks to a ferocious cyclone season earlier in the year, the sandbar blew out, taking the four-wheel drive access with it. It's only just now reforming. It'll be good to go again at the end of the year but for now it makes for a convenient launch point for us.'

And launch they did. His sea kayak was wider and flatter than a regular canoe, which made it possible for two of them to fit on a vessel technically designed for half that number. He slid down into the moulded seat well and scooted back to make room for Mila, spreading his legs along the kayak's lip so she could sit comfortably between them at the front of the seat well, with her own bent legs dangling over each side. Once she was in, he bent his knees up on either side of her to serve as some kind of amusement park ride safety barrier and unlocked his double paddle into a single half for each of them.

They soon fell into an easy rhythm that didn't fight the other, though Mila's body stayed as rigid and unyielding as the hard plastic of the kayak against his legs. Given what he now knew about her, this kind of physical contact had to be difficult for her. Not that she was snuggled up to him exactly, but the unconventional position wasn't easy for either of them. Though maybe for different reasons. *He* was supposed to be paying attention to everything around him yet he kept finding his gaze returning to the slim, tanned back and neck of the young woman seated between his knees, her now-dry ponytail hanging not quite neatly down her notched spine. She'd shrugged out of her uniform shirt and folded it neatly into her backpack but somehow—in this marine environment—the bikini top was as much of a uniform as anything.

She was in her mid-twenties—nearly a decade younger than he was—but there was something about her... As if she'd been here a whole lot longer. Born of the land, or even the sea. She just...belonged.

'Looks like we have the creek to ourselves.' Mila's soft words came easily back to him. courtesy of the gorge's natural acoustics.

Sure enough, there was not another human being visible anywhere—on the glassy water, up on the top of the massive canyon cliffs, in the car park gouged out of the limestone and dunes. Though it was easy to imagine a solitary figure, dark and mysterious, silhouetted against the sun, spear casually at hand, watching their approach far below.

It was just that kind of place.

Mila stopped paddling and he copied her, the drag of his paddle embedded in the water slowing them to almost nothing. Ahead, a pair of nostrils and a snub-nosed little face emerged from the water, blinking, checking them out. The kayak drifted silently past him on inertia. Only at the last moment did he dip back underwater and vanish to the depths of the deep canyon creek.

'Hawksbill turtle,' Mila murmured back to him once they were clear. 'Curious little guy.'

'You get curiosity for turtles?'

She turned half back, smiled. 'No. I mean he was *actually* curious. About us. I get bossy for turtles.'

They paddled on in silence. Rich battled with a burning question.

'Does it affect how you feel about some things?' he finally asked, as casually as he could. 'If your perception is negative?'

'It can.'

She didn't elaborate and he wondered if that question—or any question—held some hidden offence, but her voice when she finally continued wasn't tight.

'I'm not a huge fan of yellow fish, for instance, through no fault of their own. I read yellow as derisive and so…' She shrugged. 'But, similarly, people and things can strike me positively because of their associations too.'

'Like what?' he asked.

She paused again, took an age to answer. 'Oak moss. I used to get that when I was curled in my mother's arms as a child. I get it now when I'm wrapped up in my softest, woolliest sweater on a cold night, or snuggled under a quilt. It's impossible not to feel positive about oak moss.'

Her love came through loud and clear in her low voice and he was a bit sorry that he was neither naturally oaky nor mossy. It threw him back to a time, long ago, when he'd done the same with his own mother. Before he'd lost her at the end of primary school. Before he'd been dumped into boarding school by his not-coping father.

There'd been no loving arms at all after that.

She cleared her throat and kept her back firmly to him.

'Once, I met someone who registered as cotton candy. Hard not to respond positively to such a fun and evocative scent memory. I was probably more predisposed to like and trust him than, say, someone who I read as diesel smoke.'

Lucky cotton candy guy. Something told him that being liked and trusted by Mila Nakano was rarer than the mysteries in this gorge.

'What's the worst association you've ever made?' Curious was as close to 'accepting' as she was going to let him get.

'Earwax,' she said softly.

'Was that a person or a thing?'

The kayak sent out ripples ahead of them but it was easy to imagine they were soundwaves from her laughter. It was rich and throaty and it got right in between his ribs.

'A person, unfortunately.' She sighed. 'The one kid at primary school that gave me a chance. Whenever they were around I got a strong hit of earwax in the back of my throat and nose. Now, whenever my heart is sad for any reason at all, I get a delightful reminder...'

Imagine trying to forge a friendship—or, worse, a relationship—with someone who struck you so negatively whenever they were around. How impossible it would be. How that would put you off experimenting with pretty much anyone.

Suddenly, he got a sense of how her superpower worked. He was going to find it difficult to go out on this kayak ever again without an image of Mila's lean, long back popping into his head. Or to watch ripples radiate on still water anywhere without hearing her soft voice. The only difference was that her associations didn't need to have a foundation in real life.

Mila dug the paddle hard into the water again and turned her face up and to the right as the kayak slowed. 'Black-flanked rock wallaby.'

Rich followed her gaze up the towering cliffs that lined

both sides of the deep creek and hunted the vertical, rust-coloured rock face. 'All I see are some shadowy overhangs. What am I missing?'

'That's where the wallabies like to lurk. It's why they have evolved black markings.'

He scanned the sheer cliffs for camouflaged little faces. 'What are they, half mountain goat? Don't they fall off?'

'They're born up there, spend their lives leaping from claw-hold to claw-hold, nibbling on the plants that grow there, sleeping under the overhangs, raising their own young away from most predators. They're adapted to it. It's totally normal to them. They would be so surprised to know how impossible we find it.'

He fell back into rhythm with her gentle paddling. Was she talking about wallabies now or was she talking about her synaesthesia?

The more he looked, the more he saw, and the further he paddled, the more Mila showed him. She talked about the prehistoric-looking fish species that liked the cold, dark depths of the creek's uppermost reaches, the osprey and egrets that nested in its heights, the people who had once lived here and the ancient sites that were being rediscovered every year.

It was impossible not to imagine the tourist potential of building something substantial down the coast from a natural resource like this. An eco-resort in eco-central. Above them, small openings now occupied by wallabies hinted at so much more.

'The cavers must love it here,' he guessed. He knew enough about rocks to know these ones were probably riddled with holes.

'One year there was a massive speleologist convention and cavers from all over the world came specifically to explore the uncharted parts of the Range. They discovered nearly twelve new caves in two days. Imagine what they might have found if they could have stayed up here for a week. Or two!'

'Why couldn't they?'

'There just aren't any facilities up here to house groups of that size. Or labs to accommodate scientists or…really anything. Still, the caves have waited this long, I guess.' Her shoulders slumped. 'As long as the sea doesn't rise any faster.'

In which case the coastal range where the rock walla-bies clung would go back to being islands and the exposed rock they were exploring would eventually be blanketed in corals again.

The circle of life.

They took their time paddling the crumbled-in end of the gorge, looking closely at the make-up of the towering walls, the same shapes he'd seen out on the reef here, just fossilised, the synchronised slosh of their oars the only sounds between them.

The silence in this beautiful place was otherwise com-plete. It soaked into him in a way he'd never really felt before and he finally understood why Mila might have thought that open ocean wasn't really that quiet at all.

Because she had *this* to compare it to.

'So, I'm thinking of coming back on the weekend,' he said when they were nearly done, before realising he'd even decided. 'For a couple more days. I've obviously under-estimated what brings people here.'

They bumped back up against the re-establishing sand bar and Mila clambered out then turned to him with some-thing close to suspicion on her pretty face. After the con-nection he thought they'd just made it was a disappointing setback.

'I'm only booked for today,' she said bluntly. 'You'll have to find someone else to guide you.'

Denial surged through him.

'You have other clients?' He could get that changed with one phone call. But pulling rank on her like that would be about as popular as…earwax.

'No, but I've got things on.'

'What kind of things?'

'An aerial survey of seagrasses and some whale shark pattern work. A tagging job. And the neap tide is this weekend so I'll be part of the annual spawn collection team. It's a big deal up here.'

Rich felt his chance at continuing to get quality insider information—and his opportunity to get to know Mila a bit better—slipping rapidly away.

'Can I come along? Two birds, one stone.' Then, when she hesitated awkwardly, he added, 'Paid, of course.'

She winced. 'It's not about money. I'm just not sure whether that's okay. Most of our work isn't really a spectator sport.'

It was a practical enough excuse. But every instinct told him it was only half the truth. Was she truly so used to only ever seeing developers the one time? Well, he liked to be memorable.

'Put me to work, then. I can count seagrass or study the…spawn.'

Ten minutes ago that would have earned him another throaty laugh. Now, she just frowned.

'Come on, Mila, wasn't it you who asked when I'd last done something completely new to me? This is an opportunity. A bunch of new experiences.' He found the small tussle of wills disproportionately exhilarating. 'I'll be low-maintenance. Scout's honour.'

She shrugged as she bent to hike her side of the kayak

up, but the lines either side of her flat lips told him she wasn't feeling that casual at all.

'It's your time to waste, I guess.'

He only realised he'd been holding his breath when he was able to let it out on a slow, satisfied smile. More time to get a feel for this district and more time to get his head around Mila Nakano.

The return trip felt as if it took half the time, as return trips often did. But it was long enough for Mila to carefully pick her way out to the front of the *Portus* and slide down behind the safety barrier on one of the catamaran hulls. Rich did the same on the other and—together but apart—they lost themselves in the deep blue ocean until they reached the open waters off Coral Bay again. Over on her side, the water whooshing past sang triumphantly.

Regardless, she shifted on the deck and let her shoulders slump.

She'd been rude. Even she could see that. Properly, officially rude.

But the moment Rich had decided to return to Coral Bay for a more in-depth look she'd felt a clawing kind of tension start to climb her spine. Coming back meant he wasn't a *one* any more. Coming back meant that none of the remoteness or the politics or the environmental considerations had deterred him particularly.

Coming back meant he was serious.

She'd guided Rich today because that was her job. But she'd let herself be disarmed by his handsome face and fancy boat and his apparently genuine interest in the reef and cape. Her only comfort was that he still had to get past the Dawsons—and no one had ever managed that—but she still didn't want him to think that she somehow endorsed his plans to develop the bay.

Whatever they were.

Regardless of the cautious camaraderie that had grown between them, Richard Grundy was still her adversary. Because he was the reef's adversary.

She cast her eyes across the deep green ocean flashing by below the twin hulls. Rich sat much as she did, legs dangling, spray in his face, but his gaze was turned away from her, his focus firmly fixed on the coast as they raced south parallel to it. No doubt visualising how his hotel was going to look looming over the water. Or his resort.

Or—perish the thought—his casino.

Knowing wouldn't change anything, yet she had to work hard at not being obsessed by which it would be.

They met on the aft deck as the catamaran drew to an idling halt off Bill's Bay an hour later. Behind them, the sun was making fairly rapid progress towards the horizon.

'It was good to meet you,' she murmured politely, already backing away.

Rich frowned. 'You say that like I won't be seeing you again…'

The weekend was four days away. Anything could happen in that time, including him losing his enthusiasm for returning. Just because he was eager for it now didn't mean he'd still be hot for it after the long journey back to the city and his overflowing inbox. Or maybe she'd have arranged someone else to show him around on Saturday. That would be the smart thing to do. This could quite easily be the last she ever saw of Richard Grundy.

At the back of her throat the slightest tang began to climb over the smell of the ocean.

Earwax.

Which was ridiculous. Rich was virtually a stranger; why would her heart squeeze even a little bit at the thought of parting? But her senses never lied, even when she was lying to herself. That was unmistakably earwax she could taste.

Which made Saturday a really bad idea.

She hurried down to the dive platform on one of the *Portus*' hulls when Rich might have kissed her cheek in farewell, and she busied herself climbing aboard the tender when he might have offered her a helpful outstretched hand. But once she was aboard and the skipper began to throttle the tender out from under the *Portus* she had no real excuse—other than rudeness—not to look back at Rich, his hands shoved deeply into his pockets, still standing on the small dive platform. It changed the shape of his arms and shoulders below the T-shirt he'd put on when they'd got back aboard, showing off the sculpted muscles she'd tried so hard not to appreciate when they were snorkelling. Or when they brushed her briefly while they were paddling the kayak.

'Seven a.m. Saturday, then?' he called over the tender's thrum and nodded towards the marina. It would have sounded like an order if not for the three little forks between his blue eyes.

Doubt.

In a man who probably never second-guessed himself.

'Don't look for me,' she called back to him. 'Look for the uniform.' Just in case. Any one of her colleagues could show him the area.

She should have scrunched her nose as the tender reversed through a light fog of its own diesel exhaust, but all she could taste and smell in the back of her throat was candyfloss. The flavour she was rapidly coming to associate with Rich.

The flavour she was rapidly coming to crave like a sugary drug.

She was almost ashore before she realised that the presence of candyfloss in her mind's nose meant she'd already decided to be the one who met him on Saturday.

The first thing Mila did when she got back to her desk was jump online and check out the etymology of the word *portus*. She'd guessed Greek—some water god or something—but it turned out it was Latin…for port. *Duh!* But it also meant sanctuary, and the imposing vessel certainly was that— even up here, where everything around them was already nine parts tranquil. She'd felt it the moment she'd stepped aboard Rich's luxurious boat. She could only imagine what it was like for him to climb aboard and motor away from the busy city and his corporate responsibilities for a day or two.

No…only ever one. Hadn't he told her as much?

What were those corporate responsibilities, exactly?

It took only moments to search up WestCorp and dis- cover how many pies the corporation had its fingers in. And a couple of media stories that came back high in the search results told her that Richard Grundy was the CEO of WestCorp and had been since the massive and unexpected heart attack that had taken his father. Rich had been carry- ing the entire corporation since then. No wonder he'd been on the phone a lot that morning. No wonder he didn't have time to use his boat. The Internet celebrated the growth of WestCorp in his few short years. There were pages of re- source holdings and she lost interest after only the first few.

Suffice to say that Mr Richard Grundy was as corpo- rate as they came.

Despite that, somewhere between getting off the *Portus* and setting foot back on land she'd decided to definitely be the one to meet him on Saturday. Not just because of the candyfloss, which she reluctantly understood—biology was biology and even hers, tangled as it was with other input, was working just fine when it came to someone so high up on the Mila Nakano Secret Hotness Scale—but because of the earwax.

Her earwax couldn't be for Rich—she just didn't know him well enough—it had to be for the reef. For what a company like WestCorp could do to it. If she left him in the hands of anyone else, could she guarantee that they'd make it as abundantly clear as she would how badly this area did not need development? How it was ticking along just fine as it was?

Or should she only trust something that important to herself?

She reached for her phone.

'Hey, Craig, it's Mila…'

A few minutes later she disconnected her call, reassured that the pilot of Saturday's aerial survey could accommodate an extra body without compromising the duration of the flight. So that was Rich sorted; he would get to see a little more of the region he wanted to know about, and she…

She, what?

She'd bought herself another day or two to work on him and convince him exactly why this region didn't need his fancy-pants development. It happened to also be another day or two for Rich to discover how complicated she and her synaesthesia were to be around but, at the end of the day, the breathy anticipation of her lonely heart had to mean less than the sanctity and security of her beloved reef.

It just had to.

CHAPTER FIVE

'WE'RE MAPPING WHAT?' Rich asked into the microphone of the headset they each wore on Saturday morning as the little Cessna lifted higher and higher. Coasting at fifteen hundred feet was the only way to truly appreciate the size and beauty of the whole area.

Dugongs, Mila mouthed back, turning her face out towards a nook in the distant coast where the landforms arranged themselves into the kind of seagrass habitat that the lumbering animals preferred. 'Manatees. Sea cows.'

When he just blinked, she delved into her pocket, swiped through an overcrowded photo roll and then passed the phone back to him.

'Dugong,' she repeated. 'They feed on the seagrasses. They all but disappeared at the start of the century after a cyclone smothered the seagrasses with silt. The department has been monitoring their return ever since.'

She patted the sizeable camera that was fixed to the open window of the aircraft by two heavy-duty braces. 'Their main feeding grounds are a little south of here but more and more are migrating into these sensitive secondary zones. We're tracking their range to measure the viability of recovery from another incident like it.'

The more she impressed upon him the complexity of the environmental situation, the less likely he would be to go ahead with his plans, right? The more words like 'sensitive' and 'fragile' and 'rare' that she used, the harder development would seem up here. Either he would recognise the total lack of sense of developing such delicate coast or—at the very least—he would foresee how much red tape lay in his future.

It couldn't hurt, anyway.

Rich shifted over to sit closer to her window, as if her view was any more revealing than his. This close, she could smell him over the residual whiff of aviation fuel. Cotton candy, as always, but there was something else… Something she couldn't identify. It didn't ring any alarm bells; on the contrary, it made her feel kind of settled. In a way she hadn't stopped feeling since picking him up at the marina after four days apart.

Right.

It felt right.

'Craig comes up twice a day to spot for the whale shark cruises,' she said to distract herself from such a worrying association. To keep her focus firmly on work. She nodded down at the four white boats waiting just offshore. 'If he isn't scheduled to take tourists on a scenic flight then I hitch a lift and gather what data I can while we're up here.'

'Opportunistic,' Rich observed.

'Like the wildlife.' She smiled.

Okay, so he hadn't technically earned the smile, but she was struggling not to hand them out like sweets. What was going on with her today? She hadn't gushed over Craig when she saw him again after a week.

They flew in a wide arc out over the ocean and Rich shifted back to his own window and peered out. Below, areas of darkness on the water might have been the shadow of clouds, reef or expansive seagrass beds.

'We're looking for pale streaks in the dark beds,' Mila

said. 'That's likely to be a dugong snuffling its way along the seafloor, vacuuming up everything it finds. Where there's one, hopefully there'll be more.'

Until you saw it, it was difficult to explain—something between a snail's trail and a jet stream—but, as soon as you saw it, it was unmistakable in the bay's kaleidoscopic waters.

They flew lower, back and forth over the grasses, eyes peeled. When she did this, she usually kept her focus tightly fixed on the sea below, not only to spot an elusive dugong but also to limit the distracting sensory input she was receiving from everything else she could see in her periphery. Today, though, she was failing at both.

She'd never been as aware of someone else as she was with Rich up here. If he shuffled, she noticed. If he smiled, she felt it. If he spoke, she attended.

It was infuriating.

'Is that one?' Rich asked, pointing to a murky streak not far from shore.

'Sure is!' Mila signalled to Craig, who adjusted course and took them closer. She tossed a pair of binoculars at Rich and locked onto his eyes. 'Go you.'

Given the animal she was supposed to be fascinated by, it took her a worryingly long time to tear her eyes away from Rich's and focus on the task at hand.

Through the zoom lens of her camera it was possible to not only get some detail on the ever-increasing forage trail of a feeding dugong but to also spot three more rolling around at the surface enjoying the warmest top layer of the sea and the rising sun. Her finger just about cramped on the camera's shutter release and she filled an entire memory card with images. Maybe a dozen or so would be useful to the dugong research team but until she got back to her office she couldn't know which. So she just kept shooting.

Rich shook his head as they finished up the aerial survey. 'Can't believe you get paid to do this.'

'Technically, I don't,' Mila admitted. 'I'm on my own time today.'

He turned a frown towards her and spoke straight into her ear, courtesy of the headsets. 'That doesn't seem right.'

She looked up at him. 'Why? What else would I do with the time?'

'Uh… Socialise? Sleep in? Watch a movie?'

'This is plenty social for my liking.' She chuckled, looking between Craig and Rich. 'And why watch a movie when I can be watching dugongs feeding?'

'So you never relax? You're always doing something wildlifey?'

His judgement stung a little. And not only because it was true. 'Says the man who has an office set up on his boat so he doesn't miss an email.'

'I run a *Fortune 100* company.' He tsked. 'You're just—'

'Dude…!' Craig choked out a warning before getting really busy flying the plane. All those switches that needed urgent flipping…

'*Just?*' Mila bristled, as the cabin filled with the unmissable scent of fried chicken. 'Is that right?'

But he was fearless.

'Mila, one of the few advantages to being an employ*ee* and not an employ*er* is that you get to just…switch off. Go home and not think about work until Monday.'

Wow. How out of touch with ordinary people was he?

'My job title may not be comprised of initials, Rich, but what I do is every bit as important and *as occupying* as what you do. The only difference is that I do it for the good of the reef and not for financial gain.'

Craig shook his head without looking back at either of them.

'I'm out,' she thought she heard him mutter in the headset.

Rich ignored him. 'Oh, you're some kind of philanthropist? Is that it?'

'How many voluntary hours did *you* complete last month?'

His voice crept up, even though the microphone at his throat meant it didn't need to. 'Personally? None; I don't have the time. But WestCorp has six new staff working for us in entry level roles who were homeless before we got to them and that's an initiative *I* started.'

Mila's outrage snapped shut.

'Oh.' She puffed out a breath. 'Well… That's not on your website.'

'You think that's something I should be splashing around? Exposing those people to public scrutiny and comment?'

No, that would be horrible. But would a corporation generally care about that when there was good press to be had?

The Cessna's engines spluttered on.

'So you made good on your threat to check up on me, I see,' he eventually queried, his voice softening.

Sour milk mingled in with the bitter embarrassment of Brussels sprouts for a truly distasteful mix. Though she was hardly the only uncomfortable one in the plane. Rich looked wary and Craig looked as if he wanted to leap out without wasting time with a parachute.

'I was just curious about what you did,' she confessed.

'Find anything interesting?'

'Not really.' But then she remembered. 'I'm sorry about your father.'

The twitch high in his clenched jaw got earwax flowing again and this time it came with a significant, tangible and all too actual squeeze behind her breast. Had she hurt him with her clumsy sympathy?

But he didn't bite; he just murmured, 'Thank you.'

The silence then was cola-flavoured and she sank into the awkwardness and chewed her lip as she studied the ocean below. Craig swung the plane around and headed back towards Coral Bay.

'Okay, we're on the clock,' he said, resettling in his seat, clearly relieved to have something constructive to say. 'Whale sharks, here we come.'

Rich knew enough about this region to know what it was most famous for—the seasonal influx of gentle giants of the sea. Whale sharks. More whale than shark, the massive fish were filter feeders and, thus, far safer for humans than the other big sharks also out there. Swimming out in the open waters with any of them was a tightly regulated industry and a massive money-spinner.

But, frankly, anyone doing it for fun had to be nuts.

The water was more than beautiful enough from up here without needing to be immersed in it and all its mysteries.

'What do you need with whale sharks?' he asked, keen to undo his offence of earlier with some easier conversation.

Mila couldn't know how secretly he yearned to be relieved of the pressure of running things, just for a while. A week. A weekend even. He hadn't had a weekend off since taking over WestCorp six years before. Even now, here, he was technically on the job. Constantly thinking, constantly assessing. While other people dreamed of fancy cars and penthouse views, his fantasies were a little more…*suburban*. A sofa, a warm body to curl around and whatever the latest hit series was on TV.

Downtime.

Imagine that.

He couldn't really name the last time he'd done something just for leisure. Sport was about competitiveness, rock-climbing was about discipline and willpower. If he read a book it was likely to be the autobiography of someone wildly successful. It was almost as if he didn't *want* to be alone. Or quiet. Or thoughtful.

So when he'd commented on Mila's downtime, he hadn't meant it as a criticism. Of everything he'd seen in Coral Bay so far, the thing that had made the biggest impression on him was the way Mila spent her days.

Spectacularly simple. While also being very full.

She patted her trusty camera.

'Whale sharks can be identified by their patterning rather than by invasive tagging. The science employs the same algorithms NASA uses to chart star systems.'

A pretty apt analogy. The whale sharks he'd seen in photos were blanketed in constellations of pale spots on a Russian blue skin.

Mila turned more fully to him and her engagement lit up her face just like one of those distant suns he saw as a star. It almost blinded him with optimism. 'Generally, the research team uses crowd-sourced images submitted by the tourists that swim with them but I try and contribute when I can.'

'You can photograph them from up here?'

'Oh, we'll be going lower, mate,' Craig said, over the rattle of the Cessna's engine. 'We're looking for grey tadpoles at the surface. Shout out if you see any.'

Tadpoles? From up here? He looked at Mila.

Her grin was infectious. 'You'll see.'

He liked to do well at things—that came from results-based schooling, an all-honours university career, and a career where he was judged by his successes—so he was super-motivated to replicate his outstanding dugong-spotting performance. But this time Mila was the first to spot a cluster of whale sharks far below.

'On your left, Craig.'

They banked and the sharks came into view.

'Tadpoles,' Rich murmured. Sure enough: square-nosed, slow-swimming tadpoles far, far below. 'How big are they?'

'Maybe forty feet,' Mila said. 'A nice little posse of three.'

'That'll keep the punters happy,' Craig said and switched channels while he radioed the location of the sharks in to the boats waiting patiently but blindly below.

'We'll stay with this pod until the boats get here,' Mila murmured. 'Circle lower and get our shots while we wait.'

Craig trod a careful line between getting Mila the proximity she needed and not scaring the whale sharks away into deeper waters. He descended in a lazy circle, keeping a forty-five-degree angle to the animals at all times. While Mila photographed their markings, Rich peered down through the binoculars to give him the same zoomed-in views she was getting. Far below, the three mammoth fish drifted in interlocking arcs, their big blunt heads narrowing down into long, gently waving tail fins. As if the tadpoles were moving in slow motion. There was an enviable kind of ease in their movements, as if they had nowhere better to be right now. No pressing engagements. No board meeting at nine. No media pack at eleven.

Hard not to envy them their easy life.

'The plankton goes down deep during the day so the whale sharks take long rests up here before going down to feed again at dusk,' Mila said. 'That's why they're so mellow with tourists, because they have a full belly and are half asleep.'

'How many are there on the whole reef?'

'Right now there's at least two dozen and more arriving

every day because they're gathering for the coral spawn this weekend.'

'They eat the spawn?'

'Everyone eats the spawn. It's why the entire reef erupts all on the same night—to increase the chances of survival.' She glanced back at him. 'What?'

'You're pretty impressed with nature, aren't you?'

'I appreciate order,' she admitted. 'And nothing is quite as streamlined as evolution. No energy wasted.'

If his world was as cluttered as hers—with all her extra-sensory input—he might have a thing for order too. His days tended to roll out in much the same way day in, day out.

Same monkeys, different circus.

'If it was just about systems you'd be happy working in a bank. Why out here? Why wildlife?'

She gave the whale sharks her focus but he knew he had her attention and he could see her thinking hard about her answer—or whether or not to give it to him, maybe. Finally, she slipped the headset off her head, glanced at an otherwise occupied Craig and leaned towards him. He met her in the middle and turned his ear towards her low voice.

'People never got me,' she said, low. And painfully simple. He got the sense that maybe this wasn't a discussion she had very often. Or very easily. 'Growing up. Other kids, their parents. They didn't hate me but they didn't accept me either, because I saw or heard or smelled things that they couldn't. Or they thought I was lying. Or making fun of them. Or defective. One boy called me "Mental Mila" and it kind of…stuck.'

Huh. He'd never wanted to punch a kid so much in his life.

'I already didn't fit anywhere culturally, then I discovered I didn't fit socially.' She looked down at the reef. 'Out there every species is as unique and specialised as the one next to it yet it doesn't make them exclusive. If anything, it makes them inclusive; they learn to work their specialties in together. Nature cooperates; it doesn't judge.'

Mankind sure did.

She slid the headset back on, returned to her final photos and the moment—and Mila's confidence—passed. He could so imagine her as a pretty, lonely young girl who turned her soft heart towards the non-judgemental wildlife and made them her friends.

The sorrowful image sucked all the joy out of his day.

The Cessna kept on circling the three-strong pod of whale sharks, keeping track of them until the boats of tourists began to converge, then Craig left them to their fun and scoured up the coast for a back-up group in case those ones decided to dive deep. As soon as they found more and radioed the alternate location, their job was done and Craig turned for Coral Bay's airfield, charting a direct line down the landward side of the coast.

As they crossed back over terra firma, Rich peered through the dusty window of his door at the red earth below. He knew that land more for its features on a map than anything else. The distinctive hexagonal dam that looked like a silver coin from here, but was one of the biggest in the region from the ground. The wagon wheel of stock tracks leading to it. The particular pattern of eroded ridges in Wardoo's northwest quadrant. The green oasis of the waterhole closer to the homestead. When he was a boy he'd accompanied his father on a charter flight over the top of the whole Station and been arrested by its geometry. For a little while he'd had an eight-year-old's fantasies of the family life he might have had there, as a kid on the land with a dozen brothers and sisters, parents who sat around a table at night, laughing, after a long day mustering stock…

'That's the Station I told you about,' Mila murmured, misreading his expression as interest. 'Wardoo isn't just beautiful coastline; its lands are spectacular too. All those fierce arid ripples.'

Fierce. He forced his mind back onto the present. 'Is that what you feel when you look at the Station?'

It went some way to explaining her great faith in Wardoo as a protector of the realm if looking at it gave her such strong associations.

'Isolation,' she said. 'There's an undertone in Wardoo's red… I get the same association with jarrah. Like the timber deck on your boat. It's lonely, to me.'

He stared down at all that red geometry. Fantasy Rich and his enormous fantasy family were pretty much all that had got him through losing his mother and then being cast off in boarding school. But by the time he was old enough to consider visiting by himself, he had no reason and even less time to indulge the old crutch. He'd created a stable, rational world for himself at school and thrown himself into getting the grades he needed to get into a top university. Once at uni he'd been all about killing it in exams so that he could excel in the company he'd been raised to inherit. He'd barely achieved that when his father's heart had suddenly stopped beating and, since then, he'd been all about taking WestCorp to new and strictly governable heights. There'd been very little time for anything else. And even less inclination.

Thus, maps and the occasional financial summary were his only reminder that Wardoo even existed.

Until now.

'Actually, I can see that one.'

Her eyes flicked up to his and kind of…crashed there. As if she hadn't expected him to be looking at her. But she didn't look away.

'Really?' she breathed.

There was an expectation in her gaze that stuck in his gut like a blade. As if she was hunting around for someone to understand her. To connect with.

As if she was ravenous for it.

'For what it's worth, Mila,' Rich murmured into the headset, 'your synaesthesia is the least exceptional thing about you.'

Up front, Craig's mouth dropped fully open, but Mila's face lit up like a firework and her smile grew so wide it almost broke her face.

'That's so lovely of you to say,' she breathed. 'Thank you.'

No one could accuse him of not knowing people. And people the world over all wanted the same thing. To belong. To fit. The more atypical that people found Mila, the less comfortable she was bound to be with them. And, even though it was a bad idea, he really wanted her to be comfortable with him for the few short hours they would have together. He turned and found her eyes—despite the fact that his voice was feeding directly to her ears courtesy of the headphones—and pumped all the understanding he could into his gaze.

'You're welcome.'

The most charged of silences fell and Craig was the only one detached enough to break it.

'Buckle up,' he told them both. 'Airstrip's ahead.'

Mila shifted towards the open door of the Cessna, where Rich had just slid out under its wing. As long as his back was to her she was fine, but the moment he turned to face her she knew she was in trouble. Normally she would have guarded against the inevitable barrage of crossed sensations that being swung down bodily by someone would bring. But, in his case, she had to steel herself against the pleasure—all that hard muscle and breadth against her own little body.

Tangled sensations had never felt so good.

Twenty-four hours ago she would have found some excuse to crawl through to the other door and exit far away from Rich, or accepted his hand—*maybe*—and limit the physical skin-on-skin to just their fingers, but now... She rested her hands lightly on his shoulders and held her breath. He eased her forward, over the edge of the door, and supported her as she slid his full length until her toes touched earth. Even then he didn't hurry to release her and the hot press of his body sent her into a harpy, sugary overdrive.

Your synaesthesia is the least exceptional thing about you.

To have it not be the first thing someone thought about when they thought about her... The novelty of that was mind-blowing. And it begged the question—what *did* he associate first with her? Not something she could ever ask for shame; ridiculous to be curious about and dangerous to want, given what he did for a living.

But there it was. As uncontrollable and illogical as her superpower. And she'd learned a long time ago to accept the inevitability of those.

Her nostrils twitched as her feet found purchase on the runway; alongside the usual carnival associations there was something else. Some indefinable...closeness. She felt inexplicably drawn to Richard Grundy. She'd been feeling it all morning.

It took a moment for her to realise.

She spun on him, eyes wide. 'What are you wearing?'

He didn't bother disguising his grin. He reached up with one arm and hooked it over the strut holding the Cessna's wing and fuselage to each other. The casual pose did uncomfortable things to her pulse.

'Do you have any idea how hard it is to find a cologne with oak moss undertones on short notice?' he said.

Mila stared even as her chest tightened. 'You wore it intentionally?'

'Totally. Unashamedly,' he added, as the gravity of her expression hit him. 'I wasn't sure it was working. You seemed unaffected at first.'

That was because she was fighting the sensation to crawl into his lap in the plane and fall asleep there.

Oak moss.

'Why would you do that?' she half whispered, thinking about that murmured discussion without their headsets. The things she'd confessed. The access she'd given him into her usually protected world.

He shrugged the shoulder that wasn't stretched up towards the plane's wing. 'Because you associate it with security.'

She fought back the rush of adrenaline and citrus that he'd cared at all how she felt around him and gave her anger free rein. 'And you thought manipulating the freak would somehow make me feel safe with you?'

He lowered his arm and straightened, his comfortable expression suddenly growing serious. 'Whoa, no, Mila. That's not what—'

'Then what? Why do I need to feel safe with you?'

She'd not seen Rich look anything but supremely confident since he'd first come striding towards her with his hand outstretched at Nancy's Point. Now he looked positively bewildered. And a little bit sick. It helped ease the whiff of nail varnish that came with the devastation.

This whole conversation stank more than an industrial precinct.

'Because you're so wary and I...' He greyed just a little bit more as his actions dawned on him. 'Oh, God, Mila—'

'Way to go, bro!' Craig called as he breezed past them with a hand raised in farewell and marched towards the little shed that served as the airfield's office.

Rich was way too fixated on her face to acknowledge his departure, but it bought them both a moment to take a breath and think. Mila fought her natural inclination to distrust.

Richard Grundy was not a serial killer. He hadn't just spiked her drink in a nightclub. He wasn't keeping strangers locked up in a basement somewhere.

He'd worn something he thought would make her comfortable around him.

That was all.

Mila could practically see his mind whirring away in that handsome head. He dropped his gaze to the crushed limestone runway and when it came back up his eyes were bleak. But firm. And she registered the truth in them.

'I wanted to ask you to dinner,' he admitted, low. 'And I wanted you to feel comfortable enough around me to say yes.'

'Do I look comfortable?'

He sagged. 'Not even a little bit.'

But every shade paler Rich went helped with that. He saw his mistake now and something told her that he very rarely made them. Old habits died hard, yet something in his demeanour caused a new and unfamiliar sensation to shimmer through her tense body.

Trust.

She wanted to believe in him.

'Why would you care whether I come to dinner or not?' Which was coward-speak for, *Why do you want to have dinner at all?*

With me.

'You intrigue me,' he began. 'And not because of the synaesthesia. Or not *just* because of it,' he added when she lifted a sceptical brow. 'I just wanted to get to know you better. And I wanted you to get to know *me* better.'

'I'm not sure you improve on repeat exposure, to be honest.'

Conflict shone live in his intense gaze. He battled it for moments. Then he decided.

'You know what? This was a mistake. *My* mistake,' he hurried to clarify.

'Big call from a man who never makes mistakes.'

His laugh was half-snort. And barely even that.

'Apparently, I save them up to perpetrate in one stunning atrocity.' His chest broadened with one breath. 'I succeed in business because of my foresight. My planning. Because I anticipate obstacles and plan for them. But I'm completely out of my depth with you, Mila. I have no idea where the boundaries are, never mind how I can control them. But that's a poor excuse for trying to game you.' He stepped out from under the shade of the Cessna's wing. 'Thank you for everything you've shown me and I wish you all the best for the future.'

He didn't try and shake her hand, or to touch her in any way. He just delivered an awkward half-bow like some lord of a long-ago realm and started to back away. But at the last moment he stopped and turned back.

'I meant what I said, Mila, about you being exceptional for a whole bunch of reasons that have nothing to do with your synaesthesia. There's something about how you are on that reef, in this place… I think you and your super-connectedness to the world might just hold the secret to life. I don't understand it, but I'm envious as hell and I think I was just hoping that some of it might rub off on me.'

He nodded one last time and strode away.

A slam of freshly made toast hit her. *Sorrow.* Rich was saying goodbye just as she'd finally got to meet the real him. Just as he'd dropped his slick veneer and let her in through those aquamarine eyes—the colour that always energised her. She would never again know the harp strains of his touch, or the coffee of his easy company or the sugar-rush of his sexy smile. He would be just like every other suited stranger she'd ever guided up here.

A *one*.

She wasn't ready to assign him to those dreaded depths just yet. And not just because of the rapidly diminishing oak moss that made her feel so bereft. She'd spent her life being distanced by people and here was a man trying to close that up a little and she'd gone straight for the jugular.

Maybe she needed to be party to the distance-closing herself.

Maybe change started at home.

'Wait!'

She had to call it a second time because Rich had made such long-legged progress away from her. He stopped and turned almost as he stepped off the airfield onto the care-fully reticulated grass that lined it. Some little voice deep down inside urged her that once he'd stepped onto that surface it would have been too late, that he'd have been lost to her.

That she'd caught something—barely—before it was gone for ever. 'What about the coral spawn?'

He frowned and called back. 'What about it?'

'You can't leave before you've seen it, surely? Having come all this way.'

His face grew guarded and she got toast again as she realised that she'd made him feel as bad about himself as others had always made her feel.

'Is it that spectacular?' he called back warily.

'It's a miracle,' she said, catching up. Puffing slightly. More aware of someone than ever before in her life. 'And it should start tonight.'

He battled silently with himself again, and she searched his eyes for signs of an angle she just couldn't find.

'It would be my first miracle…' he conceded.

'And the moon has to be high to trigger it so, you know, we could grab something to eat beforehand.' She huffed out a breath. 'If you want.'

His smile, when it came, was like a Coral Bay sunrise. Slow to start but eye-watering when it came up over the ridge. It was heralded by a tsunami of candyfloss.

'That won't be weird? After…' He nodded towards the plane.

Cessna-gate?

'No,' she was quick to confirm. 'It wasn't the brightest thing you've done but I believe that you meant no harm.'

His handsome face softened with gratitude. But there was something else in there too, a shadow…

'Okay then,' he said, pushing it away. 'I'll meet you at the marina at six?'

Her breath bunched up in her throat like onlookers crowding around some spectacle. It made it hard to say much more than, 'Okay.'

It was only at the last moment that she remembered to call out.

'Bring your fins!'

CHAPTER SIX

Rᴵᴄʜ ʙʀᴀᴄᴇᴅ ʜɪs feet in the bottom of the tender as it puttered up to the busy pier, then leapt easily off onto the
unweathered timbers without Damo needing to tie up
amongst the dozen boaters also coming ashore for the
evening.

Mila had been on his mind since he'd left her earlier in
the day, until the raft of documents waiting for him had
forced her out so that he could focus on the plans.

I believe that you meant no harm, she'd said.

Purposefully wearing one of her synaesthesia scents was
only a small part of the hurt he feared he might be gear-
ing up to perpetrate on this gentle creature. A decent man
would have accepted another guide, or gone back to the city
and stayed there. Made the necessary decisions from afar.
A decent man wouldn't be finding reasons to stay close to
Mila even as he did the paperwork that would change her
world for ever. A driven man would. A focused man would.

He would.

Was there no way to succeed up here *and* get the girl?

Deep down, he knew that there probably wasn't.

Mila wouldn't be quite so quick to declare her confident
belief in him if she knew that he had the draft plans for a
reef-front resort sitting on his desk on board the *Portus*.

Or why he was so unconcerned about any eleventh-hour development barriers from the local leaseholders.

Because he *was* that final barrier.

He *was* Wardoo.

And Wardoo's lease was up for renewal right now. There was no time to come up with another strategy, or for long-winded feasibility testing. *Someone* was going to develop this coast—him, the government, some offshore third party—and if he didn't act, then he would lose the coastal strip or the lease on Wardoo. Possibly both.

Then where would Mila and her reef be?

Better the devil and all that.

He waved Damo off and watched him putter past incoming boats, back out towards the *Portus*' holding site beyond the reef. As the sun sank closer to the western horizon, it cast an orange-yellow glow over everything, reflected perfectly in the still, mirrored surface of the windless lagoon. Did Mila dislike golden sunsets the way she distrusted yellow fish? He couldn't imagine her disliking anything about this unique place.

'Beautiful, isn't it,' a soft voice said behind him. 'I could look at that every day.'

Rich turned to face Mila, standing on the marina. He wanted to comment that she *did* look at it every day but the air he needed to accomplish it escaped from his lungs as soon as he set eyes on her.

She wasn't wet, or bedraggled, or crunchy-haired. She wasn't in uniform. Or in a bikini. Or any of the ways he'd seen her up until now. She stood, weight on one leg, hands twisted in front of her, her long dark hair hanging smooth and combed around her perfectly made-up face. All natural tones, almost impossible to see except that he'd been remembering that face without its make-up every hour of the day since he'd left on Tuesday and comparing it subconsciously to every other artfully made-up female face he'd seen since then. That meant he could spot the earthy, natural colours, so perfect on her tanned skin. A clasp of shells tightly circled her long throat while a longer strand hung down across the vee of smooth skin revealed by her simple knitted dress, almost the same light brown as her skin. The whole thing was held up by the flimsiest of straps, lying over the bikini she wore underneath. She looked casual enough to walk straight out into the glassy water, or boho enough to dine in any restaurant in the city. Even the best ones.

'Mila. Good to see you again.' *Ugh, that was formal.* He held up the snorkelling gear he'd purchased on his way back to the *Portus* that morning. 'Fins.'

Her smile seemed all the brighter in the golden light of evening and some of the twist in her fingers loosened up. 'I thought you might have left them on the boat by-accident-on-purpose. To get out of tonight.'

'Are you kidding? Miss out on such a unique event?'

She chewed her lip and it was adorable. 'I should confess that not everyone finds mass spawning as beautiful as I do.'

'Seriously? A sea full of floating sex cells. What's not to love?'

She stood grinning at him long enough for him to realise that he was standing just grinning at her too.

Ridiculous.

'Want me to drive?' he finally managed to say. 'It's such a long way.'

His words seemed to break Mila's trance and her laugh tinkled. 'I think I can handle it.'

He rolled around in that laugh, luxuriating, and his mind went again to the stack of plans on his desk.

Jerk.

It only took three minutes to drive around into the heart of Coral Bay. On the way, she asked him about his day at large in town and he asked her about hers. They filled the three minutes effortlessly.

And then they ran flat out of easy conversation.

As soon as they stepped out of her four-wheel drive in front of the restaurant, Mila's body seemed to tighten up. Was she anticipating the sensory impact of sharing a meal with dozens of others, or the awkwardness of sharing a meal with him? Whichever, her back grew rigid as her hand lifted to push the door open.

'Would it be crazy to suggest eating on the beach instead?' he asked before the noise from the restaurant reached more fully out to them. 'The lagoon is too beautiful not to look at tonight.'

As was Mila.

And he didn't really feel like sharing her with a restaurant full of people.

He watched her eagerness to seek the solace of the beach wrestle with her reluctance to be so alone with him. After what he'd pulled earlier, who could blame her? Sharing a meal in a crowded restaurant was one thing; sharing it on a moonlit beach made it much harder to pretend this was all just…business.

'I'm scent-free tonight,' he assured her, holding his hands out to his sides. Trying to keep it light.

'If only,' he thought he heard her mutter.

But then she spoke louder. 'Yes, that would be great; let's order to go.'

And go they did, all of one hundred metres down to the aptly named Paradise Beach, which stretched out expansively from the parking area. The tide was returning but, still, the beach was wide and white and virtually empty. A lone man ran back and forth with a scrappy terrier, white sand flying against the golden sunset. The dog barked with exuberant joy.

'This looks good,' Rich said, unfolding the battered fish and potato scallops.

'Wait until you taste it,' she promised as the man and dog disappeared up a sandy track away from the beach. 'That fish was still swimming a couple of hours ago. They source locally and daily.'

Talking about food was only one step removed from talking about the weather and it almost pained him to make such inane small talk when his time with Mila was so limited.

He wanted to see the passion in her eyes again.

'Speaking of swimming, why exactly are we heading out into spawn-infested waters?' he encouraged. 'More volunteering?'

'This one's work-related. My whole department heads out at different points of the Northwest Cape on the first nights of the eruption to collect spawn. So we have diverse genetic stock.'

'For what?'

'The spawn bank.'

He just blinked. 'There's a spawn *bank*?'

'There is. Or…there will be, one day. Right now it's a locked chest freezer in Steve Donahue's fish shed, but some day the fertilised spawn will help to repopulate this reef if it's destroyed. Or we can intentionally repopulate individual patches that die off.' She turned to him, her eyes glowing as golden as the sunset. 'Tonight we collect and freeze, and in the future they'll culture and release the resulting embryos to wiggle their way back onto the reef and fix there.'

'That sounds—' *Desperate? A lost cause?* '—ambitious.'

'We have to do something.' She shrugged. 'One outbreak

of disease or a feral competitor, rising global temperatures or a really brutal cyclone... All of that would be gone.'

His eyes followed hers out to the darkening lagoon and the reef no longer visible anywhere above it. The water line was nearly twice as far up the beach as it had been when the *Portus* set him ashore. He didn't realise there were so many threats to the reef's survival.

Threats that didn't include him, anyway.

'And how do you know it will be tonight?'

'It's usually triggered by March's full moon.'

He glanced up at the crescent moon peeking over the eastern horizon. 'Shouldn't you have done this last week, then?'

'By the time they've grown for ten days, the moonlight is dim enough to help hide the spawn bundles from every other creature on the reef waiting to eat them.' She glanced out to the horizon. 'It will probably be more spectacular tomorrow night but I like to be in the water for the first eruptions. Not quite so soupy.'

'Sounds delicious,' he drawled.

But it didn't deter his enjoyment of his seafood as he finished it up.

'How far out are we going this time?'

He hated exposing himself with that question but he also liked to be as prepared as possible for challenges, including death-defying ones. Preparedness was how you stayed alive—in the boardroom and on the beach. There was nothing sensible about swimming out onto a reef after dark.

He'd seen the documentaries.

'The species we're after are all comfortably inside the break.'

Comfortably. Nothing about this was comfortable. It was testament to how badly he wanted to be with Mila that he was entertaining the idea at all.

They fell to silence and talked about nothing for a bit, Mila glancing now and again out to the lagoon to check that the spawning hadn't commenced while they were making small talk.

'Can I ask you something?' she eventually said, bringing her eyes back to him. 'How come the captain of the swim team doesn't like water? And don't mention your jet ski,' she interrupted as he opened his mouth. 'I'm talking about being *in* water.'

Given how she'd opened herself up to him about her synaesthesia, not returning the favour felt wrong. Yet going down this path scarcely felt any better, because of where he knew it led. And how she might judge him for that.

'I'm hurt that you've forgotten our first snorkel already...'

Her green eyes narrowed at his evasion.

He leaned forward and rested his elbows on his knees. 'I like to be the only species in the water. Swimming pools are awesome for that.'

'Spoken like a true axial predator. You don't like to share?'

'Only child,' he grunted. But Mila still wasn't satisfied. That keen gaze stayed locked firmly on his until he felt obliged to offer up more. 'I like to know what I'm sharing with.'

'You know there's more chance of being killed by lightning than a shark, right?'

'I'd like to see those odds recalculated in the middle of an electrical storm.' Which was effectively what swimming out into their domain was like. Doubly so at night. On a reef.

He could stop there. Leave Mila thinking that he was concerned about sharks. Or whales. Or Jules Verne–type squid. She looked as if she was right on the verge of believing him.

But he didn't want to leave her with that impression. Sharks and whales and squid mattered to Mila. And it mattered to *him* what she thought.

He sighed. 'Open ocean is not somewhere that mankind reigns particularly supreme.'

'Ah…' Awareness glowed as bright as the quarter-moonlight in Mila's expression. 'You can't control it.'

'I don't expect to,' he pointed out. 'It's not mine to control. I'm just happier not knowing what's down there.'

'Even if it's amazing?'

Especially if it was amazing. He was better off not knowing what he was missing. Wasn't that true of all areas of life? It certainly helped keep him on track at WestCorp— the only times he wobbled from the course he'd always charted for himself was when he paused to consider what else might be out there for him.

'As far as I'm concerned, human eyes can't see through ocean for a reason. Believing that it's all vast, empty nothing fits much better with my understanding of the world.'

Though that wasn't the world that Mila enjoyed, and it had nothing to do with her superpower.

'It is vast,' she acknowledged carefully. 'And you've probably become accustomed to having things within your power.'

'Is that what you think being CEO is about? Controlling things?'

'Isn't it?'

'It's more like a skipper. Steering things. And I've worked my whole life towards it.'

'You say that like you were greying at the temples when you stepped up. What are you now, mid-thirties? You must have been young when it happened.'

He remembered the day he'd got the call from the hospital, telling him about his father. Telling him to come. The sick feeling of hitting peak-hour traffic. The laws he'd broken trying to get there in time. Wishing for lights or sirens or *something* to help him change what was so obviously happening.

His father was dying and he wasn't there for it.

It was his mother all over again. Except, this time, he couldn't disappear into a child's fantasy world to cope.

'Adult enough that people counted on me to keep things running afterwards.'

'Was it unexpected?' she murmured.

'It shouldn't have been, the way he hammered the liquor and the cigarettes. The double espressos so sweet his spoon practically stood up in the little cup. But none of us were ready for it, him least of all. He still had lots to accomplish in life.'

'Like what?'

He hoped the low light would disguise the tightness of his smile. 'World domination.'

'He got halfway there, at least,' she murmured.

'WestCorp and all its holdings are just an average-sized fish on our particular reef.'

'I've seen some of those holdings; they're nothing to sneeze at.'

Rich tensed. That's right; she'd done her homework on him. He searched her gaze for a clue but found only interest. And compassion.

So Mila hadn't dug so deep that she'd found Wardoo. She wasn't skilled enough at subterfuge to have that knowledge in her head and be able to hide it. Of course it wouldn't have occurred to her to look. Why would it? And Wardoo—big as it was—was still only a small pastoral holding compared to some of WestCorp's mining and resource interests. She'd probably tired of her search long before getting to the smaller holdings at the end of the list.

'For a woman who hangs out with sea stars and coral for a living you seem to know a lot about the Western Australian corporate scene. I wouldn't have thought it would interest you.'

He saw her flush more in the sweep of her lashes on her cheeks in the moonlight than in her colour. 'Normally, no—'

Out on the water, a few gulls appeared, dipping and soaring, only to dip again at the glittering surface. The moon might not be large but it was high now.

'Oh! We're on!' Mila said, excitement bubbling in her voice.

Compared to the last time she'd stripped off in front of him, this time she did it with far less modesty. It only took a few seconds to slide the strings holding up her slip of a dress off her shoulders and step out of the pooled fabric, leaving only bare feet and white bikini. Her shell necklace followed and she piled both on the table with the same casual concern that she'd balled up the paper from their fish and chips. She gathered her snorkelling gear as Rich shed a few layers down to his board shorts and he followed her tensely to the high tide mark. Their gear on, she handed him a headlamp to match her own and a calico net.

There was something about doing this together—as partners. He trusted Mila not to put him in any kind of danger, and trusting her felt like an empowered decision. And empowerment felt a little like control.

And that was all he needed to step into the dark shallows.

'What do I do with this?' he asked, waving the net around his head, as if it was meant for butterflies.

'Just hold it a foot above any coral that's erupting. Ten seconds maximum. Then find a coral that looks totally different to the first and repeat the process.'

'This is high stakes.'

He meant that glibly but he knew by the pause as she studied him that, for her, it absolutely was.

'You can't get it wrong. Come on.'

She waded in ahead of him and his headlamp slashed across her firm, slim body as she went. Given they were on departmental business, it felt wrong to be checking out a fellow scientist. It would have helped if she'd worn a white lab coat instead of a white bikini.

Focus.

The inky water swallowed them up, and its vastness demanded his full attention even as his mind knew it wasn't particularly deep. He fought to keep a map of the lagoon in his head so that his subconscious had something to reference when it was deciding how much adrenaline to pump through his system.

They were on the shallow side of the drop-off, where everything was warm and golden and filled with happy little sea creatures during the day. There was no reason that should change just because it was dark. Robbed of one of his key senses, his others heightened along with his imagination. In that moment he almost understood how Mila saw the reef. The water was silky-smooth and soft where it brushed his bare skin. Welcoming.

Decidedly un-soupy.

He kept Mila's fins—two of them this time—just inside the funnel of light coming from his headlamp. Beyond the cone of both their lights it was the inkiest of blacks. But Mila swam confidently on and the sandy lagoon floor fell away from them until the first corals started to appear a dozen metres offshore.

'They need a good couple of metres of water above them to do this,' she puffed, raising her head for a moment and pushing out her snorkel mouthpiece. Her long hair glued to her neck and shoulders and her golden skin glittered wet in his lamplight. 'So that the receding tide will carry their spawn bundles away to a new site while the embryos mature. Get ready…'

He mirrored her deep breath and then submerged, kicking down to the reef's surface. At first, there was nothing. Just the odd little bit of detritus floating across his field of light, but between one fin-kick and the next he swam straight into a plume of spawning coral. Instantly, he was inside a snow dome. Hundreds of tiny bundles wafted around him on the water's current, making their way to the surface. Pink. White. Glowing in the lamplight against the endless black background of night ocean. As each one met his skin, it was like rain—or tiny reverse hailstones—plinking onto him from below then rolling off and carrying on its determined journey to the surface. As soft as a breath. Utterly surreal. All around them, tiny bait fish darted, unconcerned by their presence, and picked off single, unlucky bundles. The bigger fish kept their distance and gorged themselves just out of view and, though he knew that *even bigger* fish with much sharper teeth probably watched them from the darkness, he found it difficult to care in light of this once-in-a-lifetime moment.

Mila was right.

It was spectacular.

And he might have missed it if not for her.

He surfaced for air again, glanced at the lights of the beach car park to stay oriented and then plugged his snorkel and returned to a few metres below. Just on the edge of his lamp, Mila back-swam over a particularly active plate coral and held her net aloft, letting the little bundles just float right into its mesh embrace. He turned to the nearby staghorn and did the same. On his, the spawn came off in smoky plumes and it was hard to know which was coral and which was some local fish timing its own reproductive activity within the smokescreen of much more obvious targets. He scooped it all up regardless. For every spawn bundle he caught, thousands more were being released.

Besides, the little fish were picking off many more than he was.

Ten seconds...

A sea jelly floated across the shaft of his lamp, glowing, but it was only when a cuttlefish did the same that he stopped to wonder. He'd only ever seen them dead on the seashore—as a kid he'd used them to dig out moats on sandcastles—like small surfboards. Live and lamplit, the cuttlefish glowed with translucent beauty and busied itself chasing down a particular spawn bundle, with a dozen crazily swimming legs.

But, as he raised his eyes, the shaft of his light filled with Mila, her limbs gently waving in a way the cuttlefish could only dream of, pink-white spawn snowing in reverse all around her, her eyes behind her mask glinting and angled. He didn't need to see her smile to feel its effect on him.

She was born to be here.

And he was honoured to be allowed to visit.

The reef at night reminded him of an eighties movie he'd seen. A dying metropolis, three hundred years from now, saturated with acid rain and blazing with neon, the skies crowded with grungy air transport, the streets far below pocked with dens and cavities of danger and the underbelly that thrived there.

This reef was every bit as busy and systematic as that futuristic world. Just far more beautiful.

She surfaced for a breath near to him.

'Ready to go in?' she asked.

'Nope.' Not nearly.

She smiled. 'It's been an hour, Rich.'

He kicked his legs below the surface and realised how

much thicker the water had become in that time. 'You're kidding?'

'Time flies…'

Yeah. It really did. He couldn't remember the last time he'd felt this relaxed. Yet energised at the same time.

'I'm happy with that haul,' she said. 'I missed the *Porites* coral last year so they'll be awesome for the spawn bank.'

'Is that what I can smell?' he said, nostrils twitching at the pungent odour.

'It's probably better not to think about exactly what we're swimming in,' she puffed, staying afloat. 'But trust me when I say it's much better being out here in freshly erupted spawn than tomorrow in day-old spawn. Or the day after.'

She deftly twisted her catch net and then his so that the contents could not escape and then they turned for shore. They had drifted out further than he'd thought but still well within the confines of the lagoon. He could only imagine what a feeding frenzy this night would be beyond the flats where the outer reef spread. In the shallow water, she passed him the nets and then kicked free of her fins to jog ashore and collect the big plastic tub waiting there. She half filled it with clear seawater and then used her snorkelling mask to pour more over the top of her reversed net, swilling out the captured spawn into their watery new home. Maskful after maskful finally got all of his in too. They wrestled the heavy container up to their table together.

After the weightlessness of an hour in the dystopian underworld his legs felt like clumsy, useless trunks and he longed for the ease and effectiveness and freedom of his fins.

Freedom…

'So what did you think?' Mila asked, straightening.

Because they'd carried the tub together, she was standing much closer to him than she ever had before and her head came to just below his shoulder, forcing her to peer up at him with clear green eyes. Even bedraggled and wet, and with red pressure marks from her mask around her face, he wasn't sure he'd ever seen anything quite as beautiful. Except maybe the electric snowfield of spawning coral rising all around her as she did her best mermaid impersonation.

He'd never wanted to kiss someone so much in his life.

'Speechless,' he murmured instead. 'It was everything you said it would be.'

'Now do you get it?'

Somehow he knew what she was really asking.

Now do you get me?

He raised a hand and brushed her cheek with his knuckles, tucking a strand of soggy hair behind her ear. She sucked in a breath and leaned, almost easily, into his touch. It was the first time she hadn't flinched away from him.

His chest tightened even as it felt as if it had expanded two-fold with the pride of that.

'Yeah,' he breathed. 'I think I do. What is it like for you?'

'A symphony. So many sounds all working together.' Her eyes glittered at the memory. 'Not necessarily in harmony—just a wash of sound. The coral bundles are like tiny percussions and they build and they build as the sea fills with them and the ones that touch my skin are like—' she searched around her as if the word she needed was hovering nearby '—a mini firework. Hundreds of tiny explosions. The coral itself is so vibrant under light it just sings to me. Seduces. Breathtaking, except that I'm already holding my breath.' She dropped her head and her wet locks swayed. 'I can't explain it.'

He brought her gaze back up with a finger beneath her chin. His other hand came up to frame her cheek. 'I think I envy you your superpower right now.'

Lips the same gentle pink as the coral spawn parted slightly and mesmerised his gaze just as the little bundles had.

'It has its moments,' she breathed.

Mila was as much a product of this reef as anything he saw out there. Half-mermaid and easily as at home in the water as she was on land. Born of the Saltwater People and she would die in it, living it, loving it.

Protecting it.

This land was technically his heritage too, yet he had no such connection with it and no such protective instincts. He'd been raised to work it and maximise its yield. To exploit it.

For the first time ever he doubted the philosophy he'd been raised with. And he doubted himself.

Was he exploiting Mila too? Mining her for her knowledge and expertise? Wouldn't kissing her when she didn't know the truth about him just be another kind of exploitation? As badly as he wanted to lower his mouth onto hers, until he rectified *that*, any kiss he stole would be just that…

Stolen.

'You have spawn in your hair,' he murmured as she peered up at him.

It said something about how used to the distance of others Mila was that she was so unsurprised when he stepped back.

'I'm sure that's the least of it,' she said. 'Let's get this all back to my place and we can both clean up.'

He retreated a step, then another, and he lifted the heavy spawn-rich container to save Mila the chore. Her dress snagged on her damp skin as she wriggled back into it but then she gathered up the rest of their gear and followed him up to her truck.

CHAPTER SEVEN

IT ONLY OCCURRED to Mila as she pulled up out the front that Rich was the first person she'd ever brought into this place. When she needed to liaise with work people she usually drove the long road north to the department's branch office or met them at some beach site somewhere. She never came with them here, to the little stack of converted transport modules that served as both home and office.

Safe, private spaces.

Rich stood by her four-wheel drive, looking at the two-storey collection of steel.

'Are those…shipping containers?'

The back of her mouth filled with something between fried chicken and old leather. She looked at the corrugated steel walls in their mismatched, faded primary colours as he might see them and definitely found them wanting.

'Up here the regular accommodation is saved for the tourists,' she said. 'Behind the scenes, everyone lives in pretty functional dwellings. But we make them homey inside. Come on in.'

She led him around the back of the efficient dwelling where a weathered timber deck stretched out between the 'U' of sea containers on three sides—double-storey in the centre and single-storey adjoining on the left and right. He stumbled to a halt at the sight of her daybed—an old timber dinghy, tipped on an angle and filled with fat, inviting cushions. A curl of old canvas hung above it between the containers like a crashing wave. He stood, speechless, and stared at her handiwork.

'You're going to see a bit of upcycling in the next quarter-hour…' she warned, past the sour milk of self-consciousness.

Mila pushed open the double doors on the sea container to her left and stepped into her office. Despite the unpromising exterior, inside, it looked much like any other workspace except that her furniture was a bit more eclectic than the big city corporate office Rich was probably used to. A weathered old beach shack door for a desk, with a pair of deep filing cabinets for legs. An old paint-streaked ladder mounted lengthways on the wall served as bookshelves for her biology textbooks and her work files. The plain walls were decorated with a panoramic photograph she had taken of her favourite lagoon, enlarged and mounted in three parts behind mismatched window frames salvaged from old fishing shacks from down the coast.

Rich stared at the artwork.

'My view when I'm working,' she puffed, fighting the heat of a blush. 'Could you put that by the door?'

He positioned the opaque tub by the glass doors so that the moonlight could continue to work its magic on the coral spawn within until she could freeze them in the morning. Those first few hours of moonlight seemed critical to a good fertilisation result; why else had nature designed them to bob immediately to the surface instead of sink to the seafloor?

She killed the light and turned to cross the deck. 'I inherited this stack from someone else when I first moved out of home, but it was pretty functional then. I like to think I've improved it.'

She opened French windows immediately opposite her office and led Rich inside. His eyes had barely managed to stop bulging at her makeshift office before they were goggling again.

'You did all this?' he asked, looking around.

Her furniture mostly consisted of another timber sailing boat cut into parts and sanded within an inch of its life before being waxed until it was glossy. The stern half stood on its fat end at the end of the room and acted as a bookshelf and display cabinet, thanks to some handiwork flipping the boat's seats into shelves; its round little middle sat upturned at the centre of the space and held the glass that made it a coffee table, and its pointed bow was wall-mounted and served as a side table.

'I had some help from one of Coral Bay's old sea dogs, but otherwise, yes, I made most of this. I hate to see anything wasted. Feel free to look around.'

She jogged up polished timber steps to the bedroom that sat on top of the centremost sea container—the one that acted as kitchen, bathroom and laundry. She rustled up some dry clothes and an armful of towels and then padded back down to take a quick shower. Rich hadn't moved his feet but he'd twisted a little, presumably to peer around him. Was it in disbelief? In surprise?

In horror?

To her, it was personalised expression—her little haven filled with things that brought her pleasure. But what did Rich see? Did he view it as the junkyard pickings of some kind of hoarder?

His eyes were fixed overhead, on the lighting centrepiece of the room. A string of bud lights twisted and wove back on itself but each tiny bulb was carefully mounted inside a sea urchin she'd found on the shore outside of the sanctuary zone. Some big. Some small. All glowing their own delicate shades of pinks and orange. The whole thing tangled around an artful piece of driftwood she'd just loved.

The room filled with sour milk again and it killed her that she could feel so self-conscious about something that had brought her so much joy to create. And still did. She refused to defend it even though she burned to.

'I'll be just five minutes,' she announced, tossing the towel over her shoulder. 'Then you can clean up too.'

She scurried through the kitchen to the bathroom at the back of the sea container. If you didn't know what you were standing in you might think you were in some kind of up-market beach shack, albeit eclectically furnished. Rich had five minutes to look his fill at all her weird stuff and then he'd be in here—her eyes drifted up to the white, round lightshade to which she'd attached streaming lengths of plaited fishing net until the whole thing resembled a cheerful bathroom jellyfish—for better or worse.

When she emerged, rinsed and clean-haired, Rich was studying up close the engineering on a tiered wall unit made of pale driftwood. She moved up next to him and lit the tea lights happily sitting on its shelves. They cast a gentle glow over that side of the room.

'Will I find an ordinary light fitting anywhere in your house?' he murmured down at her.

She had to think about it. 'The lamp in the office is pretty regular.' If you didn't count the tiny sea stars glued to its stand. 'This is one of my favourites.'

She lit another tea light sitting all alone on the boat bow side table except for a tiny piece of beach detritus that sat with it. It looked like nothing more than a minuscule bit of twisted seaweed. But, as the flame caught behind it, a shadow cast on the nearby wall and Rich was drawn by the flickering shape that grew as the flame did.

'I found the poor, dried seahorse on the marina shore

when it was first built,' she said. 'Took me ages to think how I could celebrate it.'

He turned and just stared, something rather like confusion in his blue gaze.

Mila handed him a small stack of guest towels and pointed him in the direction of the bathroom. 'Take your time.'

As soon as he was safely out of view, she sagged against the kitchen bench. Nothing should have upstaged the fact that there was a naked man showering just ten feet away in her compact little bathroom, but Rich had given her spectacular fodder for distraction.

That kiss...

Not an actual kiss, but nearly. Cheek-brushing and chest-heaving and lingering looks. Enough that she'd been throbbing candyfloss while her pulse had tumbled over itself like a crashing wave. Lucky she'd built up such excellent lung capacity because she'd flat-out forgotten to breathe during the whole experience. Anyone else might have passed out.

'An almost-kiss isn't an actual kiss,' she lectured herself under her breath.

Even if it was the closest she'd come in a long, long time. Rich had been overwhelmed by his experience on the reef and had reached out instinctively, but—really—who wanted to kiss a woman soaked in spawn?

'No one.'

She rustled up a second mug and put the kettle on to boil. It took about the same time to bubble as the ninety seconds Rich did to shower and change back into his black sweater and jeans. When he emerged from the door next to her, all pink and freshly groomed, the bathroom's steam mingled with the kettle's.

'I made you tea,' she murmured.

He smiled as he took the mug. 'It's been a long time since I've had tea.'

Her eyes immediately hunted for coffee. 'You don't like it?'

'It's just that coffee's more a thing in the corporate world. I've fallen out of practice. It was a standard at boarding school until eleventh form, when we were allowed to upgrade to a harder core breakfast beverage.'

She started rummaging in the kitchen. 'I have some somewhere…'

He met her eyes and held them. 'I would like to drink tea with you, Mila.'

She couldn't look away; she could barely breathe a reply. 'Okay.'

He looked around her humble home again. 'I really like your place.'

'It's different to the *Portus*.'

He laughed. 'It's not a boat, for one thing. But it suits you. It's unique.'

Unique. Yep, that was one word for her.

'I hate to see anything wasted,' she said again. Her eyes went to her sea urchin extravaganza. 'And I hate to see beautiful things die. This is a way I can keep them alive and bring the reef inside at the same time.'

He studied her light art as if it was by a Renaissance sculptor, his brows drawn, deep in thought.

'What is your home like?' she went on when he didn't reply.

The direct question brought his gaze back to her. 'It's not a *home*, for a start. I don't feel like I've had one of those since… A long time.' He peered around again. 'But it's nothing like this.'

No. She couldn't imagine him surrounded by anything other than quality. She sank ahead of him onto one of two sofas made out of old travelling chests. The sort that might have washed up after a shipwreck. The sort that was perfect to have upholstered into insanely comfortable seats.

Rich frowned a little as he examined the seat's engineering.

'Home is something you come back to, isn't it?' he went on. 'About the only thing I have that meets that definition is the *Portus*. I feel different when I step aboard. Changed. Maybe she's my home.'

Mila sipped at her tea in the silence that followed and watched Rich grow less and less comfortable in her company.

'Is everything all right, Rich?' she finally braved.

He glanced up at her and then sighed. Long and deep.

'Mila, there's something I haven't told you.'

The cloves made a brief reappearance but she pushed through the discomfort. Trust came more easily with every minute she spent in Rich's company.

'Keeping secrets, Mr Grundy?' she quipped.

'That's just it,' he went on, ignoring her attempt at humour. 'I'm not Mr Grundy. At least… I am, and I'm not.'

She pressed back into the soft upholstery and gave him her full attention.

He lifted bleak eyes. 'Nancy Dawson married a Grundy.'

Awareness flooded in on a wave of nostalgia. 'Oh, that's right. Jack. I forgot because everyone up here knows them as Dawson. Wait…are you a relative of Jack Grundy? Ten times removed?'

'No times removed, actually.' Rich took a long sip of his tea. As if it were his last. 'Jack was my great-grandfather.'

Mila just stared. 'But that means…'

Nancy's Point. She'd stood there and lectured him about his own great-grandmother. The more immediate ramification took a little longer to sink in. She sat upright and placed her still steaming mug onto the little midships coffee table. The only way to disguise the sudden tremble of her fingers was to lay them flat on the thighs of her yoga pants. Unconsciously bracing herself.

'Are you a Dawson? Of the Wardoo Dawsons?'

Rich took a deep breath. 'I'm *the* Dawson. The only son of an only son. I hold the pastoral rights on Wardoo Station and the ten thousand square kilometres around it.'

Mila's hands dug deeper into her thighs. 'But that means…'

'It means I hold the lease on the land that Coral Bay sits on.'

The back of her throat stung with the taste of nail varnish and it was all she could do to whisper, 'You own my town?'

Rich straightened. 'The only thing I *own* is the Station infrastructure. But the lease is what has the value. And I hold that, presently.'

Her brain finally caught up and the nail varnish dissipated. 'Wardoo is yours.'

Because there was no Wardoo without the Dawsons. Just as there was no Coral Bay without them either.

Rich took a deep breath before answering. 'It is.'

Her eyes came up. 'Then you've been stopping the developers in their tracks! I thought you were one!'

His skin greyed off just a bit. Maybe he wasn't comfortable with overt gushing, but the strong mango of gratitude made it impossible for her to stop.

'WestCorp has been denying access for third-party development, yes—'

Whatever that little bit of careful corporate speak meant. All she heard was that *Rich* was the reason there were no towering hotels on her reef. *Rich* had kept everyone but the state government out of the lands bordering the World Heritage Marine Park. *Rich* was her corporate guardian angel.

Despite herself, despite everything she knew about people and every screaming sense she knew she'd be triggering, Mila tipped herself forward and threw her arms wide around his broad shoulders.

'Thank you,' she gushed, pressing herself into the hug. 'Thank you for my reef.'

CHAPTER EIGHT

RICH COULDN'T REMEMBER a time that he'd been more comfortable in someone's arms yet so excruciatingly uncomfortable as well.

Mila had only grasped half the truth.

Because he had only told half of it.

He let his own hands slide up and contribute to Mila's fervent embrace, but it was brief and it took little physical effort to curl his fingers and ease her slightly back from him. The emotional effort was much higher; she was warm and soft under his hands and she felt incredibly right there—speaking of going *home*—yet he felt more of a louse than when he'd nearly kissed her earlier.

Telling her had been the right thing to do but, in his head, this moment was going to go very differently. He'd steeled himself for her shock, her disappointment. Maybe for an escaped tear or two that he'd been keeping the truth from her. Instead, he got…this.

Gratitude.

He'd confessed his identity now but Mila only saw half the picture… The half that made him a hero, looking out for the underdog and the underdog's reef. She had no sense for the politics and game playing behind every access refusal. The prioritising.

It wasn't noble… It was corporate strategy.

'Don't be too quick to canonise me, Mila,' he murmured as she withdrew from the spontaneous hug, blushing. The gentle flush matched the colour she'd been when she came out of the bathroom. 'It's business. It's not personal. I hadn't even seen the reef until you showed me.'

Even now he was avoiding putting the puzzle fully together for her. It would only take a few words to confess that—yeah, he was still a developer and he was planning on developing her reef. But he wasn't strong enough to do that while he was still warm from her embrace.

'How could you go to Wardoo and not visit such a famous coast?' she asked.

'Actually, I've never been to Wardoo either,' he confessed further. 'I flew over it once, years ago.'

The quizzical smile turned into a gape. 'What? Why?'

'Because there's no need. I get reports and updates from the caretaking team. To me, it's just a remote business holding at the end of one of my spreadsheets.'

The words on his lips made him tense. As though the truth wasn't actually the truth.

Her gape was now a stare. 'No. Really?'

'Really.' He shrugged.

'But… It's *Wardoo*. It's your home.'

'I never grew up there, Mila. It holds no meaning for me.'

A momentary flash of his eight-year-old self tumbled beneath his determination for it to *be* the truth.

She scrabbled upright again and perched on her seat, leaning towards him. 'You need to go, Rich.'

No. He really didn't.

'You need to go and see it in its context, not in some photograph. Smell it and taste it and…'

'Taste it?'

'Okay, maybe that's just me, but won't you at least visit

the people who run it for you? Let them show you their work?'

It was his turn to frown. Her previous jibe about *minions* hit home again.

'I'm sure they'd be delighted with a short-notice visit from their CEO,' he drawled.

She considered him. 'You won't know if you don't ask.'

He narrowed his eyes. 'You're very keen for me to visit, Mila. What am I missing?'

Her expression grew suspiciously innocent. 'I *might* be thinking about the fact that you don't have a car. And that I do—'

'And you're offering to lend it to me?' he shot back, his face just as impassive. 'Thanks, that's kind of you.'

Which made it sound as if he was considering going. When had that happened?

'Actually, it's kind of hinky to drive. I'd better take you. Road safety and all.'

'You don't know the roads. You've never been out there.'

Hoisted by her own petard.

'Okay, fine. Then take me in return for the coral spawn.' She shuffled forward. 'I would give anything to see Wardoo.'

Glad one of them was so keen. 'You know there's no reef out there, right? Just scrub and dirt.'

'Come on, Rich, it's a win-win—I get to see Wardoo and you get to have a reason to go there.'

'I don't need a reason to go there.'

And he didn't particularly *want* to. Though he did, very much, want to see the excited colour in Mila's cheeks a little bit longer. It reminded him of the flush as he'd stroked her cheek. And it did make a kind of sense to check it out since he was up here on an official fact-finding mission. After all, how convincing was he going to be if that government bureaucrat discovered he'd never actually been to the property? Photos and monthly reports could only do so much.

'What time?' he sighed.

Mila's eyes glittered like the emeralds they were, triumphant. 'I have a quickish task to do at low tide, but it's on the way to Wardoo so… Eight?'

'Does this *task* involve anything else slimy, soupy or slippery?' he worried.

'Maybe.' She laughed. 'It involves the reef.'

Of course it did.

'How wet will I be getting?'

'You? Not at all. I might, depending on the tide.'

'Okay then.' He could happily endure one last opportunity to see Mila in her natural habitat. Before he told her the full truth. And he could give her the gift of Wardoo, before pulling the happy dream they were both living out from under her too.

The least he could do, maybe.

'Eight it is, then.'

Her gaze glowed her pleasure and Rich just let himself swim there for a few moments. Below it all, he knew he was only delaying the inevitable, but there really was nothing to gain by telling her now instead of tomorrow.

'I should get back to the *Portus*,' he announced, reaching into his pocket for his phone. 'Need my beauty sleep if I'm going to wow the minions tomorrow.'

Her perfect skin flushed again as she remembered her own words and who she'd been talking about all along. But she handled the embarrassment as she handled everything—graciously. She crossed the small room to get her keys off their little hook.

'I'll drive you to the marina.'

* * *

Not surprisingly, given the marina was only a few minutes away, there was no sign of Damo when they climbed out of the four-wheel drive at the deserted ramp, although Mila could clearly see the *Portus* waiting out beyond the reef. Had it done laps out there the whole night, like a pacing attendant waiting for its master?

'He won't be long,' Rich murmured as a floodlight made its way steadily across the darkness that was the sea beyond the reef. The speed limits still applied even though no one else was using the channel. They weren't there to protect the boats.

'Did you enjoy dinner?' Rich asked after a longish, silence-filled pause. He turned closer to her in the darkness.

She'd totally forgotten the eating part of the evening. All she'd been fixating on was the looking part, the touching part. The just-out-of-the-shower part.

'Very much,' she said, looking up to him. 'Always happy not to go into a crowded building.'

'Thank you for letting me tag along on the spawn; it really was very beautiful.'

It was impossible not to chuckle but—this close and in this much darkness—it came out sounding way throatier than she meant it. 'I'm pretty sure I bullied you into coming.'

Just like she'd talked her way into Wardoo tomorrow.

'Happy to have been bullied then. I never could have imagined…'

No. It really was *un*imaginable until you'd seen it. She liked knowing that they had that experience in common now. Every shared experience they had brought them that little bit closer. And now that she knew he was a Dawson… every experience would help to secure the borders against developers even more.

A stiff breeze kicked up off the water and reminded Mila that she was still in the light T-shirt and yoga pants she'd shrugged into in her steamy little bathroom inside her warm little house. Gooseflesh prickled, accompanied by imaginary wings fluttering as the bumps raced up her skin.

'You should head home,' Rich immediately said as she rubbed her arms. 'It's cold.'

'No—'

She didn't want to leave. She didn't want to wait until eight a.m. to see him again. She wasn't ready to leave this man who turned out to have had the back of everything she cared about for all these years. If he asked her back to his boat to spend the night she was ready to say yes.

'I'm good.'

Large hands found her upper arms in the light from the silvered moon and added their warmth to her cold skin. Harps immediately joined the fluttering wings.

'Here…'

Rich moved around close behind her and then rubbed his hands up and down her arms, bringing her back against his hard, warm, sweater-clad chest. He'd shifted from a client to an acquaintance somewhere around the visit to Yardi Creek, and from acquaintance to a friend when she'd agreed to have dinner. But exactly when did they become *arm-rubbing* kinds of friends? Was it when they'd stood so close by the shore this evening? When they'd shared the majesty of the spawn event? The not-quite kiss?

Did it even matter? The multiple sensations of his hands on hers, his body against hers was a kind of heaven she'd secretly believed she would never experience.

It was only when she saw the slash of the tender's arriving floodlight on the back of her eyelids that she realised they'd fluttered shut.

Rich stepped away and the harps faded to nothing at the loss of his skin on hers.

'I'll see you here at eight,' he said, far more composed than she felt. But then his big frame blocked the moonlight as he bent to kiss her cheek. His words were a hot caress against her ear and the gooseflesh worsened.

'Sleep well.'

Pfff... As if.

Before she could reply, he had stepped away and she mourned not only the warmth of his hands but now the gentle brush of his lips too. Too, too brief. He stepped down onto the varnished pier out to the tender and left her. Standing here, watching him walk away from her, those narrow jeans-clad hips swinging even in the dim moonlight, was a little too much like self-harm and so she turned to face her truck and took the few steps she needed to cross back to it.

At the last moment she heard a crunch that wasn't her own feet on the crushed gravel marina substrate.

'Mila...'

She pivoted into Rich's return and he didn't even pause as he walked hard up against her and bent again, to her lips this time. His kiss was soft but it lingered. It explored. It blew her little mind. And it came with a sensation overload. He took her too much by surprise to invoke the citrus of anticipation but it kicked in now and mingled with the strong, candy surge of attraction as a tiny corner of her mind wondered breathlessly how long his kiss could last. Waves crashed and she knew it wasn't on the nearby shore; it was what kissing gave her, though not always like this... Not always accompanied by skin harps and the crackle of fireplace that was the heat of Rich's mouth on her own. And all that oak moss...

Her head spun with want as much as the breathless surprise of Rich's stealthy return.

'I should have done that hours ago,' he murmured at last, breathing fast. 'I wanted to right after the coral.'

'Why didn't you?' Belatedly, she realised she was probably supposed to protest his presumption, or say something witty, or be grown up and blasé about it. But really, all she wanted to know was why they hadn't been kissing all evening.

'I wanted you to know about me. Who I was. So you had the choice.'

Oh, kissing him was a *choice*? That was a laugh, and not because he'd sneaked up on her and made the first move. She'd been thinking about his mouth for days now.

There was no choice.

But she was grateful for the consideration.

'I like who you are,' she murmured. 'Thank you for telling me.'

Besides, she was the last person who could judge anyone else for keeping themselves private.

He dipped his head again and sent the harps a-harping and the fire a-crackling for more precious moments. Then he straightened and stepped back.

'Tomorrow then,' he said and he and his conflicted gaze were gone, jogging down the pier towards the *Portus'* waiting tender.

Mila sagged against her open car door and watched until he was out of sight. Even then, she stared at the inky ocean and imagined the small boat making its way until it reappeared as a shadow against the well-lit *Portus*. Impossible to see Rich climb aboard at this distance but she imagined that too; in her mind's eye she saw him slumping down on that expansive sofa amid the polished chrome and glass. She tried to imagine him checking his phone or picking up a book or even stretching out on that king-sized bed and watching the night sky through the wraparound windows, but it was easier to imagine him settling in behind his laptop at the workstation and getting a few more hours of corporate in before his head hit any kind of pillow.

That was just who he was. And it was where he came from.

A whale shark couldn't change its spots.

Except this one—just maybe—could.

CHAPTER NINE

MILA TOOK A careful knife to the reef and carved out a single oyster from a crowded corner, working carefully not to injure or loosen the rest. Then she did it again at another stack. And again. And again. On the way out to this remote bay, she'd told Rich that her department's licence called for five test oysters every month and a couple of simple observational tests to monitor oyster condition and keep them free of the disease that was ravaging populations down the east coast of the country.

Rich held the little bag for her as she dropped them in one by one.

She smiled shy thanks, though not quite at him. 'For a CEO you make an excellent apprentice ranger.'

So far this morning the two of them had been doing a terrific job of ignoring exactly what it was that had gone down between them last night. The kissing part, not the sharing of secrets part. One was planned, the other... Not so much. He hadn't even known he was going to do it until he'd felt his feet twisting on the pier and striding back towards her.

'Now I understand your fashion choice,' he murmured, nodding at her high-vis vest emblazoned with the department logo. It wasn't the most flattering thing he'd seen her

in since they'd met yet she still managed to make it seem…
intriguing.

'Don't want anyone thinking they can just help themselves to oysters here,' she said. 'This is inside the sanctuary zone.'

Not that there was a soul around yet. The tide was way
too low to be of interest to snorkelers and the fishermen
had too much respect for their equipment to try tossing a
line in at this razor-ridden place.

They waded ashore and Mila laid the five knotted shells
out on the tailgate of her four-wheel drive. She placed a
dog-eared laminated number above each, photographed it
and then set about her testing. All that busyness was a fantastic way of not needing to make eye contact with him.

Was she embarrassed? Did she regret participating quite
so enthusiastically in last night's experimental kiss? Or was
she just as focused on her work as he could be when he
was in the zone? Given how distracted he'd been last night,
going over and over the proposal, it was hard to imagine
ever being in the zone again.

Mila picked one oyster up and gently knocked its semi-
open shell. It closed immediately but with no great urgency.

'That's a four,' she told him, and he dutifully wrote it
down on the form she'd given him.

The others were all fours too, and one super-speedy
five. That made her happy. She'd clearly opened an oyster or three in her time and she made quick work of sepa-
rating each one from its top shell by a swift knife move to
its hinge. She wafted the inner scent of each towards her
nostrils before dipping her finger in and then placing it in
her mouth to taste its juices. He wrote down her observa-
tions as she voiced them.

'If these five exemplars are responsive, fresh and the

flesh is opaque then it's a good sign of the health of the whole oyster community,' she said.

'What do you do with them, then—toss them back?'

'These five are ambassadors for their kind. I usually wedge the shells back in to become part of the stack, but I don't waste the meat.'

'And by that you mean…?'

'I eat them,' she said with a grin. 'Want to help?'

Rich frowned. 'Depends on whether you have any red wine vinegar on hand.'

She used the little knife to shuck the first of them and flip it to study its underside. Then she held up the oyster sample in front of her lips like a salute. *'Au naturel.'*

Down it went. She repeated the neat move and handed the finished shuck to him.

His eyebrows raised as soon as he bit down on the ultra-fresh mollusc. 'Melon!'

'Yeah, kind of. Salty melon.'

'Even to you?'

She smiled. 'Even to me. With a bonus hit of *astute*.'

Rich couldn't really see how a hibernating lump of muscle could have any personality at all but he was prepared to go with 'astute'. He'd never managed to taste the 'ambition' in vintage wine either, but he was prepared to believe that connoisseurs at the fancy restaurants he frequented could.

Maybe Mila was just a nature connoisseur.

Oyster number three and four went the same way and then there was only the one left. He offered it to Mila. 'You know what they say about oysters…'

She blinked at him. 'Excellent for your immune system and bone strength?'

He stared at her, trying to gauge whether she was serious. He loved not being able to read her. How long had it been since someone surprised him?

'Yeah, that's what they say.'

It was only when she smiled, slow and sexy, that he knew *she* knew. But obviously she wasn't about to mention it in light of last night's illicit kiss.

She gasped, scribbling in her log what she'd found on the oyster's underside. 'A pearl.'

Rich peered at the small cream mass. It wasn't much of one but it undoubtedly *was* a pearl. 'Is that a good sign?'

'Not really.' Mila poked at it carefully. 'It could have formed in response to a parasite. Too much of that would be a bad sign for these stacks.'

'Pearls are a defect?' he asked.

'"Out of a flaw comes beauty",' Mila quoted.

She might as well have been describing herself.

She lifted it out with her blade and rinsed it in the sea-water, then swallowed the last of the oyster flesh.

'Here,' she said, handing it to him. 'A souvenir.'

'Because you have so many littering your house?'

Just how many had she found in her time?

'It's reasonably rare to find a wild one,' she said, still smiling. 'This is only my second in all the time I've been working here. But I don't feel right about keeping them; I'm lucky enough just to do this for a living without prof-iting from it further. I gave the last one away to a woman with three noisy kids.'

Rich stared. She was like a whole different species to him. 'Do you know what they're worth?'

'Not so much when they're this small and malformed, I don't think.' She laid it out on her hand and let the little lump flip over on her wet palm. 'But I prefer them like this. Rough and nature-formed. Though it's weird, I don't get any kind of personality off them. I wonder why.'

She studied it a moment longer, as if *willing* it to per-form for her.

'Here…' She finally thrust her hand out. 'Something to remember Coral Bay by. Sorry it's not bigger.'

Something deep in his chest protested. Did she imagine he cared about that? When he looked at the small, imperfect pearl he would remember the small, imperfect woman who had given it to him.

And how perfect her imperfections made her.

He closed his hand around the lumpy gem. 'Thank you.'

She took the empty shell parts and jogged back into the water to wedge them back into the stacks as foundation for future generations, then she returned and packed up. Rich took the opportunity to watch her move, and work, without making her self-conscious.

He found he quite liked to just watch her.

'Okay,' she finally puffed. 'All done for the month. Shall we get going? Did you tell Wardoo you were coming?'

'Panic duly instigated, yes.'

She smiled at him and he wondered when he'd started counting the minutes between them. She'd smiled more at him in the last hour than she had in the entire time he'd known her. It was uncomfortably hard not to connect it to her misapprehension that he was some kind of crusading, conservation good guy.

'I think you'll like it. This country really is very beautiful in its own unique way.'

As he followed her up the path to her car all he could think about was an old phrase…

Takes one to know one.

Their arrival at Wardoo was decidedly low-key. If not for the furtive glance of a man crossing between one corrugated outbuilding and the next she'd have thought no one was all that interested in Rich's arrival. But that sideways look spoke volumes. It was more the kind of surreptitious

play-down-the-moment peek reserved for politicians or
rock stars.

Or royalty.

Some of the men who had worked Wardoo their whole
adult lives might never have seen a Dawson in person.
Grundy, she reminded herself.

A wide grin in a weathered, masculine face met them,
introduced himself as the Station foreman and offered to
show them, first, through the homestead.

'Jared Kipling,' he said, shaking Rich's hand. 'Kip.'

She wasn't offended that Kip had forgotten to shake her
hand in the fluster of meeting his long-absent boss. It saved
her the anxiety of another first-time touch.

It was only when she watched Rich's body language as
he stepped up onto the veranda running the full perimeter of the homestead that she realised he'd slipped back
into business mode. She recognised it from that first day
at Nancy's Point. Exactly when he'd stopped being quite
so...corporate she wasn't as sure.

'It's vacant?' Mila asked as she stepped into the dust-
free hall of Wardoo homestead ahead of the men. Despite
being furnished, there was something empty about it, and
not just because the polished floorboards exuded isolation
the way jarrah always did for her.

Wardoo was...hollow. And somehow lifeless.

How incredibly sad. Not what she had imagined at all.

'Most of our crew live in transportables on site or in
town. We keep the house for the Dawsons,' Kip said. 'Just
in case.'

The Dawsons who had never visited? The hollowness
only increased and she glanced at Rich. He kept his gaze
firmly averted.

She left the men to their discussions and explored the
homestead. Every room was just as clean and just as empty

as the one before it. She ran her fingertips along the rich old surfaces and enjoyed the myriad sensations that came with them. When she made her way back to the living room, Rich and the foreman were deep in discussion on the unused sofas. She heard the word 'lease' before Rich shot to his feet and brought the conversation to a rapid halt.

'If you've seen enough—' Kip floundered at the sudden end to their conversation '—I can show you the operations yards and then the chopper's standing by for an aerial tour.'

Rich looked decidedly awkward too. What a novelty— to be the least socially clumsy person in a room.

'You have your own chopper?' Mila asked him, to ease the tension.

It did the trick. He gifted her a small smile that only served to remind her how many minutes it had been since the last one.

Because apparently she counted, now.

He turned for the door as if she'd been the one keeping him waiting. 'It seems I do.'

'It's a stock mustering chopper,' Kip went on, tailing them. 'There's only room for two. But it's the only way to get out to the perimeter of Wardoo and back in a day.'

'The perimeter can wait,' Rich declared. 'Just show us the highlights within striking distance by road.'

Us. As if she were some kind of permanent part of the Richard Grundy show.

She trotted along behind Rich as he toured the equipment and sheds closest to the Homestead. Of course, on a property of this scale 'close' was relative. Then they piled into a late model Land Cruiser and set off in a plume of red-brown dust to the north. Mila lost herself in the Australian scrub and let time flow over her like water as Rich and Kip discussed the operations of the cattle station. She was yet to actually see a cow.

'The herds like to range inland this time of year,' Kip said when she asked. 'While the eastern dams are full. We'll see some soon.'

She lost track of time again until the brush of knuckles on her cheek tingled her out of a light doze.

'Lunchtime,' Rich murmured.

'How long have...?' Lord, how embarrassing.

'Sorry, there was a lot of shop-talk.'

And she'd only slept fitfully last night. Something to do with being kissed half to death at the marina had left her tossing and turning and, clearly, in need of some decent sleep. Mila scurried to climb out of the comfortable vehicle ahead of him.

'The missus made you this,' Kip said, passing Rich a hamper. 'She wasn't expecting two of you but she's probably over-catered so you should be right. Follow the track down that way and you'll come to Jack's Vent. A nice spot to eat,' he told them and then raised Rich's eyebrows by adding, 'No crocs.'

'No crocs...' Rich murmured as they set off. 'Good to know.'

His twisted smile did the same to her insides, and she'd grown to relish the pineapple smell when he gave her that particular wry grin. Pineapple—just when she thought she'd had every fruit known to man.

They walked in silence as the track descended and the land around them transformed in a way that spoke of regular water. Less scrub, more trees. Less brown, more colours peppering the green vegetation. Even the surface of the dark water was freckled with oversized lily pads, some flowering with vibrant colour. Out of cracks in the rock, tall reeds grew.

They reached the edge of Jack's Vent and peered down from the rocky ledge.

Mila glanced around. 'A waterhole seems out of place here where it's so dry.'

Though it certainly was a tranquil and beautiful surprise.

'I've seen this on a map,' Rich murmured. 'It's a sink-hole, not a waterhole. A groundwater vent.'

Golden granite ringed the hole except for a narrow stock trail on the far side where Wardoo's cattle came to drink their fill of the icy, fresh, presumably artesian water, and a flatter patch of rock to their right. It looked like a natural diving platform.

'Wish I'd brought my snorkelling gear,' she murmured. 'I would love to have a look deeper in the vent.'

'You're off the clock, remember?'

'I could do that while you and Kip talk business.'

He gave her his hand to step down onto the rocky platform, which sloped right down to the water's edge. She moved right down to it and kicked off her shoes.

'It's freezing!' she squealed, dipping a toe in. 'Gorgeous.'

Rich lowered the hamper and toed off his own boots, then rolled his jeans up to his knees and followed her down to a sitting position. He gingerly sank his feet.

'There must be twenty sandwiches in here,' Mila said, looking through the hamper's contents and passing him a chilled bottle of water to match her own. 'All different.'

'I guess they were covering all bases.'

'Eager to impress, I suppose. This is a big moment for them.'

Rich snorted then turned his gaze out to the water. They ate in companionable silence but Mila felt Rich's focus drift further and further from her like the lily pads floating on the sinkhole's surface.

'For someone sitting in such a beautiful spot, you look pretty unhappy to be here,' she said when his frown grew too great. Guilt swilled around her like the water at her feet; she had nagged him to bring her. To come at all.

'Sorry,' he said, snapping his focus back to the present. 'Memories.'

She kept her frown light. 'But you haven't been here before.'

'No.' And that was all he gave her. His next words tipped the conversation back her way. 'You were the one panting to come today. How's it living up to your expectations?'

She looked around them. 'It's hard to sit somewhere like this and find fault. Wardoo offers the best of both worlds—the richness of the land and the beauty of the coast. I feel very—'

What? What was the quality she felt?

'*Comfortable* here,' she said at last. 'Maybe it's some kind of genetic memory doing its thing. Oh!'

He glanced around to see what had caught her eye.

'I just realised that both our ancestors could have sat right on this spot, separated by centuries. And now here we are again. Maybe that's why I feel so connected to you.'

Those words slipped out before she thought of the wisdom of them.

Eyes the colour of the sky blazed into her. 'Do you? Feel connected?'

Sour milk wafted around them but Rich's nostrils didn't twitch the way hers wanted to. 'You don't?'

He considered her, long and hard. 'It's futile but... I do, yes.'

Her breath tightened in a way that made her wonder whether her sandwich was refusing to go down.

'Futile?' she half breathed.

'We have such different goals.' His eyes dropped away. 'You're Saltwater People and I'm…glass-and-chrome people.'

She'd never been more grateful to not fit any particular label. That way anything felt possible.

'That's just geography, though. It doesn't change who we are at heart.'

'Doesn't it? I don't know anyone like you back home. So connected to the land…earth spirit and mermaid all at once. That's nurture, not nature. You're as much a product of this environment as those waterlilies. You wouldn't last five minutes in the city, synaesthesia or not.'

Did he have so little faith in her? 'You think I wouldn't adapt?'

'I think you'd *wither*, Mila. I think being away from this place would strip the best of you away. Just like staying here would kill me.'

'You don't like the Bay?'

Why did that thought hurt so very much?

'I like it very much but my world isn't here. I don't know how long I would be entertained by all the pretty. Not when there's work to be done.'

Did he count her in with that flippant description? She had no right to expect otherwise, yet she was undeniably tasting the leather of disappointment in the back of her throat.

'Is that what I've been doing? Entertaining you?'

The obvious answer was yes, because she was paid to show him the best of the Marine Park, but they both knew what she was really asking.

'Mila, that was—' He glanced away and back so quickly she couldn't begin to guess what he was thinking. 'No. That wasn't entertainment. I kissed you because…'

Because why, Rich?

'It was an impulse. A moment. I couldn't walk off that marina without knowing whether the attraction was mutual.'

Given she'd clung to him like a remora, he'd certainly

got his answer. Heat billowed up under the collar of her Parks uniform.

'It was,' she murmured. Then she sighed. 'It *is*. I'm awash in candyfloss twenty-four-seven. I'd be sick of it if it didn't smell—' *and feel* '—so good.'

'I'm candyfloss guy?' he breathed. 'I was sure I was earwax.'

He'd eased back on one strong arm so he could turn his body fully to her for this delicate conversation. It would be so easy to lean forward and find his lips, repeat the experiment, but…to what end? She would eventually run out of things to show him in Coral Bay and then he'd be gone, back to the city, probably for good, and the kissing would be over. And he was right. She wouldn't cope in the city. Not long-term.

'Candyfloss is what I get for…' *attraction* '…for you.'

If Rich was flattered to get a scent all to himself, he didn't show it. He studied her and seemed to glance over her shoulder, his head shaking.

'The timing of this sucks.'

'Would six months from now make a difference?'

'Not a good one,' she thought she heard him mutter.

But he leaned closer, bringing his face within breathing distance, and Mila thought that even though these random kisses confused the heck out of her she could certainly get used to the sensation. Pineapple went quite well with candyfloss, after all. But his lips didn't meet hers; his right shoulder brushed her left one as he leaned beyond her for a moment. When he straightened, he had a flower in his hand, plucked with some of its stem still attached. The delicate pink blossom fanned out around a thatch of golden-pink stamens. On its underside it was paler and waxier, to help it survive the harsh outback conditions.

'One of my favourites,' she said, studying it but not taking it. If she took it he might lean back. 'Desert rose.'

'It matches your lips,' he murmured. 'The same soft pink.'

She couldn't help wetting them; it was instinctive. Rich brushed her cheek with the delicate flower, then followed it with his bare knuckles. Somewhere, harps sang out.

'Pollen,' he explained before folding her fingers around the blossom's thick-leaved stem.

But he didn't move back; he just stayed there, bent close.

'I need you to know something—' he began, a shadow in his gaze.

But no, she wasn't ready to have this amazing day intruded upon by more truths. If it was bad news it could wait. If it wasn't…it could wait too.

'Will you still be here tomorrow?'

He took her interruption in his stride. 'I'm heading back overnight. I have an important meeting at ten a.m.'

Panic welled up like the water in this vent.

Tonight… That was just hours away. A few short hours and he would be gone back to his in-tray, twelve hundred kilometres south of here. After which there were no more reasons for him to return to Coral Bay, unless it was to visit Wardoo, which seemed unlikely given he'd never had the interest before.

And they both knew it.

Mila silenced any more bad news with her fingers on his lips. 'Tell me later. Let's just enjoy today.' Then, when the gathering blue shadows looked as if they weren't going to be silenced, she added, 'Please.'

There wasn't much else to do then than close up the short distance between them again. Mila sucked up some courage and took care of that herself, leaning into the warmth of Rich's cheek, brushing hers along it, seeking out his mouth.

Their kiss was soft and exploratory, Rich brushing his lips back and forth across hers, relearning their shape. She inhaled his heated scent, clung to the subtle smell of *him* through the almost overpowering candyfloss and pineapple that made her head light. He tasted like the chutney in Kip's wife's sandwiches but she didn't care. She could eat pickle for the rest of her days and remember this place. This kiss.

This man.

Long after he'd gone.

'Have dinner with me,' he breathed. 'On the *Portus*. Tonight before I leave.'

Dinner... Was that really what he was asking? Or was he hoping to cap off his northern experience with something more...satisfying? Did she even care? She should... She'd only just begun to get used to the sensations that came with kissing; how could she go from that to something so much more irrevocable in just one evening?

Rich watched her between kisses, his blue eyes peering deeply into hers. He withdrew a little. 'Your mind is very busy...'

This moment would probably be overwhelming for anyone—even those without a superpower. She'd never felt more...normal.

'I'm going out on the water this afternoon,' she said. 'Come with me. One last visit onto the reef. Then I'll have dinner with you.'

Because going straight from this to dinner to goodbye just wasn't an option.

'Okay,' he murmured, kissing her softly one last time.

She clung to it, to him, then let him go. In the distance, the Land Cruiser honked politely.

'Back to work,' Rich groaned.

Probably just as well. Sitting here on the edge of an ancient sinkhole, older than anything either of them had ever known, it was too easy to pretend that none of it mattered. That real life didn't matter.

She nodded and watched as he pushed to his feet. When he lowered a strong hand towards her she didn't hesitate to slide her smaller fingers into his. The first time ever she didn't give a moment's thought before touching someone.

Pineapple wafted past her nostrils again.

CHAPTER TEN

'ARE YOU KIDDING ME?' Rich gaped at her. 'How danger-ous is this?'

'It's got to be done,' Mila pointed out.

Right. Something about baselines for studying dugong numbers. He understood baselines; he worked with them all the time. But not like this.

'Why does it have to be done by *you*?' he pointed out, pretty reasonably he thought, as he did his part in the equip-ment chain, loading the small boat.

'It's not just me,' she said, laughing. 'There's a whole team of us.'

Yeah, there was. Four big, strong men, experienced in traditional hunting methods. It was the only bit of comfort he got for this whole crazy idea.

'You hate teams,' he pointed out in a low voice. She loved working solo. Just Mila and the reef life. A mermaid and her undersea world.

'I wouldn't do it every day,' she conceded. 'But I'm way too distracted to think about it until it's over. You don't have to come…'

Right. If a gentle thing like Mila could get out there and tackle wild creatures he wasn't about to wuss out. Besides, if anything went wrong he wanted to be there to help make sure she came out of it okay. Finally, those captain-of-the-swim-team skills coming in useful. Though it wasn't likely she'd be doing this in the comfortable confines of Coral Bay's shallows.

The team loaded up the fast little inflatable and all five of them got in—Mila and her ranger quarterbacks—then the documentary crew that were capturing the dugong tagging exercise for some local news channel loaded into their own boat and Rich got in with them. Not close enough, maybe, but as close as he was going to get out on the open water. And the documentary crew would make sure they had a good view of the activities—which meant he would have a good view of Mila's part in it.

I'm just the tagger, she'd said and he'd thought that was a good thing. Until he realised she'd be in the open ocean down the thrashing end of a wild, defensive dugong fitting that tag.

Rich held on as they headed out. The inflatable wasted no time getting well ahead and the film crew did their thing as Rich watched.

'They've spotted a herd,' the documentary producer called to her crew. 'Twenty animals.'

Twenty? Rich swore under the engine noise and his gut fisted. Anything could happen in a herd that size.

As soon as they reached the herd, the little inflatable veered left to cut an animal off the periphery and chase it away rather than drive it into the herd and risk scattering them. Or, worse, hurting them. They ran it in a wide arc for ten minutes, wearing it down, preventing it from re-entering the herd and then he watched as three of the four wetsuit-clad Rangers got to their feet and balanced there precariously as the fourth veered the inflatable across the big dugong's wake. Mila held on for her life in the back of the little boat.

'Get ready!' the producer called to her two camera operators.

Rich tensed too.

When it happened, it all happened in a blinding flash. The puffed animal came up for a breath, then another, then a third. As soon as they were sure it had a good lungful of air, the first dugong-wrangler leapt over the edge of the inflatable and right onto the dugong's back. The two others followed suit and, though he couldn't quite see what was happening in the thrashing water, he did see Mila toss them a couple of foam tubes, which seemed to help keep the hundred-kilogram dugong incredulously afloat while the men kept its nose, flippers and powerful tail somewhat contained.

Then Mila jumped. Right in there, into that surging white-water of death, with the tracking gear in her tiny hands. Rich's heart hammered almost loud enough to hear over the engine of the documentary boat and he leapt to his feet in protest. Her bright red one-piece flashed now and again above the churning water and kept him oriented on her. The video crew were busy capturing the rest of what was happening, but he had eyes for only one part of that animal—its wildly thrashing back end and Mila where she clung to it, fitting the strap-on tracker to the narrowest point of its thick tail. How that could possibly be the lesser of jobs out there...

She and the dugong both buffeted against the small boat and he realised why they used an inflatable and not a hard shell like the one he was in. Its cushioned impact protected the animal and bounced Mila—equally harm-free—back onto the dugong's tail and helped keep her where she needed to be to finally affix the tracker.

While he watched, they measured the animal in a few key spots and shouted the results to the inflatable's skipper, who managed to scrawl it in a notebook while also keeping the boat nice and close.

Then…all of a sudden, it was over. The whole thing took less than three minutes once the first body hit the water. The aggravated dugong dived deep the moment it was released and the churning stopped, the water stilled and the five bodies tumbling around in its turbulence righted themselves and then swam back to the inflatable. The men hauled Mila in after them and they all fell back against the rubber, their chests heaving. One of the neoprene-suited quarterbacks threw up the stomachful of water he'd swallowed in the melee.

Rich's own heart was beating set to erupt from his chest. He couldn't imagine what theirs were like.

Of all the stupid things that she could volunteer to help with…

Mila fell back against the boat's fat rim and stared up into the blue sky. Then she turned and sought out his boat. His eyes. And as soon as she found them she laughed.

Laughed!

Who was this woman leaping into open ocean with a creature related more closely to an elephant than anything else? What had she done with gentle, mermaid Mila? The woman who took such exquisite care of the creatures on the reef, who didn't even tread on an ant if she could avoid it. Where was all this strength coming from?

He sank back down onto his seat and resigned himself to a really unhappy afternoon. This activity crossed all the boxes: dangerous, deep and—worst of all—totally uncontrollable. Beyond a bit of experience and skill, their success was ninety per cent luck.

It occurred to him for a nanosecond that experience, skill and luck were pretty much everything he'd built his business on.

All in all, they tagged six animals before the team's collective exhaustion called a halt to the effort. Science would glean a bunch of something from this endeavour but Rich didn't care; all he cared about was the woman laid out in the back of the inflatable, her long hair dangling in the sea as the inflatable turned for shore and passed the film crew's boat.

Rich was the first one off when it slid up onto the beach, but Mila was the last one off the inflatable, rolling bodily over its fat edge, her fatigued legs barely holding her up. In between, he stood, fists clenched, bursting with tension and the blazing need to wrap his arms around Mila and never let her go.

Ever.

'Rich!' she protested as he slammed bodily into her, his arms going around to hold her up. 'I'm drenched.'

'I don't care.' He pressed against her cold ear. 'I *so* don't care.'

What was a wet shirt when she'd just risked her life six times over? Mila stood stiffly for a moment but the longer he held onto her, the more she relaxed into his grip and the more grateful she seemed for the strength he was lending her. Her little hands slid up his back and she returned his firm embrace.

Around them, the beach got busy with the packing up of gear and the previewing out of video and the relocation of vessels but Rich just stood there, hugging her as if his life depended on it.

In that moment it felt like absolute, impossible truth.

'Ugh, my legs are like rubber,' Mila finally said, easing back. She kept one hand on his arm to steady herself as her fatigued muscles took back reluctant responsibility for her standing. She glanced up at him where a Mila-shaped patch clung wetly to his chest.

'Your shirt—'

'Will dry.' He saw the sudden goose pimples rising on her skin. 'Which is what you need to be. Come on.'

'I'm not cold,' she said, low, but moved with him up the beach compliantly.

'You're trembling, Mila.'

'But not with cold,' she said again, and stared at him until her meaning sank in. 'I'm having a carnival moment.'

Oh. Candyfloss.

The idea that his wet skin on hers had set her shivers racing twisted deep down in his guts. He wanted to be at least as attractive to her as she was to him. Though that was a big ask given how keyed-up he was whenever she was around. Yet still his overriding interest was to get her somewhere warm…and safe. Like back into his arms.

That was disturbingly new.

And insanely problematic given he was leaving tonight. And given that he'd vowed to finish the conversation he'd wanted to have out at the sinkhole.

He stopped at their piled-up belongings on the remote beach and plucked the biggest towel out of the pile, wrapping it around her almost twice. He would much rather be her human towel but right now the heat soaked through it was probably more useful to her. She stood for minutes, just letting the lactic acid ease off in her system and walking off the fatigue. Then she passed him the towel and pulled on her shorts and shirt with what looked a lot like pain. She glanced at her team, still packing up all their gear.

'I should help,' she murmured.

Rich stopped her with a hand to her shoulder. 'You're exhausted.'

'So are they.'

'I'm not. I'll help in your place.'

'I'm not an invalid, Rich.'

'No, but it's something I can do to feel useful. I'd like to do this for you, Mila.' When was the last time he'd felt as…impotent…as he had today? Out on that boat, on all that water, witness to Mila risking her life repeatedly while he just…watched. And there was nothing he could do to help her.

It was like sitting in traffic while his father's heart was rupturing.

His glare hit its target and Mila acquiesced, nodding over mumbled thanks.

Rich turned and crossed to help with the mounded pile of equipment from his boat.

He didn't want her gratitude; a heavy hauling exercise was exactly what he needed to get his emotions back in check. The more gear he carried back and forth across the sand, the saner he began to feel—more the composed CEO and less the breathless novice.

Though maybe in this he *was* a novice. It certainly was worryingly new territory.

He was attracted to everything that was soft about Mila—her kindness, her gentleness; even her quirky super-power was a kind of fragile curiosity. Attraction he could handle. Spin out the anticipation and even enjoy. But this… this was something different. This was leaning towards *admiration*.

Hell, today was downright *awe*.

Gentle, soft Mila turned out to be the strongest person he knew, and not just because she'd spent the day wrestling live dugongs. How much fortitude did it take to engage with a world where everyone else experienced things completely differently to you? Where you were an alien within your own community? Every damned day.

So, *attraction* he could handle. *Admiration* he could troubleshoot his way through. *Awe* he would be able to smile and enjoy as soon as the adrenaline spike of today wore off. But there was something else… Something that tipped the scales of his comfort zone.

Envy.

He was coveting the hell out of Mila and her simple, happy, *vivid* life. Amid all the complexity that her remote lifestyle and synaesthesia brought, Mila just stuck to her basic philosophy—protect the reef. Everything else fell into place behind that. Her goals and her strengths were perfectly aligned. No wonder she could curl up in that quirky little stack-house surrounded by all her treasures and sleep deep, long and easy.

When had he ever slept the night through?

When he'd come to Coral Bay on a fact-finding mission, his direction had been clear. Get a feel for the issues that might hamper his hotel development application. The hotel he needed to build to keep the lucrative coastal strip in Wardoo's lease.

Simple, right?

But now nothing was simple. Mila had more than demonstrated the tourism potential of the place but she'd also shown him how inextricably her well-being was tangled up with the reef. They were like a symbiotic pair. Without Mila, the reef would suffer. Without the reef, Mila would suffer.

They were one.

And he was going to put a hotel on her back.

His eyes came up to her as she joined in on the equipment hauling, finding strength from whatever bottomless supply she had. He could yearn like a kid for Mila's simple, focused life and he could yearn like a grown man for her body—but this *need* for her, this *fear* for her… Those weren't feelings that he could master.

And he didn't do powerless. Not any more.

Mila Nakano never was for him. And he was certainly no good for her. If anything, he was the exact opposite of what was good for her.

And he wasn't going to leave tonight without letting her know how much that was true.

CHAPTER ELEVEN

THE *PORTUS* WAS closer by a half-hour than Mila's little stack-house in Coral Bay town centre and, given she was coming to him for dinner anyway, Rich had called his crew up the coast and had the tender pick them both up at the nearest authorised channel in the reef. The last time she'd been aboard she had done everything she could not to touch either of the men wanting to help her board safely; it was probably wrong to feel so much satisfaction at the fact that she didn't even hesitate to put her hand into his now.

Or that she'd looked at him with such trust as he'd helped her aboard.

It warmed him even as it hurt him.

He'd led her into the *Portus*' expansive bow bedroom, piled her up with big fluffy towels, pointed her in the direction of his bathroom and given her a gentle shove. Then he'd folded back the thick, warm quilt on his bed in readiness so that she could just fall into it when she was clean, warm and dry.

That was two hours ago and he'd been killing time ever since, vacillating between wanting to wake her and spend what little time he could with her, and putting off the inevitable by letting her sleep. In the end, he chose sleep and told himself it wasn't because he was a coward. She'd been almost wobbling on her feet as he'd closed the dark bedroom doors behind him; she needed as much rest as he could give her.

Now, though, it was time for Sleeping Beauty to wake. He'd made sure to bang around on boat business just outside the bedroom door in the hope that the sounds would rouse her naturally, but it looked as if she could sleep through a cyclone—*had he ever slept that well in his life?*—so he had to take the more direct approach now.

'Mila?' He followed up with a quiet knock on the door. Nothing.

He repeated her name a little louder and opened the door a crack to help her hear him. Still not so much as a rustle of bedclothes on the other side. He stepped onto the bedroom's thick carpet and took care to leave the door wide open behind him. If she woke to find him standing over her he didn't want it to be with no escape route. He also didn't want it to be *over* her.

'Mila?' he said again, this time crouched down to bed level.

She twitched but little else, and he took a moment to study her. She looked like a child in his massive bed, curled up small, right on the left edge, as though she knew it wasn't her bed to enjoy. As though she was trying to minimise her impact. Or maybe as though she was trying to minimise its impact *on her.* He studied the expensive bedding critically—who knew what association was triggered by the feel of silk against her skin?

Yet she slept practically curled around his pillow. Embracing it. Would she do that if she wasn't at least a little comfortable in this space? She'd been exhausted, yes, but not so shattered that she couldn't have refused if curling up in a bed other than her own had been in any way disturbing to her. There was no shortage of sofas she could have taken instead.

Rich reached out and tucked a loose lock of hair back in with its still-damp cousins. Mila twitched again but not away from him. She seemed to curl her face towards him before burrowing down deeper into his pillow. Actually, his was on the other side of the bed but he would struggle, after he'd left this place, not to swap it for the one Mila practically embraced. Just to keep her close a little longer. Until her scent faded with Coral Bay on the horizon behind him.

He placed a gentle hand on her exposed shoulder. 'Mila. Time to wake up.'

She roused, shifted. Then her beautiful eyes flickered open and shone at him, full of confused warmth as she tried to remember where she was. It only took a heartbeat before she mastered them, though, and looked around the space.

'How did you sleep?' he asked, just to give her an excuse to look back at him.

She pushed herself up, and brought his quilt with her.

'This bed…' she murmured, all sleepy and sexy.

His chest actually hurt.

'Best money could buy,' he squeezed out.

'How do you even get out of it?' Her voice grew stronger, less dreamy with every sentence she uttered. 'I'm not sure I'm going to be able to.'

That was what he wanted; the kind of sleep the bed promised when you looked at it, lay on it. The kind of sleep that Mila's groggy face said she'd just had. And now that he'd seen his bed with her in it, that was what he wanted too.

But *wanting* didn't always mean *having*.

'Damo will have dinner ready in a half hour,' he said. 'Do you want to freshen up? Maybe come out on deck for some air?'

It was only then that the darkness outside seemed to dawn on her. She pushed up yet straighter.

'Yes, I'm sorry. It was only supposed to be a nap—'

'Don't apologise. After the day you've had, you clearly needed it.' He pushed to his feet. 'I'll see you on deck when you're ready.'

He left her there, blinking a daze in his big bed, and retreated up the steps to the galley, where he busied himself redoing half the tasks his deckhand had already done. Just to keep busy. Just to give Mila the space he figured she would appreciate. He lifted the clear lid on the chowder risotto steaming away beneath it and then, at Damo's frustrated cluck, abandoned the galley, went out on the aft deck and busied himself decanting a bottle of red.

'Gosh, it's even more beautiful at night,' a small voice eventually said from the galley doorway.

His gaze tracked hers across the *Portus'* outer deck. He took it for granted now, but the moody uplights built into discreet places along the gunnel did cast interesting and dramatic shapes along the cat's white surfaces.

'I forget to appreciate it sometimes.'

'Human nature,' she murmured.

But was it? Mila appreciated what she had every single day. Then again, he wasn't at all sure she was strictly human. Maybe all mermaids had synaesthesia.

'What smells so good?'

'No crayfish on the menu tonight,' he assured her. 'I believe we're having some kind of chowder-meets-risotto. What are your feelings about rice?'

Her dark eyes considered that. 'Ambivalent.'

'And clams?'

'Clams are picky,' she said immediately. 'I'm sure they would protest any use you made of them, chowder or otherwise.'

The allusion brought a smile to his lips. 'But you eat them?'

'Honestly? After today, I would happily eat the cushions on your lovely sofa.'

She laughed and he just let himself enjoy the sound. Because it was the last time he ever would.

He led her to the sofa and poured two glasses of Merlot. 'This isn't going to help much with the sleepiness, I'm afraid.'

Mila wafted the glass under her nose and her eyes closed momentarily. 'Don't care.'

He followed her down onto the luxurious sofa that circled the low table on three sides. Her expression made him circle his glass with liquid a few extra times and sip just a little slower. Craving just a hint of whatever it was that connected Mila so deeply with life.

Pathetically trying to replicate it.

They talked about the dugong tagging—about what the results would be used for and what that meant for populations along this coast. They talked about the coral spawn they'd collected and how little it would take to destroy all that she'd ever collected. One good storm to take out the power for days, one fuel shortage to kill Steve Donahue's generator and the chest freezer they were using would slowly return to room temperature and five years' worth of spawn would all perish. They talked about the two big game fishermen who'd gone out to sea on an ill-prepared boat during the week, and spent a scary and frigid few nights being carried further and further away from Australia on the fast-moving Leeuwin Current before being rescued and how much difference an immediate ocean response unit would have made.

Really he was just raising anything to keep Mila talking.

She listened as well as she contributed and her stories were always so engaging. These were not conversations he got to have back in the city.

He thought that he was letting her talk herself almost out of breath because he knew this might well be the last opportunity he had to do it. But the longer into the night they talked, the more he had to admit that he was letting her dominate their conversation because it meant he didn't have to take such an active part. And if he took a more active part then he knew he would have to begin the discussion he was quietly dreading.

'I'm sorry,' Mila said as she forked the last of the double cream from her dish with the last of her tropical fruit. A gorgeous shade of pink stained her cheeks. 'I've been talking your ear off since the entree.'

'I like listening to you,' he admitted, though *like* wasn't nearly strong enough. But he didn't have the words to describe how tranquil he felt in her presence. As if she were infecting him with her very nature.

That, itself, was warning enough.

'Besides,' he said, beginning what had to be done, 'this might be my last chance.'

Mila frowned. 'Last chance for what?'

'To hear your stories. To learn from you.' Then, as she just stared, he added, 'I have what I need now. There's no reason for me to come back to Coral Bay.'

Yeah, there was. Of course there was. There was Wardoo and there was his proposed development and there was Mila. She was probably enough all by herself to lure him back to this beautiful place. What he meant, though, was that he *wouldn't* be coming back, despite those things.

She just blinked at him as his words sank into her exhausted brain. What kind of a jerk would do this to someone so unprepared?

'No reason? At all?'

He shrugged, but the nonchalance cost him dear. 'I have what I came for.'

It was hard to define the expression that suffused her face

then: part-confusion, part-sorrow, part-disappointment. 'What about Wardoo?'

It was impossible not to mark the perfect segue into the revelation he wanted so badly not to make. To hurt this gentle creature in a way that was as wrong as taking a spear gun to some brightly coloured fish just going about its own business on the reef.

But he'd already missed several opportunities to be strong—to be honest—and do the right thing by Mila.

He wasn't about to leave her thinking the best of him.

Not when it was the last thing he deserved.

'Mila, listen—' Rich began.

'I wasn't making any assumptions,' she said in a rush. 'I know I don't have any claims on you. That I'm necessarily anything more than just…'

Entertainment.

Though the all too familiar and awkward taste of cola forming at the back of her throat suggested otherwise.

Mila, listen…was as classic an entrée into the *it's-not-you-it's-me* speech as she'd ever heard. Except she well knew the truth behind that now.

It was *always* her.

Just because she'd found someone that she could be comfortable around—with—didn't necessarily mean Rich felt the same way. Or, even if he did, that it was particularly unique for him. There were probably a lot of women back in the city that he felt comfortable around. More business-like women with whom he could discuss current affairs. More suitable women that he could take to important functions. More cognitively conventional women that he could just be normal with.

The cola started to transition into the nose-scrunching earwax that she hated so much.

'We've spent days together,' he began. 'We've eaten together and we've kissed a couple of times. It's not unreasonable for you to wonder what we are to each other, Mila.'

He spoke as if he were letting an employee go. Impersonal. Functional. Controlled. It was hard not to admire the leader in him, but it was just as impossible not to resent the heck out of that. He'd clearly had time to prepare for this moment whereas she'd walked into it all sleepy-eyed and Merlot-filled.

Yet, somehow, this felt as prepared as she was ever going to get.

'And what is that, exactly?' she asked.

'There's a connection here,' he said, leaning in. 'I think it would be foolish to try and pretend otherwise. But good chemistry doesn't necessarily make us a good fit.'

She blinked at him. *They* didn't fit? He would fit in anywhere. He was just that kind of a man. Which meant...

'You mean *I'm* not.'

'That's not what I was saying, but you have to admit that you would fit about as well in my world as I've fit in yours.'

'You fit in mine just fine.' Or so she'd thought.

His laugh wasn't for her. 'The man who can't go in open water? That novelty wouldn't last long.'

She refused to let him minimise this moment. 'Do you not like it here?'

'I didn't say I haven't enjoyed it. I said I don't *fit* here.'

Why? Because he was new to it? 'You haven't really given it much of a chance.'

It was so much easier to defend the place she loved than the heart that was hurting.

Rich sighed. 'I didn't come here looking for anything but information, Mila...'

'Why *did* you come, Rich?' she asked. He'd avoided the

question twice before but asking that bought her a few moments to get her thoughts in order. To chart some safe passage out of these choppy emotional waters.

He took a deep, slow breath and studied her, tiny forks appearing between his eyes. Then he leaned forward with the most purpose she'd seen in him and she immediately regretted asking.

'The government is proposing a re-draft of the boundaries of the leaseholdings on the Northwest Cape,' he began. 'They want to remove the coastal strip from Wardoo's lease.'

His words were so unlike the extreme gravity in his face it took her a moment to orient. That was not the terrible blow she'd steeled herself for.

'Why?'

'They want to see the potential of the area fulfilled and remove the impediments to tourism coming in.'

Impediments like the Dawsons protecting the region by controlling the access.

'It's a big deal that this is a World Heritage Marine Park,' he went on. 'They want the world to be able to come see it. But until now they haven't been able to act.'

There was a point in all this corporate speak, somewhere. Mila grappled for it. 'What's changed now?'

'Wardoo's fifty-year lease is up. They're free to renegotiate the boundaries as they wish.'

Ironic that the very listing that was supposed to recognise and protect the reef only made it more attractive for tourists. And all those people needed somewhere to stay.

'And redrawn boundaries are bad?'

'The new leasehold terms will make it nearly impossible to turn a reasonable profit from this land. Without the coastal strip.'

Was she still feeling the effects of her not-so-power nap?

Somehow, she was failing to connect the dots that Rich was laying out. 'What has the coastal strip got to do with Wardoo's profitability?'

Rich's broad shoulders lifted high and then dropped slowly as he measured his words.

'Every business that operates in Coral Bay pays a percentage to WestCorp for the opportunity to do so. Tourism has been keeping Wardoo afloat for years.'

The stink of realisation hit her like black tar. She sagged against the sofa back. *That* was why the Dawsons were so staunchly against external developers in Coral Bay.

'So…you weren't protecting the reef,' she whispered. 'You were protecting your profits?'

'WestCorp is a business, Mila. Wardoo is just one holding amongst three dozen.'

She pushed her empty dish away. 'Is that why you were up here? To check up on your tenants?' It hit her then. 'Oh, God! A percentage of my rent probably goes to you too. You should have said it was a rental inspection, I would have tidied up—'

'Mila—'

She pushed to her feet as her stomach protested the mix of yeast and cherry that came with all the anger and confusion—on top of the clam chowder, red wine and utter stupidity, it threatened a really humiliating resurgence.

'Excuse me, I need a moment.'

She didn't wait for permission. Before Rich could even rise to his own feet, she'd crossed the room and started negotiating the steps down to his bedroom. Once in the spacious en suite bathroom, she braced her hands either side of the sink until she was sure that her churning stomach was not going to actually broil over. Then she pressed a damp cloth to her face and neck until the queasiness eased off.

This was not the first time she'd had synaesthesia-prompted nausea. Her body really couldn't discriminate between actual tastes and imagined, so some combinations, usually reserved for really complicated moments, ended up in long sojourns to a quiet, cool place.

She sagged down onto her elbows on the marble vanity and pressed the cloth to her closed eyes.

If she'd given it any real thought she wouldn't have been surprised to discover Wardoo was getting kickbacks from the local businesses. If they were in the city they'd definitely have been paying rent to someone.

No, the churning cherry was all about how stupid she had been to just assume that Rich would find the *reef* the most valuable part of the Bay. If he liked the reef at all, it was secondary to the income that the tenants could bring him. He was still here for the money.

He was all about the money.

WestCorp is a business, Mila...

He'd even hinted at as much, several times. But she hadn't listened. She and Rich saw the world completely differently. She had no more right to judge him for the way he perceived the world than he had to judge her synaesthesia.

They just came at life from very different places.

Too different.

Leveraging a bunch of cafés and caravan parks and glass-bottom boat operators for a percentage did not make him a bad person.

It just meant he was no white knight to her reef after all.

She'd have to carry on doing her own white knighting.

She patted her face dry, pinched her cheeks to encourage a little colour into them and switched off the fancy lights as she stepped back into the bedroom. Such a short time ago she'd curled up in that bed—in amongst Rich's lingering scent—and thought drowsily how nice it would be to stay there for ever. Now, that moment felt as dream-like as the past few days.

When viewed with the cold, hard light of reality.

She'd stumbled against Rich's office chair as she'd staggered into the bedroom a few minutes earlier and she took a moment now to right it, sliding it back into the cavity under the workstation and setting to rights the documents she'd splayed across the desktop with her falter. As she did, her eyes slashed across a bound wad of pages that had slipped out from under a plain file.

The word 'Coral Bay' immediately leapt out at her.

She glanced at the empty doorway and then lifted the corner on the cover page like a criminal.

Words. Lots and lots of words. Some kind of summary introduction. She flipped to the next page and saw a map of the coast—as familiar to her as the shape of her own hand. A large area was shaded virtually across the coast road from Nancy's Point.

That was where she stopped being covert.

Mila pulled out the chair, let her wobbly legs sink her into it and unclipped the binder so she could turn the pages more fully. Another plan showing massive trenching down from Coral Bay township—water, power, sewer. Over the page another, showing side elevations of a mass-scale construction—single, two and three storeys high in different places. Swathes of parking. Irrigation. Gardens.

A helipad, for crying out loud.

Her fingers trembled more with every page she turned. Urgent eyes scanned the top of every plan and found the WestCorp logo. Waves of nausea rolled in again and Mila concentrated on slowing her patchy breathing. She bought herself more time by tidying the pages and fixing the binding. Just before she stood, she glanced again at the summary introduction and her eyes fell to the page bottom. An elaborate signature in ink. Rich's signature.

And that was yesterday's date beside it.

The *Portus* seemed to lurch beneath her as if it had been hit by some undersea quake.

Rich was developing the reef—a luxury resort on the coast of Wardoo's land. No wonder he protested the government's plans to excise the coastal strip.

He had *this* under development.

And he'd signed off on it after he'd seen the coral spawn. After he'd first kissed her.

She wobbled to her feet and pressed the incriminating evidence to her chest as she returned to the aft deck. Rich rose politely as she came back out but if he noticed what she was clinging to he showed no sign.

Mila dropped the report on the table between them and let it lie there like some dead thing.

Rich's eyes fell shut briefly, but then found hers again—one hundred per cent CEO. 'WestCorp isn't a charity, Mila. I have shareholders and other ventures to protect.'

No. That wasn't what he was supposed to protect.

'You're forsaking the reef?' she cut in. 'And the Bay.'

And me, a tiny, hurt voice whimpered.

'I admit it is beautiful, Mila. And diverse. UNESCO obviously agreed to give it World Heritage status. But without the revenue from tourism activity, without the coastal strip, I can't see how I can justify maintaining Wardoo.' His chest rose high and then fell.

Couldn't justify it? Did every part of his world have to pay for itself? Did life itself come with a profit margin?

Her voice fell to a hoarse whisper. 'It's your heritage, Rich. Your roots are here. You're a Dawson. Does that not matter?'

'That's like me saying that your roots are in Tokyo be-cause your surname is Nakano. Do you *feel* Japanese, Mila?'

She'd never fully identified with any one culture in her crazy patchwork quilt family. That had always been part of her general disconnection with the world until the day she'd woken up and realised that where she belonged was *here*. The reef was her roots. Regardless of the many where-elses she had come from.

She identified as *Mila*. Wildlife was her people.

And she would defend them against whoever came.

'You're Saltwater People too, Rich. You just don't know it. Look at who you become on the *Portus*. Look at where you go to find peace.'

'Peace doesn't put food on the table.'

'Does everything have to revolve around the almighty dollar?'

'We can't all live in shipping containers and spend our days frolicking with sea life, Mila. Money matters. Choos-ing it isn't a bad choice; it's just not your choice.'

Her beautiful little home had never sounded so tawdry—nor her job so unimportant—and when those two things formed at least half of your world believing in them mattered.

A lot.

She pushed to her feet. Words tumbled up past the ear-wax taste of heartbreak and she had to force them over her tight lips so they could be heard up on the fly bridge. Though there was no chance on earth that the crew hadn't heard their most recent discussion.

'Damo? I would like to go to shore, please.'

Rich rose too. 'Mila, we're not done…'

'Oh, yes. We are.' *Completely*. 'As soon as you're free, Damo.'

There was enough anxiety in her voice to get anyone's attention.

'Mila,' Rich urged, 'you don't understand. If it's not me, it will be someone else…'

'I understand better than you think,' she hissed. 'You used me and you lied to me. About why you were here. About who you are. I squired you around the district like some royal bloody tour and showed you all its secrets, and I thought I was making a difference. I thought you saw the Bay the way I do. And maybe you actually did, yet you're *still* happy to toss it all away with your trenches and your pipes and your helipads.'

Her arms crept around her middle. 'That was my mistake for letting my guard down for you; I won't be so foolish again.'

She stepped up to him as he also rose to his feet.

'But if you think for one minute that I am going to let anyone hurt the place and people that I love, then you—' she pushed a finger into his chest '—don't understand me. I will whip up a PR nightmare for WestCorp. I'll get every single tourist who visits this place to sign my petition and every scientist I know to go on record with the damage that commercialisation does to reefs. You go ahead and throw the Bay to the wolves. You go make your money and spend it on making more money and don't worry about any of us. But I want you to think on something as you sit on your big stockpile of cash, tossing it over your head and letting it rain down on you…'

She flicked her chin up.

'What are you keeping the money for, exactly, if not to allow you to have ten thousand square kilometres of gorgeous, red, barely productive land in your life? Or an ocean. Or a reef. Or a luxury catamaran. Things that might not make any money but are completely priceless because of what they bring you. Money is a means to an end; it's not the end itself. Surely wealth is meaningless unless it buys you freedom or love or—'

She stumbled on the word as soon as it fell across her lips because she hadn't meant to say it. And she hadn't meant to feel it. But the subtlest undertones of pineapple told her that she did.

Richard Grundy, of all people…

She took a steadying breath.

'Or sanctuary! It won't keep you warm at night and it won't fill the great void inside you that you try so hard to disguise.'

'I don't have a void—'

'Of course you do. You pack your money down into it like a tooth cavity.' She frowned and stepped closer. 'What if wealth is the thing that people like you are raised to believe matters in lieu of the things that actually matter?'

'People like me?' he gritted.

'Disconnected people. Empty people. Lonely people.'

Rich's strong jaw twitched and he paled a little. 'Really, Mila? The poster-child for dysfunction wants to counsel me on being disconnected?'

His hard words hit home, but she could not deny the essential truth in them.

'Has it not occurred to you yet that I am far richer than you could ever be? *Will* ever be? Because I have all of this.' She held her hands out to the moonlight and the ocean and the reef they couldn't see and the wonders they both knew to be on it. 'And I have my *place* within it. The certainty and fulfilment of that. All of this is more wealth than anyone could ever need in a dozen lifetimes.'

Damo appeared at the bottom of the steps down from the bridge, looking about as uncomfortable as she suddenly felt. Here, in this place that she'd already started to think of as a second home.

Mila turned immediately to follow him down to the tender.

'If WestCorp opts not to renew the lease then who knows who would come in or what they might do with it? The only thing that will keep the government from excising the coastal strip is significant capital investment in the area,' he called after her. 'I need to build something.'

She called back over her shoulder. 'Why don't you build an undersea hotel? That would be awesome.'

She refused to think of what she'd seen on his desk as a reasonable compromise. And she refused to let herself believe that the project was still open to amendment, any more than she could believe that *she* made the slightest difference to his secret plans.

He'd *signed* it. In ink.

'Or, better yet, don't build anything. Just let Wardoo stand or fall on its own merits.'

'It will fall.'

'Then give up the lease, if that's what it takes.'

'I don't *want* to give it up. I'm trying to save it.'

She stared at him, her chest heaving. Even he looked confused by that.

'If I surrender the lease,' he went on after the momentary fumble, 'then anyone could take it up. You could end up with a million goats destroying the land. If I keep the lease and don't develop then the government will excise the strip and someone else will come in and do it. Someone who doesn't care about the reef at all.'

'Funny,' she spat. 'I thought that was you.'

For a moment she thought that Rich was going to let her go with the last word still tasting like nail varnish on her lips. But he was a CEO, and people with acronyms for titles probably never surrendered the final word. On principle.

'Mila, don't go. Not like this.'

But final words could sometimes be silent. And she was determined that hers should be. Besides which, her lungs were too full of the scent of earwax for adequate speech and the last thing she wanted was for Richard Grundy to hear her croak. So she kept moving. Her feet reached the timber dive platform. The jarrah deck's isolation practically pulsed through her feet. Resonating with a kindred spirit, perhaps. She accepted Damo's hand without thought and stepped into the tender, sinking down with her back firmly to the man she'd accepted so readily into her life.

Nothing.

No solo trumpet at Damo's touch. No plinking ball bearings at the breeze rushing under the *Portus*. No fluttering of wings as her skin erupted in gooseflesh.

It was as if every part of her was as deadened as her heart.

Had he not taken enough from her this night? Now he'd muted her superpower.

Behind her, Rich stood silent and still. Had she expected an eleventh-hour apology? Some final sense of regret? An attitudinal about-face?

Just how naive was she, really?

Richard Grundy was making decisions based on the needs and wants of his shareholders. She couldn't reasonably expect him to put anyone else's needs ahead of his own. And certainly not hers. She was his tour guide, nothing more. A curiosity and an entertainment. A woman he'd known only days in the greater scheme of things. It was pure folly to imagine that she would—or even could—affect any change in his deep-seated attitudes.

Then again, folly seemed to be all Rich thought she was

capable of here. In her quaint little shack with her funny little job…

Damo had the good sense to stay completely silent as he ran her back to the marina and dropped her onto the pier. She gave him the weakest of smiles in farewell and didn't wait to watch him leave, climbing down onto the beach and turning towards town. The tide was far enough out that she could wade around the rocks to get back to town and, somehow, it felt critical that she put her feet back in the water, that she prove to herself that Rich had not muted her senses for good.

That he had not broken her.

But there was no symphony as the water swilled around her bare feet. And as she turned to look out to the reef, imagining what was down there, there was no sound or sensation at all.

Everything was as deadened as her heart.

It was impossible to imagine a world without her super-power to help her interpret it. Or without her reef to help her breathe. And, though she hated to admit it after such a spectacularly short time, she was struggling to even imagine a world without Rich in it.

To help her live.

How had he done that? So quickly. So deeply. And— knowing what he'd done—how could she ever trust any of her senses ever again?

CHAPTER TWELVE

'I'VE GOT NEWS,' her supervisor said down the telephone, his voice grave. 'But you're not going to like some of it.'

Mila took a deep breath. There had been much about the past nine weeks that she didn't like, least of all her inability to get the treacherous Richard Grundy completely from her mind. Whether she was angry at herself for failing to heed her own instincts or angry at him for turning out to be such a mercenary, she couldn't tell.

All she knew was that time had not healed that particular wound, no matter what the adage promised. And no matter how many worthy distractions she'd thrown at it.

It was her own stupid fault that many of her favourite places were now tainted with memories of Rich in them. She had to go showing them off…

'Go ahead, Lyle.'

'First up… Wardoo's lease has been renewed.'

Her stomach clenched. *Renewed*, Lyle had said. Not *re-filled*.

Part of the emotional swell she'd been surfing these past months—up, down, up, down—was due to the conflict between wanting Rich to keep his heritage and wanting him to surrender his resort plans. If Rich kept Wardoo it meant he must have kept the coastal strip, which meant going ahead with the resort. But if he dropped the resort, it meant he must have given up Wardoo. And giving up Wardoo meant there was no conceivable reason for Rich to ever be in Coral Bay again.

So, secretly craving an opportunity to see Rich again meant secretly accepting commercialisation of her beloved coast.

'By the Dawsons?'

How her stomach could leap quite that high while still fisted from nerves she didn't know but it seemed to lurch almost into her throat, accompanied by the delicious hot chocolate of hope behind her tongue.

'Looks like they're staying.'

He's staying. Impossible to think of Wardoo as West-Corp's. Not when she'd eaten sandwiches with and stood in the living room with—and *kissed*—the the man who owned it.

'I'm looking at a copy of an agreement that I'm probably not supposed to have,' Lyle admitted. 'Friends in high places. It's not the whole thing, just highlights.'

'And the coastal strip?'

Please… There was still a chance that Rich had negotiated a different outcome. That he'd dropped the resort plans. Or that he'd found a way to keep Wardoo profitable without the coastal strip.

Not the perfect outcome, but one she only realised in this moment that she would accept. As long as it wasn't *Rich* trashing her reef…

'It's staying in the leasehold,' Lyle admitted and her heart sank. 'Not without conditions, though. That's what I want to talk to you about.'

She'd been the one to tell her boss about the government's plans for the coastal strip, but she never told him about Rich's development. Or that she was on a first name basis with the Dawsons.

The hopeful hot chocolate wavered into a cigarettey kind of mocha.

'What kind of conditions?' she asked suspiciously. Though, really, she knew.

The helicopters were probably circling Coral Bay right now, waiting for that helipad.

'Government has approved a development for the Bay,' he said.

Courtesy of a two-month head start, that news didn't send her to water, but it still hurt hearing it. Had she really imagined he would change his multi-million-dollar plans…?

For her?

The hot chocolate completely dissipated and Mila wrapped the arm not holding the phone around her middle and closed her eyes. She asked purely because she was not supposed to already know.

'What kind of development, Lyle?'

'Like I said, I've only got select pages,' he started. 'But it's big, some kind of resort or hotel. Dozens of bathrooms or kitchens; it's hard to tell. No idea why they'd need quite that many, so far from the accommodation,' Lyle flicked through pages on his end of the phone, 'but there's lots of that too. Looks like a theatre of some kind, and a massive wine cellar, maybe? Underground, anyway, temperature-controlled. And a helipad of all things. It's hard to say what it is. But it's not small, Mila. And it can't be a coincidence that it's coming up just as Wardoo's lease is resolved.'

No. It was no coincidence.

'Do you know where it's approved for?' she breathed.

This was her last hope. Maybe he'd shifted its site further south, out of the Marine Park. Though really, wouldn't that defeat the purpose?

'There is a sketch map. Looks like it's about a half-hour south of you. Nancy's Point, maybe?'

Ice began to crystallise the very cells in her flesh.

So it was done. And at his great-grandmother's favourite point, of all places.

'Lyle, look through the documents. Is there any reference to a company called WestCorp anywhere in them?'

Lyle shuffled while Mila died inside.

'Yeah, Mila. There is a WestCorp stamp on one of the floor plans. Who are they?'

Mila stared at the blank space on the wall opposite her.

'WestCorp is the Dawsons,' she breathed down the line.

Lyle seemed as speechless as she was. 'Dawsons? You're kidding. They're the last ones I would have thought—'

'We don't know them,' Mila cut in. 'Or what they're capable of. They're just a family who loved this land once. They haven't lived here for decades.'

'But still—'

'They're not for the reef any more, Lyle.' She realised she was punishing him for Rich's decisions. 'I'm sorry, I have to go. Can you send me those documents?'

This time his hesitation was brief. 'I can't, Mila. I'm not even supposed to have seen them. This was just a heads-up.'

Right. Like a five-minute warning siren that a tsunami was coming. What was she supposed to do with that?

'I understand,' she murmured. 'And I appreciate it. Thank you, Lyle.'

It took no time to lock up her little office and get into her four-wheel drive. Then about a half-hour more to get down to Nancy's Point, half expecting to see site works underway—survey pegs, vehicle tracks, a subterranean wine cellar. But there was nothing, just the same rocky outlook she'd visited a hundred times. The place Rich had first come striding towards her, his big hand outstretched.

Impotence burned as bourbon in her throat. She tried to imagine the site filled with tourists, staff, power stations and treatment plants and found she couldn't. It was simply inconceivable.

And in that moment she decided to tell Rich so.

If she didn't fight for her reef, who would?

There had been no communication between them since he'd left all those weeks ago but this was worth the precedent— now that it was a reality. But she wasn't brave enough to talk to him face to face or even voice to voice. A big part of her feared what it would do to her heart to hear his voice right inside her ear, and what it would do to her soul to have to endure his justification for this monstrosity. She had a smartphone and she had working fingers, and she could tap him one heck of a scathing email telling him exactly what she thought of his plans to put a resort at Nancy's Point. And she could do it right now while she was still angry enough to be honest and brave.

Brave in a way she hadn't been when she'd fled the *Portus* that night.

She climbed back into her car and reached into her dashboard for her phone, then swiped her way through to her email app. She gave a half-moment's consideration to a subject line that he couldn't ignore and then began tapping on letters.

Subject: Nancy will turn in her grave!

'All right, folks, time to get wet!'

Mila sat back and let the excited tourists leap in ahead of her. If they'd been nervous earlier, about snorkelling in open ocean, the anxiety dissipated completely when they spotted their first whale shark, the immense shape looming as a shadow in the water ahead. There were two out here, but the boat chose this one to centre on while another vessel chugged their passengers closer to the other one. But not too close…there were rules. It was up to the tourists to swim the distance and close up the gap between them.

Not everyone was a natural swimmer and so every spare member of crew got in the water with them and shepherded a small number of snorkelers each. Each leader took an underwater whiteboard so they could communicate with their group without having to get alongside them or surface constantly. Easier when you were navigating an animal as big as a whale shark to be able to keep your eyes on its every move.

The last cluster slipped off the back of the boat and into the open water in an excited, splashy frenzy.

That left Mila to go it alone—just how she liked it. She'd eased herself right out onto the front of the big tourist boat where none of them thought to go and so she hadn't had to sit amongst them with the smells and sounds of unfamiliar people. Now, she gave the captain a wave so he knew she was in, and slid down quietly and gently into the silken water.

It was normally completely clear out here, barring the odd cluster of weed floating along or balls of fish picking at the surface, but the churning engines of two boats and the splashing of the associated snorkelling tourists made the water foggy with a champagne of bubbles in all directions. Easy to forget what was out here with them when she couldn't see it, but Mila swam a wide arc to break out of the white-water. As the boats backed away from the site, the water cleared, darkened and then settled a little. The surface turbulence still rocked her but, with her head under, it was much calmer. Calm enough to get on with the job. She looked around her at the light streaming down into the deep blue, converging on some distant point far below, her eyes hunting for the creature so big it seemed impossible that it could hide out here.

The first clue that it was with them was the frenzied flipper action of the nearby tourists, then a great looming shape materialised in slow motion out of the blue below them straight towards her. The whale shark's camouflage—the very thing she'd come to photograph—made it hard for Mila to define its distinctive shape until it was nearly upon her, but it did nothing more dramatic than cruise silently by, its massive tail fanning just once to propel it the entire distance between the other tourists and her group. Everyone else started swimming to keep up with it while Mila back-pedalled madly to get herself out of its way.

She dived under as it passed her, and she got a good view of the half-dozen remoras either catching a ride on the shark's underside or using its draught to swim against its pale underbelly. She swung her underwater camera up and took a couple of images of the patterning around its gills—the ones that the star-mapping software needed—and then watched it disappear once again into the deep blue. But she knew it wouldn't be gone long. Whale sharks seemed to enjoy the interaction with people and this one circled around and emerged out of nothing again to swim between them once more. Mila photographed it on the way back through in case it wasn't the same one at all, then set off after its relaxed tail, swimming back towards the main group of tourists. Two boatloads were combined now, all eager to see the same animal.

As she approached, a staff member in dive gear held up a whiteboard with four letters on it.

R U OK?

Mila gave him an easy thumbs-up and he turned and focused on the less certain swimmers. It was more exhausting than many expected, being out here in the open current and trying to swim clear of a forty-foot-long prehistoric creature.

Mila let herself enjoy the shark, the gorgeous light filtering down through the surface and the sensations both brought with them. She attributed whale sharks with regal qualities—maybe her most literal association yet—and this one was quite the prince. Comparatively unscarred, spectacular markings, big square head, massive gaping mouth that swallowed hundreds of litres of seawater at a time. When it wasn't gulping, it pressed its lips together hard to squeeze the headful of water out through its gills and then swallow what solids were left behind in its massive mouth. To Mila, the lips looked like a vaguely wry smirk.

Her chest squeezed and not because of exertion.

She'd seen that smirk before. But not for months.

She back-swam again, to maintain the required safety distance, and watched the swimmers on the far side of the animal move forward as it swam away from them. Another carried a whiteboard, but he wasn't a diver and he wasn't in one of the company wetsuits. Mila tipped her head and looked closer.

The snorkeler wrote something on his board with waterproof marker then held it aloft in the streaming light.

NOT...

She had to wait for the long tail of the whale shark to pass between them before she could read it properly.

NOT EN SUITES... LABS.

What? What did that mean? She straightened to read it again, certain she'd misread some diving instruction.

The man wiped it off with his bare arm and wrote again. Something about the way he moved made her spine ratchet straighter than even the circling whale shark did. But she could not take her eyes off his board. He held it up again and the words were longer and so the letters were smaller. Mila had to swim a little closer to read them.

ROOMS NOT 4 TOURISTS.
4 RESEARCHERS.

Her heart began to pound. In earnest. She tried to be alert to what the shark was doing but found it impossible to do anything other than stare at that whiteboard and the man holding it.

'Rich?'

She couldn't help saying it aloud and the little word must have puffed out of the top of her snorkel into the air above the surface to be lost on the stiff ocean breeze.

He held the board up again, the words newly written.

NOT U/GROUND WINE CELLAR...

The whale shark swam back through between them, doing its best to drag her eyes off the man wiping the board clean again and back onto the *true* ocean spectacle, but Mila paid it no heed, other than to be frustrated by the spectacular length of the shark as it blocked her view of Rich. As soon as it passed, she read the two words he'd replaced on the board. Her already tight breath caught altogether.

SPAWN BANK.

She pushed her feet and gasped for air above the surface. Water splashed and surged against her body, buffeting her on two sides. Using the clustered snorkelers for reference, she stroked her way towards them with already weary muscles. Just out of voice range, another snorkeler rose above the splash. The only head other than hers poking out of the water while the massive shark dominated attention below.

Rich.

They swam directly towards each other, oblivious to any monsters of the deep still doing graceful laps below them. But when they got close, Mila pulled up short and slid her mask up onto her head.

'What are you doing here?' Her arms and legs worked in opposition to keep her stable in the undulating water.

'I got your email,' Rich answered, raising his mask too. His thick hair spiked up in all directions.

'You could have just replied,' she gasped as the gently rolling seas pitched her in two directions at once.

Rich swam a little closer and Mila turned to keep some distance between them. As life-preserving as the four metres' clearance she was supposed to give the whale shark. They ended up swimming in a synchronised arc in the heaving swell, circling each other.

'Yeah, I could have. But I wanted to see you.'

Hard enough to speak as all her muscles focused on keeping her afloat without the added complication of a suddenly collapsing chest cavity.

She didn't waste time with coyness. 'Why? To break the news in person?'

His voice was thick as he answered. 'It's not a resort, Mila. It's a technology centre. The Wardoo Northern Studies Centre.'

Labs. Accommodation for researchers.

Incongruous to smell hot chocolate over the smell of fresh seawater and marine diesel, but that was hope for you...

'It has a helipad, Rich.'

He ignored her sarcasm and answered her straight. 'For a sea rescue chopper.'

She just blinked. Hadn't they talked about that the night on the *Portus*? The difference it would make to lives up here?

Her voice was as weak as her breath, suddenly. 'And the spawn bank?'

'Subterranean. Temperature-controlled. Solar-powered. You can't keep that stuff in a fish freezer, Mila. It's too important.'

She circled him warily in the water.

'Why?'

There it was again. Such a simple little word but it loomed as large as the whale shark now swimming away in the distance.

A wave splashed Rich full in the face. 'Is this really where you want to have this discussion?'

'You picked it,' she pointed out.

Mila could see all the tourists making their way back to their respective boats, ready to go and find another shark at another location. But, in the distance between them, she saw something else. The flashing white double hull of the *Portus*. Poised to whisk Rich away from her once again.

He puffed, as the swell bobbed them both up and down.

'A state-of-the-art research and conference facility appealed to the government's interest in improving the region.' He swam around her as he spoke but kept his eyes firmly locked on hers. Effort made every word choppy. 'It satisfies the need for facilities for all the programmes running up here.'

The scientists, the researchers. Even the cavers. They would all have somewhere local to work now.

She wanted to reply but didn't. Breathing was hard

enough without wasting air on pointless words. Besides which, she didn't trust herself to speak just yet.

His eyes darted to the *Portus*, to his sanctuary, but it was too far away to provide him with any respite now. 'They didn't have the funding for something like that; it had to be private investment.'

And who else was going to invest in a region like this for something like that, if not a local?

Mila lifted her mouth above the waterline. 'I can't imagine Wardoo will ever make enough to pay for a science centre. Even with kickbacks from your tenants.'

'The centre should pay for itself eventually. With grants. And conference business. The emergency response bit, WestCorp will be covering.'

His breath-stealing revelation was interrupted by the burbling arrival of Mila's charter boat alongside them; it towered above and dozens of strangers' eyes peered over the edge at them. Rich passed the little whiteboard back to whoever he had borrowed it from and waited until she was able to scrabble aboard the dive platform. Gravity immediately made its presence felt in muscles that had been working so hard to keep her afloat and away from the whale sharks. Rich had a quick word with the crew and the charter chugged happily over to the *Portus* and waited as they transferred from one dive deck to the other.

Moments later, the twenty curious tourists were happily heading off after another whale shark sighting signalled by Craig in his Cessna high above them.

A science centre. Rich was planning on building an entire facility so that all the work being done on the reef could be done locally, properly and comfortably. No more long-haul journeys. No more working out of rust-flecked transportables or four-wheel drives. No more vulnerable, fish-filled freezers for her spawn. The researchers of Coral

Bay would have facilities at least as good as the visitors who flocked here in the high season.

It was a godsend in so many ways.

But Rich has used it to buy his way to holding onto the revenue-rich coastal strip, a flat inner voice reminded her.

He could have just freed himself of Wardoo and run, a perkier voice said. *He didn't have to come back.*

Is he even 'back'? the cynical voice said. *He's owned and run it for years without ever setting foot on the property. You still might never see him again.*

I'm seeing him now, aren't I...?

Yes. She was. Fulfilling her most secret hopes. The ones she'd pushed down and down until the only place they could be expressed was in her dreams. Mila stripped off her mask and snorkel and dropped them on the dive deck but left her flippered feet dangling in the deep.

Ready for a fast getaway.

'Do you even want Wardoo?' she challenged without looking at him.

'I thought I didn't,' he admitted, casting the words to the sea like she had. 'Not if I couldn't make it profitable. I thought it was just a business like any other to me. A means to an end. A millstone even.'

'But it's not?'

'Turns out I'm more northern than I thought,' he quipped. 'I didn't know how much until that night on the *Portus.* After we'd been there and I was able to conceptualise what I'd be losing.'

Mila studied her waving fins in the undulating water below the *Portus.*

'Wardoo was an emotional sanctuary when my mother died, and I'd forgotten how much. I let myself forget. I painted a picture of what it could be—full of children, full of love—and all of that came rushing back when I faced the reality of losing it. That's why I was reluctant to go out there; I feared it wouldn't make my decision any easier.'

She remembered his quietness at Jack's Vent. Were those the thoughts he'd been struggling with?

'And what about the reef?' she pressed. 'How was discovering that going to help you make your decision?'

'I needed to know what I was up against with the development. See it as the government sees it.'

'Sure.' She looked sideways at him. 'Who better to ask than a government employee?'

'I wasn't expecting you, Mila. Someone with your passion and connectedness. I thought I was just getting a guide to show me around. I didn't mean to exploit your love for the reef.'

'Okay, so you're sorry. Is that what you came all this way to say?'

Rich frowned. 'You likened Wardoo to the *Portus*, that last day I saw you,' he said. 'And I spent a lot of time thinking about that, of all the reasons it wasn't true. Except that, eventually, I realised it was. I don't hesitate to let other areas of WestCorp's operations pay for maintaining and running the *Portus* because she's become a fundamental part of my survival. She makes me…happy. She's important.'

'Except the land isn't important to you,' she reminded him.

He found her eyes. Stared. 'It is to you.'

A whale shark bumping up against her legs couldn't have rocked her more. Cherry-flavoured confusion whirled in her head.

'You signed a fifty-year lease—' she grappled '—you're building an entire science and rescue facility. You're changing all your big corporate plans…to please *me*? Someone you've known for a few days at most?'

No. There had to be another angle here. Some kind of money trail at work.

Rich turned side on to face her.

'Mila, you have a handle on life that I'm only beginning to understand. You are just…in tune. You dive into life with full immersion. Before I met you I would have scoffed at how important that was in life. I'm pretty sure I did scoff at it, until I saw it in action. In *you*.' He brought them closer, but still didn't touch her. 'I envy what you have, Mila. And I absolutely don't want to be the one to take it from you.'

Uneasiness washed around them.

'You're not responsible for me, Rich,' she said tightly.

'I don't feel responsible, Mila. I feel…grateful.' He swung his legs up under him and pushed to standing. 'Come on, let's get warm.'

She was plenty warm looking up at all that hard flesh, thanks very much.

Without accepting his aid, she also stood and used the short, arduous climb up the *Portus'* steps to get her thoughts in order. On deck, Rich patted at his face and shoulders with one of the thick towels neatly piled there.

'I'm a king in the city, Mila. Well-connected, well-resourced. I have colleagues and respect and a diary full to overflowing with opportunity. Busy enough to mask any number of voids inside. But you called me empty and dis-connected—' *and lonely* '—and you named all the things I'd started to feel so dramatically when I came here. To this place where none of those city achievements meant squat. A place that stripped me back to the essence of who I am. I hated being that exposed because it meant I couldn't kid myself any more.'

'About what?'

He tucked himself deeper into the massive towel.

'Losing my mother so young hit me hard, Mila. Being

sent away to school just added to that. I was convinced then that if I played by life's rules then I would be rewarded with the certainty that had just been stripped away from me. The rules said that if you worked hard you would be a success, and that with success came money and that people with money got the power.'

'And you wanted power?' she whispered.

'As a motherless eight-year-old abandoned in boarding school? Yes, I did. I never wanted life to happen *to* me again.'

Mila could only stand and stare. 'Did it work?'

'Yeah, everything was going great. All my sacrifices were paying off and I was rising through the ranks nicely. And then my father's heart ruptured one day while I was busy taking an international conference call and I couldn't get there in time and he died alone. Life stuck it to me, just to remind me it could. So I worked harder and I earned more. I forsook everything else and I stuck it back to life.'

'And did *that* work?' she breathed, knowing the answer already.

Rich slid her a sideways look and it was full of despair. 'I thought so. And then I came here. And I met you and I saw how you didn't need to compete with life because you just worked with it. Symbiotically. Like the creatures on the reef you told me about with all their diversity, working together, cooperatively. You *owned* life.'

Rich looked towards the coastline—burnished red against the electric blue of the coastal reef lagoons.

'I don't own it, Rich. I just live it. As best I can.'

'I'd worked my whole life to make sure that *I* got life's best, Mila. I upskilled and strategised and created this sanitised environment where everything that happened to me happened *because* of me. Not because of someone else and sure as heck not because of capricious life! And then

I discover that you're just getting it organically…just by being you.'

'Rich…'

'This is not a complaint, Mila. Just an explanation. I got back to Perth and I was all set to go ashore for that critical ten a.m., and then it hit me, right between my eyes.'

'What did?'

'That I didn't want to be a Grundy any more.'

Mila frowned. 'What do you want to be?'

His brows dipped and then straightened. His blue eyes cleared and widened with resolve. 'I think I want to be a Dawson.'

She gasped.

'*The* Dawson—the one you described to me that first day we met and spoke of with such respect. Protector of the reef. Part of the land up here. Part of the history. I want you to look at me like someone who built something here, not just…mined it for profits.'

She realised. 'That's why you wanted to keep the Wardoo lease?'

'Now I just have to learn how to run it.'

Mila thought through the ramifications of his words. 'You'd give up WestCorp?'

He shook his head. 'I'll transform it. Play to my own strengths and transition away from the rest. Get back to fundamentals.'

Nothing was quite as fundamental as grazing the animals that fed the country.

'You have zero expertise in running a cattle station,' she pointed out.

'I have expertise in buying floundering businesses and building them back up. That's how WestCorp got its start. About time I applied that to our oldest business, don't you think? See what it could be with some focus. Besides, as you so rightly pointed out, I have minions. Very talented minions.'

She could see it. Rich as a Dawson. Standing on Wardoo's wrap-around verandas, a slouch hat shielding him from the mid-morning sun, even if it was only once a month. But she wasn't in that picture. And, despite saying all the right things, he wasn't inviting her.

This was just a *mea culpa* for everything that had gone down between them. Nothing more.

'If anyone can do it,' she murmured, 'you can.'

Her heart squeezed just to say it. Having him be twelve hundred kilometres away was hard enough. Having him here in Coral Bay yet not *be* with him would be torture. But she'd done hard things before. And protecting herself was second nature.

'Nancy would be proud of you, Rich.'

It was impossible not to feel the upwelling of happiness for him; that this good man had found his way to such a good and optimistic place.

'I'm glad someone will because the rest of my world is going to be totally and utterly bemused. I'm going to need your help, Mila,' he said, eyes shining. 'To make a go of it.'

Earwax flooded her senses. She knew he didn't mean to be cruel, but what he asked… It was too much. Even for a woman who had hardened herself against so much in the past. She couldn't put herself through that.

She wouldn't.

He would have to find someone else to be his cheer squad as he upturned his life.

'You don't need me,' she said firmly. 'Now that you know what you want to do.'

Confusion stained his handsome face. 'But you're the one that inspired me.'

'I'm not some kind of muse,' she said, pulling her hair

up into something resembling a soggy ponytail. 'And I'm not your staff.'

He reeled back a little. 'No. Of course. That's not what I—'

Tying up her hair was like breathing to her—second nature. Yet she couldn't even manage that with her trembling hands. She abandoned her effort and clenched them as the smell of processed yeast overruled the heartbreak.

'I recognise that I'm a curiosity to you and that my *quirky* little life here is probably adorably idyllic from your perspective, particularly at a time when you're facing some major changes, but I never actually invited you to share it. And I'm not obliged to, simply because you've had an epiphany about your own life.'

Rich frowned. Stared. Realised.

'I've lost your faith,' he murmured.

'It's been nine weeks!' Anger made her rash but it was pain that made her spit. 'And you just roll up out of the blue wanting something from me yet again. Enough to even hunt me down two kilometres off—'

She cut herself off on a gasp. *Offshore...*

'You were in the deep!' she stammered. 'Way beyond the drop-off.'

Rich grimaced. 'I was trying not to think about it.'

'You came out into the open ocean to find me.' Where life was utterly uncontrollable. 'With sharks and whales and...and...'

'Sea monsters,' he added helpfully.

Maybe that was her cue to laugh. Maybe that would be the smart thing to do—laugh it off and move on with her life. But Rich had gone *into the deep*. Where he never, ever went.

The yeast entirely vanished, to make way for a strong thread of pineapple.

Love.

The thing she'd been struggling against since the day she'd sat, straddled between his thighs, on the sea kayak on Yardi Creek. The thing she'd very determinedly not let herself indulge since the night she'd motored away from him all those weeks ago.

No one had ever put themselves into danger for her. Or even vague discomfort. All her life *she* was the one who'd endured unease for the ease of others.

Yet Rich had climbed down into the vast unknown of open water and swum with a whale shark…

And he'd done it to get to *her.*

'Why are you really here, Rich?' she whispered.

He'd apologised.

He'd had an epiphany…all over the place.

But he hadn't told her why he'd come in person.

He studied her close, eyes tracking all over her face, and she became insanely self-conscious about what she must look like, fresh out of the water with a face full of mask pressure marks.

'I have something for you, Mila.' He reached for another towel and carefully draped it around her shoulders, tucking it into her cold hands. 'Come on.'

He discarded his own towel and Mila padded silently into the galley behind him as he crossed to a shelf beside the interior sofa and tucked something there into his fist. Gentle hands on her shoulders urged her down onto the sofa as he squatted in front of her. All that bare flesh and candyfloss was incredibly distracting.

'I should have reached out to you, Mila,' he started. 'Not left it nine weeks.' His eyes dropped to his fist momentarily, as though to check that whatever was in there was *still* in there. 'But it took me half of that to get my head around the things that you'd said. To get my head right.'

That still left several weeks…

'And then I didn't want to come back to you until I had something tangible to offer you. Development permission on the Northern Studies Centre. A plan. Something I could give you that would show how much I—'

His courage seemed to fail him just at the crucial moment. He blew a long, slow breath out and brought his gaze back to hers.

'This is harder than stepping into that ocean,' he murmured, but then he straightened. 'I don't have planning approval to give you, Mila. That's still a week or two away. But I have this. And it's something. A place-holder, if you like.'

He opened his white-knuckled hand to reveal a small silk pouch.

Mila stared at it and the tang of curiosity added itself to all the pineapple to create something almost like a delicious cocktail.

'What is it?'

'A gift. An apology.' He took a deep breath, hand outstretched. 'A promise.'

That word stalled her hand just as it hovered over the little pouch. But he didn't expand on it, just held his palm flat and not quite steady.

That made her own shake anew.

But the pouch opened easily and a pale necklace slid out. A wisp of white-gold chain and hanging from it…

'Is that your pearl?'

The one from the oyster stacks that day. The one she'd given him as a memento of the reef. The one that was small and a little bit too malformed to be of actual value.

It hung on its cobweb-fine chain as if it was as priceless as any of its more perfect spherical cousins.

More so because it came from Rich.

'It's your pearl,' he murmured. 'It always was.'

She lifted her eyes to his.

'I should have known better than to try and stage-manage this whole reunion,' he said. 'I guess I have a way to go in giving up control over uncontrollable things.'

Her heart thumped even harder.

This was a *reunion*?

Her eyes fell back to the pearl on its beautiful chain. 'But I gave this to you.'

He nodded. 'To remember you by. I would rather have the real deal.'

She stared at him, wordless.

'I know you've done it tough in the past,' he went on. 'That you consider yourself as much a misfit as your grandmother. And I know that's made it hard for you to trust people. Or believe in them. But you believed in me when we met and I came to hope that maybe you trusted me a little bit too.'

Still she could do nothing but stare. And battle the myriad incompatible tastes swamping the back of her throat and nose.

'I'm hoping we can get that back. With time. And a fair amount of effort on my part.'

'You lied to me, Rich.' There was no getting around that.

'I was lying to me, too. You raised too many *what-ifs* in my nice ordered life, Mila. And I didn't deal in ifs, I only dealt in certainties.'

Did he mean to use the past tense?

'You threw into doubt everything I'd been raised to believe, and I...panicked. I fell back on what I knew best. And what I started to feel for you... It was as uncontrollable as everything I'd ever fought against.'

'You said your world was in the city,' she whispered. Saying it aloud was too scary because what if she reminded

him? What if she talked him out of what she was starting
to think he was saying?

But she had to know.

And he had to say it.

'That's because I had no idea then that you were about
to become my world,' he attested. 'My world is wherever
you are.'

Pineapple suffused every other scent trying to get her
attention. But every other scent had no chance. Not while
she sat here, so near to a half-naked Rich with truth in his
eyes and the most amazing miracle on his gorgeous lips.

'We barely know each other.'

Did she need to test him again? Or did she just not trust
it?

Rich leaned closer. 'I know everything I need to know
about you. And you have a lifetime to get to know me better.'

'What exactly are you saying?'

'I'm saying that you can swim Wardoo's sinkhole whenever you want. And you can use the *Portus* any time you
need a ride somewhere. And you'll have your own swipe
key for the Science Centre and sole management of the
spawn bank.'

He forked his fingers through her hair either side of
her face.

'I'm saying that you have a standing welcome in any
part of my life. I'm through putting impediments of any
kind between myself and the most spectacularly unique
and beautiful woman I could ever imagine meeting. I'm
saying that your synaesthesia does not entertain me or con-
fuse me or challenge me. It delights me. It reminds me what
I've been missing in this world.' His fingers curled gently
against her scalp to punctuate his vow. 'I will make it my
life's work to understand it—and you—because the Daw-

son kids are probably going to have it and I'd like them to always feel loved and supported, even by their poor, superpower-deficient dad.'

Dawson *kids*?

Her heart was out-and-out galloping now.

'I'm saying that all of this will happen on *your* schedule, as soon as I've won back your trust and faith in me. You and I are meant to be together, Mila. I don't think it's any coincidence that we first met at a place that was so special to my great-grandmother. Nancy had my back that day.'

He pressed his lips against hers briefly.

'I'm asking you to be with me, Mila Nakano. To help me navigate the great unknown waters ahead. To help me interpret them.' Then, when she just stared at him, still wordless, he added, 'I'm saying that I love you, Mermaid. Weirdness inclusive. In fact, especially for that.'

Mila just stared, overcome by his words, and by the pineapple onslaught that swamped her whole system. It seemed to finally dawn on Rich that she hadn't said a word in a while.

A very long while.

'Have I blown it?' he checked softly, setting himself back from her. 'Misjudged your interest?' She still didn't speak but he braved it out. 'Or am I the creepiest stalker ever to live, right now?'

Mila caressed the smooth undulations of the imperfect pearl resting in her fingers. Grounding herself. She traced the fine chain away from it and then back again. But the longer she did it, the clearer the pearl's personality became.

Rich's soft voice broke into her meditation.

'Is that a happy smile or a how-am-I-going-to-let-him-down-gently smile?'

She found his nervous eyes.

'It's the pearl,' she breathed. 'My subconscious has finally given them a personality.'

'Oh.' The topic change seemed to pain him, but he'd just promised not to rush her. 'What is it?'

Maybe her subconscious had been waiting for him all this time so that she'd know it when she saw it. 'Smitten.'

Her cotton candy stole back in as a cautious smile broke across Rich's face.

'Smitten is a good start,' he said, nodding his appraisal. 'I can work with smitten.'

'You won't need to. It's a small pearl,' she murmured on a deep, long breath. 'It only reflects a small percentage of what I'm feeling.'

This time, the hope in Rich's expression was so palpable it even engendered a burst of hot chocolate on his behalf.

Well, that was a first.

'Mila, you're killing me…'

'Payback.' She smiled, then slipped the pearl chain around her neck and fiddled with the clasp until it was secure. Made him wait. Made him sweat, just a little bit. After nine weeks, it was the least she could do.

And after a lifetime of strict caution, it was almost the best she could do.

'It killed me to walk away from you the last time I was on the *Portus*,' she said. 'I'm not doing it again. I may need to take things slow for a bit, but—' she took a deep breath '—yes, I would love to explore whatever lies ahead. With you,' she clarified, to be totally patent.

Rich hauled her to her feet and whipped the massive towel from around her until it circled him instead. Then he brought her right into its fluffy circle, hard up against him, and found her mouth with his own.

'I think I first fell for you during the coral spawn,' Rich murmured around their kisses. 'Literally in the middle of the snow globe. And then the truth slammed into me like you slammed into that dugong and I was a goner.'

'Yardi Creek for me,' she murmured. 'So I guess I've loved you longer.'

His smile took over his face. 'But I guarantee you I've loved you deeper.'

She curled her arms around his neck and kept him close.

'I guess we can call that a draw then. Although—' she fingered the little pearl on the chain '—I think the oyster might have known before either of us.'

He bent again for another kiss. 'Oysters always were astute.'

* * * * *

If you enjoyed this book by Nikki Logan,
look out for
STRANDED WITH HER RESCUER
also by Nikki Logan.

Or, if you'd love to read about another
gorgeous billionaire, we hope you enjoy
THE UNFORGETTABLE SPANISH TYCOON
by Christy McKellen.

Both available as eBooks!

"What do you think we should do about this chemistry between us?"

Cassie choked on her latte. "Excuse me?"

"I'm stumbling here," Braden acknowledged. "Because it's been a long time since I've been attracted to a woman."

She eyed him warily. "Are you saying that you're attracted to me?"

"Why else would I be here when there are at least a dozen coffee shops closer to my office?"

"I thought you came to the library to return the train your daughter took home."

"That was my excuse to come by and see you. When I found the train, I planned to leave it with my mother for her to return. And when I dropped Saige off this morning, I had it with me, but for some reason, I held on to it. As I headed toward my office, I figured I'd give it to her later. Except that I couldn't stop thinking about you."

Cassie wiped her fingers on her napkin, then folded it on top of her plate.

"This would be a good time for you to admit that you've been thinking about me, too."

* * *

Those Engaging Garretts!—
The Carolina Cousins!

BABY TALK & WEDDING BELLS

BY
BRENDA HARLEN

MILLS & BOON

First Published in Great Britain 2017
By Mills & Boon, an imprint of HarperCollins*Publishers*
1 London Bridge Street, London, SE1 9GF

© 2017 Brenda Harlen

ISBN: 978-0-263-92273-8

23-0217

Our policy is to use papers that are natural, renewable and recyclable products and made from wood grown in sustainable forests. The logging and manufacturing processes conform to the legal environmental regulations of the country of origin.

Printed and bound in Spain
by CPI, Barcelona

Brenda Harlen is a former attorney who once had the privilege of appearing before the Supreme Court of Canada. The practice of law taught her a lot about the world and reinforced her determination to become a writer—because in fiction, she could promise a happy ending! Now she is an award-winning, national best-selling author of more than thirty titles for Mills & Boon. You can keep up to date with Brenda on Facebook and Twitter or through her website, www.brendaharlen.com.

For Sheryl Davis—a fabulous friend,
dedicated writer and librarian extraordinaire.
Thanks for showing me "a day in the life," answering
my endless questions and sharing my passion
for hockey—which has absolutely nothing
to do with this story but needed to be noted!

Chapter One

By all accounts, Braden Garrett had lived a charmed life. The eldest son of the family had taken on the role of CEO of Garrett Furniture before he was thirty. A year later, he met and fell in love with Dana Collins. They were married ten months after that and, on the day of their wedding, Braden was certain he had everything he'd ever wanted.

Two years later, it seemed perfectly natural that they would talk about having a baby. Having grown up with two brothers and numerous cousins in close proximity, Braden had always envisioned having a family of his own someday. His wife seemed just as eager as he was, but after three more years and countless failures, her enthusiasm had understandably waned.

And then, finally, their lives were blessed by the addition of Saige Lindsay Garrett.

Braden's life changed the day his tiny dark-haired, dark-eyed daughter was put in his arms. Eight weeks later, it changed again. Now, more than a year later, he was a single father trying to do what was best for his baby girl—most of the time not having a clue what that might be.

Except that right now—at eight ten on a Tuesday morning—he was pretty sure that what she needed was breakfast. Getting her to eat it was another matter entirely.

"Come on, sweetie. Daddy has to drop you off at Grandma's before I go to work for a meeting at ten o'clock."

His daughter's dark almond-shaped eyes lit up with anticipation in response to his words. "Ga-ma?"

"That's right, you're going to see Grandma today. But only if you eat your cereal and banana."

She carefully picked up one of the cereal O's, pinching it between her thumb and forefinger, then lifted her hand to her mouth.

Braden made himself another cup of coffee while Saige picked at her breakfast, one O at a time. Not that he was surprised. Just like every other female he'd ever known, she did everything on her own schedule.

"Try some of the banana," he suggested.

His little girl reached for a chunk of the fruit. "Na-na."

"That's right, sweetie. Ba-na-na. Yummy."

She shoved the fruit in her mouth.

"Good girl."

She smiled, showing off a row of tiny white teeth, and love—sweet and pure—flooded through him. Life as a single parent was so much more difficult than he'd anticipated, and yet, it only ever took one precious smile from Saige to make him forget all of the hard stuff. He absolutely lived for his little girl's smiles—certain proof that he wasn't a total screw-up in the dad department and tentative hope that maybe her childhood hadn't been completely ruined by the loss of her mother.

He sipped his coffee as Saige reached for another piece

of banana. This time, she held the fruit out to him, offering to share. He lowered his head to take the banana from her fingers. Fifteen months earlier, Braden would never have imagined allowing himself to be fed like a baby bird. But fifteen months earlier, he didn't have the miracle that was his daughter.

He hadn't known it was possible to love someone so instantly and completely, until that first moment when his baby girl was put into his arms.

I want a better life for her than I could give her on my own—a real home with two parents who will both love her as much as I do.

It didn't seem too much to ask, but they'd let Lindsay down. And he couldn't help but worry that Saige would one day realize they'd let her down, too.

For now, she was an incredibly happy child, seemingly unaffected by her motherless status. Still, it wasn't quite the family that Lindsay had envisioned for her baby girl when she'd signed the adoption papers—or that Braden wanted for Saige, either.

"I'm not going anywhere," he promised his daughter now. "Daddy will always be here for you, I promise."

"Da-da." Saige's smile didn't just curve her lips, it shone in her eyes and filled his whole heart.

"That's right—it's you and me kid."

"Ga-ma?"

"Yes, we've got Grandma and Grandpa in our corner, too. And lots of aunts, uncles and cousins."

"Na-na?"

He smiled. "Yeah, some of them are bananas, but we don't hold that against them."

She stretched out her arms, her hands splayed wide open. "Aw dun."

"Good girl." He moistened a washcloth under the tap to

wipe her hands and face, then removed the tray from her high chair and unbuckled the safety belt around her waist.

As soon as the clip was unfastened, she threw herself at him. He caught her against his chest as her little arms wrapped around his neck, but he felt the squeeze deep inside his heart.

"Ready to go to Grandma's now?"

When Saige nodded enthusiastically, he slung her diaper bag over his shoulder, then picked up his briefcase and headed toward the door. His hand was on the knob when the phone rang. He was already fifteen minutes late leaving for work, but he took three steps back to check the display, and immediately recognized his parents' home number. *Crap*.

He dropped his briefcase and picked up the receiver. "Hi, Mom. We're just on our way out the door."

"Then it's lucky I caught you," Ellen said. "I chipped a tooth on my granola and I'm on my way to the dentist."

"Ouch," he said sympathetically, even as he mentally began juggling his morning plans to accommodate taking Saige into the office with him.

"I'm so sorry to cancel at the last minute," she said.

"Don't be silly, Mom. Of course you have to have your tooth looked at, and Saige is always happy to hang out at my office."

"You can't take her to the office," his mother protested.

"Why not?"

"Because it's Tuesday," she pointed out.

"And every Tuesday, I meet with Nathan and Andrew," he reminded her.

"Tuesday at ten o'clock is Baby Talk at the library."

"Right—Baby Talk," he said, as if he'd remembered. As if he had any intention of blowing off a business meeting to take his fifteen-month-old daughter to the library instead.

"Saige loves Baby Talk," his mother told him.

"I'm sure she does," he acknowledged. "But songs and stories at the library aren't really my thing."

"Maybe not, but they're Saige's thing," Ellen retorted. "And you're her father, and it's not going to hurt you to take an hour out of your schedule so that she doesn't have to miss it this week."

"I have meetings all morning."

"Meetings with your cousins," she noted, "both fathers themselves who wouldn't hesitate to reschedule if their kids needed them."

Which he couldn't deny was true. "But…Baby Talk?"

"Yes," his mother said firmly, even as Saige began singing "wound an' wound"—her version of the chorus from the "Wheels on the Bus" song that she'd apparently learned in the library group. "Miss MacKinnon—the librarian— will steer you in the right direction."

He sighed. "Okay, I'll let Nate and Andrew know that I have to reschedule."

"Your daughter appreciates it," Ellen said.

He looked at the little girl still propped on his hip, and she looked back at him, her big brown eyes sparkling as she continued to sing softly.

She truly was the light of his life, and his mother knew there wasn't anything he wouldn't do for her.

"Well, Saige, I guess today is the day that Daddy discovers what Baby Talk is all about."

His daughter smiled and clapped her hands together.

The main branch of the Charisma Public Library was located downtown, across from the Bean There Café and only a short walk from the hospital and the courthouse. It was a three-story building of stone and glass with a large open foyer filled with natural light and tall, potted plants.

The information desk was a circular area in the center, designed to be accessible to patrons from all sides.

Cassandra MacKinnon sat at that desk, scanning the monthly calendar to confirm the schedule of upcoming events. The library wasn't just a warehouse of books waiting to be borrowed—it was a hub of social activity. She nodded to Luisa Todd and Ginny Stafford, who came in together with bulky knitting bags in hand. The two older women—friends since childhood—had started the Knit & Purl group and were always the first to arrive on Tuesday mornings.

Ginny stopped at the desk and took a gift bag out of her tote. "Will you be visiting with Irene this week?" she asked Cassie, referring to the former head librarian who now lived at Serenity Gardens, a seniors' residence in town.

"Tomorrow," Cassie confirmed.

"Would you mind taking this for me?" Ginny asked, passing the bag over the desk. "Irene always complains about having cold feet in that place, so I knitted her a couple pairs of socks. I had planned to see her on the weekend, but my son and daughter-in-law were in town with their three kids and I couldn't tear myself away from them."

"Of course, I wouldn't mind," Cassie told her. "And I know she'll love the socks."

Luisa snorted; Ginny smiled wryly. "Well, I'm sure she'll appreciate having warm feet, anyway."

Cassie tucked the bag under the counter and the two women continued on their way.

She spent a little bit of time checking in the materials that had been returned through the book drop overnight, then arranging them on the cart for Helen Darrow to put back on the shelves. Helen was a career part-time employee of the library who had been hired when Irene Houlahan was in charge. An older woman inherently distrustful of technology, Helen refused to touch the computers and spent most of her time finding books to fill online and call-in requests of patrons, putting them back when they were returned—and shushing anyone who dared to speak above a whisper in the book stacks.

"Hey, Miss Mac."

Cassie glanced up to see Tanya Fielding, a high school senior and regular at the Soc & Study group, at the desk. "Good morning, Tanya. Aren't you supposed to be in school this morning?"

The teen shook her head. "Our history teacher is giving us time to work on our independent research projects this week."

"What's your topic?"

"The role of German U-boats in the Second World War."

"Do you want to sign on to one of the computers?"

"No. Mr. Paretsky wants—" she made air quotes with her fingers "—real sources, actual paper books so that we can do proper page citations and aren't relying on made-up stuff that someone posted on the internet."

Cassie pushed her chair away from the desk. "Nonfiction is upstairs. Let's go see what we can find."

After the teen was settled at a table with a pile of books, Cassie checked that the Dickens Room was ready for the ESL group coming in at ten thirty and picked up a stack of abandoned magazines from a window ledge near the true crime section.

She put the magazines on Helen's cart and returned to her desk just as George Bowman came in. George and his wife, Margie, were familiar faces at the library. She knew all of the library's regular patrons—not just their names and faces, but also their reading habits and preferences. And, over the years, she'd gotten to know many of them on a personal level, too.

She was chatting with Mr. Bowman when the tall, dark and extremely handsome stranger stepped into view. Her heart gave a little bump against her ribs, as if to make sure she was paying attention, and warm tingles spread slowly through her veins. But he wasn't just a stranger, he was an outsider. The expensive suit jacket that stretched across his broad shoulders, the silk tie neatly knotted at his throat and the square, cleanly shaven jaw all screamed "corporate executive."

She would have been less surprised to see a rainbow-colored unicorn prancing across the floor than this man moving toward her. Moving rather slowly and with short strides considering his long legs, she thought—and then she saw the little girl toddling beside him.

The child she *did* recognize. Saige regularly attended Baby Talk at the library with her grandmother, which meant that the man holding the tiny hand had to be her dad: Braden Garrett, Charisma's very own crown prince.

A lot of years had passed since Braden was last inside the Charisma Public Library, and when he stepped through the front doors, he had a moment of doubt that he was even in the right place. In the past twenty years, the building had undergone major renovations so that the address was the only part of the library that remained unchanged.

He stepped farther into the room, noting that the card catalogue system had been replaced by computer terminals and the checkout desk wasn't just automated but self-serve—which meant that the kids borrowing books or other materials weren't subjected to the narrow-eyed stare of Miss Houlahan, the old librarian who marked the cards inside the back covers of the books, her gnarled fingers wielding the stamp like a weapon. He'd been terrified of the woman.

Of course, the librarian had been about a hundred years old when Braden was a kid—or so she'd seemed—so he didn't really expect to find her still working behind the desk. But the woman seated there now, her fingers moving over the keyboard as she conversed with an elderly gentleman, was at least twenty years younger than he'd expected, with chin-length auburn hair that shone with gold and copper highlights. Her face was heart-shaped with creamy skin and a delicately pointed chin. Her eyes were dark—green, he guessed, to go with the red hair— and her glossy lips curved in response to something the old man said to her.

Saige wiggled again, silently asking to be set down. Since she'd taken her first tentative steps four months earlier, she preferred to walk everywhere. Braden set her on her feet but held firmly to her hand and headed toward the information desk.

The woman he assumed was Miss MacKinnon stopped typing and picked up a pen to jot a note on a piece of paper that she then handed across the desk to the elderly patron.

The old man nodded his thanks. "By the way, Margie wanted me to tell you that our daughter, Karen, is expecting again."

"This will be her third, won't it?"

"Third *and* fourth," he replied.

Neatly arched brows lifted. "Twins?"

He nodded again. "Our seventh and eighth grandchildren."

"That's wonderful news—congratulations to all of you."

"You know, I keep waiting for the day when you have big news to share."

The librarian smiled indulgently. "Didn't I tell you just this morning that there's a new John Grisham on the shelves?"

Mr. Bowman shook his head. "Marriage plans, Cassie."

"You've been with Mrs. Bowman for almost fifty years—I don't see you giving her up to run away with me now."

The old man's ears flushed red. "Fifty-one," he said proudly. "And I didn't mean me. You need a handsome young man to put a ring on your finger and give you beautiful babies."

"Until that happens, you keep bringing me pictures of your gorgeous grandbabies," she suggested.

"I certainly will," he promised.

"In the meantime—" she picked up a flyer from the counter and offered it to Mr. Bowman "—I hope you're planning to come to our Annual Book & Bake Sale on the fifteenth."

"It's already marked on the calendar at home," he told her. "And Margie's promised to make a couple dozen muffins."

"I'll definitely look forward to those."

The old man finally moved toward the elevator and Braden stepped forward. "Miss MacKinnon?"

She turned toward him, and he saw that her eyes weren't green, after all, but a dark chocolate brown and fringed with even darker lashes.

"Good morning," she said. "How can I help you?"

"I'm here for…Baby Talk?"

Her mouth curved, drawing his attention to her full, glossy lips. "Are you sure?"

"Not entirely," he admitted, shifting his gaze to meet hers again. "Am I in the right place?"

"You are," she confirmed. "Baby Talk is in the Bronte Room on the upper level at ten."

He glanced at the clock on the wall, saw that it wasn't yet nine thirty. "I guess we're a little early."

"Downstairs in the children's section, there's a play area with puzzles and games, a puppet theater and a train table."

"Choo-choo," Saige urged.

Miss MacKinnon glanced down at his daughter and smiled. "Although if you go there now, you might have trouble tearing your daughter away. You like the trains, don't you, Saige?"

She nodded, her head bobbing up and down with enthusiasm.

Braden's brows lifted. He was surprised—and a little disconcerted—to discover that this woman knew something about his daughter that he didn't. "Obviously she spends more time here than I realized."

"Your mom brings her twice a week."

"Well, since you know my mother and Saige, I guess I should introduce myself—I'm Braden Garrett."

She accepted the hand he offered. He noted that hers was soft, but her grip firm. "Cassie MacKinnon."

"Are you really the librarian?" he heard himself ask.

"One of them," she said.

"When I think of librarians, I think of Miss Houlahan."

"So do I," she told him. "In fact, she's the reason I chose to become a librarian."

"We must be thinking of different Miss Houlahans," he decided.

"Perhaps," she allowed. "Now, if you'll excuse me, I need to check on something upstairs."

"Something upstairs" sounded rather vague to Braden, and he got the strange feeling that he was being brushed off. Or maybe he was reading too much into those two words. After all, this was a library and she was the librarian—no doubt there were any number of "somethings" she had to do, although he couldn't begin to imagine what they might be.

As she walked away, Braden found himself admiring

the curve of her butt and the sway of her hips and thinking that he might have spent a lot more time in the library as a kid if there had been a librarian like Miss MacKinnon to help him navigate the book stacks.

Chapter Two

By the time he managed to drag Saige away from the trains and find the Bronte Room, there were several other parents and children already there—along with Cassie MacKinnon. Apparently one of the "somethings" that she did at the library was lead the stories, songs and games at Baby Talk.

She nodded to him as he entered the room and gestured to an empty place in the circle. "Have a seat," she invited.

Except there were no seats. All of the moms—and yes, they were *all* moms, there wasn't another XY chromosome anywhere to be found, unless it was tucked away in a diaper—were sitting on the beige Berber carpet. He lowered himself to the floor, certain he looked as awkward as he felt as he attempted to cross his legs.

"Did you bring your pillow, Mr. Garrett?"

"Pillow?" he echoed. His mother hadn't said anything about a pillow, but when he looked around, he saw that all of the moms had square pillows underneath their babies.

"I've got an extra that you can borrow," she said, opening a cabinet to retrieve a big pink square with an enormous daisy embroidered on it.

He managed not to grimace as he thanked her and set the pillow on the floor, then sat Saige down on top of it. She immediately began to clap her hands, excited to begin.

Ellen had told him that Baby Talk was for infants up to eighteen months of age, and looking around, he guessed that his daughter was one of the oldest in the room. A quick glance confirmed that the moms were of various ages, as well. The one thing they had in common: they were all checking out the lone male in the room.

He focused on Cassie, eager to get the class started and finished.

What he learned during the thirty-minute session was that the librarian had a lot more patience than he did. Even when there were babies crying, she continued to read or sing in the same soothing tone. About halfway through the session, she took a bin of plastic instruments out of the cupboard and passed it around so the babies could jingle bells or pound on drums or bang sticks together. Of course, the kids had a lot more enthusiasm than talent—his daughter included—and by the time they were finished, Braden could feel a headache brewing.

"That was a great effort today," Cassie told them, and he breathed a grateful sigh of relief that they were done. "I'll see you all next week, and please don't forget the Book & Bake Sale on the fifteenth—any and all donations of gently used books are appreciated."

Despite the class being dismissed, none of the moms seemed to be in a hurry to leave, instead continuing to chat with one another about feeding schedules and diaper rashes and teething woes. Braden just wanted to be gone but Saige had somehow managed to pull off her shoes, forcing him to stay put long enough to untie the laces, put the shoes back on her feet and tie them up again.

While he was preoccupied with this task, the woman who had been seated on his left shifted closer. "I'm Heather Turcotte. And this—" she jiggled the baby in her lap "—is Katie."

"Braden Garrett," he told her, confident that she already knew his daughter.

"You're a brave man to subject yourself to a baby class full of women," she said, then smiled at him.

"I'm only here today because my mom had an appointment."

"That's too bad. It would be nice to have another single parent in the group," she told him. "Most of these women don't have a clue how hard it is to raise a child on their own. Of course, I didn't know, either, until I had Katie. All through my pregnancy, I was so certain that I could handle this. But the idea of a baby is a lot different than the reality."

"That's true," he agreed, only half listening to her as he worked Saige's shoes back onto her feet. Out of the corner of his eye, he saw Cassie talking to one of the other moms and cleaning the instruments with antibacterial wipes, which made him feel a little bit better about the bells that his daughter had been chewing on.

"Of course, it helps that I have a flexible schedule at work," Heather was saying. "As I'm sure you do, considering that your name is on the company letterhead."

"There are benefits to working for a family business," he agreed.

Cassie waved goodbye to the other woman and her baby, then carried the bin of instruments to the cupboard.

"Such as being able to take a little extra time to grab a cup of coffee now?" Heather suggested hopefully.

He forced his attention back to her, inwardly wincing at the hopeful expression on her face. "Sorry, I really do need to get to the office."

She pouted, much like his daughter did when she didn't get what she wanted, but the look wasn't nearly as cute on a grown woman who had a daughter of her own.

"Well, maybe we could get the kids together sometime. A playdate for the little ones—" she winked "—*and* the grown-ups."

"I appreciate the invitation, but my time is really limited these days."

"Oh. Okay." She forced a smile, but he could tell that she was disappointed. "Well, if you change your mind, you know where to find me on Tuesday mornings."

"Yes, I do," he confirmed.

Somehow, while he'd been putting on her shoes, Saige had found his phone and was using it as a chew toy. With a sigh, he pried it from her fingers and wiped it on his trousers. "Are you cutting more teeth, sweetie?"

Her only answer was to shove her fist into her mouth.

He picked her up and she dropped her head onto his shoulder, apparently ready for her nap. He bent his knees carefully to reach the daisy pillow and carried it to the librarian. "Thanks for the loan."

"You're welcome," she said. Then, "I wanted to ask about your mother earlier, but I didn't want you to think I was being nosy."

"What did you want to ask?"

"In the past six months, Ellen hasn't missed a single class—I just wondered if she was okay."

"Oh. Yes, she's fine. At least, I think so," he told her. "She chipped a tooth at breakfast and had an emergency appointment at the dentist."

"Well, please tell her that I hope she's feeling better and I'm looking forward to seeing her on Thursday."

"Is that your way of saying that you don't want to see me on Thursday?" he teased.

"This is a public library, Mr. Garrett," she pointed out. "You're welcome any time the doors are open."

"And will I find you here if I come back?" he wondered.

"Most days," she confirmed.

"So this is your real job—you don't work anywhere else?"

Her brows lifted at that. "Yes, this is my real job," she said, her tone cooler now by several degrees.

And despite having turned down Heather's offer of coffee only a few minutes earlier, he found the prospect of enjoying a hot beverage with this woman an incredibly appealing one. "Can you sneak away for a cup of coffee?"

She seemed surprised by the invitation—and maybe a little tempted—but after a brief hesitation, she shook her head. "No, I can't. I'm working, Mr. Garrett."

"I know," he said, and offered her what he'd been told was a charming smile. "But the class is finished and I'm sure that whatever else you have to do can wait for half an hour or so while we go across the street to the café."

"Obviously you think that 'whatever else' I have to do is pretty insignificant," she noted, her tone downright frosty now.

"I didn't mean to offend you, Miss MacKinnon," he said, because it was obvious that he'd done so.

"I may not be the CEO of a national corporation, but the work I do matters to the people who come here." She moved toward the door where she hit a switch on the wall to turn off the overhead lights—a clear sign that it was time for him to leave.

He stepped out of the room, and she closed and locked the door. "Have a good day, Mr. Garrett."

"I will," he said. "But I need one more thing before I go."

"What's that?" she asked warily.

"A library card."

Cassie stared at him for a moment, trying to decide if he was joking. "*You* want a library card?"

"I assume I need one to borrow books," Braden said matter-of-factly.

"You do," she confirmed, still wondering about his angle—because she was certain that he had one.

"So where do I get a card?" he prompted, sounding sincere in his request.

But how could she know for sure? If her recent experience with the male species had taught her nothing else, she'd at least learned that she wasn't a good judge of their intentions or motivations.

"Follow me," she said.

He did, and with each step, she was conscious of him beside her—not just his presence but his masculinity. The library wasn't a female domain. A lot of males came through the doors every day—mostly boys, a few teens and some older men. Rarely did she cross paths with a male in the twenty-five to forty-four age bracket. Never had she crossed paths with anyone like Braden Garrett.

He was the type of man who made heads turn and hearts flutter and made women think all kinds of naughty thoughts. And his nearness now made her skin feel hot and tight, tingly in a way that made her uneasy. Cassie didn't want to feel tingly, she didn't want to think about how long it had been since she'd been attracted, on a purely physical level, to a man, and she definitely didn't want to be attracted to this man now.

Aside from the fact that he was a Garrett and, therefore, way out of her league, she had no intention of wasting a single minute of her time with a man who didn't value who she was. Not again. Thankfully, his disparaging remark about her job was an effective antidote to his good looks and easy charm.

Taking a seat at the computer, she logged in to create a new account. He took his driver's license out of his wallet so that she could input the necessary data. She noted that his middle name was Michael, his thirty-ninth birthday was coming up and he lived in one of the most exclusive parts of town.

"What kind of books do you like to read?" she inquired, as she would of any other newcomer to the library.

"Mostly historical fiction and nonfiction, some action-thriller type stories."

"Like Bernard Cornwell, Tom Clancy and Clive Cussler?"

He nodded. "And John Jakes and Diana Gabaldon."

She looked up from the computer screen. "You read Diana Gabaldon?"

"Sure," he said, not the least bit self-conscious about the admission. "My cousin, Tristyn, left a copy of *Outlander* at my place on Ocracoke and I got hooked."

For a moment while they'd been chatting about favorite authors, she'd almost let herself believe he was a normal person—just a handsome single dad hanging out at the library with his daughter. But the revelation that he not only lived in Forrest Hill but had another house on an island in the Outer Banks immediately dispelled that notion.

"My brothers tease me about reading romance," he continued, oblivious to her thought process, "but there's a lot more to her books than that."

"There's a lot more to most romance novels than many people believe," she told him.

"What do you like to read?" he asked her.

"Anything and everything," she said. "I have favorite authors, of course, but I try to read across the whole spectrum in order to be able to make recommendations to our patrons." She set his newly printed library card on the counter along with a pen for him to sign it.

He did, then tucked the new card and his identification back into his wallet. By this time, Saige had lost the battle to keep her eyes open, and the image of that sweet little girl sleeping in his arms tugged at something inside of her.

"Congratulations," she said, ignoring the unwelcome tug. "You are now an official card-carrying member of the Charisma Public Library."

"Thank you." He picked up one of the flyers advertising the Book & Bake Sale along with a monthly schedule of classes and activities, then slid both into the side pocket of Saige's diaper bag. "I guess that means I'll be seeing you around."

She nodded, but she didn't really believe him. And as she watched him walk out the door, she assured herself that was for the best. Because the last thing she needed was to be crossing paths with a man who made her feel tingles she didn't want to be feeling.

His daughter slept until Braden got her to the office. As soon as he tried to lay her down, Saige was wide-awake and wanting his attention. He dumped the toys from her diaper bag into the playpen—squishy blocks and finger puppets and board books—so that she could occupy herself while he worked. She decided to invent a new game: throw things at Daddy. Thankfully, she wasn't strong enough to fling the books very far, but after several blocks bounced across the surface of his desk, he decided there was no point in hanging around the office when he obviously wasn't going to get anything accomplished.

There were definite advantages to working in a family business, and since his baby wouldn't be a baby forever, he decided to take the rest of the day off to spend with her. He took her to the indoor play center, where she could jump and climb and swing and burn off all of the energy she seemed to have in abundance. Then, when she was finally tired of all of that, he took her to "Aunt" Rachel's shop—Buds & Blooms—to pick out some flowers, then to his parents' house to see how Ellen had fared at the dentist.

"Ga-ma!" Saige said, flinging herself at her grandmother's legs.

"I didn't think I was going to get to see you today," Ellen said, ruffling her granddaughter's silky black hair. "And I was missing you."

"I'm sure she missed you more," Braden said, handing the bouquet to his mother. "She was not a happy camper at the office today."

"Offices aren't fun places for little ones." Ellen brought the flowers closer to her nose and inhaled their fragrant scent. "These are beautiful—what's the occasion?"

"No occasion—I just realized that I take for granted how much you do for me and Saige every day and wanted to show our appreciation," he told her. "But now that I see the swelling of your jaw, I'm thinking they might be 'get well' flowers—what did the dentist do to you?"

"He extracted the tooth."

"I thought it was only a chip."

"So did I," she admitted, lowering herself into a chair, which Saige interpreted as an invitation to crawl into her lap. "Apparently the chip caused a crack that went all the way down to the root, so they had to take it out."

He winced instinctively.

"Now I have to decide whether I want a bridge or an implant."

"And I'll bet you're wishing you had oatmeal instead of granola for breakfast," he noted, filling a vase with water for her flowers.

"It will definitely be oatmeal tomorrow," she said. "How was Baby Talk?"

"Fine," he said, "aside from the fact that I was the only man in a room full of women, apparently all of whom know my life story."

"They don't know your whole life story," his mother denied.

"How much do they know?"

"I might have mentioned that you're a single father."

"Might have mentioned?" he echoed suspiciously.

"Well, in a group of much younger women, it was immediately apparent that Saige isn't my child. Someone— I think it was Annalise—asked if I looked after her while her mother was at work and I said no, that I looked after her while her dad's at work because Saige doesn't have a mother."

"Hmm," he said. He couldn't fault his mother for answering the question, but he didn't like the way she made him sound like some kind of "super dad" just because he was taking care of his daughter—especially when they both knew there was no way he'd be able to manage without Ellen's help.

"And you're not the only single parent with a child in the group," she pointed out. "There are a couple of single moms there, too."

"I met Heather," he admitted.

"She's a pretty girl. And a loving mother."

"I'm not interested in a woman who's obviously looking for a man to be a father to her child," he warned.

"She told you that?"

"She gave me the 'single parenthood is so much harder than most people realize' speech."

"Which you already know," she pointed out.

He nodded again.

"So maybe you should think about finding a new mother for Saige," she urged.

"Because the third time's the charm?" he asked skeptically.

"Because a little girl needs a mother," she said firmly. "And because you deserve to have someone in your life, too."

"I have Saige," he reminded her, as he always did when she started in on this particular topic. But this time the automatic response was followed by a picture of the pretty librarian forming in his mind.

"And no one doubts how much you love her," Ellen acknowledged. "But if you do your job as a parent right— and I expect you will—she's going to grow up and go off to live her own life one day, and then who will you have?"

"I think I've got a few years before I need to worry about that," he pointed out. "And maybe by then, I'll be ready to start dating again."

His mother's sigh was filled with resignation.

"By the way," he said, in a desperate effort to shift the topic of conversation away from his blank social calendar, "Cassie said that she hopes you feel better soon."

As soon as he mentioned the librarian's name, a speculative gleam sparked in his mother's eyes that warned his effort had been for naught.

"She's such a sweet girl," Ellen said. "Smart and beautiful, and so ideally suited for her job."

Braden had intended to keep his mouth firmly shut, not wanting to be drawn into a discussion about Miss Mac-Kinnon's many attributes. But the last part of his mother's statement piqued his curiosity. "She's a librarian—what kind of qualifications does she need?"

His mother frowned her disapproval. "The janitor who scrubs the floors of a surgery is just as crucial as the doctor who performs the operation," she reminded him.

"But she's not a surgeon or a janitor," he pointed out. "She's a librarian." And he didn't think keeping a collection of books in order required any particular knowledge outside of the twenty-six letters of the alphabet.

"With a master's degree in library studies."

"I didn't know there was such a discipline," he acknowledged.

"Apparently there are a lot of things you don't know," she said pointedly.

He nodded an acknowledgment of the fact. "I guess, when I went into the library, I was expecting to find someone more like Miss Houlahan behind the desk."

His mother chuckled. "Irene Houlahan's been retired more than half a dozen years now."

"I'm relieved to know she's no longer terrifying young book borrowers."

"She wasn't terrifying," Ellen chided. "You were only afraid of her because you lost a library book."

"I didn't lose it," he denied. "I just couldn't find it when it was due. And you made me pay the late fines out of my allowance."

"Because you were the one who misplaced it," she pointed out logically.

"That's probably why I buy my books now—I'd rather pay for them up front and without guilt."

Which didn't begin to explain why he was now carrying a library card in his wallet—or his determination to put it to use in the near future.

Chapter Three

Cassie stood with her back against the counter as she lifted the last forkful of cheesy macaroni to her mouth.

"You might be surprised to hear that I like to cook," she said to Westley and Buttercup. "I just don't do it very often because it's not worth the effort to prepare a whole meal for one person."

Aside from the crunch of the two cats chowing down on their seafood medley, there was no response.

"Maybe I should get a dog," she mused. "Dogs at least wag their tails when you talk to them."

As usual, the two strays she'd rescued from a box in the library parking lot ignored her.

"Unfortunately, a dog would be a lot less tolerant of the occasional ten-hour shift at the library," she noted.

That was one good thing about Westley and Buttercup—they didn't really need her except when their food or water bowls were empty. And when she was away for several hours at a time, she didn't worry because they had one another for company.

But she did worry that she was turning into a cliché—the lonely librarian with only her cats and her books to keep her company. Since Westley and Buttercup were more interested in their dinner than the woman who fed it to them, she put her bowl and spoon in the dishwasher, then went into the living room and turned her attention to the tightly packed shelves.

The books were her reliable companions and steadfast friends. She had other friends, of course—real people that she went to the movies with or met for the occasional cup of coffee. But most of her friends were married now, with husbands and children to care for. It wasn't that Cassie didn't want to fall in love, get married and have a family, but she was beginning to wonder if it would ever happen. The few serious relationships she'd had in the past had all ended with her heart—if not broken—at least battered and bruised. When she'd met Joel Langdon three years earlier, she'd thought he was finally the one. Three months after he'd put a ring on her finger, she'd realized that her judgment was obviously faulty.

Thankfully, she was usually content with her own company. And when she wasn't, she could curl up with Captain Brandon Birmingham or Dean Robillard or Roarke. But tonight, she reached out a hand and plucked a random book from the shelf. A smile curved her lips when she recognized the cover of a beloved Jennifer Crusie novel.

She made herself a cup of tea and settled into her favorite chair by the fireplace, happy to lose herself in the story and fall in love with Cal as Min did. But who wouldn't love a man who appreciated her shoe collection, fed her doughnuts and didn't want to change a single thing about her? All of that, and he was great in bed, too.

She sighed and set the book aside to return her empty mug to the kitchen. Of course Cal was perfect—he was fictional. And she wasn't looking for perfect, anyway—she just wanted to meet a man who would appreciate her for who she was without trying to make her into someone different. He didn't have to be mouthwateringly gorgeous or Rhodes Scholar smart, but he had to be kind to children and animals and have a good relationship with his family. And it would be a definite plus if she felt flutters in her tummy when he smiled at her.

As she pieced together the ideal qualities in her mind, a picture began to form—a picture that looked very much like Braden Garrett.

Braden planned to wait a week or so before he tried out his library card to avoid appearing too eager. He figured seven to ten days was a reasonable time frame, and then, if he saw Cassie again and had the same immediate and visceral reaction, he would consider his next move.

He'd been widowed for just over a year and married for six years prior to that, so it had been a long time since he'd made any moves. How much had the dating scene changed in those years? Were any of the moves the same? Was he ready to start dating again and risk jeopardizing the precious relationship he had with his daughter by bringing someone new into their lives?

Except that Cassie was already in Saige's life—or at least on the periphery of it. And by all accounts, his little girl was enamored of the librarian. After only one brief meeting, he'd found himself aware of her appeal. Which was just one reason he'd decided to take a step back and give his suddenly reawakened hormones a chance to cool down.

But when he picked up his daughter's clothes to dump

them into the laundry basket, he found the red engine that she'd been reluctant to let go of at the train table earlier that day. He had a clear memory of prying the toy from her clenched fist and setting it back on the track, but apparently—maybe when he turned his back to retrieve her diaper bag—his daughter had picked it up again.

Wednesday morning he dropped Saige off at his parents' house, then headed toward his office as usual. But, conscious of the little red engine in his pocket, he detoured toward the library on his way. He'd considered leaving the train with his mother so that she could return it, but the "borrowed" toy was the perfect excuse for him to see the pretty librarian again and he was going to take advantage of it.

For the first six months after Dana's death, his mother hadn't pushed him outside of his comfort zone. Ellen understood that he was grieving for his wife and adjusting to his role as a new—and now single—dad. But since Christmas, she'd started to hint that it was time for him to move on with his life and urged him to get out and meet new people. More recently, she'd made it clear that when she said "people" she meant "women."

He knew she was motivated by concern—that she didn't want him to be alone. But whenever he dared to remind her that he wasn't alone because he had his daughter, she pointed out that Saige needed a mother. Saige deserved a mother. And that was a truth Braden could not dispute.

A real home with two parents.

He shook off the echo of those words and the guilt that weighed on his heart. He wasn't interested in getting involved with anyone right now. He had neither the time nor the energy to invest in a romantic relationship.

Getting some action between the sheets, on the other hand, held some definite appeal. But he knew that if he was just looking for sex, he should not be looking at the local librarian. Especially not when the woman was obviously adored by both his mother and his daughter.

But if he took the train back to the library, well, that was simply the right thing to do. And if he happened to see Cassie MacKinnon while he was there, that would just be a lucky coincidence.

Cassie didn't expect to ever see Braden again.

Despite his request for a library card, she didn't think he would actually use it. Men like Braden Garrett didn't borrow anything—if he wanted something he didn't have, he would buy it. And considering how busy the CEO and single father must be, she didn't imagine that he had much free time to read anything aside from business reports.

All of which made perfect, logical sense. What didn't make any sense at all was that she found herself thinking about him anyway, and wishing he would walk through the front doors in contradiction of her logic.

She tried to push these thoughts from her mind, annoyed by her inexplicable preoccupation with a man she was undeniably attracted to but wasn't sure she liked very much. A man who wasn't so very different from any other member of the male species who came through the library.

Okay, that was a lie. The truth was, she'd never met anyone else quite like Braden Garrett. But there were a lot of other guys in the world—good-looking, intelligent and charming guys. Some of them even came into the library and flirted with her and didn't regard her job as inconsequential. Rarely did she ever think about any of them after they were gone; never did she dream about any of them.

Until last night.

What was wrong with her? Why was she so captivated by a guy she'd met only once? A man who wasn't only gor-

geous and rich but a single father undoubtedly still grieving for the wife he'd lost only a year earlier.

Because even if he was interested in her, and even if it
turned out that he wasn't as shallow and judgmental as her
initial impressions indicated him to be, she had no intention
of getting involved with a man who was still in love with
another woman. No way. She'd been there, done that already, and she still had the bruises on her heart to prove it.

So it was a good thing she would probably never see
Braden Garrett again. A very good thing.

Or so she thought until she glanced up to offer assis-
tance to the patron who had stopped at her desk—and
found herself looking at the subject of her preoccupation.

Her heart skipped a beat and then raced to catch up. She
managed a smile, determined not to let him know how he
affected her. "Good morning, Mr. Garrett. Are you looking for some reading material today?"

He shook his head. "Returning some smuggled mer-
chandise." He set a red engine on top of her desk. "Apparently Saige loves the trains more than I realized."

It wasn't the first toy to go missing from the playroom,
and she knew it wouldn't be the last. Thankfully, the "borrowed" items were usually returned by the embarrassed
parents of the pint-size pickpockets when they were found.

"Universal toddler rules," she acknowledged. "If it's in
my hand, it's mine."

"Sounds like the kind of wisdom that comes from experience," he noted, his gaze shifting to her left hand. "Do
you have kids?"

She shook her head and ignored the emptiness she felt
inside whenever she thought about the family she might
have had by now if she'd married Joel instead of giving
him back his ring. "No," she said lightly. "But I've spent
enough time in the children's section to have learned a lot."

"What about a husband?" he prompted. "Fiancé? Boy-friend?"

No, *no* and *no*. But she kept those responses to her-self, saying only, "Thank you for returning the train, Mr. Garrett."

"I'll interpret that as a no," he said, with just the hint of a smile curving his lips.

And even that hint was potent enough to make her knees weak, which irritated her beyond reason. "You should in-terpret it as none of your business," she told him.

Her blunt response had no effect on his smile. "Except that if you'd had a husband, fiancé or boyfriend, you would have said so," he pointed out reasonably. "And since there's no husband, fiancé or boyfriend, maybe you'll let me buy you a cup of coffee and apologize for whatever I did that put your back up."

Before she could think of a response to that, Megan hur-ried up to the desk. "I'm sorry I got caught up with Mrs. Lynch and made you late for your break, Cassie."

"That's okay," she said. "I wanted to finish logging these new books into the system before I left the desk."

"I can do that," her coworker offered helpfully.

Cassie thanked Megan, though she was feeling any-thing but grateful. Because as much as she was desperate for a hit of caffeine, she suspected that Braden would tag along on her break and his presence would make her jit-tery for a different reason.

"I guess you're free for that coffee, then?" he prompted.

"I'm going across the street for my break," she con-firmed, unlocking the bottom drawer of the desk to retrieve her purse. "And while I may not be a corporate executive, I can afford to buy my own coffee."

"I'm sure you can," he agreed. "But if I pay for it, you might feel obligated to sit down with me to drink it."

And apparently her determination to remain unaffected was no match for his effortless charm, because she felt a smile tug at her own lips as she replied, "Only if there's a brownie with the coffee."

Growing up a Garrett in Charisma, Braden wasn't accustomed to having to work so hard for a woman's attention. And while he was curious about the reasons for Cassie's reluctance to spend time with him, he decided to save the questions for later.

He pulled open the door of the Bean There Café and gestured for her to precede him. There were a few customers in line ahead of them at the counter, allowing him to peruse the pastry offerings in the display case while they waited. He ordered a lemon poppy-seed muffin and a large coffee, black; Cassie opted for a salted caramel brownie and a vanilla latte.

"How's this?" he asked, gesturing to a couple of leather armchairs close together on one side of the fireplace, further isolated by a display of gift sets on the opposite side of the seating.

"Looks…cozy," she said.

He grinned. "Too cozy?"

She narrowed her gaze, but he suspected that she wouldn't turn away from the challenge. A suspicion that was proven correct when she sat in the chair closest to the fire.

The flickering flames provided light and warmth and the soft, comfy seating around the perimeter of the room provided a much more intimate atmosphere than the straight-back wooden chairs and square tables in the center. Braden relaxed into the leather seat beside Cassie and set his muffin on the small table between them.

"Are you going to let me apologize now?" he asked her.

She eyed him over the rim of her cup as she sipped. "What are you apologizing for?"

"Whatever I said or did to offend you."

"You don't even know, do you?" she asked, her tone a combination of amusement and exasperation.

"I'm afraid to guess," he admitted. But he did know it had happened the previous morning, sometime after Baby Talk, because her demeanor toward him had shifted from warm to cool in about two seconds.

She shook her head and broke off a corner of her brownie. "It doesn't matter."

"If it didn't matter, you wouldn't still be mad," he pointed out.

"I'm not still mad."

He lifted his brows.

"Okay, I'm still a little bit mad," she acknowledged. "But it's not really your fault—you didn't do anything but speak out loud the same thoughts that too many people have about my work."

"I'm still confused," he admitted. "What did I say?"

"You asked if working at the library was my real job."

He winced. "I assure you the question was more a reflection of my interest in learning about you than an opinion of your work," he said. "And probably influenced by a lack of knowledge about what a librarian actually does."

"My responsibilities are various and endless."

"I'll admit, I was surprised to see so many people at the library yesterday. I figured most everyone did their research and reading on their own tablets or computers these days."

"To paraphrase Neil Gaiman, an internet search engine can find a hundred thousand answers—a librarian can help you find the right one."

"My mother's a big fan of his work," Braden noted.

"I know," she admitted. "Anytime we get a new book with his name on it, I put it aside for her."

"She's a fan of yours, too," he said.

Her lips curved, and he felt that tug low in his belly again. There was just something about her smile—an innocent sensuality that got to him every time and made him want to be the reason for her happiness.

"Because I put aside the books she wants," Cassie said again.

"I think there's more to it than that," he remarked. "How long have you known her?"

"As long as I've worked at CPL, which is twelve years."

"Really?" He didn't know if he was more surprised to learn that she'd worked at the library for so many years or that she'd known his mother for that amount of time.

"I started as a volunteer when I was still in high school," she explained. "And in addition to being an avid reader, Ellen is one of the volunteers who delivers books to patrons who are unable to get to the library."

"I didn't know that," he admitted. "Between the Acquisitions Committee of the Art Gallery, the Board of Directors at Mercy Hospital and, for the past year, taking care of Saige three to five days a week for me, I wouldn't have thought she'd have time for anything else."

"She obviously likes to keep busy," Cassie noted. "And I know how much she adores her grandchildren. Ever since Ryan and Harper got custody of little Oliver almost three years ago, I've seen new pictures almost every week.

"Of course, hundreds of pictures when Vanessa was born, and hundreds more when Saige was born," she continued. "And I know she's overjoyed that Ryan and Harper are moving back to Charisma—hopefully before their second child is born."

"You're probably more up-to-date on my family than I

am," he admitted. "I don't even know my sister-in-law's due date."

"August twenty-eighth."

"Which proves my point." He polished off the last bite of his muffin.

She broke off another piece of brownie and popped it into her mouth. Then she licked a smear of caramel off her thumb—a quick and spontaneous swipe of her tongue over her skin that probably wasn't intended to be provocative but certainly had that effect on his body and thoughts.

"I only remember the date because it happens to be my birthday, too," she admitted.

He sipped his coffee. "As a librarian, how much do you know about chemistry?"

"Enough to pass the course in high school." She smiled. "Barely."

"And what do you think we should do about this chemistry between us?" he asked.

She choked on her latte. "Excuse me?"

"I'm stumbling here," he acknowledged. "Because it's been a long time since I've been attracted to a woman—other than my wife, I mean."

She eyed him warily. "Are you saying that you're attracted to me?"

"Why else would I be here when there are at least a dozen coffee shops closer to my office?"

"I thought you came to the library to return the train Saige took home."

"That was my excuse to come by and see you," he said.

She dropped her gaze to her plate, using her fingertip to push the brownie crumbs into the center.

"You didn't expect me to admit that, did you?"

"I didn't expect it to be true," she told him.

"I was a little surprised myself," he confided. "When I

found the train, I planned to leave it with my mother, for her to return. And when I dropped Saige off this morning, I had it with me, but for some reason, I held on to it. As I headed toward my office, I figured I'd give it to her later. Except that I couldn't stop thinking about you."

She wiped her fingers on her napkin, then folded it on top of her plate.

"This would be a good time for you to admit that you've been thinking about me, too," he told her.

"Even if it's not true?"

He reached across the table and stroked a finger over the back of her hand. She went immediately and completely still, not even breathing as her gaze locked with his.

"You've thought about me," he said. "Whether you're willing to admit it or not."

"Maybe I have," she acknowledged, slowly pulling her hand away. "Once or twice."

"So what do you think we should do about this chemistry?" he asked again.

"I'm the wrong person to ask," she said lightly. "All of my experiments simply fizzled and died."

"Maybe you were working with the wrong partner," he suggested.

"Maybe." She finished her latte and set the mug on top of her empty plate. "I really need to get back to work, but thanks for the coffee and the brownie."

"Anytime."

He stayed where he was and watched her walk away, because he'd never in his life chased after a woman and he wasn't going to start now.

Instead, he took his time finishing his coffee before he headed back to his own office—where he thought of her throughout the rest of the day, because he knew he would be seeing the sexy librarian again. Very soon.

Chapter Four

When Cassie left work later that afternoon, she headed to Serenity Gardens to visit Irene Houlahan. Almost three years earlier, the former librarian had slipped and fallen down her basement stairs, a nasty tumble that resulted in a broken collarbone and femur and forced her to sell her two-story home and move into the assisted-living facility for seniors.

The septuagenarian had never married, had no children and no family in Charisma, but once upon a time, she'd changed Cassie's life. No, she'd done more than change her life—she'd saved it. And Cassie knew that she'd never be able to repay the woman who was so much more to her than a friend and mentor.

Since Irene had taken up residence at Serenity Gardens, Cassie had visited her two or three times a week. The move had been good for Irene, who was now surrounded by con-temporaries who encouraged her to take part in various social activities on the property. And then, just after the New Year, Jerry Riordan had moved in across the hall.

His arrival had generated a fair amount of buzz among the residents and staff, and Cassie had overheard enough to know that he was seventy-two years old, a retired civil engineer and widower with three children and eight grandchildren, all of whom lived out of state. He was close to six feet tall, slender of build and apparently in possession of all of his own teeth, which made him the object of much female admiration within the residence.

But far more interesting to Cassie was her discovery that the newest resident of the fifth floor was spending a fair amount of time with the retired librarian. One day when Cassie was visiting, she'd asked Irene about her history with Jerry. Her friend had ignored the question, instead instructing Cassie to find *To Kill a Mockingbird* on her shelf. Of course, the woman's personal library was as ruthlessly organized as the public facility, so Cassie found it easily—an old and obviously much-read volume with a dust jacket curling at the edges.

"You've obviously had this a very long time."

"A lot more years than you've been alive," Irene acknowledged.

Cassie opened the cover to check the copyright page, but her attention was caught by writing inside the front cover. Knowing that her friend would never deface a work of art—and books undoubtedly fit that description—the bold strokes of ink snagged her attention.

Irene held out her hand. "The book."

The impatience in her tone didn't stop Cassie from taking a quick peek at the inscription:

To Irene—who embodies all the best characteristics of Scout, Jem and Dill. One day you will be the

*heroine of your own adventures, but for now, I hope
you enjoy their story.
Happy Birthday,
Jerry*

She closed the cover and looked at her friend. "Jerry—as in Jerry Riordan?"

"Did someone mention my name?" the man asked from the doorway.

"Were your ears burning?" Irene snapped at him.

Jerry shrugged. "Might have been—my hearing's not quite what it used to be." Then he spotted the volume in Cassie's hand and his pale blue eyes lit up. "Well, that book is familiar."

"There are more than thirty million copies of it in print," Irene pointed out.

"And that looks like the same copy I gave to you for your fourteenth birthday," he said.

"Probably because it is," she acknowledged, finally abandoning any pretense of faulty memory.

"I can't believe you still have it," Jerry said, speaking so softly it was almost as if he was talking to himself.

"It's one of my favorite books," she said. "Why would I get rid of it?"

"Over the years, things have a tendency to go missing or be forgotten."

"Maybe by some people," the old woman said pointedly.

"I never forgot you, Irene," Jerry assured her.

Cassie continued to stand beside the bookcase, wondering if she was actually invisible or just felt that way. She didn't mind being ignored and she had no intention of interrupting what was—judging by the unfamiliar flush in her friend's usually pale cheeks—a deeply personal moment.

Years ago, when Cassie had asked Irene why she'd never

married, the older woman had snapped that it wasn't a conscious choice to be alone—that sometimes the right man found the right woman in someone else. Of course, Cassie hadn't known what she meant at the time, and Irene had refused to answer any more questions on the subject. Watching her friend with Jerry now, she thought she finally understood.

"Are you going to sit down and read the book or just stand there?" Irene finally asked her.

Cassie knew her too well to be offended by the brusque tone. "I was just waiting for the two of you to finish your stroll down memory lane," she responded lightly.

"I don't stroll anywhere with six pins in my leg and I wouldn't stroll with him even if I could," Irene said primly.

"Thankfully, it's just your leg and not your arms that are weak," Jerry teased. "Otherwise you'd have trouble holding on to that grudge."

Cassie fought against a smile as she settled back into a wing chair, turned to the first page and began reading while Jerry lowered himself onto the opposite end of the sofa from Irene.

She read three chapters before she was interrupted by voices in the hall as the residents started to make their way to the activity room for Beach Party Bingo. Irene professed to despise bingo but she was fond of the fruit skewers and virgin coladas they served to go with the beach party theme.

When Cassie glanced up, she noted that Jerry had shifted on the sofa so that he was sitting closer to Irene now. Not so close that she could find his ribs with a sharp elbow if the mood struck her to do so, but definitely much closer. Apparently the man still had some moves—and he was making them on her friend.

"I think that's a good place to stop for today," she decided, sliding a bookmark between the pages.

"Thank you for the visit," Irene said, as she always did.

Cassie, too, gave her usual response. "It was my pleasure."

She set the book down on the coffee table, then touched her lips to her friend's soft, wrinkled cheek.

Irene waved her away, uncomfortable with the display of affection.

"What about me?" Jerry said, tapping his cheek with an arthritic finger. "I'd never wave off a kiss from a pretty girl."

"Isn't that the truth?" Irene muttered under her breath.

Cassie kissed his cheek, too. "Good night, Mr. Riordan. I'll see you on Friday, Irene."

"There's a trip to Noah's Landing on Friday," her friend said. "We're not scheduled to be back until dinnertime."

"Then I'll come Friday night," Cassie offered.

"That's fine."

"No, it's not," Jerry protested. "You can't ask a beautiful young woman to spend her Friday night hanging out with a bunch of grumpy old folks."

"I didn't ask, Cassandra offered," Irene pointed out. "And she comes to visit *me*, not any other grumpy old folks who decide to wander into my room uninvited."

"Well, I'm sure Cassandra has better things to do on a Friday night," he said, glancing at Cassie expectantly.

"Actually, I don't have any plans," she admitted.

He scowled. "You don't have a date?"

She shook her head.

"What's wrong with the young men in this town?" Jerry wondered.

"They're as shortsighted and thickheaded now as they were fifty years ago," Irene told him.

"And on that note," Cassie said, inching toward the door.

"I'll see you in a few days," Irene said.

"Don't come on Friday," Jerry called out to her. "I'm going to keep Irene busy at the cribbage board."

"I have cataracts," she protested.

"And I have a deck of cards with large print numbers."

Cassie left them bickering, happy to know that her friend had a new beau to fill some of her quiet hours. And eager to believe that if romance was in the air for Irene, maybe it wasn't too late for her, either.

Of course, if she wanted to fall in love, she'd have to be willing to open up her heart again, and that was a step she wasn't sure she was ready to take. Because what she'd told Braden about her struggles with chemistry was only partly true. About half of her experiments had fizzled into nothingness—the other half had flared so bright and hot, she'd ended up getting burned. And she simply wasn't willing to play with fire again.

While Braden wouldn't trade his baby girl for anything in the world, there were times when he would willingly sacrifice a limb for eight consecutive hours of sleep.

"Come on, Saige," he said wearily. "It's two a.m. That's not play time—it's sleep time."

"Wound an' wound," she said, clapping her hands.

He reached into her crib for her favorite toy—a stuffed sock monkey that had been a gift from her birth mother—and gave it to Saige. "Sleep. Sleep. Sleep."

She immediately grabbed the monkey's arm and cuddled it close. Then she tipped her head back to look at him, and when she smiled, he gave in with a sigh. "You know just how to wrap me around your finger, don't you?"

"Da-da," she said.

He touched his lips to the top of her head, breathing in the familiar scent of her baby shampoo.

She was the baby he and Dana had been wanting for most of their six-year marriage, the child they'd almost given up hope of ever having. In the last few weeks leading up to her birth, they'd finally, cautiously, started to transform one of the spare bedrooms into a nursery. They'd hung a mobile over the crib, put tiny little onesies and sleepers in the dresser, and stocked up on diapers and formula.

At the same time, they'd both been a little hesitant to believe that this time, finally, their dream of having a child would come true. Because they were aware that the birth mother could decide, at the last minute, to keep her baby. And they knew that, if she did, they couldn't blame her.

But Lindsay Benson had been adamant. She wanted a better life for her baby than to be raised by a single mother who hadn't yet graduated from college. She wanted her daughter to have a real family with two parents who would care for her and love her and who could afford to give her not just the necessities of life but some extras, too.

Within a few weeks, Braden had begun to suspect that he and Dana wouldn't be that family. For some reason that he couldn't begin to fathom—or maybe didn't want to admit—his wife wasn't able to bond with the baby. Every time Saige cried, Dana pushed the baby at him, claiming that she had a headache. Every time Saige needed a bottle or diaper change, Dana was busy doing something else. Every time Saige woke up in the middle of the night, Dana pretended not to hear her.

Yes, he'd seen the signs, but he'd still been optimistic that she would come around. That she just needed some more time. She'd suffered so much disappointment over the years, he was certain it was her lingering fear of los-

ing the child they'd wanted so much that was holding her
back. He refused to consider that Dana might be unhappy
because their adopted daughter was so obviously not their
biological child.

Then, when Saige was six weeks old, Dana made her
big announcement: she didn't really want to be a mother
or a wife. She told him that she'd found an apartment and
would be moving out at the end of March. Oh, and she
needed a check to cover first and last month's rent.

And Braden, fool that he was, gave it to her. Because
they'd been married for six years and he honestly hoped that
the separation would only be a temporary measure, that after
a few months—or hopefully even sooner—she would want
to come home to her husband and daughter. Except that a
few weeks later, she'd died when her car was T-boned by a
semi that blew through a red light.

He hadn't told anyone that Dana was planning to leave
him. He'd been blindsided by the announcement, embarrassed that he hadn't been able to hold his marriage together. As a result, while his family tried to be supportive,
no one could possibly understand how complicated and
convoluted his emotions were.

He did grieve—for the life he'd imagined they might
have together, and for his daughter, who had lost another
mother. But he was also grateful that he had Saige—her
innocent smile and joyful laugh were the sunshine in his
days.

If he had any regrets, it was that his little girl didn't
have a mother. Her own had given her up so that she could
have a real family with two parents. That dream hadn't
even lasted three months. Now it was just the two of them.

"Well, the two of us and about a thousand other Garretts," he said to his little girl. "And everyone loves you,

so maybe I should stop worrying that you don't have a Mommy."

"Ma-ma," Saige said.

And despite Braden's recent assertion, he sighed. "You've been listening to your grandma, haven't you?"

"Ga-ma."

"You'll see Grandma tomorrow—no," he amended, glancing at his watch. "In just a few hours now."

She smiled again.

"And I bet you'll have another three-hour nap for her, won't you?"

"Choo-choo."

"After she takes you to the library to play with the trains," he confirmed.

She clapped her hands together again, clearly thrilled with his responses to her questions.

Of course, thinking about the library made him think about Cassie. And thinking about Cassie made him want Cassie.

The physical attraction was unexpected but not unwelcome. If anything, his feelings for the librarian reassured him that, despite being a widower and single father, he was still a man with the usual wants and needs.

Unfortunately, Cassie didn't seem like the kind of woman to indulge in a no-strings affair, and he wasn't prepared to offer any more than that.

Cassie had updated the bulletin board in the children's section to suggest Spring into a Good Book and was pinning cardboard flowers to the board when Stacey found her.

"I've been looking all over for you," her friend and co-worker said.

"Is there a problem?"

"Nothing aside from the fact that I'm dying to hear all of the details about your hottie," Stacey admitted.

"Who?"

"Don't play that game with me," the other woman chided. "Megan told me you went for coffee with a new guy yesterday."

Cassie acknowledged that with a short nod. "Braden Garrett."

"As in the Garrett Furniture Garretts?"

She nodded.

"Not just hot but rich," Stacey noted. "Does this mean you've decided to end your dating hiatus?"

"Not with Braden Garrett," she said firmly.

"Because hot and rich men aren't your type?" her friend asked, disbelief evident in her tone.

"Because arrogant and insulting men aren't my type," Cassie clarified, as she added some fluffy white clouds to the blue sky.

"Which button of yours did he push?" Stacey asked, absently rubbing a hand over her pregnant belly.

"He asked if this was my real job."

"Ouch. Okay, so he's an idiot," her coworker agreed. "But still—" she held out her hands as if balancing scales "—a hot and rich idiot."

"And then he apologized," she admitted.

"So points for that," Stacey said.

"Maybe," Cassie allowed. "He also told me he's attracted to me."

"Gotta love a guy who tells it like it is."

"Maybe," she said again.

Stacey frowned at her noncommittal response. "Are you not attracted to him?"

"A woman would have to be dead not to be attracted to

him," she acknowledged. "But he's also a widower with a child."

"And you love kids," her friend noted.

"I do." And it was her deepest desire to be a mother someday. "But I don't want to get involved in another relationship with someone who might not actually be interested in me but is only looking for a substitute wife."

"You're not going to be any kind of wife if you don't start dating again," Stacey pointed out to her.

"I'm not opposed to dating," she denied. "I'm just not going to date Braden Garrett."

"How about my cute new neighbor?" her friend suggested. "He's a manager at The Sleep Inn, recently transferred back to Charisma after working the last three years in San Diego."

Cassie shook her head. "You know I don't do blind dates."

"In the past two years, you've hardly had *any* dates," Stacey pointed out. "You need to move on with your life."

She looked at her friend, at the enormous baby bump beneath her pale blue maternity top, and felt a familiar pang of longing. She was sincerely happy for Stacey and her husband who, after several years and numerous fertility treatments, were finally expecting a child, but she couldn't deny that her friend's pregnancy was a daily reminder that her own biological clock was ticking. "You're right," she finally agreed.

"So I can give your number to Darius?"

"Why not?" she decided, and left her friend grinning as she headed upstairs.

Toddler Time was scheduled to start at 10:00 a.m. on Thursdays. By nine fifty, almost all of the usual group were assembled, but Saige wasn't there yet. Cassie found herself watching the clock, wondering if she was going to show and, if she did, whether it would be her father or grandmother who showed up with her.

At nine fifty-seven, Ellen Garrett entered the room with the little girl. Cassie was happy to see the both of them—and maybe just a tiny bit disappointed, too.

The older woman's jaw still looked a little swollen and bruised, but she insisted that she was feeling fine. They didn't have time for more than that basic exchange of pleasantries before the class was scheduled to begin, and Cassie didn't dare delay because she could tell the children were already growing impatient. When the half hour was up, she noticed that Ellen didn't linger as she sometimes did. Instead, she hastily packed up her granddaughter's belongings, said something about errands they needed to run, then disappeared out the door.

It was only after everyone had gone and Cassie was tidying up the room that she discovered Saige Garrett's sock monkey under a table by the windows.

Chapter Five

Braden was just about to leave the office at the end of the day when his mother called.

"I need you to do me a favor," Ellen said.

"Of course," he agreed. Considering everything that his mother did for him, it never occurred to him to refuse her request.

"I can't find Saige's sock monkey. I think she might have left it at story time today."

His daughter never released her viselike grip on her favorite stuffed toy, which made him suspect that Saige hadn't *accidentally* left the monkey anywhere. "And you want me to go by the library to see if it's there," he guessed.

"Well, it is on your way from the office."

"Not really," he pointed out.

"If it's too inconvenient, I can get it tomorrow," Ellen said. "But you'll be the one trying to get Saige to sleep without it tonight."

Unfortunately, that was true. His daughter was rarely without the monkey—and she never went to sleep without it. Still, he could see what his mother was doing. She obviously liked Cassie MacKinnon and was trying to put the pretty librarian in his path as much as possible. And Braden didn't have any objection, really, but he suspected that Cassie might not appreciate his mother's maneuverings.

So he would stop by the library, per his mother's request, and apologize to Cassie for the situation. He would admit that Ellen was probably attempting to do a little matchmaking and suggest that maybe they should have dinner sometime, just to appease her.

Cassie might try to refuse, but he knew she liked his mother and he wasn't opposed to working that angle. In fact, he had the whole scenario worked out in his mind when he walked into the library just after five o'clock. He recognized the woman at the desk as the one who had nudged Cassie along to her coffee break. Megan, if he remembered correctly. He smiled at her. "Hi. I'm looking for Miss MacKinnon."

"I'm sorry, she isn't here right now," Megan told him.

"Oh." He felt a surprisingly sharp pang of disappointment, as if he hadn't realized how much he was looking forward to seeing her again until he was there and she wasn't.

"Is there something I can help you with?" she offered.

"I hope so," he said, because he did have a legitimate reason for this detour. "My daughter, Saige, was here for Toddler Time today and—"

"The sock monkey," Megan realized.

He nodded.

She pulled a clear zipper-seal bag out from under the

desk. Saige's name had been written on the bag with black marker, and her favorite soft toy was inside.

"That's it," he confirmed. "Now we'll both be able to get some sleep tonight."

She smiled. "Is there anything else I can help you with?"

"Can you tell me if Miss MacKinnon is working tomorrow?"

Megan shook her head. "I can't give out that kind of information." Then she sent him a conspiratorial wink. "But if you were to stop by around this time tomorrow, she might be able to tell you herself."

Braden smiled. "Thanks, I just might do that."

At first when Cassie put the phone to her ear and heard the deep masculine voice on the line, her pulse stuttered. When the caller identified himself as Darius Richmond, she experienced a twinge of regret followed by a brief moment of confusion as she tried to place the name.

"Stacey's neighbor," he clarified, and the conversation with her coworker immediately came back to her.

"Of course," she said, mentally chastising herself for thinking—and hoping—that it might have been Braden calling.

"I'm sorry it's taken me so long to call," he apologized. "Stacey gave me your number last week but I've been tied up in meetings with my staff."

"Understandable," she said. "Settling into a new job is always a challenge."

"But I'm free tonight and I'd really like to have dinner with you."

"Tonight," she echoed, her brain scrambling for a valid reason to decline. Then she remembered why she'd agreed to let Stacey give him her number: because she was trying to move on with her life. Because she'd only been out on a handful of dates since breaking up with Joel, and staying home and thinking about Braden Garrett—who, judging by his absence from the library for the past eight days, obviously wasn't thinking about her—wasn't going to help her move on.

"I know it's short notice," he said.

"Actually, tonight is fine," Cassie told him, determined not just to go out but to have a fabulous time.

"Seven o'clock at Valentino's?" he suggested.

"Perfect," she agreed, mentally giving him extra points for his restaurant selection. "I'll see you then."

Cassie disconnected the call and set her phone aside. As much as setups made her nervous, her friend and co-worker was right: she wasn't ever going to find her real-life happily-ever-after hanging out in the library.

She did have some lingering concerns about going out with one man when she couldn't get a different one out of her mind, but since the day Braden had bought her coffee, she hadn't heard a single word from him. She hadn't seen Ellen or Saige this past week, either, but at least Ellen had called to let her know that they would be absent from Baby Talk and Toddler Time because Saige had a nasty cold and Ellen didn't want her to share it with the other children.

And then, almost as if her thoughts had conjured the woman, Ellen was standing there.

"Who's the lucky guy?" she asked. Then she smiled. "Forgive me for being nosy, but that sounded like you were making plans for a date."

Cassie felt her cheeks flush. "I was. He's the neighbor of a friend."

"Oh," she replied, obviously disappointed. "A blind date?"

Cassie nodded, then asked, "How's Saige doing?"

"Much better," the little girl's grandmother said. "Though it's been a rough week for both of them."

"Both of them?"

"Braden was under the weather, too. Of course, that's what happens when you take care of a sick child. In fact, today will be his first day back at work—he's leaving Saige with me this afternoon and going into the office for a few hours."

"Well, I'm glad to hear they're both doing better—and that you managed to avoid whatever is going around. Because something is definitely going around," she noted. "Even Megan, who never calls in sick, did so today—and we have three school groups coming in for tours and story time this afternoon."

"In that case, I won't keep you from your work any longer," Ellen promised. "I really just wanted to check in to see if Braden stopped by last week to pick up Saige's sock monkey."

"He must have," Cassie told her. "I left it under the desk in a bag with Saige's name on it and it was gone when I got in the next morning."

"So you weren't here when he came in?" the other woman asked, sounding disappointed.

"No, I leave at two on Tuesdays and Thursdays, and then I'm back at seven for Soc & Study," she explained, referring to the teen study group that ran Monday through Friday nights.

Cassie was happy to supervise two nights a week and would have done more if required, because she understood how important it was for students to have a place to escape from the stress and drama of their homes. As a teen with three younger siblings and a short-tempered stepfather, she'd spent as much time as possible at the library. But of course she didn't mention that to Ellen, because she never told anyone about her past, and especially not about Ray.

In an effort to shift the direction of her own thoughts, she said, "Is there anything I can help you find today?"

"I'm just here to pick up a few travel books for Mabel Strauss," Ellen explained. "She hasn't left her own home in more than three years, but she still seems to find joy in planning trips that she's never going to take."

"What's her destination this time?" Cassie asked.

"Japan."

She smiled. "Well, if you're going to dream, dream big, right?"

"Absolutely," Ellen agreed. "Although, in Mabel's case, I think she's just going alphabetically now. It was Italy last week and India the week before that."

"Then you probably don't need me to steer you in the right direction," Cassie noted.

The older woman shook her head. "Thanks, but I know exactly where I'm going."

Several hours later, Cassie wished she wasn't going anywhere. After a busy day, she just wanted to go home, put her feet up and pet her cats. She considered canceling her plans with Darius, but she knew that she'd have to answer to Stacey if she did. She also knew that if she didn't want to spend the rest of her life alone with her cats, she had to get out and meet new people. Specifically, new men.

Unbidden, an image of Braden Garrett formed in her mind. Okay—he was new and she'd met him without leaving the safe haven of the library, but a man who'd lost his first wife in a tragic accident wasn't a good bet for a woman who'd vowed not to be anyone's second choice ever again.

She hadn't dated much since she'd given Joel back his ring. Her former fiancé hadn't just broken her heart, he'd made her question her own judgment. She'd been so wrong about him. Or maybe just so desperate to become a wife and a mother that she'd failed to see the warning signs. She'd fallen for a man who was all wrong for her because she didn't want to be alone.

That realization had taken her aback. For the first ten years of her life, her Army Ranger father had been away more than he'd been home, and her mother—unable to tolerate being alone—had frequently sought out other male companionship. Then her father had been killed overseas and her mother had dated several other men before she'd met and exchanged vows with Ray Houston.

Their marriage had been a volatile one. Naomi was a former beauty queen who basked in the adoration of others; Raymond was proud to show off his beautiful wife and prone to fits of jealousy if she went anywhere without him. Even as a kid, Cassie had decided she'd rather be alone than be anyone's emotional—and sometimes physical—punching bag, and she'd vowed to herself that she wouldn't ever be like her mother, so desperate for a man's attention that she'd put up with his mercurial moods and fiery temper.

For the most part, she was happy on her own and with her life. She had a great job, wonderful friends, and she was content with her own company and the occasional affectionate cuddle with her cats. And then Braden Garrett had walked into the library with his daughter.

So really, it was Braden's fault that she'd agreed to go out with Darius. Because he stirred up all kinds of feelings she'd thought were deeply buried, she'd decided those feelings were a sign that she was ready to start dating again. Because after more than two years on her own, she realized that she wasn't ready to give up. She wanted to fall all the way in love. She wanted to get married and have a family. And while she wasn't all starry-eyed and weak-kneed at the prospect of dinner with Stacey's new neighbor, she wasn't ready to write him off just yet, either.

So she brushed her hair, dabbed some gloss on her lips, spritzed on her perfume and headed out, determined to focus on Darius Richmond and forget about Braden Garrett.

Except that as soon as she walked through the front door of Valentino's, she found herself face-to-face with the man she was trying to forget.

"Hello, Cassie."

She actually halted in mid-stride as the low timbre of his voice made the nerves in her belly quiver. "Mr. Garrett—hi."

He smiled, and her heart started beating double-time. "Braden," he reminded her.

"I…um… What are you doing here?" Her cheeks burned as she stammered out the question. She never stammered, but finding him here—immediately after she'd vowed to put him out of her mind—had her completely flustered.

"Picking up dinner." He held up the take-out bag he carried. "And you?"

"I'm…um…meeting someone." And she was still stammering, she realized, with no small amount of chagrin.

"A date?" Braden guessed.

She nodded, unwilling to trust herself to respond in a complete and coherent sentence.

Of course, that was the precise moment that Darius spotted her. He stood up at the table and waved. She lifted a hand in acknowledgment.

"With Darius Richmond?" The question hinted at both disbelief and disapproval.

"You know him?" And look at that—she'd managed three whole words without a pause or a stutter.

"He went to school with my brother, Ryan," Braden

said, in a tone clearly indicating that he and Stacey's neighbor were *not* friends. "But last I heard, he was living in San Diego."

"He recently moved back to Charisma," she said, repeating what she'd been told.

"How long have you been dating him?"

"I'm not… I mean, this is our first date. And possibly our last, if I keep him waiting much longer." She glanced at the silver bangle watch on her wrist, resisting the urge to squirm beneath Braden's narrow-eyed scrutiny. She had no reason to feel guilty about having dinner with a man. "I was supposed to meet him at seven and it's already ten after."

"He knows you're here," Braden pointed out. "It's not as if he's sitting there, worrying that you've stood him up. Although, if that's what you want to do, I'd be happy to share my penne with sausage and peppers."

"Isn't your daughter waiting for her dinner?" she asked, relieved that she was now managing to uphold her end of the conversation.

But he shook his head. "I worked late trying to catch up after four days away from the office, so she ate with my parents."

"Your mom mentioned that you'd both been under the weather," she noted.

"Saige had the worst of it," he said. "But we're both fully recovered now."

"That's good," she said.

He looked as if he wanted to say something more, but in the end, he only said, "Enjoy your dinner."

"Thanks," Cassie said. "You, too."

Braden forced himself to walk out of the restaurant and drive home, when he really wanted to take his food into the dining room to chaperone Cassie on her date. Unfortunately, he suspected that kind of behavior might edge a little too close to stalking, even if he only wanted to protect her from the womanizing creep.

Because, yeah, he knew Darius Richmond, and he knew the guy had a reputation for using and discarding women. And, yeah, it bothered him that Cassie was on a date with the other man.

Or maybe he was jealous. As uncomfortable as it was to admit, he knew that his feelings were possibly a result of the green-eyed monster rearing its ugly head. Cassie's unwillingness to explore the attraction between them had dented his pride. Discovering that she was on a date with someone else was another unexpected blow, because it proved that she wasn't opposed to dating in general but to dating Braden in particular.

He couldn't figure it out. He knew there was something between them—a definite change in the atmosphere whenever they were in close proximity. What he didn't know was why she was determined to ignore it.

She was great with kids, so he didn't think she was put off by the fact that he had a child. Except that liking children in general was undoubtedly different than dating a guy with a child, and if she had any reservations about that, then she definitely wasn't the right woman for him.

Not that he was looking for "the right woman"—but he wouldn't object to spending time with a woman who was attractive and smart and interested in him. And the only way that was going to happen was if he managed to forget about his attraction to Cassie.

Which meant that he should take a page out of the librarian's book—figuratively speaking—and look for another woman to fulfill his requirement.

The problem was, he didn't want anyone but Cassie.

* * *

Cassie was tidying up the toys in the children's area late Saturday morning when Braden and Saige came into the library. The little girl made a beeline for the train table, where two little boys were already playing. Aside from issuing a firm caution to his daughter to share, Braden seemed content to let her do her own thing. Then he lowered himself onto a plastic stool where he could keep an eye on Saige and near where Cassie was sorting the pieces of several wooden puzzles that had been jumbled together.

"So…how was your date last night?" he asked her.

She continued to sort while she considered her response. "It was an experience," she finally decided.

"That doesn't sound like a rousing endorsement of Darius Richmond."

"Do you really want to hear all of the details?"

"Only if the details are that you had a lousy time and were home by nine o'clock," he told her.

She felt a smile tug at her lips. "Sorry—I wasn't home by nine o'clock." She put three puzzle pieces together. "It was after nine before I left the restaurant and probably closer to nine twenty before I got home."

He smiled. "Nine twenty, huh?"

She nodded.

"Alone?"

She lifted a brow. "I can't believe you just asked me that question."

"A question you haven't answered," he pointed out.

"Yes," she said. "Alone. As I told you last night—it was a first date."

"And you never invite a guy home after a first date?"

"No," she confirmed. "And why don't you like Darius?"

"Because he's a player," Braden said simply.

"So why didn't you tell me that last night?"

"I was tempted to. But if I'd said anything uncomplimentary about the man, you might have thought I was trying to sabotage your date, and I was confident that you'd figure it out quickly enough yourself."

"I knew within the first five minutes that it would be a first and last date," she admitted.

"What did he do?"

"When I got to the table, he told me that he'd ordered a glass of wine for me—a California chardonnay that he assured me I would enjoy. Which maybe I shouldn't fault him for, because he doesn't know me so how could he know that I generally prefer red wine over white? And maybe I wouldn't have minded so much if he was having a glass of the chardonnay, too, but he was drinking beer."

"You don't like guys who drink beer?" he guessed.

"I don't like guys who assume that women don't drink beer," she told him.

He nodded. "So noted."

"And when the waitress came to tell us about the daily specials, his gaze kept slipping from her face to her chest."

"You should have walked out then," he told her.

"Probably," she agreed. "Then he ordered calamari as an appetizer for us to share. And I hate squid."

"But again, he didn't ask you," Braden guessed, glancing over at the train table to check on his daughter.

"Not only did he not ask—he ignored my protests, as if he knew what I wanted more than I did.

"But still, I was hopeful that the evening could be salvaged," she admitted. "Because Valentino's does the most amazing three-cheese tortellini in a tomato cream sauce. And when I gave my order to the waitress—vetoing his suggestion of the veal Marsala—he suggested, with a blatantly lewd wink, that I would have to follow my meal with some intense physical activity to burn off all of the calories in the entrée."

Braden's gaze narrowed. "Is *that* when you walked out?"

"No," she denied. "I ordered the tortellini—with garlic bread—and I ate every single bite."

He chuckled. "Good for you."

"Then I had cheesecake for dessert, put money on the table for my meal and said good-night. And he seemed genuinely baffled to discover that I didn't intend to go home with him." She shook her head. "I mean, it was obvious early on that the date was a disaster, and yet he still thought I'd sleep with him?"

"When it comes to sex, men are eternally optimistic creatures."

"He was more delusional than optimistic if he believed for even two seconds that I would get naked with him after he counted the calories of every bite I put in my mouth."

"Note to self—never comment on a woman's food choices."

"I'm sure you didn't need to be told that."

"You're right," he admitted. "But obviously I'm doing something wrong, because you shot me down when I asked you to go out with me."

"You never actually asked me out," she said.

He frowned at that. "I'm sure I did."

She shook her head. "You only asked what we should do about the chemistry between us."

"And you said the chemistry would fizzle," he said, apparently remembering that part of the conversation.

She nodded.

"But it hasn't," he noted.

She kept her focus on the puzzles she was assembling.

"So what do you propose we do now?"

"Right now, I'm trying to figure out how to tell Stacey that last night's date was a complete bust," she admitted.

"You could tell her you met someone that you like more," he suggested.

She finally looked up to find his gaze on her. "I do like you," she admitted. "But you're a widower with a child."

He frowned. "Which part of that equation is a problem for you?"

"It doesn't really matter which part, does it?" she said, sincerely regretful.

"You're right," he agreed. "But I'd still like to know."

Thankfully, before he could question her further, Saige came running over with a train clenched in each fist.

"Choo-choo," she said, in a demand for her daddy to play with her.

And Cassie took advantage of the opportunity to escape.

Chapter Six

She wasn't proud of the way she'd ended her conversation with Braden, but she'd done what she needed to do. If she tried to explain her reasons and her feelings, he might try to change her mind. And there was a part of her—the huge empty space in her heart—that wished he would.

She left the library early that afternoon and headed over to Serenity Gardens. When she arrived at the residence, she saw that a group of women of various shapes and sizes was participating in some kind of dance class in the front courtyard. Some were in sweats and others in spandex, and while they didn't seem to be particularly well choreographed, they all looked like they were having a good time.

"Geriatric Jazzercise," a familiar male voice said from behind her.

Cassie choked on a laugh as she turned to Jerry. "That's not really what they call it?"

He held up a hand as if taking an oath. "It really is."

"Well, exercise is important at any age," she acknowledged. "Unfortunately, I can't imagine Irene participating in something like this."

"Can't you?" he asked, his eyes twinkling. "Check out the woman in the striped purple top."

Cassie looked more closely at the group, her eyes widening when they zeroed in on and finally recognized the former librarian. "I don't know what to say," she admitted.

"You could say you'll have a cup of coffee with me," Jerry told her. "As I was told, in clear and unequivocal terms, that the jazzercise class is for women only."

"I'd be happy to have coffee with you," Cassie said, falling into step beside Jerry as he headed back toward the building.

"What's that you've got there?" he asked, indicating the hardback in her hand. "A new book for Irene?"

She nodded. "One of the advantages of being head librarian—I get dibs on the new releases when they come in."

"My name's on the waiting list for that one," he admitted.

"Irene's a fast reader—maybe she'll let you borrow it when she's done."

"I'm a fast reader, too," he told her. "Maybe *I* could give it to Irene when *I'm* done."

"That would work," she agreed.

Peggy's Bakery and Coffee Shop, on the ground floor of the residence, offered a variety of hot and cold beverages and baked goods, and the air was permeated with the mouthwatering scents of coffee and chocolate.

"What will you have?" Jerry asked her.

Cassie perused the menu, pleased to note that they had her favorite. "A vanilla latte, please."

"And I'll have a regular decaf," Jerry said.

"Can I interest you in a couple of triple chocolate brownies still warm from the oven?" Peggy asked.

"One for sure," Jerry immediately responded, before glancing at Cassie in a silent question.

"Brownies are my weakness," she admitted.

"Make it two," he said.

"You go ahead and grab a seat," Peggy said. "I'll bring everything out to you."

"Can we sit outside?" Cassie asked.

"Anywhere you like," the other woman assured them.

They sat on opposite sides of a small round table, beneath a green-and-white-striped awning. Peggy delivered their coffee and brownies only a few minutes later.

Jerry poured two packets of sugar into his coffee, stirred. "The first time I saw you here, visiting Irene, I thought you must be her granddaughter. Then I found out that she never married, never had any children."

"No, she didn't," Cassie confirmed.

"So what is your relationship?" he wondered. "If you don't mind me asking."

"I don't mind," she told him. "And although our relationship has changed a lot over the years, Irene has always played an important part in my life—from librarian to confidante, surrogate mother, mentor and friend."

"You've known her a long time then?"

"Since I was in fourth grade."

"I've known her a long time, too," Jerry said. "We grew up across the street from one another in the west end, went to school together, dated for a while when we were in high school. I'm sure both my parents and hers thought we would marry someday." He cut off a piece of brownie with his fork. "In fact, I was planning to propose to her at Christmas, the year after we graduated."

"What happened?"

He chewed on the brownie for a long minute, his eyes focused on something—or maybe some time—in the distance. "I met someone else that summer and fell head over heels in love." He shifted his attention back to Cassie, his gaze almost apologetic. "I'd fallen in love with Irene slowly, over a lot of years. And then Faith walked into my life and the emotions hit me like a ton of bricks. Everything with her was new and intense and exciting."

"And you married her instead," Cassie guessed.

He nodded. "She was the love of my life and I'm grateful for the almost fifty years we had together."

"And now you've come full circle," she noted.

"Do you disapprove of my friendship with Irene?"

"Of course not," she denied. "But I don't want to see her get hurt again."

"Neither do I," he told her.

She considered his response as she nibbled on her own brownie, savoring the rich chocolate flavor.

"Have you ever been in love, Cassie?"

"I was engaged once."

"Which isn't necessarily the same thing," he pointed out.

"I haven't had much luck in the love department," she acknowledged.

"It only takes once," he told her. "You only need one forever-after love to change your whole life."

She sipped her coffee. "I'll keep that in mind."

"It's not about the mind," Jerry admonished. "It's about the heart. You have to keep an open heart."

Cassie thought about Jerry's advice for a long time after she'd said goodbye to him and left Serenity Gardens. A week later, his words continued to echo in the back of her mind.

She headed to the library much earlier than usual, eager to get started on the setup for the Book & Bake Sale. The forecast was for partly sunny skies with a 25 percent chance of precipitation, but that was not until late afternoon. Cassie hoped they would be sold out and packed up before then.

The event was scheduled to start at 8:00 a.m. but she was on-site by six thirty to meet with a group of volunteers from the high school to set up the tents and the tables. There were boxes and boxes in the library basement—old books that had been taken out of circulation and donations from the community.

Over the past several weeks, Tanya and a couple of her friends from the high school had sorted through the donations, grouping the books into genres. Some of the books were horribly outdated—such as *Understanding Windows 2000*—but she decided to put them out on display anyway, because local crafters often picked up old books to create new things. In addition to the books, there were board games and toys and DVDs.

The student volunteers were almost finished setting up the tents when Braden showed up just after seven. It was the first time she'd seen him since she'd abruptly ended their conversation the previous Saturday morning—though she'd heard from Megan that he'd checked out some books when she was on her lunch break a few days earlier—and she wasn't sure what to make of his presence here now.

"The sale doesn't start until eight," she told him.

"I know, but I thought you might be able to use an extra hand with set up."

"We can always use extra hands," she admitted.

"So put me to work," he suggested.

"Where's Saige?" she asked.

"Having pancakes at my parents' house."

"Lucky girl."

He smiled. "My mom's going to bring her by later."

"Okay," she said. "Most of the tents have been set up, Tanya and Chloe know how to arrange the tables, which Cade and Jake are bringing out, so why don't you help Ethan and Tyler haul boxes up from the basement?"

"I can do that," he confirmed.

She led him down to the basement and introduced him to the other helpers, then went back outside to help Brooke arrange the goodies on the bake table. With so many volunteers from the high school—most of them students who were regulars at Soc & Study—there wasn't a lot for her to do, and she found herself spending an inordinate amount of time watching Braden and pretending that she wasn't.

"Is there somewhere else you're supposed to be?" he asked, when he caught her glancing at her watch for about the tenth time.

"Serenity Gardens in half an hour."

"Aren't you about fifty years too early for Serenity Gardens?"

"So maybe we were talking about the same Miss Houlahan," he mused.

"She's been retired for several years, but she never misses any of our fund-raising events."

"I didn't know she was still alive," he admitted. "She seemed about a hundred years old when I was a kid."

"I'm seventy-one," a sharp voice said from behind him. "And not ready for the grave yet."

Braden visibly winced before turning around. "Miss Houlahan—how lovely to see you again."

Behind square wire-rimmed glasses, the old woman's pale blue eyes narrowed. "You're just as cheeky now as you were when you were a boy, Braden Garrett."

Cassie seemed as surprised as he was that the former librarian had remembered him well enough to be able to distinguish him from his brothers and male cousins—all of whom bore a striking resemblance to one another.

"I was planning to pick you up," Cassie interjected.

"Jerry decided he wanted to come and get some books, and it didn't make sense to drag you away if he was heading in this direction," Miss Houlahan said.

"Where is Mr. Riordan?"

"He dropped me off in front, then went to park the car."

"Well, we're not quite finished setting up, but you're welcome to wander around and browse through the books we've got on display."

"I'm not here to shop, I'm here to work," Irene said abruptly.

Cassie nodded, unfazed by the woman's brusque demeanor. "Was there any particular section you wanted to work in?" she asked solicitously.

"Put me near history," the former librarian suggested. "Most people assume old people are experts on anything old."

"We've got history set up—" Cassie glanced at the tables queued along the sideway "—four tables over, just this side of the card shop. Give me a second to finish this display and I'll show you."

"I've got a box of history books right here," Braden said. "I can show her."

"It's 'Miss Houlahan' not 'her,'" Irene corrected him. "And I know where the card shop is."

"I'm heading in that direction anyway, *Miss Houlahan*," he told her.

But she'd already turned and started to walk away, her steps slow and methodical, her right hand gripping the handle of a nondescript black cane. Braden fell into step beside her, the box propped on his shoulder so that he had a hand free in case *Miss Houlahan* stumbled.

She didn't say two words to him as they made their way down the sidewalk. Not that they were going very far—the history/political science table wasn't more than thirty feet from the library's main doors—and not that he expected her to entertain him with chatter, but the silence was somehow not just uncomfortable but somehow disapproving. Or maybe he was projecting his childhood memories onto the moment.

When they reached the table, he eased the box from his shoulder and dropped it on the ground, perhaps a little more loudly than was necessary, and got a perverse sense of pleasure when she jolted at the noise, then glared at him. As he busied himself unpacking the books, he reminded himself that he was no longer a child easily intimidated but a CEO more accustomed to intimidating other people.

He'd just finished unpacking when he heard the sweetest sound in the world: "Da-da!"

Tucking the now-empty box under the table, he turned just in time to catch Saige as she launched herself into his arms. "There's my favorite girl," he said, giving her a light squeeze.

"Choo-choo, Da-da! Choo-choo!" she implored.

"Later," he promised.

Unhappy with his response, she turned her attention to her grandmother, who was following closely behind her. "Choo-choo, Ga-ma!"

"We can go find the trains in a minute," Ellen told her, before greeting Irene Houlahan.

While his mother was chatting with the old librarian, Braden slipped away to get a chair for Miss Houlahan. By the time he got back, his mother and Saige were gone again.

Miss Houlahan thanked him, somewhat stiffly, for the chair before she said, "Your daughter doesn't look much like you."

He smiled at her blunt statement of the obvious fact that so many other people tried to tiptoe around. "Her paternal grandmother was Japanese."

"You adopted her then?" she guessed.

He nodded.

"Adoption is a wonderful way to match up parents who want a child with a child who needs a family," she noted.

He appreciated not just the sentiment but her word choice. He didn't want to count the number of times that someone had referred to children placed for adoption as "unwanted," because that description couldn't be further from the truth. Perhaps untimely in the lives of the women who birthed them, those babies were desperately wanted by their adoptive parents. And in the case of his own daughter, he knew that Lindsay had wanted her child but, even more, she'd wanted a better life for Saige than she'd felt she would be able to give her.

"There was a time I considered adopting a child myself," Miss Houlahan surprised him by confiding. "But that was about forty years ago, when unmarried women weren't considered suitable to take on the responsibilities of raising a child, except maybe a child who was in the foster care system."

"I'm not sure much has changed," he admitted.

"Back then, not a lot of men would be willing to raise an infant on their own, either," she noted.

"I'm a Garrett," he reminded her. "There are currently thirty-one members of my immediate family in this town—believe me, I haven't done any of this on my own."

Miss Houlahan smiled at that, the upward curve of her lips immediately softening her usually stern and disapproving expression. "It takes a village," she acknowledged. "And a willingness to rely on that village."

"Believe me, I'm not just willing but grateful. I don't know how I would have managed otherwise."

"Where does Cassie fit into the picture?" Irene asked.

He didn't insult her by pretending to misunderstand the question. "I'd say that's up to her."

"Hmm," she said. Before she could expand on that response, a tall, silver-haired man ambled over. "I let you out of my sight for five minutes, and you're already chatting up other men," he teased Miss Houlahan.

She pursed her lips in obvious disapproval but introduced the newcomer as Jerry Riordan to Braden, and the two men shook hands.

"You're not trying to steal away my girl, are you?" Jerry asked.

Braden held up his hands in surrender. "No, sir. I can promise you that."

"I'm not anyone's *girl* and I'm not *your* anything," Miss Houlahan said firmly to her contemporary. "And Braden has his eye on Cassie."

"Then I'd say he's got a good eye," Jerry said, sending a conspiratorial wink in Braden's direction.

Miss Houlahan sniffed disapprovingly. "She's a lot more than a pretty face, and she deserves a man who appreciates her sharp mind and generous heart, too."

Braden silently acknowledged the validity of her concerns, because as much as he appreciated Cassie's pretty face and sharp mind, he had no interest in her heart—and even less in putting his own on the line again.

Chapter Seven

The library didn't spend much money to advertise the Book & Bake Sale, relying mostly on word of mouth to draw people to the event. As Cassie looked around the crowds gathered at the tables and milling on the sidewalk, she was satisfied the strategy had succeeded.

She wandered over to the children's tent—always one of the more popular sections—where, in addition to the books and games and toys for sale, balloon animals were being made and happy faces were being painted. Chloe, a straight-A student and an incredible artist, was turning boys and girls into various jungle animals and superheroes, and the lineup for this transformation seemed endless. While Cassie was there, a pint-size dark-haired toddler came racing toward her, baring tiny white teeth. "Raar!"

In response to the growl, Cassie hunkered down to the child's level. "Well, who is this?" she asked, peering closely at the little girl's face. "She looks a little bit like Saige and a lot like a scary lion."

"Raar!" Saige said again, then held out the train in her hand for Cassie's perusal.

"What have you got there?"

"Choo-choo."

She glanced at Braden. "Daddy finally caved and bought you a train, did he?"

Though the little girl probably didn't understand all of the words, she nodded enthusiastically.

"Not Daddy, Grandma," he corrected. "My mother spoils her rotten."

"If that was true, she'd be rotten and she's not," Ellen Garrett protested as she joined them. "In fact, she's so sweet I could gobble her right up." Then she scooped up her granddaughter and pretended to nibble on her shoulder, making Saige shriek with laughter.

"That doesn't change the fact that you indulge her every whim," Braden pointed out.

"Unfortunately, I can't give her what she really needs," his mother said.

He sighed. "Mom."

The single word was a combination of wariness and warning that gave Cassie the distinct impression she was in the middle of a familiar argument between the son and his mother.

"But I can give her a cookie," Ellen said, apparently heeding the warning.

"Kee?" Saige echoed hopefully.

Braden nodded. "*One* cookie," he agreed. "And then I need to get her home for her nap."

"I can take her back to my house," Ellen offered.

"You already had her for most of the morning," he pointed out.

"Is there a reason I shouldn't spend more time with my granddaughter?"

"You know there isn't," he said. "And you know how much I appreciate everything you do for us."

Cassie kept her attention on Saige, quietly entertaining the little girl with the "Handful of Fingers" song while her father and grandmother sorted out their plans.

"Then maybe you could do something for me," his mother suggested.

"Of course," he agreed readily.

"Stick around here to help Cassie with the cleanup—and make sure she gets something to eat."

"Oh, that isn't necessary," Cassie interjected. "We have plenty of volunteers."

"But you can always use extra hands," Braden reminded her of the statement she'd made only a few hours earlier.

"That's settled then," Ellen said happily. "Come on, Saige. Let's go get that cookie."

Braden stole a hug and a kiss from his daughter before he let her head off to the bake table with her grandmother.

"You really don't have to stay," Cassie told him. "You've already done so much to help."

"I do need to stay—my mother said so."

She smiled at that. "Do you always do what your mother tells you to?"

"Usually," he acknowledged. "Especially when it's what I want to do, anyway."

"There must be something else you'd rather do with your Saturday."

"You don't think supporting a community fund-raiser for the local library is good use of my time?" he countered.

"You're deliberately misunderstanding me."

"And you're tiptoeing around the question you really want to ask," he told her.

"You're right," she agreed, a teasing glint in her eye. "What I really want to know is why you got arrested."

He frowned. "Why would you think I was arrested?"

"Because your sudden determination to volunteer seems like a community service thing to me," she told him.

He chuckled at that. "You really do have a suspicious mind, don't you?"

"Not suspicious so much as skeptical," she told him.

"I wanted to help out," he said. "Although yes, I did have an ulterior motive."

"I knew it."

"To spend some time with you," he said, and slung a companionable arm across her shoulders. "Now let's go see if there's anything left at the bake table."

"There's probably not much more than crumbs," she warned. "I know for a fact that all of Mrs. Bowman's muffins were gone within the first half hour."

"How many of those did you take?"

"Four."

He lifted his brows. "Two were my breakfast," she explained. "I took the other two for Irene and Jerry."

"And none for me," he lamented.

"Sorry."

"You can make it up to me by going out with me for some real food when this is over and done," he suggested.

"Are you asking me on a date?"

"I am," he confirmed.

"Then I'm sorry to have to decline," she said. "Because the only reason half these kids are here to help with the takedown is that they know I always get pizza and soda for the volunteers when we're done."

"Does that mean I get to hang around for pizza and soda?"

"Only if you stop slacking and get back to work," she told him.

He grinned. "Yes, ma'am."

* * *

Cassie couldn't fault his work ethic. Braden did what he was told and with a lot less grumbling than she got from some of the teens who were helping out. He might spend his days sitting behind a desk, but he didn't look soft. In fact, the way his muscles bunched and flexed while he worked, he looked pretty darn mouthwatering and close to perfect.

And if she felt uncomfortable that he was hanging around, well, that was on her. He'd done absolutely nothing to suggest that his reasons for being there weren't as simple and straightforward as he claimed. But every once in a while, she'd catch a glimpse of him out of the corner of her eye, and she'd feel a little tingle course through her veins. Or she'd find him looking at her and he'd smile, unashamed to be caught staring, and her heart would flutter inside her chest as if she was a teenage girl. And maybe being surrounded by so many fifteen-to-seventeen year-olds was the reason for her immature and emotional response to the man.

"Is everything okay, Miss Mac?"

She dragged her attention away from Braden to focus on Ethan Anderson—a senior honor student and first-string football player. "Of course, Ethan."

"Who's the old guy hanging around?"

She couldn't help but smile at that. Not because Braden was old but because she understood that to most teens anyone over thirty was ancient—a status she was close to attaining herself. "Braden Garrett," she said. "His daughter is in a couple of the preschool programs."

"Is he your boyfriend?"

"No," she said quickly, unexpectedly flustered by the question.

"Then why is he here?" Ethan wanted to know.

"To help out," she said. "Just like everyone else."

"He's keeping a closer eye on you than anyone else," the teen noted.

"The tables," she reminded him, attempting to shift his attention back to the task at hand.

"You told me to keep this one set up for the pizza."

"Oh. Right."

Ethan eyed her speculatively, his lips curving. "Maybe he's not your boyfriend, but you like him, don't you?"

"What?" She pretended not to understand what he was asking, but she suspected the flush in her cheeks proved otherwise.

"I just noticed that you're keeping a pretty close eye on him, too," he remarked.

"It's my responsibility to keep an eye on *all* of the volunteers," she reminded him.

"So why haven't you told Cade and Jake to stop fooling around?"

She hadn't even noticed that the fifteen-year-old twins were roughhousing on the other side of the room until Ethan directed her gaze in that direction. "Cade, Jake," she called out. "If you don't stop fooling around, I won't sign off on your volunteer hours."

Cade reluctantly released his brother from his headlock and Jake took his elbow out of his twin's side.

Ethan's smile only widened.

Thankfully, before he could say anything else, Tanya announced that the pizza had arrived. While she and Chloe got out the drinks and plates and napkins, Cassie took out the money she'd tucked into her pocket. But when she looked up again, the delivery guy was already halfway back to his car.

"I didn't pay him," Cassie said, frowning.

"I did," Braden told her.

"You didn't have to do that—I've got the money right here."

But he shook his head when she tried to give it to him. "I'm beginning to suspect this might be the only way I ever get to buy you dinner."

Before she could respond, the volunteers descended on the boxes.

"You better grab a slice while you can," she told him.

He nodded and reached for a plate.

Although Braden knew this wasn't quite what his mother had in mind when she asked him to make sure that Cassie got something to eat, he was glad he'd stayed. Not only to lend a hand but to see her interact with the teen group. Although she was an authority figure, he could tell that they didn't just respect her, they genuinely liked her. And they were undoubtedly curious about who he was and why he was hanging around.

There was a lot of talk and laughter while everyone chowed down. The kids were an eclectic group: there was the good girl, the jock, the geek, the cheerleader, the artist. They probably didn't interact much at school, if their paths crossed at all, but here they were all—if not friends—at least friendly.

"Who's the kid in the red hoodie with the fat lip and angry glare?" he asked.

"That's Kevin," Cassie told him. "An eleventh grader at Southmount."

"What's his story?"

She looked at him curiously. "Why do you think he has any more of a story than any of the other kids here?"

"The way you look at him—like you understand what he's all about," he said.

"He hangs out at the library because he's got four

younger siblings at home, it's not all that difficult to understand," she told him.

Maybe not, but he suspected it wasn't quite that simple, either. "What happened to his lip?"

She shrugged. "How would I know?"

But her deliberately casual tone made him suspect that she did know—and wasn't nearly as unconcerned as she wanted him to believe.

"Does he get knocked around at home?" he asked quietly.

"Again—how would I know?"

But he saw it, just a flicker in her eyes, before she answered. And he realized that not only did she know, she'd been there. Who? When? These questions and more clamored for answers, but he knew this wasn't the time and place. Instead, he reached for another slice of pizza.

When everyone had eaten their fill, Cassie wrapped up the extra slices and discreetly slipped them into certain backpacks. After the food was cleared away, the teens started to head out.

Braden noticed that Ethan was the last to leave—after carrying the sole remaining table to the library basement, and even then he seemed reluctant to go.

"Are you sure you don't need anything else, Miss Mac?" the teen asked Cassie.

"I'm sure," she said. "Thanks for all of your help today."

"Anytime," Ethan said.

"So long as it's before June, right?" Cassie said. "After you graduate, you'll be throwing a football at college somewhere."

"Ohio State University," he told her proudly. "I'm going to be a Buckeye."

"Congratulations, Ethan. That's wonderful news."

"I'm glad you think so—Alyssa isn't so thrilled."

"Because she's got another year of high school before she goes off to college," Cassie acknowledged. "But I know she's proud of you."

Ethan checked his phone, grimaced. "And she's going to be annoyed with me if I'm late picking her up for our date tonight."

"Then you should get going," she advised.

He nodded, casting a sidelong glance toward Braden before he headed out. "Have a good night, Miss Mac."

"I don't think your football player likes me," Braden noted.

"He doesn't know you," Cassie clarified, heading into the building.

He followed. "And he's very protective of you."

"He does have a protective nature," she agreed. "But he's a good kid." She sighed when she saw the empty boxes all over the basement but didn't say anything else as she picked one up and broke it apart.

Braden picked up another and did the same. "I noticed most of the kids call you Miss Mac."

"They like nicknames."

But he knew it was more than that—it was a sign of acceptance and camaraderie. "I wonder if anyone ever considered giving Miss Houlahan a nickname," he mused. "How does 'Hoolie' sound?"

"Not very flattering," she said, but he could tell she was fighting a smile.

He grinned. "You don't think she'd like it?"

"I think you like to rile Miss Houlahan," she said, continuing to collapse the empty boxes.

"She was all about the rules and I was never a big fan of them," he explained.

"Your tune will change in a few years," Cassie warned

him. "When your daughter grows up and boys start coming around."

"Nah, I'll just put a padlock on her bedroom door," he decided.

"And then she'll sneak out her bedroom window," she warned.

"Is that what you did when you wanted to go out with a guy you knew your father wouldn't approve of?"

She shook her head. "My dad died when I was ten."

"I'm sorry."

"It was a long time ago," she said.

"Still, I imagine that losing a parent isn't an experience you forget about after a few years."

"No," she agreed. "But you shouldn't worry that Saige will be scarred by the loss of her mother—she's obviously happy and well loved."

"I wasn't thinking about Saige but about you," he told her.

"It was a long time ago," she said again.

She'd left only the biggest box intact and now stuffed the folded cardboard inside of it. "Thanks for your help today. We usually have a good number of volunteers, but the kids sometimes forget why they're here, so it was nice to have another adult around to keep them on task."

"You have an interesting group of kids," he said, turning his attention to stacking the stray chairs with the others that lined the wall. "I couldn't help but notice that they come from several different area high schools."

She nodded. "We advertise our programs widely—in all the schools and at local rec centers—to ensure all students are aware of our programs. For the most part, the ones who come here want the same thing, so they don't bring their issues or rivalries inside."

"That's impressive," he said. "Kids usually carry their grudges wherever they go."

"Only kids?" she challenged, doing a final visual scan of the basement.

"No." He breached the short distance that separated them. "But most adults have better impulse control."

She tipped her head back to meet his gaze. "You think so?"

"Usually," he clarified.

And then he gave in to his own impulses and kissed her.

Cassie was caught completely unaware.

One minute they were having a friendly conversation while they tidied up the basement storage area, and the next, his mouth had swooped down on hers.

In that first moment of contact, her heart stuttered and her mind went blank. And somehow, without even knowing what she was doing, she wound her arms around his neck and kissed him back.

It was all the encouragement Braden needed. He slid his hands around her back, drawing her closer. Close enough that her breasts grazed his chest, making her nipples tighten and the nerves in her belly quiver.

She was suddenly, achingly aware that it had been more than two years since she'd had sex. Twenty-eight months since she'd experienced the thrill of tangling the sheets with a man. For most of that time, she hadn't missed the sharing of physical intimacy. Truth be told, she'd barely thought about it.

But she was definitely thinking about it now.

Braden tipped her head back and adjusted the angle of his mouth on hers, taking his time to deepen the kiss and explore her flavor. Her fingers tangled in the silky ends of his hair, holding on to him as the world tilted on its axis. She sighed and his tongue delved between her parted lips to dance with hers in an erotically enticing rhythm.

He was turning her inside out with a single kiss, obliterating her ability to think. And she needed to think. She needed to be smart. And inviting this man to her home, to her bed, would not be smart.

But it would feel good.

If the man made love even half as masterfully as he kissed, she had no doubt that it would feel *really* good.

She forced herself to push that taunting, tempting thought aside, and to finally, reluctantly, push him away, too.

"What…" She took a moment to catch her breath. "What was that?"

"I think that's what happens when you try to douse a flame with gasoline," he said, sounding a little breathless himself.

"Explosive."

He nodded. "And proof that the chemistry between us hasn't fizzled. You're a dangerous woman, Cassie MacKinnon."

"Me? You're the one who started the fire."

"You're the first woman I've kissed in fifteen months," he admitted. "You're the only woman—aside from my wife—that I've kissed in eight years."

The ground was starting to feel a little more stable beneath her feet, but her heart was still struggling to find a normal rhythm. "That might explain why your technique is a little rusty."

But her unsteady tone belied her words, and his smile widened. "I'd be happy to show you a few other unpracticed talents."

She put her hand on his chest, holding him at a distance. "Maybe another time."

"Is that an invitation or a brush-off?" he asked.

She blew out a breath. "I'm not sure."

Chapter Eight

Several hours later, Braden couldn't stop thinking about the scorching hot kiss he'd shared with the sexy librarian.

Finally back home after picking Saige up from his parents' house and settling her into her crib, he sat down in front of the television as he did on so many other nights. Impulsively, he picked up the remote, clicked off the power and picked up the book he'd borrowed from the library.

But half an hour later, he hadn't turned a single page. He couldn't focus on the words because he couldn't stop thinking about Cassie. He closed the cover and set it aside.

Maybe he shouldn't have kissed her.

Maybe he shouldn't have *stopped* kissing her.

Maybe he should have his head examined.

Definitely he should have his head examined.

He wasn't accustomed to indecision. He was a Garrett—and Garretts didn't vacillate. Garretts set goals and devised clear strategies to get what they wanted.

Braden wanted Cassie, and he didn't doubt that she wanted him, too. But while he was confident that taking her to bed would satisfy their most immediate and basic needs, he knew that he had to think about what would happen after.

He wanted sex. After sleeping alone for more than fifteen months, he desperately wanted the blissful pleasure of joining together with a warm, willing woman. But he wanted more than that, too. One of the things he missed most about being married was the companionship—having someone to talk with about his day, someone to eat dinner with and watch TV with. Someone to snuggle with at night—not necessarily as a prelude to sex but as an affirmation that he wasn't alone in the world.

Oh, who was he kidding? A man snuggled when he wanted sex—other than that, he didn't want anyone encroaching on his territory. Except that after sleeping alone in his king-size bed for so many months, he realized he might not object to a little encroaching. Especially if Cassie was the one invading his space.

If he closed his eyes, he could picture her there—in his bedroom, sprawled on top of the covers in the middle of his mattress, wearing nothing but a smile. He didn't dare close his eyes.

The fact that she was acquainted with his mother and his daughter was both a comfort and a complication. If he decided to pursue a relationship with the librarian, he knew he wouldn't face any obstacles from his family. But if he subsequently screwed up that relationship, it could be incredibly awkward for all of them.

He wasn't looking for a one-night stand, but he wasn't looking to fall in love, either. He had no desire to go down that path again. And while he wasn't opposed to the idea of sharing his life with someone special, his main focus right now was Saige and what was best for his little girl.

But when he finally did sleep, it was Cassie who played the starring role in his dreams.

After she'd finished catching Irene up on all the latest happenings at the library and read a couple chapters of a new book to her, Cassie headed to the grocery store to do her weekly shopping. With her list in hand, she methodically walked up and down the aisles.

She paused at the meat cooler and surveyed the selection of pork roasts. Several weeks earlier, she'd found a recipe that she was eager to try, but the roasts seemed like too much for one person. Of course, she could freeze the leftovers for future meals—or maybe invite Irene and Jerry to come over.

After selecting what she needed from that department, she moved to the fresh food section and from there on to the nonperishable aisles. Cat food was on sale, so she stocked up on Westley's and Buttercup's favorite flavors. Then she remembered that she needed kitty litter, too, and added a bag of that to her cart.

And then she rounded the corner and nearly collided with Braden Garrett.

"I guess it's a popular day for grocery shopping," she said lightly.

Saige was seated in the cart facing her father, but twisted around when she recognized Cassie's voice, a wide smile spreading across her face.

"I'm here at least three times a week," Braden admitted. "Because I never seem to remember everything I need to get it all done in one trip."

"You don't make a list?"

"I usually do, and then I usually forget the list on the table at home."

Cassie smiled as Saige offered her a package of string cheese. "Those look yummy," she commented.

The little girl nodded her enthusiastic agreement.

"What other treats does Daddy have for you in there?"

Saige dropped the package of cheese and picked up a box of yogurt tubes. "Chay-wee."

The flavor noted on the box helped Cassie interpret. "You like the cherry ones best," she guessed.

Saige nodded again.

"Me, too," Cassie confided, as she glanced from Braden's shopping cart to her own. His was almost filled with family-size boxes of cereal, multipacks of juice, and bags of fresh fruits and vegetables; Cassie's basket wasn't even half full and her biggest purchases were the cat food and kitty litter.

"We're on our way to the prepared foods section, because I forgot to take dinner out of the freezer this morning," Braden told her. "Why don't you come over to eat with us?"

"Thanks, but I have to get my groceries home and put away."

"You could come over after," he suggested.

She considered the offer for about two seconds before declining. Because as much as she didn't want to be the lonely old cat lady, she also didn't want to be the broken-hearted librarian. Again. And since the kiss they'd shared in the basement of the library four days earlier, it would be foolish to continue to deny the chemistry between them. The only thing she could do now was avoid situations in which that chemistry might heat up again.

"I could get a tray of three-cheese tortellini," he said enticingly. "It's not Valentino's, but it's not bad."

She ignored the temptation—of the food and the man. "Maybe another time."

His direct and steady gaze warned that he could read more of what she was thinking and feeling than she wanted him to.

"We're at twenty-eight Spruceside in Forrest Hill, if you change your mind," he finally said.

But she knew that she wouldn't—she couldn't. "Enjoy your tortellini."

When Cassie was finished making and eating her own dinner, she turned on her tablet to check her email. Then she snapped a picture of the cats wrestling on the carpet in front of her and posted it to her Facebook page. Scrolling through her newsfeed, she saw that a friend from high school—who had married in the Bahamas just before Christmas—was expecting a baby. She noted her congratulations, adding hearts and celebratory confetti emojis to the message.

Buttercup jumped up onto the couch and crawled into her lap. She stroked her back, her feline companion purring contentedly as Cassie's fingers slid through her soft, warm fur.

She had so many reasons to be grateful: terrific friends and a great job that allowed her to spend much of her time working with children. But recently, after spending even just a little bit of time with Braden and Saige, she was suddenly aware of the emptiness inside herself, a yearning for something more.

She was twenty-nine years old with a history of broken or dead-end relationships—it would be crazy to even think about getting involved with a widowed single father to an adorable baby girl who made all of her maternal instincts sit up and beg "pick me." And while Braden had flirted with her a little, and kissed her exactly once, she didn't know what he wanted from her. But she knew what she wanted: a husband, children, a house with a second chair on the front porch and a tire swing in the backyard.

Unfortunately, she had a habit of jumping into relationships, falling in love before she had a chance to catch her breath. Most of the time, it was infatuation rather than love, but she usually only realized the truth after the relationship was over.

She wondered whether it was some kind of legacy from her childhood, if losing her family had created a desperate yearning in her for a meaningful connection. She didn't have a list of qualities that she was looking for in a partner, although she wouldn't object to meeting a man who would make her heart beat from across a room and her insides quiver with a simple touch—and Braden Garrett checked both of those boxes.

She also liked the way he interacted with his little girl, leaving absolutely no doubt about how much he loved his daughter. And she liked the way he talked about his family—not just his parents and siblings but his aunts, uncles and cousins and all of their kids.

And she really liked the way she felt when he looked at her.

She hadn't felt that stir of attraction in a long time—and she didn't want to be feeling it for this man now. Because as gorgeous and charming as he was, she'd vowed to stay away from men who had already given their hearts away.

But she couldn't deny that she was intrigued to see his house in Forrest Hill—or maybe she was just looking for an excuse to see him again. Whatever the reason, she set her tablet aside and picked up her keys.

Braden settled Saige into her high chair with a bowl of tortellini while he put the groceries away. She used both of her hands to shove the stuffed pasta into her mouth, ignoring the spoon he'd given to her. When her bowl was empty, she had sauce—and a happy grin—spread across her face.

"Did you like that?" he asked her.

She nodded and pushed her empty bowl to the edge of her tray. "Mo'."

"Do you want more pasta or do you want dessert?"

She didn't hesitate. "Zert!"

"Yeah, that was a tough question, wasn't it?" He chuckled as he wiped her face, hands and tray.

He was looking in the fridge, considering dessert options, when the doorbell rang.

He unbuckled Saige and lifted her out of her high chair, then went to respond to the summons. He wasn't expecting company, but it wasn't unusual for his parents or his brother Justin, or any of his cousins to stop by if they were in the neighborhood. The absolute last person he expected to see when he opened the door was Charisma's sexy librarian.

"I changed my mind," Cassie said.

Despite the assertion, she looked a little uncertain, as if she might again change her mind and turn right back around.

"I'm glad," he said, and moved away from the door so that she could enter. "Saige and I have already eaten, but there is some pasta left."

"Zert!" Saige said.

Cassie smiled at his daughter. "I had dinner," she said. "And then I decided I was in the mood for ice cream, so I went back to the grocery store and came out with all of this."

He glanced at the bags as she stepped into the foyer. "That looks like a lot of ice cream."

"It's not just ice cream. There's also chocolate sauce,

marshmallow topping, chopped peanuts, toffee bits, sprinkles and maraschino cherries."

"I cweam?" Saige said hopefully.

Braden chuckled. "Yes, Cassie brought ice cream. And it sounds like a whole sundae bar, too," he noted, taking the bags and leading her through the living room.

Cassie shrugged. "I didn't know what you and Saige liked."

"What do you like?"

"Everything," she admitted.

He grinned. "A woman after my own heart."

But Cassie shook her head. "I'm only here for the ice cream." Then her gaze shifted, to take in the surroundings as she followed him toward the kitchen. "How long have you lived here?"

"Almost six years."

"So you've had time to paint—if you wanted to," she noted.

"Dana picked the colors," he admitted.

She squinted at the walls, as if looking for the color, and he chuckled.

"I know it's hard to see the difference, but the foyer is magnolia blossom—no, the original color was magnolia blossom," he remembered. "Now it's spring drizzle or summer mist or something like that, the living and dining rooms are vintage linen...I think, and the kitchen is French vanilla."

"In other words, every room is a different shade of white," she commented.

"Pretty much," he admitted, depositing the grocery bags on the counter so he could put Saige back in her high chair.

"I cweam!" Saige demanded.

"Yes, we're going to have ice cream," he promised.

His little girl clapped her hands together.

"Do you like chocolate sauce?" Cassie asked his daughter.

"Chay-wee."

"I brought some cherries, too," she said. Then, to Braden, "What I didn't bring was an ice-cream scoop."

He opened a drawer to retrieve the necessary implement, then reached into an overhead cupboard for bowls while she unpacked the bags.

"You should make Saige's sundae," she said, nudging the tub of vanilla ice cream toward him. "Because you know what she likes and what she can have."

"She likes everything, too," he told her. "Although she probably shouldn't have the toffee bits or peanuts. Or a lot of chocolate."

"Which is why you should do it," she said again.

So he scooped up a little bit of ice cream, added a drop of chocolate sauce, a dollop of marshmallow topping, a few sprinkles and three cherries on top.

"You need to use a spoon for this," he told Saige, setting the bowl in front of her.

"'Kay," she agreed, wrapping her fingers around the plastic handle of the utensil.

"How many scoops do you want?" Cassie asked him.

"How many can I have?"

She put three generous scoops of ice cream into the bowl, covered them with chocolate sauce, nuts, toffee bits, marshmallow topping, sprinkles and cherries. Then she prepared a second, much smaller bowl of the same for herself.

"I'm not sure why you came all this way to bring us dessert, but I'm glad you did," he told her, digging into his sundae.

"Bingeing on ice cream seems like one of those things that shouldn't be done alone."

"I seem to be the only one bingeing," he pointed out.

"And as good as this ice cream is, I can think of other and more satisfying things that shouldn't be done alone, either."

Her cheeks turned a pretty shade of pink as she dipped her spoon into her bowl.

"And maybe I wanted to have a real conversation with another human being as much as I was craving ice cream," she admitted.

"Conversation, huh?" He scooped up more ice cream. "That wasn't exactly what I had in mind, but okay. Anything in particular you want to talk about?"

"No." She slid her spoon between her lips, humming with pleasure as she closed her eyes. "Oh, this is good."

He knew she wasn't being deliberately provocative, but he recognized her expression as that of a woman lost in pure, sensual pleasure, and he found himself wishing that he'd been the one to put that look on her face. Because her blissful smile, combined with the sensual sound emanating from deep in her throat, had all of the blood draining from his head into his lap. To cool the heat pulsing in his veins, he shoved another spoonful of ice cream into his mouth.

"What did you have for dinner?" Braden asked, hoping that conversation would force her to open her eyes and stop making those noises that were making him aroused.

"A microwaveable chicken and rice bowl," she admitted.

"That sounds…incredibly unappealing," he decided.

She licked her spoon. "It wasn't that bad." And then she shrugged. "I do occasionally cook, but it's not a lot of fun to prepare meals for only one person."

"You can make dinner for me anytime," he told her.

"That's a generous offer," she said dryly.

He grinned. "I'm a generous guy."

"Hmm," was all Cassie said to that, as she spooned up more ice cream.

"Aw dun!" Saige announced.

He shifted his attention away from Cassie. "And it looks like you put more in your belly than on your face this time," he noted. "Good girl."

She smiled and rubbed her belly. "Mo?"

He shook his head. "No more ice cream for you or I'll never get you to sleep tonight."

"Chay-wee?" she said hopefully.

Before he could respond, Cassie had scooped one of the cherries out of her bowl and held her spoon out to Saige, who snagged the piece of fruit and popped it into her mouth. Then she smiled again, showing off the cherry caught between her front teeth, making Cassie laugh.

His attention shifted back to her, noted her curved lips and sparkling eyes. He'd always thought she was beautiful, but looking at her here now—in his kitchen, with his daughter—she almost took his breath away.

"Chay-wee?" Saige said again.

"I've got one more," Cassie said, this time looking to Braden for permission before she offered it.

He shrugged. At this point, he didn't think one more cherry was going to make any difference.

So Cassie gave Saige her last cherry, then pushed away from the table to clear away their empty bowls. While she was doing that, he got a washcloth to wipe off Saige's face and hands. He was returning the cloth to the sink just as Cassie closed the dishwasher and turned around, the action causing her breasts to brush against his chest.

She sucked in a breath and took half a step back—until she bumped against the counter. "Oh. Um. Sorry."

He held her gaze, watched her pupils dilate until there was only a narrow ring of dark chocolate around them. "Close quarters," he noted.

She looked around, managed a laugh. "This is not close quarters. You should see my kitchen."

"Is that an invitation?" he asked.

She tilted her head, as if considering. "Maybe."

He smiled and took a half step forward, so there was barely a breath between them. "I think we're making progress."

The tip of her tongue swept over her bottom lip, leaving it glistening with moisture. "Are we?"

He dipped his head, so that his mouth hovered above hers. "I haven't stopped thinking about our first kiss," he admitted.

"First implies the beginning of a series," she pointed out.

He'd noticed that she had a habit of reciting definitions and facts when she was nervous. Apparently he was making her nervous; she was definitely making him aroused.

"Uh-huh," he agreed.

"And I haven't decided if there's going to be a second," she said, the breathless tone undercutting her denial.

"That's okay—because I have," he said, and brushed his lips against hers.

Her eyelids fluttered and had just started to drift shut when the phone rang.

She immediately drew back; he cursed under his breath but didn't move away.

"Aren't you going to answer that?" she asked him.

"If my choices are answering the phone or kissing you, I opt for door number two," he told her.

But when the phone rang again, she lifted her hands to his chest and pushed him away. "I need to get home," she said.

With a resigned sigh, he stepped back.

A cursory glance at the number on the display panel had a whole different kind of tension taking hold of him.

"I'm sorry," he said, "but I do have to answer this."

"Of course," she said easily.

Nothing was easy about the emotions that coursed through his system as he lifted the receiver to his ear. "Hello?"

"Hi, Mr. Garrett."

"Lindsay?"

"Yeah, it's me," she confirmed.

He hadn't heard from Saige's biological mother in months, and the last he'd heard, she was in London. The 330 exchange, though, was Ohio, which meant that she was back at her parents' house.

As endless thoughts and questions tumbled through his mind, he vaguely registered Cassie lifting a hand in a silent goodbye before she stepped out of the room and then, out the front door.

Chapter Nine

Cassie didn't hear from Braden again until Friday afternoon when he came into the library. She was guiding an elderly patron through the self-checkout process and showing her how to unlock the DVDs she wanted to borrow. He waited patiently until she was finished, pretending to peruse the books on the Rapid Reads shelf, but she felt him watching her, his gaze almost as tangible as a caress.

"Can I help you with something, Mr. Garrett?" she asked when Elsa Ackerley had gone.

"You could accept my apology," he said.

"What are you apologizing for?"

"Not having a chance to say good-night before you left the other night."

"You were obviously focused on your conversation with...what was her name?"

"Lindsay," he told her.

"Right—Lindsay." She kept her tone light, feigning an

indifference she didn't feel. Pretending it didn't bother her that less than a minute after his mouth had been hovering over hers and anticipation had been dancing in her veins, he'd forgotten she was even there as he gave his full and complete attention to *Lindsay*. Proving to Cassie, once again, how unreliable her instincts were when it came to the opposite sex.

"And it's not what you think," Braden said to her now.

"I'm not thinking anything," she lied.

He opened his mouth as if to say something else, then closed it again when Helen approached the desk. After retrieving the basket of recently returned DVDs, she steered her cart away again.

"Have dinner with me tonight and give me a chance to explain," he said when Helen had gone.

"You don't owe me any explanations," she assured him. "And I'm working until seven, anyway."

"Then you'll probably be hungry when you're done," he pointed out.

"Which is why I have a pork roast in my slow cooker at home." Although she hadn't been able to firm up plans with Irene and Jerry, she'd impulsively decided to cook the roast anyway, figuring she'd take the leftovers to her friend on the weekend.

"I was offering to take you out for dinner, but that sounds even better," he decided.

She blinked. "What?"

"Dinner at your place is an even better idea than going out."

"I didn't—"

But he'd already turned and walked away.

Cassie huffed out a breath as she watched him disappear through the door. She didn't know if she was more amused or exasperated that he'd so easily manipulated the situation to his advantage, but there was no doubt the man knew how to get what he wanted—though she was still uncertain about what he wanted from her.

And while the prospect of sharing a meal with Braden filled her with anticipation, she couldn't help but wonder if he only wrangled dinner with her because Lindsay had other plans.

He wasn't waiting outside the door when she left the library and he wasn't in the parking lot, either. Cassie exhaled a sigh as she headed toward home and told herself that she was relieved he'd changed his mind. But she was a little confused, too. Braden had deliberately twisted her words to suggest an invitation she'd never intended, and then he didn't even bother to follow up on it. Maybe she hadn't planned to invite him, but she still felt stood up.

She shook off the feeling that she refused to recognize as disappointment and focused on admiring the many colorful flowers that brightened her path as she walked to her modest one-and-a-half story home that was only a few blocks from the library. The spring season was evident in the sunny yellow jessamine, vibrant pink tulips, snowy bloodroot and bright purple irises, and she felt her mood lifting a little with every step.

Her steps slowed when she spotted an unfamiliar vehicle parked on the street in front of her house. A late model silver Mercedes sedan. And leaning against the hood of the car, looking ridiculously handsome, was Braden Garrett with a bottle of wine in one hand and a bouquet of flowers in the other.

He smiled when he saw her, and her resolve melted away like ice cubes in a glass of sweet tea on a hot summer day.

"You said you were cooking a pork roast," he said by

way of greeting. "And while some people claim that pork is the other white meat, you once mentioned that you preferred red wine so I picked up a bottle of my favorite Pinot Noir." He offered her the bouquet. "I also brought you flowers."

"Why?" she asked, unexpectedly moved by the commonplace gesture. Because commonplace or not, it had been a long time since any man had brought her flowers.

"It's been a long time since I've had a first date, but I always thought flowers were a nice gesture."

"This isn't a date," she told him.

"Then what is it?"

"It's you mooching my dinner."

"I offered to take you out," he reminded her.

She nodded in acknowledgment of the point. "And then you deliberately misinterpreted my refusal as an invitation."

"You weren't asking me to come here for a meal?" he asked, feigning surprise—albeit not very convincingly.

"The pork roast isn't anything fancy," she told him, as she unlocked the front door. "And there's nothing for dessert."

"No cheesecake?" he asked, disappointed.

She was helpless to prevent the smile that curved her lips. "Sorry—no."

"Well, I'm glad to be here, anyway," Braden said, following her into the house.

Waning rays of sunlight spilled through the tall windows that flanked the door, illuminating the natural stone floor. The walls in the entranceway were painted a warm shade of grayish blue and the wide trim was glossy and white.

He was barely inside the door when he felt an unexpected bump against his shin. "What the—" He glanced down to see a cat with pale gold fur rubbing against his pant leg. "You have a cat."

"Two actually." She glanced over her shoulder. "That's Buttercup. She's much more sociable than Westley."

It took him a minute to figure out why the names sounded familiar. "*The Princess Bride*?" he guessed, carefully stepping around the cat to follow her into the bright and airy kitchen.

She seemed surprised that he'd connected the names to the story. "You've read the book?"

He frowned. "It's a book?"

Cassie shook her head despairingly, but another smile tugged at the corners of her mouth. "It was a book long before it was a movie."

"I haven't read the book," he admitted, as he looked around to admire the maple cupboards, granite countertops and mosaic tile backsplash. "But it was a great movie."

"One of my favorites." She took a meat thermometer out of a drawer and lifted the lid of the slow cooker to check the temperature of the roast. "And the book was even better."

"You're a librarian—you probably have to say that."

"Why don't I lend it to you, then you can judge for yourself?" she suggested.

"Sure," he agreed. "Mmm…that smells really good."

"Hopefully it tastes as good," she said. "It's a new recipe I'm trying out."

"So I'm a guinea pig?" he teased.

"As a result of your own machinations," she reminded him.

"I'm here for the company more than the food, anyway." He looked over her shoulder and into the pot. "Are those parsnips?"

"You don't like parsnips?" she guessed.

"Actually, I do. And sweet potatoes, too," he said, chunks of which were also in the pot. "I just didn't think anyone other than my mother cooked them."

"How lucky that you decided to invite yourself to dinner tonight," she said dryly, replacing the lid.

He grinned. "I was just thinking the same thing."

"Why don't you open the wine while I take care of these flowers?"

"Corkscrew?"

She pointed. "Top drawer on the other side of the sink. Glasses are above the refrigerator."

While he was opening the bottle, she slipped out of the room. The cat stayed with him, winding between his legs and rubbing against him.

He glanced down at the ball of fur and remarked, "Well, at least one of the females here is friendly."

"She's an attention whore," Cassie told him, returning with a clear glass vase.

"Where's Westley?"

"Probably sleeping by the fireplace—he spends most of his day lazing in his bed until he hears his food being poured into his bowl." Setting the vase aside, she opened the door of the pantry and pulled out a bag. She carried it to an alcove beside the fridge, where he saw now there were two sets of bowls neatly aligned on mats, and crouched down to pour the food.

As the first pieces of kibble hit the bottom of the bowl, he heard a distant thump of paws hitting the floor then saw a streak of black and white shoot across the kitchen floor. The plaintive meow made Braden realize it wasn't his bowl that Cassie had filled first. Her attention diverted by her sibling's call, Buttercup padded over to her bowl and hunkered down to feast on her dinner while Westley waited for his own.

"I've never seen a cat reluctant to eat out of another animal's bowl," he noted.

"Neither of them does," she told him. "Which makes it easier for me when I need to put drops or supplements in their food, because I know they've each gotten the right amount."

"Did you train them to do that?"

She smiled at that. "You've obviously never tried to train a cat to do anything."

"I'm guessing the answer to my question is no."

"No," she confirmed. "It's just a lucky quirk of their personalities. Or maybe it has something to do with the fact that, as kittens, they were crammed into a boot box with four other siblings. Now they appreciate having their own space—not just their own bowls but their own litter boxes and beds." Although they usually curled up together in one or the other when it was time to go to sleep, because apparently even feline creatures preferred not to sleep alone.

"Six kittens and you only ended up with two?" he teased.

"I wanted to take them all," she admitted. "But I'm not yet ready to be known as the crazy old cat lady."

"You're too young to be old," he assured her.

She lifted a brow. "I notice you didn't dispute the 'crazy' part."

"I don't really know you well enough to make any assertions about your state of mind," he pointed out. Then, "So what happened to the other kittens?"

"Tanya—you met her at the Book & Bake Sale—took Fezzik, Mr. and Mrs. Bowman—regular patrons of the library—chose Vizzini, Mr. Osler—the old bachelor who lives across the street—wanted Inigo, and Megan—one of the librarian assistants—took Prince Humperdinck, but she just calls him Prince."

"You named them all," he guessed.

"I found them," she said logically.

"That seems fair," he agreed, watching as she snipped the stems of the flowers and set them in the vase she'd filled with water. She fussed a little with the colorful blooms, so he knew she liked them. A fact she further confirmed when she set the vase on the windowsill above the sink and said, "Thank you—they're beautiful."

"They are beautiful," he agreed. "That's why they made me think of you."

"You always have the right line, don't you?"

"Do I?" he asked, surprised. "Because I often feel a little tongue-tied around you."

"I find that hard to believe."

"It's true," he told her.

While Cassie sliced the meat, Braden set the table, following her directions to locate the plates and cutlery. Then they sat down together to eat the pork roast and vegetables and drink the delicious Pinot Noir he'd brought to go with the meal.

"You're not going to ask, are you?" Braden said, as he stabbed his fork into a chunk of sweet potato.

She shook her head. "It's none of my business."

"Well, I'm going to tell you anyway—Lindsay is Saige's birth mother."

"Oh." Of all the possible explanations he might have given, that one had never occurred to her.

"When Dana and I adopted Saige, we promised Lindsay that we would keep in touch. But not long after the papers were signed, she went to London to do a year of school there, and although I routinely sent photos and emails, I hadn't actually spoken to her in more than a year."

"Why was she calling?" Cassie asked curiously.

"Because she's back in the US and wants to see Saige."

"Oh," she said again. "How do you feel about that?"

"Obligated," he admitted. "We agreed to an open adoption—of course, we would have agreed to almost anything to convince Lindsay to sign the papers—so I can't really refuse. And I do think it is important for Saige to know the woman who gave birth to her, but I'm a little concerned, too."

"About?" she prompted gently.

He picked up his glass of wine but didn't drink; he only stared into it. "Lindsay gave up her baby because she wanted her to be raised in a traditional family with two parents who would love her and care for her. And now that I'm a single parent, I can't help worrying that Lindsay will decide she wants Saige back."

She considered that as she sipped her wine. "I don't know much about adoption laws, but I would think it's a little late for her to change her mind, isn't it?"

"Most likely," he acknowledged. "The first thing I did when I hung up the phone after talking to Lindsay was call my cousin, who's a lawyer. Jackson assured me that judges generally don't like to reverse adoptions. But he also warned me that if Lindsay decided to take it to court and got a sympathetic judge, she *might* be able to claim a material change in circumstances and argue that Saige's best interests would be served by vacating our contract."

Cassie immediately shook her head, horrified by the possibility. "There's no way anybody who has ever seen you with your daughter would believe it's in her best interests to be anywhere but with you."

He managed a smile at that. "I appreciate the vote of confidence."

His smile did funny things to her insides—or maybe she was hungry. She decided to stop talking and start eating.

Braden's plate was almost empty before he spoke again. "Tell me something about you," he said.

"What do you want to know?"

"Have you been dating anyone—other than Darius Richmond—recently?"

She shook her head. "No. In fact, until a few months ago, I hadn't dated at all in a couple of years."

"Bad break-up before that?" he asked sympathetically.

But she shook her head. "The break-up was good—the relationship was bad."

His dark green eyes took on a dangerous gleam. "Was he abusive?"

"No, nothing that dramatic," she assured him. "I was twenty-six when I met him and eager to move on to the next stage in my life."

"Marriage," he guessed.

She nodded. "And kids. I wanted so desperately to get married and start a family that I saw what I wanted to see…right up until the minute the truth slapped me in the face—figuratively speaking."

"Were you married?"

"No," she said again. "Just engaged for a few months."

She thought back to that blissful moment when Joel Langdon proposed. They'd quickly set the date for their wedding and booked the church and the reception venue, and she'd been so excited for their future together, believing they were on their way to happily-ever-after.

"Until I discovered that he was still in love with his ex-wife," she continued.

Braden winced. "How did that happen?"

"As we talked about the wedding, I realized that Joel had some specific ideas about how he wanted his bride to look. A strapless dress wasn't appropriate for a church wedding, white satin would make my skin look pasty, and the princess-style ball gown would overwhelm my frame.

Instead, he'd suggested a more streamlined style, perhaps ivory in color with long sleeves covered in ecru lace."

"That's pretty specific," he noted.

She nodded. And although she'd been disappointed by her fiancé's assessment, she'd been pleased he was taking such an interest in the details of their special day.

"He also suggested that I should let my hair grow out, so that I could wear it up under my veil—but I hadn't planned to wear a veil. And maybe I could consider adding a few blond highlights, to tone down the auburn. The more suggestions he made, the more I realized that he was trying to change who I was—or at least how I looked."

She shook her head, lamenting her own foolishness for not seeing then what was so obvious to her now. She knew he'd been married before, but Joel hadn't talked about his ex-wife. He certainly never said or did anything to suggest to Cassie that he was still in love with her.

"It was only after I moved in with him that I found his wedding album with the date engraved on the front—the same month and day he'd chosen to marry me."

And the date had been *his* choice. She'd thought that a fall wedding might be nice, but he'd urged her to consider spring, so that she could carry a bouquet of white tulips—her favorite flowers. She hadn't much thought about what flowers she wanted for the wedding, and while she wouldn't have said tulips were her favorite, she liked them well enough.

"Then I opened the cover and saw a picture of his ex-wife, in her long-sleeved lace gown with a bouquet of white tulips in her hand." She'd slowly turned the pages, trying to make sense of what she was seeing. "And on the last page, the close-up photo of the bride's and groom's hands revealed that my fiancé had proposed to me with his ex-wife's engagement ring.

"The rest of it I might have been able to ignore," she admitted. "But when I saw the diamond cluster on her finger—the same diamond cluster that was on my finger—I felt sick to my stomach.

"And when I confronted him about it, he didn't even try to deny it—he just said he'd paid a lot of money for the ring. So I took it off my finger and told him that I hoped the next woman he gave it to wouldn't mind being his second choice."

All of which was why she'd barely dated in the more than two years that had passed since her broken engagement. Because in the space of the few hours that had passed between finding the wedding album hidden in the back of her fiancé's closet and his return to the apartment, she'd been shocked—and a little scared—by some of the thoughts that had gone through her own mind.

During that time, she'd actually tried to convince herself that she was making the discovery of those photos into more than it needed to be. She'd even considered putting the album back and pretending that she'd never seen it, to let it go so they could move forward with their plans.

Because she'd been desperate to feel connected to someone, desperate to be part of a family again. Even aware that marriage to a man who was still in love with another woman didn't bode well for their long-term future together, her eagerness to be a wife and then a mother almost made her willing to overlook that fact. *Almost.*

In the end, it was this desperation to not be alone that made her rethink her plans. Her mother hadn't ever been able to find happiness or even contentment on her own. Not even her daughters had been enough for her. She'd needed to be with a man; she'd needed his adoration and approval to justify her existence. The possibility that she might be like her mother—that she could make the same destructive choices and ruin not only her own life but that of any children she might have in the future—compelled her to take that step back.

Actually, she'd taken a lot of steps back. For a long time after she'd given Joel back the ring, she'd been afraid to even go out on a date. Her desperation to be a wife and a mother had made her question her own judgment and fear her own motivations. Thankfully, she had her job at the library to give her another focus, and she found both pleasure and fulfillment in working with children and teens.

She'd vowed then not to waste any more time with the wrong men. Unfortunately, the wrong men didn't always come with a warning label, as her recent experience with Darius Richmond had demonstrated. And if she wanted to find the right man, she had to be open to meeting new people.

Over the past few months, she'd started to do that, but none of the guys she'd gone out with had made her think "maybe this one." None of their good-night kisses had made her pulse race and her heart pound. In fact, none of their kisses made her want a second date.

No one had made her want anything more—until Braden kissed her.

Chapter Ten

"Cassie?"

She glanced up to find Braden watching her, his expression one of concern. She forced a smile. "Sorry—my mind just wandered off for a moment."

"How long ago was it that you gave him back the ring?" he wondered.

"Two years."

He set his cutlery on his empty plate and swallowed the last of the wine in his glass. "Did you live with him here?"

"No," she said again, smiling a little at this happier memory as she pushed away from the table to begin the cleanup. "I found this place when Stacey and I spent most of a rainy Sunday afternoon going through open houses. I think this was the third—or maybe the fourth—house we saw, and as soon as I saw the den with the fireplace and the built-in bookcases, I wanted it."

"I think I need to see the den," he remarked.

So she led the way through the dining room to her favorite room in the house. As he stepped inside, she tried to see it through his eyes. She knew it was modestly sized, as was the rest of the house, but there wasn't anything else about the room that she would change. Not the hardwood floors or the natural stone fireplace or the trio of tall narrow windows—each with a cushy seat from which she could enjoy the view of her postage-stamp-sized backyard—and especially not the floor-to-ceiling bookcases that covered most of three walls and were filled with her books.

"Well, it doesn't look as if you'd ever run out of reading material." He ventured farther into the room to examine the array of titles that filled her shelves and reflected her eclectic taste. From Jane Austen's *Pride and Prejudice* to J.R. Ward's *Dark Lover*; from Anthony Burgess's *A Clockwork Orange* to Shel Silverstein's *The Giving Tree*; from John Douglas's *Mindhunter* to Eckhart Tolle's *The Power of Now*. There were also biographies of historical figures, entrepreneurs and movie stars; books about auto mechanics and dogs and feng shui. "You have almost as many books here as there are at the library."

"Hardly."

"How many have you actually read?" he wondered.

"All of them—except for that bottom shelf," she said, pointing. "Those are new."

"You've read every other book on these shelves?" he asked, incredulous.

"Some of them more than once." She moved to the other side of the room and reached up to the third shelf. "Do you want to borrow this one?"

He took the book from her hand and glanced at the cover. "*The Princess Bride: S. Morgenstern's Classic Tale of True Love and High Adventure* by William Goldman."

He frowned. "Who's the author—Morgenstern or Goldman?"

She just smiled. "Read the book."

They returned to the kitchen and the task of cleaning up. "I'm sorry I don't have anything for dessert," she said.

"But you weren't expecting company," he said, speaking the words before she could.

"I guess I've made the point a few times."

"A few," he acknowledged, starting to load the dishwasher while she packed the rest of the meat and vegetables into a plastic container. "I'm still not sorry that I crashed your dinner party for one."

"I'm not sorry you did, either," she said, lifting her glass to her lips. "This is good wine."

He smiled. "I didn't think you'd admit that."

"That I like the wine?"

"That you like my company."

She opened the refrigerator to put the leftovers inside. "I never said that."

He chuckled as he closed the dishwasher. "I was reading between the lines."

She put the stoneware from the slow cooker in the sink and filled it with soapy water, then dried her hands on a towel.

When she turned away from the sink, he was right in front of her, trapping her between the counter and his body. *Déjà vu*, she thought. And in her kitchen, they really were in close quarters.

Braden lowered his head toward her. She went still, completely and perfectly still, as his lips moved closer to her own. Then he shifted direction, his mouth skimming over her jaw instead. The unexpected—and unexpectedly sensual caress—made her breath catch in her throat, then shudder out between her lips.

"Wh-what are you doing?"

"Well—" his mouth moved toward her ear, nibbled on the lobe "—you said there wasn't anything for dessert, and I was in the mood for something sweet."

Lust pulsed through her body, a relentless and throbbing ache. "And you think I'm...sweet?"

"I think you are incredibly sweet," he told her, his mouth skimming leisurely down her throat.

"Um—" she had no idea what to say to that "—thank you?"

She felt him smile, his lips curving against the ultrasensitive spot between her neck and collarbone. "You really have no idea how you affect me, do you?"

"I know how you affect me," she admitted.

"Tell me," he suggested, his mouth returning to brush lightly over hers.

"You make me feel things I haven't felt in a very long time."

His lips feathered across her cheekbone. "What kind of things?"

Her fingers dug into his shoulders. "Hot. Needy. Weak."

"You make me feel all of those things, too," he assured her.

"When you kiss me...when you touch me...you make me forget all the reasons this is a bad idea."

He put his hands on her hips and lifted her onto the counter so that they were at eye level. He spread her thighs and stepped between them. "So maybe this isn't such a bad idea," he suggested, then covered her mouth again.

As if of their own volition, her legs wrapped around him, drawing him closer. So close that she could feel the ridge of his arousal beneath his zipper. She pressed shamelessly against him, wanting to feel his hardness against her. Inside her.

His hands slipped under her top, skimming up her belly to her breasts. She couldn't remember what kind of underwear she'd put on that morning—whether it was cotton or satin or lace. Lace, she decided, as his thumbs brushed over the nipples through the whisper-thin fabric, sending sharp arrows of sensation from the beaded tips to her core.

He made her want with an intensity and desperation that she'd never experienced before. Even in high school, when many of the other girls were slaves to their hormones, she'd spent most nights at home, alone. She'd been the quiet girl, the geeky girl. Most of the boys hadn't looked at her twice. She was too smart and flat-chested to warrant their notice. And that was okay—because she didn't want to be distracted from her plans and she especially didn't want to be like her mother.

She imagined that Braden had been one of the popular boys. Smart and rich and devastatingly good-looking. He certainly kissed like a man who had a lot of experience. And he knew just where and how to touch her so that her only thoughts were *yes* and *more*.

He was the type of guy who'd dated the most popular girls—the cheerleaders or varsity athletes. The type who never would have noticed her. And although they weren't in high school now, he was the CEO of a national corporation and she was a small-town librarian. In other words, he was still way out of her league.

But somehow, by some twist of fate, he was here with her now. Kissing her and touching her, and she was incredibly, almost unbearably, aroused. "Braden—"

He clamped his hands on the edge of the countertop and drew in a deep breath. "You want me to stop?"

She should say yes. She should shout it at the top of her lungs. What was happening between them was too much, too fast. She hadn't known him long and she certainly didn't know him well, but she knew that she wanted him and she hadn't felt such an immediate and intense attraction to a man in a very long time.

"Cassie?" he prompted.

"No." She shook her head. "I don't want you to stop."

"Tell me what you do want."

She lifted her eyes to his. "I want you to take me to bed."

The library had been Cassie's absolute favorite room in the house when she bought it, but since she'd converted the attic to a master bedroom suite, that had become a close second. The deeply sloped ceilings and dormer-style windows created a bright and cozy space that was, in her mind, the perfect place to snuggle under the covers.

To Braden, who stood about six inches taller than her, the space probably felt a little cramped. But he didn't complain when she led him up the narrow stairs and over to the queen-size four-poster bed set up in the middle of the room. Of course, that might have been because his mouth was preoccupied with other matters—namely kissing her senseless.

And his hands, those wide and strong hands, were touching her in all the right places, further heating the blood that coursed through her veins. He found the tiny zipper at the back of her skirt with no trouble at all, and then the skirt itself was on the floor at her feet. Less than a minute later, her blouse had joined it, leaving her clad in only a pale pink bra and matching bikini panties.

She wanted to touch him, too, but her fingers fumbled as they attempted to unfasten the buttons of his shirt. She'd only worked her way through half of them when he eased his lips from hers long enough to yank the garment over his head and toss it aside. Then her hands were sliding over warm, taut skin and deliciously sculpted muscles. He was so strong, so male, so perfect.

He hooked his fingers in the straps of her bra and tugged them down her arms as he skimmed kisses down her throat, across her collarbone. Then the front clasp of her bra was undone and he slowly peeled back the cups. She bit down on her tongue to prevent herself from apologizing for the small size of her breasts, because Braden didn't seem to have any complaints. And when his thumbs scraped over the nipples…*ohmy*, the frissons that sparked through her body.

Then he lowered his head to continue his exploration, and her own fell back as pleasure coursed through her body. He teased her with his tongue and his teeth, and when he took her breast in his mouth and suckled, her knees almost gave way.

He must have felt her tremble, because he eased her back onto the bed, and she drew him down with her. Though he was still half-dressed, she automatically parted her legs to fit him between them. His arousal was unmistakable and as her hips tilted instinctively to meet his, the glorious friction of the thick denim against the wisp of lace caused a soft, needy moan to escape from between her lips.

He pulled away from her just long enough to shed the rest of his clothes, then yanked her panties over her hips and tossed them aside, too. She wiggled higher up on the mattress, so that her head was cushioned on the mountain of pillows and so that his legs wouldn't be hanging off the end. He rejoined her on the bed and his mouth came down on hers again. Stealing a kiss. Stealing her breath.

If she'd thought about it, she would have come up with all kinds of reasons that this shouldn't happen. But with his mouth on hers and his hands stroking over her body, rational thought was impossible. Even coherent speech seemed beyond her grasp as she responded with only throaty sighs and needy whimpers.

And then, one desperate word, as common sense nudged its way into the middle of her true-life erotic fantasy.

"Condom," she gasped.

He groaned. "I don't have one."

Which probably wasn't surprising considering that he'd been married for so many years and, by his own admission, celibate in the year since his wife had died. Thankfully, she'd prepared for this possibility, remote though it had seemed at the time when she'd hidden the box of condoms among a variety of other items she'd purchased from the pharmacy.

"Top drawer of the night table."

He yanked open the drawer and found the box, tearing it open in his haste and scattering the strips of condoms all over the floor.

He swore; she giggled.

Finally, he had one of the little square packets in hand. Cassie tried to take it from him, but he held it out of reach.

"Not this time," he said. "I'm afraid if you touch me now, it will be over before we even get started."

"I think we've started," she said. "I'm so ready for you, I feel as if I'm going to explode."

"Sounds promising." He covered himself with the latex sheath, then parted her thighs and drove into her in one smooth thrust that made her cry out with pleasure.

Braden groaned his assent. "This…being inside of you… is even more incredible than I imagined."

Her cheeks flushed with pleasure. "You've imagined this?"

"Every night since I met you," he admitted.

She tilted her pelvis, pulling him even deeper. "So what happens next?"

He proceeded to tell her, in raw and graphic detail, how he wanted to pleasure her body. His words both shocked and aroused her, further heightening her anticipation. When he stopped talking, he focused his attention on doing everything that he'd promised. And it was exactly what she'd needed—and so much more.

When he was able to summon enough energy to move, Braden rolled off Cassie and onto his back. Now that blood flow had been restored to his brain, his mind was going in a dozen different directions. "I think we just shattered the world record for fastest simultaneous orgasms."

A surprised laugh bubbled out of her. "I feel so proud."

"You feel so good," he said, tightening his arms around her.

"If I'd had even an inkling that this might happen tonight, I would never have let you into my house," she told him.

"I didn't plan this. If I had, I would have been prepared," he said. "But I'm not the least bit sorry."

"Right now, I'm not sorry, either," she admitted.

It had been nearly a decade since he'd made love with a woman who wasn't his wife, and he'd expected to feel a little bit guilty after doing so. Regardless of the fact that his relationship with Dana had been deteriorating over the past several years, she'd still been his wife. But the minute he'd taken Cassie in his arms, all thoughts of Dana had been swept from his mind.

From the first moment that his lips touched hers, he hadn't thought of anyone but Cassie. He hadn't wanted anyone but Cassie.

"So where do we go from here?"

She nudged him toward the edge of the mattress. "You need to go home."

He didn't know whether to be insulted or amused by her ineffectual efforts to push him out of her bed. "You're kicking me out?"

"Don't you have to pick up Saige from your parents' house?"

He shook his head. "She's sleeping over tonight."

"Oh."

He slid his arm up her back and drew her closer. "Why are you so determined to draw lines and boundaries around what's happening between us?"

"Because if I don't, I'll try to turn this into something that it isn't," she admitted.

"Something like what?" he asked curiously.

"Like a happily-ever-after fantasy."

The admission gave him pause. Because he liked Cassie—and he *really* liked making love with Cassie—but he had no intention of falling in love with her. "You don't believe we can have a mutually satisfying physical relationship without making a big deal out of it?"

"I know that a couple of orgasms are not the foundation of a lasting relationship—"

"Three," he interjected. Then, in response to her blank look, he clarified. "You had three orgasms."

She blushed but didn't dispute his count. "The number is irrelevant. You have to—"

He silenced her words with a quick kiss. "Hold that thought."

She frowned at the command but didn't say anything else when he slipped from her bed. He'd noticed the small three-piece bathroom tucked near the stairs when she led him up to her bedroom. Thinking only of the necessity of dispensing with the condom, he wasn't paying attention to the shape of the space and, when he turned, rapped his head smartly on the sloped ceiling.

When he returned to the bedroom, rubbing his head, he saw that Cassie had wrapped herself in a short, silky robe and had scooped up the condoms that were scattered on the floor and stuffed them back into the broken box. He caught the edge of the drawer as it was closing and withdrew a strip from the box to set it on top of the table.

She looked at him, the arch of her brow as much a challenge as a question.

"I want to see if we can set another record," he told her. "For the world's slowest simultaneous orgasms this time."

"I'm not sure there really is such a record," she said dubiously.

"I don't care," he admitted. "I want to make love with you again."

Make love.

Those two little words stirred something inside of Cassie's heart. She was probably reading too much into the expression, especially considering that she would have been offended if he'd used the common crude vernacular. Still, there were other ways to describe the act, various euphemisms that he might have relied upon—such as the "mutually satisfying physical relationship" he'd already referenced. But she wanted to believe that what they'd shared was lovemaking, because she wanted to believe that hers wasn't the only heart involved in what was happening between them.

Except that she was trying to keep her heart *un*involved.

Yes, the experience of being naked with Braden had been beyond incredible, but she needed to maintain perspective here. He was a single father with a young daughter—a widower who had lost his wife barely a year earlier. It would be a mistake to believe that what they'd just shared was anything more than the result of an intense and mutual attraction or that it could lead to anything more than that.

"I have a habit of falling hard and fast," she admitted, as he eased her back down onto the mattress.

"Don't fall for me," he said. But with his lips skimming down her throat, and lower, it was really hard to concentrate on his words.

"I know I shouldn't," she acknowledged. "Because falling in love with a man who's still in love with the woman he married is a heartbreak waiting to happen."

He lifted his head to look at her. "You think I'm still in love with my dead wife?"

"It's okay, I know—"

"No," he said. "You don't."

She frowned at the certainty in his tone as much as the interruption.

He took a moment to gather his thoughts before he finally said, "The truth is, I'm only a widower because my wife was involved in a fatal car accident before she could divorce me."

"What?" she said, unable to make sense of what he was telling her.

"A few weeks before the crash…Dana told me that she wanted to move out," he admitted.

She couldn't imagine why a woman—especially a new mother—would choose to break up her family. Unless her husband was abusive or unfaithful. And though she couldn't imagine Braden being guilty of either of those offences, she was obviously missing something. "But… why?"

"Things hadn't been good between us for a long time," he confided. "I thought it was the stress of not being able to have a baby, and maybe that was a contributing factor, but obviously there was more going on than I realized. Only six weeks after we brought Saige home, Dana decided she couldn't do it—that she didn't really want to be a mother after all."

Cassie was stunned. She didn't understand why anyone would pursue adoption unless they were desperate to have a baby—or how anyone, when finally given the incredible gift of a child to raise, would suddenly decide that they didn't want to be a parent. "Oh, Braden," she said, her tone filled with anguish for him and what he'd been through.

"I'm only telling you this so you know that I'm not still missing my dead wife. I did grieve that her life was cut so tragically short—and I grieved for the loss of the life that I thought we were building together. But the truth is, the love we'd shared died long before she did."

"I'm so sorry," she said.

"The point of sharing that sordid tale wasn't to elicit sympathy," he told her. "It was to let you know that I'm with you because I want to be with *you*, because I don't want anyone but you."

Her heart began to fill with cautious joy and tentative hope. "Then this isn't…a one-night stand?"

"I sincerely hope not," he said.

The simple and earnest words tugged at her, but she struggled to maintain her balance. Because there was still a lot of distance between "not a one-night stand" and "forever after" and it would be a mistake to believe otherwise.

He tipped her chin up and brushed his lips over hers. "Now can we stop talking and start taking advantage of the hours we have left in this night?"

She lifted her arms to link them behind his head. "You don't want to hear all of my deep dark secrets?" she teased, in an effort to lighten the mood.

"Everyone has secrets," he said. "But unless you have six previous lovers buried in your backyard, I don't need to know all of them right now."

"Not six previous lovers, only one."

He paused, just a beat. "You only had one previous lover?"

She smiled sweetly. "No, I only buried one in the backyard."

His lips curved just before they settled on hers. "I'm willing to take my chances."

Chapter Eleven

Saturday dawned bright and sunny—a perfect day for a trip to Frazer's Butterfly Farm made even more perfect by the fact that Braden had persuaded Cassie to join him and Saige on their outing. As they toured the facility, his daughter was mesmerized by the graceful fluttering wings of the colorful insects and happy to watch them swoop and glide. When one landed on Braden's shoulder, he slowly bent down so that she could get a closer look. Saige's eyes grew wide and she clapped her hands excitedly.

Of course, the sudden movement and sharp noise startled the butterfly and it flew away again. But there were so many of them that it wasn't long before another one—and then two and three—ventured over to feed from the sugar paper Cassie carried in her hand. And while Saige obviously enjoyed watching them from a distance, she screamed like a banshee when one of them dared to land on the guardrail of her stroller.

But the winged creature didn't go far—flying away from Saige's stroller only to settle again on top of Cassie's head.

"I'm holding sugar paper in my hand—why do they keep landing on my head?" Cassie wondered.

"Because your hair smells like peaches," Braden noted.

"You think that's what's attracting the butterflies?" she asked skeptically.

"It's attracting me," he told her, dipping his head to nuzzle her ear.

Despite the warmth of the day, Cassie felt shivers trickle down her spine and goose bumps dance over her skin. She put a hand on his chest and pushed him away. Braden grinned but backed off—for now.

They walked through the education center, where they could view butterflies at various stages of development—from egg to larva to chrysalis to butterfly. They even got to see a butterfly emerging from its chrysalis. One of the expert guides advised them that it was about to happen, pointing out the wings clearly visible through the now-translucent casing and contrasting it to other encasements that were opaque and green in color. The emergence didn't take very long, and though Saige didn't really seem to understand what was happening, she was content to sit in her stroller and munch on some cereal O's while Braden and Cassie watched.

"I've never seen anything like this before," Braden admitted, as the butterfly unfurled its vibrant orange-and-black wings.

"It is incredible, isn't it?" she said.

"One of Saige's favorite stories is that one about the caterpillar that eats and eats and eats until it becomes a beautiful butterfly."

Of course, as a librarian, Cassie was familiar with the story. "She's probably disappointed to see these caterpillars aren't eating through cherry pie and lollipops."

"I think she's just enjoying being here," Braden countered. "But speaking of eating—are you hungry?"

"A little," Cassie admitted.

"Why don't we go find someplace to have our lunch?" he suggested.

"That sounds like a good idea to me."

So they made their way outside, where there were walking paths and gardens and picnic areas and play structures. As they followed along the path, Cassie noticed a trio of butterflies circling around the stroller. She leaned down beside the little girl to draw her attention to the pretty insects, only to discover that Saige was fast asleep.

"If she's tired, she can sleep anywhere, anytime," Braden told her.

Which she remembered from the first day he was with Saige at the library, when the little girl had fallen asleep in his arms. "It must be nice, to be that young and carefree, with no worries to keep you awake or interfere with happy dreams," she mused.

"What kind of worries keep you awake?" he asked, steering the stroller off the path and toward the dappled shade of a towering maple tree.

"Oh, just the usual," she said dismissively.

He took a blanket from beneath the stroller and spread it out on the grass. "Job? Bills? Family?"

Cassie helped him arrange the cover, then sat down on top of it, leaning back on her elbows and stretching out her legs. "Actually, I love my job, I live within my means and I don't have a family."

After checking on Saige to ensure that she was comfortable, he stretched out beside Cassie. "No one?"

She shook her head.

"I can't imagine what my life would be like without

my parents, brothers, aunts, uncles and cousins and their spouses and children," he said.

"You're lucky to have them," she noted. Then, "This is an unexpected side of you—I never would have guessed that you were the type to watch butterflies in the sky or eat lunch on the grass."

"It's a new side," he admitted. "I used to be focused on the business of Garrett Furniture almost to the exclusion of all else. And then, when Dana and I decided it was time to start a family, I shifted my focus to the business of having a baby."

"Sounds romantic," she said dryly.

He managed a wry smile. "It was at first. Candlelight dinners and midday trysts. But when nearly a year passed with no results, it became an endless succession of tests and doctor appointments and schedules."

"Did they ever figure out why she couldn't conceive?"

"She had a condition called anovulation. It's a pretty generic term with numerous possible causes and, depending on the origin, there are various treatment options, some of them highly successful. But not for Dana."

"I'm sorry," she said sincerely.

"It was a difficult time for both of us," he said. "And then, six months after we finally decided to pursue adoption, we got a call to meet Saige's mom."

"That must have been exciting."

"Exciting and daunting, because we knew that she was meeting with four other couples, too, in an effort to find the best home for her baby. Our odds were, at best, twenty percent, because there was always the possibility that she would decide none of the couples was suitable and expand her search.

"And then, even when she did choose us, we knew there was still a possibility that she might, at the last minute, change her mind about the adoption entirely and decide to keep her baby."

"I can only imagine what an emotional roller coaster that must have been."

He nodded. "We were so excited—and so afraid to admit that we were excited in case the baby that was finally so close at hand would be snatched out of our grasp." He looked at that baby stretched out and sleeping in her stroller now, and a smile touched the corners of his mouth. "Since she was born, not a single day has passed that I haven't thought about how incredibly lucky I am to have her in my life.

"But still, aside from the fact that I was getting a lot less sleep, my day-to-day life didn't change a lot. And I was pretty proud of myself that I managed to squeeze fatherhood into my busy schedule.

"Then, one morning when I was getting Saige dressed, she was looking at me and babbling nonsense and I saw something in her mouth. Actually two somethings. She'd cut her first teeth. Not that they looked much like teeth at that point—more like tiny little buds poking through her gums. But it suddenly struck me that those two teeth hadn't been there the day before. Except, when I thought about it, I couldn't say for certain that was true. It was a normal milestone in a baby's life—but it was huge to me because I'd almost missed it.

"That was when I forced myself to slow down a bit and vowed to not just appreciate but savor at least five minutes with my daughter every day."

"She's a lucky girl," Cassie said softly.

"I'm the lucky one," he insisted. "I just wish…"

"What do you wish?" she prompted.

"Lindsay said that she chose us because we could give her daughter what she couldn't—two parents."

"There was no way you could have known that your wife would die only a few months after Saige was born."

"But even if the accident had never happened, we wouldn't be together now," he reminded her. And he'd been devastated not just that Dana's senseless death obliterated any hope of a reconciliation, but because it meant he'd failed his daughter, that the family he'd promised to give to her wasn't ever going to exist.

Cassie touched a hand to his arm, a silent show of support.

"When I got to the hospital and talked to the officer who had responded to the accident scene and he told me what had happened, do you know what my first thought was?"

She shook her head.

"I thought, 'Thank God, the baby wasn't in the car with her.' Even through the shock of losing my wife, there was relief that Dana didn't have Saige with her when she was hit—that our baby was safe."

"And you feel guilty about that," she realized.

"Hell, yes," he admitted. "I'd just found out that my wife was dead and, instead of being grief-stricken, I was relieved."

"You weren't relieved that she'd died—you were relieved that you hadn't lost your child, too," Cassie pointed out gently.

Braden nodded, accepting that she was right. And he was grateful that he'd found the courage to tell her about the feelings he'd never been able to speak about before, because her understanding helped him to finally attain a small measure of peace.

Cassie gave his hand a reassuring squeeze.

"Now—you said something about food," she reminded him.

He unpacked the contents of the cooler: buns piled high

with meats and cheeses, carrot and celery sticks, seedless grapes and miniature chocolate chip cookies. There was even a bottle of sweet tea for them to share and a couple of juice boxes for Saige, paper plates and napkins—and antibacterial hand wipes.

"You sure know how to pack a picnic," Cassie remarked.

"There's nothing very complicated in here."

"Those cookies look homemade," she noted.

"Not by me."

"Your mom?" she guessed.

He nodded.

"Did you tell her that you'd invited me to spend the day with you and Saige?"

"No," he assured her. "The last thing I want to do is encourage my mother's matchmaking efforts."

Cassie smiled at that as she unwrapped a sandwich. "Are you sure that's what she's trying to do?"

"There's no way she would ever 'forget' Saige's sock monkey anywhere unless it was on purpose."

"And what do you think was her purpose?"

"To put you in my path—or attempt to."

"She did seem disappointed to learn I wasn't there when you showed up to get the monkey," she acknowledged, nibbling on her sandwich.

"And since that failed, I'm guessing her next move will be to invite you to dinner at her house—and then she'll invite me and Saige, too," he warned.

"Do you really think she'd be that obvious?"

"She thinks she's subtle," Braden told her. "She invited the neighbor's single granddaughter to my brother Justin's thirty-fifth birthday party because she felt it was time he met a nice girl and settled down."

"And how did that work out?"

"Not the way she'd planned. Of course, she didn't

know—no one knew—that he'd already hooked up with Avery by then. And since they're happily married now, my mother considers it a win, especially since they've given her another grandchild. But she wants lots of little ones running around, which is why she's turned her attention to me again."

Cassie popped a grape into her mouth. "And how do you feel about that?"

"Well, I certainly can't fault her taste," he said.

"I have a horrible track record with men," she confided. "I tend to fall hard and fast and always for the wrong guys. Megan thinks that's because I grew up without a dependable father figure."

"Because your dad died when you were young," he remembered.

"And because he was an Army Ranger who, even before he died, was gone a lot more than he was home."

"Do you remember much about him?"

"Not really," she admitted. "Mostly I remember my mom always being so excited when he was coming home. She'd make sure the house was clean from top to bottom, she'd buy a new outfit, spritz on her favorite perfume, cook his favorite foods. She'd even dress me up in my prettiest clothes and braid ribbons into my hair.

"I loved my dad, but I didn't know him. Even when he was home, he seemed so distant and unapproachable. Now I would probably say haunted, although back then I just thought he was grumpy. I didn't look forward to him coming home, because I always knew he would go away again. And when he did, my mom would cry for days.

"She was a true Southern belle," Cassie explained. "Born in Savannah and accustomed to the attention and adoration that were her reward in the beauty pageant circuit. From what I've been told, my father fell for her, hard and fast. They had a whirlwind courtship and married after knowing each other only three weeks.

"After he died, she dated a few other guys, but none of them stuck around for long. I think I was twelve when she met Ray—an Episcopalian minister, widowed, with two sons. Eric and Ray Jr.—we called him RJ. My mom was a widowed military spouse with two daughters. I think she had some kind of image of us being a modern day Brady Bunch."

"So you have a sister?" he prompted.

She shook her head and wrapped her sandwich up again, her gaze focused on the task. "Had. Amanda was four years younger than me, and only ten when she died."

"What happened?"

Cassie took a minute, carefully wiping her fingers on a napkin, sipping the sweet tea he'd poured for her. "She'd gone fishing with Eric and RJ—just out to the pond at the back of Ray's property. They didn't usually catch anything, but they would spend hours out there trying, anyway. Amanda loved to follow the boys around—" she shook her head, her eyes shining with unshed tears "—no, she loved to follow *me* around, to pepper me with questions about everything until I told her to get lost.

"She wanted me to play some kind of game with her… I don't even remember what it was…but I told her I was busy and suggested that she go bug the boys. So she did, and they gave her a fishing pole and let her tag along. And I stayed in the house, studying for a science test because I was barely holding on to an A-minus and I knew I wouldn't be able to get a scholarship if my grade dropped."

"You were thinking about scholarships in tenth grade?" he asked, not just because he was surprised by the fact but because the anguish in her voice warned him where the story was going and he wanted to give her the option of a detour.

"When you grow up with limited financial resources, you need to think about all other options," she told him matter-of-factly. Then she fell silent for a moment before she steered the conversation back onto its original path. "So Amanda went off with the boys and I went back to my books, grateful for the peace and quiet.

"It was a long time later before RJ came racing back to the house. Apparently Amanda caught a small sunfish and was leaning forward to pull it out of the water when she lost her balance and fell in. But she was a good swimmer, so the boys weren't worried at first. They just watched the surface of the water, waiting for her to come up." Her gaze dropped away, but not before he saw that tears were now trembling on the edge of her lashes.

"Mom and Ray weren't home, so I was the only one there when RJ came running back to the house. I jumped into the pond where they said she'd gone in, and I pulled her out of the water."

There was nothing he could say to ease the pain he heard in her voice, a pain he knew she still felt deep in her heart, so he only put his arms around her and held her tight.

"Eric called 9-1-1 while I tried to remember the basic CPR I'd been taught in my babysitting course, but I knew she was already gone."

"I'm so sorry, Cassie."

"I was devastated." The admission was barely a whisper. "But my mother…my mother never recovered from losing Amanda. I don't know if she blamed herself for not being there or if losing both a husband and a child proved to be too much for her.

"She started to drink, as if the alcohol might fill up the emptiness inside of her, and she didn't stop. Six months later, she was dead, too—hit by a car when she was walking home from the bar one night."

And as horrific as it must have been for her mother to have lost that husband and child, he could not begin to imagine how much worse it had been for Cassie to have lost her father, her sister and then her mother. He wondered how she'd survived the devastation—and marveled over the fact that she had.

"The police ruled it an accident, but I'm not so sure," she admitted. "Maybe she was so drunk that she unknowingly stumbled into the middle of the road—or maybe she saw the headlights and wanted to make the pain go away forever."

He didn't know what to say to that. He wanted to reassure her that no mother grieving the loss of one child would willingly abandon another, but he didn't really know what her mother's state of mind had been. Maybe she had been so focused on everything she'd lost, she couldn't see what she had left.

"Ray, regularly prone to fits of temper, was always angry after that. He was furious with my mother for leaving him—and for leaving him with another kid. He'd frequently used scripture not as a comfort but as a weapon, and after my mother died, it got even worse. I went to church every Sunday, and sat beside the boys as he pontificated about sin. But even at home, the preaching never stopped, and when the words stopped being enough to satisfy his rage…he started to use his hands."

"He hit you?"

"Not just me," she said quietly, then shrugged. "Although I was the usual target."

"Did you tell anyone?"

"Who was I going to tell? I had no one. My father, my sister, my mother…they were all gone."

Listening to her talk about the experience, he couldn't even imagine what she'd gone through, how she must have felt. He only knew how he felt right now—furious and impotent—and he knew that if he could, he would go back in time and use his own hands on her stepfather.

"Please tell me that somebody did something," he implored.

"I spent a lot of time at the library when I was in high school," she reminded him. "And there's not much that gets past Irene. She took me to the hospital so there would be a documented record of my bruises, which prompted interviews by the police and family services. Of course, Ray had alternate explanations for my injuries—not the least of which was that I was absentminded and clumsy, never paying attention to where I was going and walking into things.

"The police officer who came to talk to Ray was sympathetic to the twice-widowed father trying to raise a teenage stepdaughter who wouldn't listen to anything he said—as Ray described the situation. Family services took a slightly harder line, offering counseling and insisting that he take an anger management course."

Braden was incredulous. "They didn't remove you from the home?"

"He was a minister—a pillar of the community."

He shook his head. "Sometimes the system really sucks."

"Sometimes it does," she agreed. "But the next time he knocked me around, Irene insisted on taking me to church for the Sunday service, and she wouldn't let me cover up any of the bruises. After the service, she met with the church elders, who later suggested that Ray might benefit from a change of scenery and offered him a position in Oregon."

"They should have offered him a position in the chaplain's office at Central Prison."

She managed a small smile. "He might have preferred that. In his eyes, losing the church in Charisma—where both his father and grandfather had preached before him—was a harsher punishment than being behind bars."

"Not harsh enough," Braden insisted.

"So Ray went to Oregon, RJ and Eric went to live with their maternal grandparents and I was supposed to be placed in a group home."

"Why a group home?"

"Because not many foster parents want an angry and grieving teenager living under their roof," she explained. "But I got lucky. By some miracle, a woman came forward for consideration as a foster parent and she was willing to take in an older child. A few days later, I was placed in her care."

And though Cassie didn't mention the woman's name, Braden knew—and he realized that he had severely misjudged Irene Houlahan.

Chapter Twelve

Cassie enjoyed the time she spent with Braden and Saige at the Butterfly Farm, but she was glad to go home alone at the end of the day. She'd poured her heart out to him—told him things that she'd never told to anyone else. And she suspected he'd done the same when he'd revealed the personal details of his marriage.

Somehow, the sharing of confidences seemed more intimate even than the physical joining of their bodies. As a result, she needed some space and time to think about everything that had happened on the weekend—and how to categorize their relationship. Were they friends? Friends with benefits? More?

Did he want more?

Did she?

She had yet to answer that question in her own mind when he called Wednesday afternoon while she was still at the library.

"How about dinner at my place tonight?" he suggested.

"What are you making?"

"Shrimp and grits," he told her.

"Mmm… I haven't had shrimp and grits in…years," she admitted.

"Is that a yes to dinner?"

"That's a definite yes."

"What time do you want to eat?" he asked.

"I finish at four today, so anytime after is good," she told him.

"Our usual dinner time is six, so we'll stick with that," he decided. "Do you want us to pick you up?"

"No, I'll drive myself so that you don't have to drag Saige out again to take me home."

"Okay," he relented. "I'll see you tonight."

"I'll see you tonight," she confirmed, and disconnected the call.

"Who are you seeing tonight?" Megan asked curiously from behind her.

Cassie sighed. "There is absolutely no privacy around here."

"What do you expect in a *public* library?" her friend teased.

"Good point," she acknowledged.

"So?" Megan prompted. "Was that the very handsome and rich Braden Garrett on the phone?"

"Yes," she admitted.

"And what is the plan for tonight?"

"Dinner."

"At his place," her friend mused.

Cassie frowned. "How long were you listening?"

"Long enough to know that shrimp and grits are on the menu," her coworker admitted unapologetically. "But the real question is…what's for dessert?"

Of course, that inquiry made Cassie remember the night she hadn't offered Braden any dessert, when his craving for something sweet had led to him kissing her—and the kissing had led to her bedroom.

"Well, well, well." Megan folded her arms on the counter and grinned. "The man is certainly doing something right if that dreamy look in your eyes and the flush in your cheeks is any indication."

"It's not the big deal you're making it out to be," Cassie protested.

"But the two of you are…dating?"

"No." She wondered how her friend would respond if she said, "just sleeping together," but decided the shock value of the revelation wasn't worth the plethora of questions that would inevitably follow.

Her friend arched a brow. "Having dinner together sounds like a date to me."

"I'm having dinner with Braden *and his daughter*."

Megan ignored the clarification. "And you and Braden have really hot chemistry together."

Cassie shook her head. "I never should have told you about that kiss."

"The way the temperature soars whenever he's around you, I'm thinking there's been more than that one kiss." Which proved that she'd been keeping a close eye when Braden visited the library to return books he'd borrowed and check out new ones.

"It doesn't matter how many kisses—" or how much more than kisses "—there have been," she told her.

"I'm just happy to see that you're putting out—I mean, putting yourself out there," Megan teased.

Cassie felt her cheeks burn. "I think I'm going to call him back and cancel."

"Don't you dare," her friend admonished.

"Why not?"

"Because in the end, we always regret the chances we didn't take."

She lifted her brows. "Why does that sound like 'quote of the day' relationship advice?"

"Maybe because I read it on Pinterest."

Cassie couldn't help smiling as she shook her head. "Isn't that Introduction to Social Media group waiting for you in the Chaucer Room?"

"I'm on my way. But remember," Megan said, as she headed away from the desk, "those who risk nothing often end up with nothing."

"Apparently you spend too much time on Pinterest."

"It's an addiction," her friend admitted. "But since I don't have a handsome man offering to make me dinner, I've only got a computer to go home to at night."

Of course, Megan disappeared before Cassie could respond, leaving her alone with her thoughts and concerns—and a niggling suspicion that her friend was right, and if she didn't take a chance with Braden, she might regret it.

But taking a chance required opening up her heart, and that was easier said than done. It wasn't just her failed engagement that made her reluctant to want to risk loving—and losing—again. In fact, her relationship with Joel was the least cause of concern to Cassie. Far more troubling was the fact that everyone she'd ever loved had left her in the end: her father, her sister, her mother and, yes, most recently her fiancé. Was it any wonder that she'd put up barriers around her heart when she found herself alone—again—after giving back Joel's ring?

Maybe she was a coward. Certainly she knew plenty of other people who had just as much reason to be wary but still found the courage to open up their hearts again. Like her coworker Stacey, who was thirty-nine years old, twice divorced and finally about to become a mother for the first time. Her first marriage had ended after only ten months when her husband decided that he just didn't want to be married anymore; her second marriage lasted for almost ten years before she finally left her abusive partner. It had taken years of counseling for Stacey to move on after that, but she'd finally done so, and she was blissfully happy with her new spouse and excited about having a family with him.

Obviously Stacey was braver than Cassie. Because as much as she wanted the happily-ever-after that her coworker had finally found, she was starting to suspect that some people were just meant to be alone. And maybe that was okay. Irene Houlahan was a perfect example of someone who'd never married or had any children of her own, and she seemed perfectly content with her life.

But even Cassie had to admit that, after seeing Irene in the company of Jerry Riordan these past few weeks, her friend had seemed more than content—she'd seemed happy. So maybe there was no harm in spending some time with Braden and enjoying his company.

Besides he'd promised her shrimp and grits, and she was hungry.

Cassie made a quick stop at home to feed the cats and change her clothes, opting for a pair of jeans and a short-sleeved knit sweater layered over a tank top because the wrap-style dress she'd worn to work only required a tug of the bow at her waist to come undone. And then, not wanting to show up at his house empty-handed after he'd brought wine and flowers for her, she made another quick stop on the way to his Forrest Hill address.

The contemporary two-story brick home on Spruceside Crescent was set back from the road and surrounded by large trees that gave the illusion of privacy despite the neighbors on each side. She pressed a finger to the bell, and heard the echo of a melodic chime that somehow suited the house and upscale neighborhood. He greeted her with a warm smile and a quick kiss, and it was only when he stepped carefully away from the door that she realized Saige was holding on to her father's pant leg.

The little girl tipped her head to peek around him and grinned at Cassie. "Hi."

"Hello, Saige."

"What's in the bag?" Braden asked curiously.

"It's for your daughter," she said, offering it to the little girl.

Saige reached her hand inside and pulled out the package of box cars. Not knowing what trains she had, Cassie had opted for the accessory cars that would attach to any of the engines. When the little girl realized what they were, her eyes grew wide.

"Ope!" she said, shoving the package at her daddy. "Ope!"

"Please," he reminded her.

"Ope, p'ease," she said obediently.

He tore open the package, freeing the box cars for his daughter.

"Now you say thank you to Cassie," he said, when he gave Saige the cars.

"Dan-koo," she piped up.

"You're very welcome," Cassie told her.

"P'ay?" Saige implored.

"You want me to play?"

The little girl nodded so vigorously her ponytails bounced up and down.

"I'd love to play, if your daddy doesn't need any help in the kitchen."

"I certainly wouldn't object to your company," he told Cassie, 'but if you'd rather play with Saige, that's okay with me."

So Cassie let Saige lead her to the living room where, in place of the coffee table she'd seen on her last visit, there was an enormous train table covered with curving tracks that went over bridges and through tunnels, winding this way and that with switches and turnouts and railway crossings, ascending pieces and risers, towers and moving cranes and even a roundhouse.

"Wow," Cassie said. "This is quite the setup."

"P'ay," Saige said again, setting her box cars on the track and linking them to the red engine—obviously her favorite.

She looked at the various engines and specialty cargo cars on the track. "What train do I get to play with?"

The little girl crinkled her forehead as she considered. She decided on a green engine and turned to hand it to Cassie, then abruptly changed her mind and set it back down again. Next she selected a blue engine, then put that one down again, too. At last she decided on an orange one.

"I'm guessing orange is not your favorite color," Cassie said.

Of course, Saige didn't respond. She was already engrossed in driving her engine and box cars around the track, halting obediently at a railway crossing as she steered a purple engine pulling a passenger coach through on another part of the track.

After about ten minutes, Cassie realized why it had been so difficult for the little girl to decide which engine to let her play with, because she took turns with all of them, hitching and unhitching box cars and cargo cars to each of them in turn as she did laps around the table. Cassie stayed near the quarry, using her engine to haul imaginary cargo from the work site to the storage shed—and moving out of Saige's way whenever she raced past with one of her engines, obviously driving an express and in a hurry to get wherever she was going.

"Who's hungry?" Braden asked, poking his head into the living room.

Saige responded by immediately abandoning her trains and racing to the kitchen.

"Your daughter's definitely worked up an appetite," Cassie told him.

"She loves that train table," he noted.

"Who wouldn't?" she agreed.

"Now to see if you love my shrimp and grits," he told her.

"Well, they smell delicious."

He had a bottle of his favorite Pinot Noir in his wine rack and though she protested that she had to drive home, he opened it, anyway. She decided she would have one glass and no more—because she didn't want to give herself any excuses for staying, no matter how much she wanted to.

Of course, the man himself was much more potent than any amount of alcohol, and the more time she spent with him the more time she wanted to spend with him. And after her first taste of the meal he'd prepared, she realized that he'd seriously understated his culinary capabilities. The flavors enticed her tongue—his shrimp and grits every bit as good as what her mother used to make.

"Is something wrong?" Braden asked.

"No," she immediately responded. "Why would you think that?"

"Because you stopped eating and started pushing your food around on your plate."

"This is really delicious," she assured him, stabbing her fork into a shrimp, and then popping it into her mouth.

"So where did your mind wander off to?"

She finished chewing, swallowed. "I was remembering the last time my mom made shrimp and grits."

"Good memories?" he prompted hopefully.

She nodded. "Very good."

He topped up her glass of wine.

"I'm driving," she reminded him.

"Eventually," he agreed.

She picked up her glass and took a tiny sip. "Your daughter is obviously a fan of your cooking," she remarked.

"Saige is a fan of food," he told her.

"You're lucky—some kids can be finicky eaters."

He nodded. "My cousin's daughter, Maura, was an incredibly finicky eater when she was little. For almost two years, she hardly ate anything more than chicken fingers, sweet potatoes—but only if they were in chunks, not mashed—and grapes."

"Well, at least she was getting some protein, vegetable and fruit," Cassie noted.

"True," he acknowledged. "And while Saige doesn't turn her nose up at too many things, I'm not sure how much food actually ends up *in* her rather than *on* her."

Cassie had noticed that the little girl's determination to feed herself resulted in a fair amount of food on her face, dribbled down her shirt and in her hair. "I'm guessing that bath time follows dinnertime."

"And you'd be right."

"Mo," Saige said, shoving her empty plate toward him.

"How about dessert?" Braden suggested, catching the plate as she pushed it over the edge of the high chair tray.

"Zert!" she agreed happily, clapping her sticky hands together.

"Cassie?" he prompted.

"I very rarely say no to dessert," she admitted. "But I don't think I could eat another bite."

"Not even a bite of lemon meringue pie?"

She groaned. "You do know how to tempt a girl."

He grinned. "Is that a yes?"

"It's an I wish but still no."

"Zert!" Saige demanded.

"Coming right up," Braden promised his daughter.

He carried the stack of dinner plates into the kitchen. Cassie wanted to help him clear up, but she didn't want to leave Saige unattended, so she stayed where she was and did her best to clean up the little girl with her napkin.

When Braden returned, she saw that he carried a wet cloth in addition to the bowl containing his daughter's dessert. He set the bowl on the table and pretended to look around for her. "Saige? Where are you?"

The little girl giggled.

He turned his head from left to right and back again. "I can hear her but I can't see her."

Saige giggled again.

"Wait a minute—" He held out the cloth, then swiped it over his daughter's face, scrubbing away the remnants of her dinner. "There you are. You were hiding behind all those cheesy grits."

Saige grinned as she held out her hands for him to clean, too, in what was obviously a post-dinner ritual. Braden complied, then set the bowl on her tray table.

The little girl's dessert was flavored gelatin cut into squares that she could easily pick up, and she immediately dipped her hand into the bowl.

"Apparently you are a man of many talents," Cassie noted.

Braden shook his head. "I can't take credit for dessert.

My mother made the Jell-O squares, and the pie that you said you don't want came from The Sweet Spot."

The downtown bakery he credited was legendary for its temperamental pastry chef—and its decadent desserts. "Now I'm really sorry I don't have room for pie."

"We can always have our dessert after."

"After what?" she asked warily, watching as Saige curled her fingers around a square and lifted it from the bowl to her mouth.

He smiled. "Whatever."

"Braden," Cassie began, but the rest of what she intended to say was forgotten as Saige held a second square of gelatin out to her in silent offering. "Oh…um…is that for me?"

"Zert," Saige told her.

"Well, there's always room for Jell-O, isn't there?" she said, and opened her mouth.

It was his own fault that he'd been caught unaware.

Braden had been so focused on enjoying the time that he was spending with Cassie—and watching Saige and Cassie together—that he'd forgotten about Lindsay's telephone call only a week and a half earlier. He'd forgotten that his happiness was like a precarious house of cards, and that an unexpected puff of air—or an unannounced visitor—could cause it to tumble down around him.

Saige was finishing up her Jell-O when the doorbell rang, and he left Cassie in the kitchen with his daughter while he responded to the summons.

He opened the door, and his heart stalled. "Lindsay."

"Hello, Mr. Garrett." A smile—quick and a little uncertain—immediately followed her greeting. "I'm sorry to drop by uninvited, but I've been driving around for hours, not sure if I was actually headed in this direction."

"Did you want to come in?"

She nodded. "I want to see Saige."

Braden stepped away from the door. "You know you're always welcome."

"I know that visitation was part of our original agreement—but a lot of things have changed since Saige was born. In fact…I'm getting married at the end of the summer."

"Congratulations."

"Thanks." She tucked her hands in her pockets and rocked back on her heels. "The thing is…"

Whatever else she intended to say was temporarily forgotten as her gaze moved past him, and he knew, even before he turned, that Cassie was there with Saige in her arms.

"There's your daddy," Cassie said, halting abruptly when she saw that he wasn't alone. "Oh, I'm sorry. I didn't realize you had company."

"This is Lindsay," he told her. "Saige's birth mother."

"Oh," she said again, her gaze shifting from Braden to Lindsay and back again. "Hi."

Lindsay returned the greeting stiffly.

"Da-da!" Saige, oblivious to the tension, lifted her arms to reach out to him, and Cassie transferred the baby to him.

Lindsay's tear-filled gaze followed the little girl. "She's grown so much," she said softly. "She's even bigger than she was in the photos you sent of her first birthday."

He nodded.

"I'm, um, going to finish up in the kitchen," Cassie said, backing away.

"Nanny?" Lindsay asked, when Cassie had gone.

"No." He set Saige on her feet by the train table and settled into a chair, then gestured for Lindsay to sit.

She perched on the edge of the sofa, her hands twisting the strap of her oversize purse as if she needed to keep them busy to prevent herself from reaching out to the little girl.

"Saige doesn't have a nanny. She's with me most of the time and, when I'm at work, my mom takes care of her."

"It's nice that your family helps out," Lindsay acknowledged, opening her purse now and withdrawing an envelope. "But a little girl needs a mother." Then she lifted her chin and handed the envelope to him. "And I *am* her mother."

Chapter Thirteen

Even before Braden opened the flap and pulled out the papers, he knew what he would find inside: an application to reverse Saige's adoption. And though he understood and even—to an extent—empathized with her position, he had to believe that the law was on his side. That belief was all that allowed him to maintain a semblance of calm when he was feeling anything but.

"Not according to the State of North Carolina," he finally responded to her claim, his tone gentle but firm.

"An adoption can be reversed," she insisted.

He slid the papers back into the envelope and set it on the table beside him. "Usually only with the consent of the adoptive parents."

She frowned at that.

"I don't know who's giving you legal advice, Lindsay, but I can assure you that no judge is going to overturn an adoption sixteen months after the fact."

"But what if it's in the best interests of the child?" she persisted.

"She hasn't seen you in more than a year," he pointed out. "Do you really think it would be in her best interests to be taken away from everything she knows, and everyone who loves her, and placed in your care just because there's a biological bond between you?"

Lindsay's lower lip quivered as her eyes filled with tears. "I love her, too."

"I know you do," he acknowledged. "That's why you wanted a better life for her than you could give her on your own."

"But I'm not on my own now. And when I told Charles that I had a child, why I gave her up, and about you now being a single parent to Saige, he said she would be better off with us."

"I appreciate that you're thinking about what's best for Saige," he said, "but I promise you, staying here—where she's lived her entire life and where she has the love and support of my extended family and with whom she's bonded emotionally—is the best thing for her."

Lindsay swiped at the tears that spilled onto her cheeks.

"Look at her, Lindsay," he instructed, though the young woman hadn't stopped doing that since Saige had entered the room. "Do you really want to tear her away from the only home she's ever known? The only parent she's ever known?"

She choked on a sob, the ragged sound drawing Saige's attention from her trains to her visitor.

"Choo-choo," she said, holding up her favorite red engine.

Lindsay sniffled. "That's a pretty awesome choo-choo," she said, and was rewarded with a beaming smile.

"P'ay?" Saige invited.

She dropped to her knees on the floor beside the table and reached for a green engine. Saige immediately snatched it away.

"Saige," he admonished softly. "What have I told you about sharing?"

She set the green engine on Braden's knee, indicating her willingness to share with her daddy, then selected a yellow engine from the track for the visitor.

Lindsay, apparently happy just to be interacting with the little girl, began to move it around the winding track.

"So...the woman in the kitchen," she said, glancing up at him through red-rimmed eyes. "Is it serious?"

He knew that the question didn't indicate a shift in the topic of their conversation but was actually an extension of it. And of course, the honest answer was that his relationship with Cassie was still too new to be categorized. However, he knew that response wouldn't assuage her concerns, so he gave her one that would. "Yes, it is."

Lindsay was quiet for a moment before she said, "Saige seems to like her."

"Saige adores Cassie—and the feeling is mutual."

She watched the little girl play for several more minutes. "She seems happy," she finally acknowledged. "Here. With you."

"She is happy," he confirmed.

Her eyes again filled with tears as she watched Saige abandon her trains and raise her arms toward Braden, a silent request to be picked up. He lifted her onto his lap, and she immediately rubbed her cheek against his shoulder and stuffed a thumb in her mouth.

"I guess I just needed to see her again, to know it was true," she admitted softly. "I thought maybe she needed me...but it's obvious that she doesn't."

"Not being needed isn't the same as not being wanted," he told her.

She seemed surprised by that. "You'd still be willing to let me visit?"

"That was always our agreement," he reminded her.

She managed a smile. "Maybe I knew what I was doing when I chose you for Saige."

"I like to think so."

"I'll talk to my lawyer about withdrawing the court application," she said.

"I'd appreciate that."

His daughter yawned and tipped her head back to look at him. "Kee?"

"You can have your monkey after your bath," he promised.

Lindsay blinked. "Monkey?"

He nodded. "The sock monkey you gave to her when she was born—she won't go to sleep without it."

This time, Lindsay's smile came more easily. "And she's obviously ready for sleep now," she decided. "So I should be going."

Braden rose from the chair with Saige in his arms. "Can you say bye-bye to Lindsay?"

"Bye-bye," she said, and yawned again.

After a brief hesitation, Linday stepped forward and touched her lips to Saige's cheek. "Night-night, sweetie."

"Bye-bye," the little girl repeated.

"I'll come back to visit again," Lindsay told him. "But next time, I'll call first."

Cassie was just putting the last pot away when Braden and Saige returned to the kitchen. "Where's Lindsay?"

"She's gone," Braden told her.

"That was a short visit," she said cautiously. "Is everything okay?"

"I hope so," he said. "We cleared the air about a few things while you were clearing up in here—so thank you."

Though she had a ton more questions about the young woman's obviously impromptu visit, she held them back, saying only, "Thank *you* for the delicious meal."

"Why don't you relax with a glass of wine now while I get this one—" he glanced at Saige "—bathed and ready for bed?"

"Can I help?"

"If you want, but I should warn you—the whole bathroom can become a splash zone."

"I won't melt," she assured him.

As Cassie followed Braden up the stairs, she saw that the monochromatic color scheme continued on the upper level. His house was beautiful but incredibly bland and she wondered why he hadn't made any changes to the decor since his wife's death. Of course, the little girl in his arms was probably the answer to that question—no doubt Saige kept him so busy that painting was the last thing on his mind. But she couldn't help but think his daughter would benefit from a little color being added to her surroundings.

So she was pleasantly surprised to see that Saige's bedroom was beautiful and colorful. The room was divided horizontally by white chair rail, with the lower part of the walls painted a rich amethyst color and the upper part done in pale turquoise. On the wall behind Saige's crib, her name had been painted in dark purple script with the dot above the *i* replaced by a butterfly. A kaleidoscope of butterflies in various shapes and sizes flew across the other three walls so that the overall effect was colorful and fun and perfect for a little girl.

"This is amazing," Cassie said, as she traced the outline of a butterfly and realized it wasn't a decal but hand-painted.

"My cousin, Jordyn, helped decorate in here."

"She's incredibly talented," she noted. "Of course, she is Jay Addison, the illustrator of graphic novels."

"How did—" He shook his head, realizing the answer even before he'd finished asking the question. "My mother."

Cassie nodded. "She was at the library when I was un-packing the latest installment of A. K. Channing's series."

"Apparently she spends a lot more time at the library than I ever realized."

"Some people golf, others knit, your mother likes to read." She noted the bookshelf above the little girl's dresser. "And she's obviously passed her love of books on to her granddaughter."

"Saige never goes to sleep without a story," he admitted.

"Wee?" his daughter echoed hopefully.

"*After* your bath."

Which turned out to involve a lot of plastic toys and plenty of splashing, resulting in a more exhausting and time-consuming process than Cassie had anticipated. When Saige was finally clean and dry and dressed for bed, Braden asked Cassie if she could keep an eye on the baby while he cleaned up the bathroom. She happily agreed.

"P'ay?" Saige said hopefully.

"No play," her father said firmly. "It's bedtime."

"Wee?"

"Yes, Daddy will read you a story in a little bit," he promised. "Why don't you let Cassie help you pick out a book?"

His daughter took Cassie's hand and led her across the room to the bookshelf. Apparently she knew what story she wanted, because as soon as Cassie lifted her up, she grabbed *Goodnight Moon* and hugged the book to her chest.

"Kee," Saige said.

"Hmm…you're going to have to help me with that one," Cassie said. At the Book & Bake Sale, the little girl had said "kee" when she wanted a cookie, but Cassie didn't think that was what she wanted now.

"Kee," she said again, stretching out her free hand toward her bed.

"Ahh, *monk*ey," Cassie realized, plucking the toy out of the crib.

Saige took the monkey from her and hugged it to her chest, too.

"All set now?"

The little girl nodded, even as her mouth opened wide in a yawn.

Cassie carried her to the rocking chair by the window and sat down with the baby in her lap.

Saige looked toward the door. "Da-da?"

"He'll be finished up in a minute—after he wipes up all the water you splashed on the bathroom floor," Cassie guessed.

Saige responded by snuggling in to her embrace, the back of her head dropping against Cassie's shoulder. She lifted a fist—the one still clutching the sock monkey—to rub her eye.

"You're a sleepy girl, aren't you?"

Saige's only response was another yawn.

"Do you want me to read your story or are you waiting for Daddy?"

"Wee," Saige replied, offering her the book.

So Cassie took it from her hand and opened the cover. She began to read, not needing to look at the page to recite the words of the classic story she'd read aloud at the library more times than she could count.

And although it wasn't a long story, Saige's eyelids had

drifted shut before the little bunny had wished good night to half of the objects in the great green room. But Cassie read all the way to the last page before setting the book aside. Still, the baby didn't stir.

Cassie continued to sit with her, the weight of the little girl in her arms filling her heart and reminding her of the dreams she'd tried to put aside. Dreams that had teased and tempted for many years but so far remained unfulfilled.

Tonight, Braden had given her a glimpse of the life she'd always imagined in her future. A home, a husband, a family. It wasn't so much—and yet it was everything she'd always wanted. And being with Braden and Saige, she was tempted to let herself dream again. To believe that she might one day be part of a family again, maybe even *this* family.

Of course, she was getting way ahead of herself. She hadn't known Braden very long and didn't know him very well, and it would be foolish to hope that one night could lead to a lifetime together.

You can't start the next chapter of your life if you keep rereading the last one.

Great—not only was Megan quoting words of wisdom from Pinterest, now those words were echoing in the back of Cassie's head.

Maybe it was clichéd advice—and maybe it was true. Maybe it was her own past experiences that were preventing her from moving forward with her life. And maybe, if she let herself open her heart, she might discover that Braden and Saige weren't just characters in her next chapter but in every chapter of the rest of her life.

It didn't take Braden long to wipe out the tub and dry off Saige's toys, but when he made his way across the hall after completing those tasks, his daughter was already asleep. And in that moment, looking at Saige snuggled contentedly in Cassie's arms, he knew: she was the one.

Cassie was the perfect mother for his little girl—the mother that Saige deserved.

Now he only had to convince her of that fact.

He didn't think it would be too difficult. Cassie had admitted that she wanted to be a wife and a mother and, coincidentally, he needed a wife and a mother for his daughter. It was, from his perspective, a win-win.

The fact that he didn't—wouldn't—love her, didn't have to be a barrier to a future for them together. He could be a good husband—affectionate and faithful—without opening up his heart. And he would do everything in his power to make Cassie happy, to show her how much he appreciated her presence in their lives.

"I think you have the touch," he said, speaking quietly from the doorway.

"It doesn't require any special magic to get an exhausted child to sleep," Cassie pointed out.

"If you were ever here at two a.m., you'd know that's not true," he commented dryly.

"She doesn't sleep through the night yet?"

"Most nights she does," he acknowledged. "But lately she's decided that two a.m. is playtime. She doesn't wake up because she's wet or hungry, she just wants to play. And then, after being up for half the night, she has a three-hour nap at my mother's house."

"Fiona, one of the moms in Toddler Time, went through something like that with her little guy," Cassie told him. "He would sleep at day care but not at home. According to her pediatrician, it's not uncommon with babies who want to spend time with their working parents."

"Well, giving up my job isn't really an option," he noted.

"And my mom's trying to break her of the habit by limiting her naptime during the day."

"That might be why she fell asleep so easily tonight," Cassie noted.

"Or maybe you tired her out, making her chase all of those trains around the track."

"You're giving me too much credit," she told him.

He shook his head. "I don't think so. I've seen you with the kids at the library—from babies to teens," he reminded her. "You have an instinctive ability to empathize and relate to all of them."

"I love working with kids."

"Did that broken engagement destroy all hope of having your own?"

"No," she denied. "But I would like to have a husband before the kids and, so far, that hasn't worked out."

"Well, maybe you'll luck out someday and meet a fabulous guy who already has a child," he suggested. "Perhaps an adorable little girl."

"That would be lucky," Cassie said lightly.

"Or maybe you've already met him."

"Maybe I have," she acknowledged. "And maybe I specifically recall the fabulous guy with the adorable little girl warning me not to fall for him."

He leaned down to lift his sleeping daughter from her arms and touch his lips to Cassie's. "But that was before he started falling for you."

He tucked Saige into her crib, ensuring that her sock monkey was beside her, then he took Cassie's hand and led her back downstairs.

"Why don't you sit down by the fire?" he suggested. "I'll be there in just a sec."

She went into the living room, but when he returned with their glasses and the rest of the bottle of wine, he saw that she was standing by the fireplace, looking at the photographs lined up on the mantel. Several were of Saige, the rest were various other members of his family.

She set down the picture in her hand—a candid shot taken at Lauryn and Ryder's wedding—and accepted the wine he offered.

"It was big news when they got married," she commented. "A daughter of Charisma's most famous family stealing the heart of America's hottest handyman."

He nodded. "But not quite as big as when my brother Ryan married Harper, daughter of soap actor Peter Ross. We had actual paparazzi in town to cover that event."

"It really is a small world, isn't it?" she mused. "The first time I ever saw Ryder Wallace was on *Coffee Time with Caroline*, which was produced by your sister-in-law, and now he's married to your cousin."

"And his sister is married to my brother Justin."

"Apparently it's even smaller than I realized."

"Especially if you're a Garrett," Braden remarked. "I swear, I can't move in this town without bumping into someone I'm related to. And it will only get worse when Ryan and Harper move back from Florida and Lauryn and Ryder return from Georgia."

"But you don't really mind," Cassie guessed. "I can tell by all these photos—and your mother's stories—that your family is close."

"We are," he agreed. "As much as they drive me crazy at times, I don't know what I would do without them."

"I miss that," she admitted.

"Being driven crazy?"

She smiled as she shook her head. "Being part of a family."

"A Day with the Garrett Clan might cure you of that,"

he suggested. And if she didn't run screaming, that would be his cue to take the next step.

"A Day with the Garrett Clan sounds like an event you'd sell tickets to," she teased.

"Maybe I'll suggest that in advance of the next family gathering, but this one is an informal welcome home barbecue at my parents' place on Sunday for Ryan, Harper and Oliver. You should come."

"If the whole family is going to be there, I'm sure your parents won't want extra people underfoot."

"Are you kidding? My mother is happiest in complete chaos—and I know she'd be thrilled to see you there."

"Aren't you worried that she might make a big deal out of me being there with you?" she asked cautiously.

He grinned. "*Everyone* will make a big deal out of you being there with me."

"Are you trying to talk me *into* or *out of* going to this barbecue?"

"Into," he assured her. "I very much want you there with me. I want you to meet my family and I want them to meet you."

Still, she hesitated. "I just think it might be too soon."

"Why?"

"Because I have a really lousy track record with relationships," she admitted.

"Most people go through a few failed relationships before they figure out how to make it work—or even realize that they want to." He slid his arms around her, drawing her closer. "We can make this work, Cassie."

"Do you really think so—or are you just saying that to get me into bed again?"

"If I wanted to get you into bed again, I wouldn't waste my breath on words," he said.

"What would—" She shook her head. "Forget it. I don't want to know."

He dipped his head, but paused with his lips hovering just a fraction of an inch above hers. "I think you do want to know. And I think you really want me to kiss you."

She responded by lifting her chin to breach the scant distance and press her mouth to his.

He believed what he'd said to her—that they could make a relationship work—and the powerful chemistry between them was only one of the many reasons. And when she was in his arms, it was an unassailable reason.

He knew a relationship required more than physical attraction. Passion was the icing on the cake rather than the base layer, more decorative than essential. But it was also able to transform something good into something spectacular. And making love with Cassie was spectacular.

He liked who she was and everything about her. She was warm and kind and compassionate, beautiful and smart and funny. He enjoyed spending time with her, talking to her and making love with her—but he wasn't going to fall in love with her.

It wasn't just that he was unwilling to risk heartbreak again—it was that he didn't have anything left in his heart to give to anyone else. The failure of his marriage—and the sense that he had failed the woman he'd vowed to love, honor and cherish—had undoubtedly broken a piece of his heart. But only a piece, because the rest was filled with the pure love he felt for Saige, and he didn't want or need anything more than that.

But his daughter did, and he owed it to Saige to give her the life that her birth mother wanted for her. A real family. A whole family. He didn't believe Lindsay would ever be able to take Saige away—and hopefully, after their conversation today, she wouldn't even try—but he did agree that his little girl needed a mother. And he couldn't imagine a woman who would be more perfect for the role than the one he was kissing right now.

They were both breathless when she finally eased away from him. He lifted a finger to her chin, tilting her head back so that he could look into her beautiful dark eyes. "Will you stay with me tonight?" he asked.

"For a while," she agreed.

"That's a start," he said, and led her down the hall.

Chapter Fourteen

Cassie was in way over her head.

She knew it, and she didn't care. When she was with Braden, when his hands were on her body, it was difficult to care about anything but how good he made her feel. And he instinctively knew how to make her feel really good.

She'd never had a lover who was so closely attuned to the wants and needs of her body, but Braden was nothing if not attentive. He used her sighs and gasps and moans to guide his exploration of her body, and his own lips and his hands to lead her slowly and inexorably toward the ultimate pinnacle of pleasure.

She followed not just willingly but eagerly, their discarded clothing marking the path to his bedroom. Somewhere in the back of her mind, she knew that they were venturing into dangerous territory—but she didn't care. Her body already knew him and wanted him and her heart refused to heed the warnings of her mind.

His hands stroked down her back, over the curve of her bottom, drawing her closer. She touched her mouth to his chest, and let her tongue dart out to taste his skin. He tasted good. Hot. Salty. Sexy. She skimmed her lips down his breastbone, then flicked her tongue over his nipple, eliciting a low growl of approval. She reached down between their bodies as her mouth moved to his other nipple, and wrapped her hand around the rigid length of him. She felt him jerk against her palm, and was pleased to know that he wanted her as much as she wanted him.

She started to move lower, her mouth trailing kisses down his belly, but he caught her arms and hauled her up again, his tongue sliding deep into her mouth in a kiss that was so hot and hungry it made her head spin and her knees tremble.

She tumbled onto the mattress, dragging Braden down with her. He pulled away only long enough to sheathe himself with a condom, then he parted her thighs and thrust into her. She gasped with pleasure, instinctively tilting her hips so that they were joined as deeply and completely as possibly.

He filled all her senses. She could see nothing but the intensity of his deep green eyes locked with her own; hear nothing but the roar of blood through her veins; taste nothing but the sweetest passion when his mouth covered hers again; feel nothing but the most exquisite bliss as their bodies merged and mated and…finally…leaped over the precipice together.

She was still waiting for her heart to stop racing when she heard a soft sound somewhere in the distance. While she was attempting to decipher what it was and from where it had come, Braden was already sliding out from beneath the covers that he'd yanked up over their naked bodies sometime after they'd collapsed together.

"I'll be right back," he said, brushing a quick kiss over her lips, having shifted gears from lover to father in the blink of an eye.

A moment later, she heard the soft murmur of his voice through the baby monitor that she now realized was on the bedside table. She couldn't hear what he was saying, but his tone was soothing, reassuring.

A few minutes later, she heard his footsteps enter the room again. She lifted her arm away from her forehead and peeled open one eyelid—then the second, when she saw that he was carrying an enormous wedge of lemon meringue pie on a plate.

"I thought you went to check on Saige."

"I did. She's fine," he assured her. "But I thought you might be ready for dessert now."

"That's for me?"

"It's for both of us," he said.

She wiggled up to a sitting position, tucking the sheet under her armpits to ensure she was covered.

He grinned. "It's a little late for modesty, don't you think?"

"I'm not going to sit here naked and eat pie," she protested.

He shrugged, broke off the tip of the pie with the fork and held it toward her—then pulled it away and ate the bite himself.

She frowned.

"Mmm…this is really good. The lemon is the perfect balance of sweet and tart and the meringue—" he cut off another piece, popped it into his mouth "—is so incredibly light and fluffy."

"You said that was to share," she reminded him.

"You give up the sheet and I'll give you some pie."

"Seriously?"

"Those are my terms," he told her.

She hesitated; he took another bite of the pie.

Her mouth watered as she watched the fork slide between his lips, swallowing up the flaky crust, tart filling and fluffy meringue, and she decided he was right—it was a little late for modesty.

She dropped the sheet; he grinned. This time, when he scooped up a forkful of pie, he held it close for her to sample. She could smell it—the tangy sweet scent—just before she parted her lips to allow him to slide the fork into her mouth.

She closed her eyes and sighed with blissful pleasure. "Oh, yeah. This is really good."

He lifted the fork again, but the pie slid off the tines and onto her thigh, near her hip. She yelped. "That's cold."

"Sorry," he said, even as he lowered his head to clean up the dessert with his mouth. He licked her skin thoroughly, making her suspect that the mishap might not have been an accident after all.

"Two can play that game," she warned him, and scooped some of the meringue off the pie with her finger, then smeared it on his belly before cleaning it up with her mouth.

He retaliated by dabbing lemon filling on each of her nipples and suckling the rigid peaks until she was gasping and squirming.

And so they went back and forth, taking turns savoring the dessert from one another's bodies. Then they made love again, the remnants of the pie creating a sticky friction between them and necessitating a quick shower afterward.

A shower that ended up not being so quick, as the slow, sensual soaping of one another's bodies had their mutual passion escalating again. When Braden finally twisted the knob to shut off the spray, it had started to go cold, and they were still dripping with water when they tumbled onto his bed again.

As Cassie drifted to sleep in his arms, she realized that she'd gone and done what she'd promised herself she wouldn't: she'd fallen head over heels in love with Braden Garrett.

Braden's maternal grandmother had been a resident of Serenity Gardens for the last ten years of her life. Of course, she'd passed away more than a dozen years earlier and the residence had undergone significant renovations and benefitted from a major addition since then. Thankfully, the main reception desk was in the same place and, after buzzing up to Irene Houlahan's room, he and Saige were cleared to find their way to Room 508 in the North Wing.

When they arrived at her door, it was ajar. He remembered that his grandmother had often left her door open, too, to welcome any neighbors who wanted to drop in for a visit. Still, he knocked on the portal and waited for Miss Houlahan's invitation before pushing the door wider.

The old woman was seated at one end of an overstuffed sofa in the living room, a thick hardcover book open in her lap. The permanent furrow between her brows relaxed marginally when her gaze lit on his daughter by his side, and she closed her book and set it aside. "Hello, Saige."

His little girl didn't have a shy bone in her body, and while he hovered on the threshold, she happily toddled across the room to the sofa. Once there, she climbed up onto the cushions, surprising Braden as much as Irene when she pursed her lips and kissed the old woman's wrinkled cheek.

"Well," Irene said, as if she wasn't quite sure how to

respond to the gesture. "It's not often that I have the pleasure of such a young visitor." Then she lifted her gaze to
Braden's. "And since you're not the Grim Reaper, you can
come in, too."

He fought against a smile as he stepped farther into
the room.

"I don't imagine you were just 'in the neighborhood,'"
Irene said.

"Not really," he admitted, setting the vase on the table
beside the sofa. "We came to deliver these."

Saige, having noticed the stack of photo books on the
coffee table, slid off the sofa again and reached for the one
on top. Braden caught her hands and gently pried them
from the cover. "Those are Miss Houlahan's books—
they're not for little girls."

"I always believed books were intended to be read by
anyone who was interested," Irene contradicted him. "But
I don't imagine pictures of coffee tables would be of much
interest to a toddler."

Braden had been so focused on ensuring his daughter
didn't damage the item he hadn't taken note of the cover,
but he did now. "A coffee table book about coffee tables?"

"Cassie's idea of a joke." She shifted forward and removed a different book from the bottom of the pile: *A Vibrant History of Pop Art.*

"This has some strange stuff in it but at least the pictures are colorful," she told him. Then she turned to his
daughter and asked, "Do you want to look at this one?"

Saige nodded and Irene set the book on the table in front
of her, then opened it up to the middle. Saige lifted all of
the pages from the front cover and pushed them over so
that she could start at the front.

"She knows how to read a book," Irene noted.

"We read every night before bed, and my mother takes her to the library a couple of times a week."

"A child who reads will be an adult who thinks," the former librarian said approvingly. "Now tell me what the flowers are for, because I'm not so old that I've forgotten when my birthday is and I know it's not today."

"Why does there need to be an occasion?" he countered.

"Because I've never known a man to bring flowers to a woman without one."

"Then maybe you've known the wrong men," he told her.

"You're trying to sweeten me up so I'll say good things about you to Cassie, aren't you?" she guessed.

He suspected it would take a lot more than a bouquet of flowers to do that, but he bit down on his tongue to prevent the thought from becoming words. "No," he denied. "I'm trying to say thank you."

"For what?" she asked, obviously still suspicious.

"For being there for Cassie when no one else was."

She scowled. "I don't know what you think I did—"

"I think you saved her life."

Irene snorted. "I did nothing of the sort."

"I don't mean literally," he explained. "But she told me about everything that happened the year her sister—and then her mother—died."

Irene peered at him over the rim of her glasses, her gaze speculative. "Cassie doesn't often talk about her family," she noted.

"She also told me that you appealed to the church to have her stepfather sent away—and gave family services the evidence they needed to ensure that he couldn't take Cassie with him."

"I didn't realize that she knew anything about that," Irene admitted.

"And then, because you recognized that she was just as terrified of the system as she was of her abusive step-father, you took her into your home."

"It wasn't a sacrifice to give her an extra bedroom."

He glanced at Saige, who was braced on her arms on the table, leaning close to scrutinize the details in the pictures.

"You gave her more than that," he said to Irene. "You gave her security, guidance and direction. You helped her focus on and achieve her goals."

"I didn't do any of it for thanks," she told him.

"I know, but I'm thanking you, anyway."

"Well, it was a nice gesture," she admitted, just a little begrudgingly.

He held back his smile. "If you give me a chance, you might find that I'm a nice guy."

"Maybe I will," she conceded, with just the hint of a smile tugging at her mouth.

The next day, when Cassie was visiting Irene, she saw the vase of colorful blooms prominently displayed on the coffee table.

"I see Jerry brought you flowers again," she noted.

"Those aren't from Jerry," Irene told her.

"Really?" She grinned. "You have another suitor in competition for your affections?"

Her friend sniffed. "Not likely. Those are from *your* suitor."

Cassie lifted a brow.

"Braden Garrett came to see me yesterday."

"He did?"

Irene nodded. "Brought his little girl with him—goodness, she's just a bundle of sweetness and joy, isn't she?"

"Saige is a very happy child," Cassie agreed.

"You've been spending a lot of time with them lately?"

"I guess I have," she agreed cautiously.

"A man like that, with a young child to raise, is a package deal," Irene warned her.

"I know."

"And you love them both already, don't you?"

There was no point in telling the old woman it wasn't any of her business. When Irene had taken an angry and grieving fifteen-year-old girl into her home, Cassie's business had become her business. Since that time, she'd been Cassie's legal guardian and surrogate mother, and she'd never hesitated to ask Irene for guidance and advice when she needed it. In the current situation, she decided that she needed it because her feelings for Braden and Saige had become so muddled with her own hopes and dreams that she feared she'd lost perspective.

"I do," she admitted.

"Why don't you sound happy about it?"

"Because I didn't want to fall in love with Braden," she admitted. "I didn't want to give him the power to break my heart."

"Loving someone is always a risk," Irene acknowledged.

"Please don't start quoting Pinterest advice to me."

"You don't need any advice—you just need to follow your heart."

"Because that's never steered me wrong in the past," Cassie noted dryly.

"Stop dwelling on the past and focus on the future," her friend suggested.

"That definitely sounds like Pinterest advice."

Irene handed Cassie the book she'd been reading during her previous visit.

"There's a lot of good stuff on Pinterest," she said. "But not a lot of men like Braden Garrett in the world."

* * *

Maybe Cassie should have made an excuse to get out of attending the welcome home party for Braden's brother and sister-in-law, but she was curious to see him interact with the whole family, and she wanted to be able to tell Megan—who was a huge fan of *Ryder to the Rescue*—that she'd met Ryder Wallace. Although his crew was still in Georgia finishing up the restoration of an antebellum mansion, he and his wife and their kids had returned to Charisma for the family event.

"It's a good thing your parents have a huge backyard," Cassie said, when they arrived at Ellen and John's residence.

"And that the weatherman was wrong in forecasting rain for today," Braden noted.

She looked up at the clear blue sky. "I guess even Mother Nature knows not to mess with Ellen Garrett's plans."

He chuckled. "You might be right about that."

As they made their way around the gathering, he introduced her to his aunts, uncles and cousins. When they crossed paths with Ellen, who was in her glory with so many little ones underfoot, she immediately whisked Saige away to play with her cousins. It seemed that everywhere Cassie looked, there were children and babies. And more than one expectant mother in the crowd, too.

Not long after they'd arrived, John dragged Braden away to man one of the extra grills that had been set up in the backyard. He was reluctant to leave Cassie's side, but she assured him that she would be fine. Although the words were spoken with more conviction than she felt, he took them at face value and accepted the chef's apron and long-handled spatula his father gave him.

"There's a gate by the garage," a pretty dark-haired woman said to her.

"Sorry?"

"You had that slightly panicked look in your eyes, as if you were searching for the nearest exit."

"Oh." Cassie blew out a breath and managed a smile. "I guess I am feeling a little overwhelmed. And I'm sorry—I know Braden introduced us, but I don't remember your name."

"Tristyn," the other woman said. "And there's no need to apologize. I sometimes feel overwhelmed at these gatherings, too, and I'm related to all of these people."

"When Braden said the whole family would be here, I didn't realize what that meant."

"There are a lot of us," his cousin agreed. "More and more every year, with all the babies being born."

"Do any of the little ones belong to you?"

"No," Tristyn said quickly, firmly. "I'm just a doting aunt—actual and honorary—to all of the rug rats running around."

The words were barely out of her mouth when a preschooler raced over to them, giggling as he was chased by a chocolate Lab that was as big as the child. Tristyn swept the little boy up into her arms and planted noisy kisses on each of his cheeks.

The dog plopped on its butt at their feet, tail swiping through the grass and tongue hanging out of its mouth.

Since Tristyn was fussing over the child, Cassie dropped to her knees beside the dog. Pleased with the attention, she immediately rolled onto her back. "Aren't you just the cutest thing?" she said, dutifully rubbing the animal's exposed belly.

The dog showed her agreement by swiping Cassie's chin with her tongue.

She chuckled softly. "Who does she belong to? And will they notice if I take her home with me?"

"What do you think, Oliver?" Tristyn asked the boy. "Would you notice if Cassie took Coco home with her?"

Oliver nodded solemnly.

"Well, as adorable as she is, I would never want to come between a boy and his dog," Cassie said.

"But there is supposed to be a leash between the boy and his dog," a different female voice piped up.

Cassie turned to see Braden's sister-in-law Harper with the leash in hand.

"But Coco wanted to meet Cassie," Oliver told her.

"Is that so?" his mother said, a smile tugging at her lips as she glanced at Cassie. "And have they been properly introduced now?"

Oliver nodded. "Coco gave her kisses and she didn't say 'yuck.'"

"That doesn't mean her kisses aren't yucky," Harper noted, bending down—not an easy task with her pregnant belly impeding her—to clip the leash onto the dog's collar. "Just that Cassie has better manners than your dog."

Coco looked at Harper with big soulful eyes, silently reproaching her for putting restrictions on her freedom.

She handed the leash to her son. "Please take her into the house so that she's not underfoot while Grandpa's grilling. And don't bug Grandma for a snack before dinner."

The little boy sighed but obediently trotted away with the dog in tow.

Harper watched him go, then her gaze shifted to encompass all of the people gathered in the backyard. "Now that we're back in Charisma, I find myself wondering how we ever stayed away so long."

"It might have had something to do with your contract with WMBT and *Mid-Day Miami*," Tristyn noted.

Harper nodded. "And maybe it was the right move for us at the time, but now…I'm so glad we're home."

"We all are," Tristyn told her. "If you'd stayed in Florida to have that baby, there would have been a convoy of Garretts down the I-95."

The expectant mother laughed. "Somehow, I don't doubt it," she said, then she turned her attention to Cassie. "Is this your first family event?"

Cassie nodded. "I've known Ellen for years and, through her, Saige since she was about six months old, but I only met Braden in March."

"The man moves fast," his sister-in-law noted, a suggestive sparkle in her eye.

Cassie felt her cheeks heat and hoped the reaction might be attributed to the afternoon sun. "We're friends," she said.

"Uh-huh," Harper agreed, smiling.

"It's true," Tristyn piped up in Cassie's defense. Or so she thought until the other woman spoke again. "In fact, they were very friendly in the shed just a little while ago."

"We were looking for a soccer ball for the kids," Cassie explained.

"And Braden thought a soccer ball might be hiding in your clothes?"

Now her cheeks weren't just hot, they were burning.

Harper chuckled but showed mercy by shifting her cousin's attention away from Cassie. "I'm going to make sure Coco isn't tripping up everyone in the kitchen."

"I should probably go in, too," Cassie said. "To give Ellen a hand."

"She has all the help she needs in the kitchen," Tristyn assured her. "The aunts have been managing family get-togethers for more years than I've been alive, and the meal preparation is more expertly choreographed than the dancers in a Beyoncé video."

Cassie couldn't help but smile at the mental image the other woman's words evoked. "I don't doubt that's true."

"The bar, on the other hand, looks abandoned," Tristyn said, linking her arm through Cassie's and guiding her in that direction.

"We're going to work the bar?"

Braden's cousin grinned. "No, we're going to get you a drink to accompany the dish I'm going to give you on my cousin."

Chapter Fifteen

Cassie would gladly have paid admission to spend a Day with the Garrett Clan—as Braden referred to it. It was a little chaotic and a lot of fun and she loved watching the interactions of his family. There was also much talking and teasing and more food than she'd ever seen in one place in her life. So she ate and she mingled and she found herself falling even more in love—not just with the man but with his whole family.

It was hard to keep track of who were siblings and who were cousins, because they were all "aunt" and "uncle" to little ones. Cassie had no experience with close-knit families like the Garretts. Growing up, she vaguely remembered a set of grandparents in Utah—her father's parents—who had sent cards at Christmas and on birthdays, but they'd both died a couple of years before Amanda did. Her mother had refused to talk about her family, so if she had any relatives on that side, Cassie had never known them.

For almost two years, the first two years after her mom had married Ray, Cassie had felt as if she was part of a real family. For the first time that she could remember, she'd lived with both a mother and a father, her sister and two stepbrothers, and it had been nice. Normal.

Even when she'd cringed at demonstrations of Ray's temper, she'd thought that was normal because she'd never really known anything different. But this was even better than that—this was the family she'd always dreamed of having someday, and being here with Braden gave her hope that the dream might be within her grasp.

"You sure do know how to throw a party," Cassie said to the hostess, when Ellen brought out a fresh pitcher of sweet tea and set it on the table with a stack of plastic glasses.

Braden's mom beamed proudly. "It's always fun getting the family together."

"It's nice that they could all be here," she commented.

And she meant it. She envied Braden having grown up with Ellen and John as parents, and she was glad that Saige, despite not having a mother, would grow up secure in the knowledge that she was loved.

"Family means a lot to all of us," Ellen said. "And although I understood why Ryan and Harper wanted to move to Florida, I can't deny that—for the past three years—I've felt as if a part of my heart was missing."

"I guess a mother never stops worrying about her children—even when they have children of their own."

"That's the truth," Ellen confirmed. "But now that all of my boys are home and happy, I'm looking forward to focusing on and enjoying my grandchildren—and maybe planning another wedding in the not-too-distant future."

Cassie suspected that Ellen was hoping for some insights about her relationship with Braden, but she had none to give her. "Speaking of your grandchildren," she said, because she didn't dare comment on the latter part of Ellen's remark, "it looks like Saige wore more ice cream than she ate. I'm going to wash her up before she puts her sticky fingers on everything."

"There's a change table in the first bedroom at the top of the stairs," Ellen told her.

"Great," Cassie said, then scooped up the little girl and made her escape.

Braden was catching up with his middle brother when he caught a glimpse of Saige out of the corner of his eye. She'd been sitting on a blanket spread out on the grass with several other kids, all of them enjoying ice-cream sandwiches under the watchful eye of Maura, one of the oldest cousins. Having finished her frozen treat, Saige stood up and turned toward the house. He saw then that she hadn't actually eaten her dessert but painted her face and shirt with it.

He started to excuse himself to take her inside to wash up, but before he could interrupt Justin's ER story, he saw Cassie pick up his daughter and carry her toward the house. He couldn't hear what she said, but whatever it was, it made Saige giggle.

He never got tired of watching Cassie with Saige. She was so good with his daughter, so easy and natural. The first day he'd attended Baby Talk at the library, he'd been impressed by her humor and patience. If there was ever a woman who was meant to be a mother—and hopefully Saige's mother—it was Cassie.

"You haven't heard a word I've said," Justin accused.

"What?"

His brother shook his head. "Never mind."

"Why are you grinning?" Braden asked suspiciously.

"Because I never thought I'd see you like this," Justin admitted.

"Like what?" Braden asked.

"Head over heels. And—more important—happy."

He scowled. "What are you talking about?"

"I don't know if you really thought you were fooling anyone, but we could all tell that you were miserable in the last few years of your marriage, at least until Saige came along."

Braden couldn't deny it.

"It's nice to see you happy again," Justin said. "And if Cassie's the reason for that, you'd be smart to hold on to her."

"I intend to," he said, and headed into the house.

He found Cassie in the nursery—formerly Ryan's childhood bedroom that his parents had redone in anticipation of their first grandchild. It had been several more years before they'd actually needed it, but the room was in frequent use now whenever Ellen and John looked after Vanessa for Justin and Avery, or—even more frequently—Saige for Braden. In fact, his parents were talking about adding a second crib and a couple of toddler beds to ensure they'd be able to accommodate all of the grandchildren now that Ryan and Harper were back in Charisma with Oliver and another baby on the way.

"I wondered where you disappeared to," Braden said to Cassie.

She glanced over and smiled at him. "Saige had ice cream all over her, so I brought her in to wash up and change her clothes, then she started yawning and I realized it was getting close to her bedtime, so I decided to put her pajamas on her instead."

"You could have asked me to do it," he protested.

"You were busy with your brother, and I didn't mind," she said, as she fastened the snaps of Saige's one-piece sleeper.

The little girl lifted her arms, indicating her desire to be picked up. As soon as Cassie had done so, Saige laid her head on her shoulder and closed her eyes.

"I think all the excitement today has worn her out," Cassie said.

"No doubt," he agreed. "How about you?"

"I had a great day," she said. "I really enjoyed being here, watching you with your family. It's rare to see so many members of three different generations and all of them so close."

He lifted Saige from her arms and carried his daughter over to the crib, setting her gently down on the mattress, before turning back to Cassie again. "I'm glad that Saige has cousins of a similar age, although I haven't given up hope that she might have a brother or a sister—or both—someday, too."

"You should have more kids," Cassie said. "You're a wonderful father."

"Thanks, but first I'd have to find a woman who's willing to take on the challenges of a widower and his adopted daughter."

"I don't think you'll have too much trouble with that," she said, her tone light and teasing. "Your little girl is pretty darn cute."

"What about her dad?" he prompted.

Cassie smiled. "He's not hard to look at, either."

"Of course, she'd also have to be willing to put up with my family."

"Your family is wonderful," she assured him.

"Most of the time," he agreed. "I'm glad to see that you survived your first Garrett family gathering without any visible signs of trauma."

"First?"

He took her hands and linked their fingers together. "I

hope it's only the first of many, because being here with you today, I realized that this is where you belong—with me and Saige."

And then he released one of her hands to reach into the side pocket of his cargo shorts and pull out a small velvet box.

Cassie's eyes went wide when he offered it to her, but she made no move to take it.

So he flipped open the hinged lid with his thumb, revealing a princess-cut diamond solitaire set on a simple platinum band. "I'm asking you to marry me, Cassie. To be my wife and a mother to my daughter—and any other children we may have."

She stared at the ring in his hand, stunned.

Because while she had undeniably thought about the possibility of a future with Braden and Saige, she'd counseled her eager heart to be patient. Even if she believed Braden's claim that he wasn't still mourning the death of his wife, he'd experienced a lot of changes in his life over the past seventeen months and she didn't imagine that he was eager to make any more right now. And although he'd recently hinted that he was falling for her, she hadn't expected this.

"I know it's fast," he acknowledged, when she failed to respond. "And if it's too soon, I can wait. But I don't want to wait. I want to start the rest of my life with you as soon as possible."

And with those words, her heart filled with so much joy, her chest actually ached. "I want that, too," she finally said.

His lips curved then, and the warmth and happiness in his smile arrowed straight to her heart. Maybe this was fast—certainly a lot faster than she'd expected—but it felt so right. And when he took her hand and slid the ring onto her finger, it fit right, too.

* * *

"I didn't think we were ever going to get away," Braden said, when they finally left his parents' house a few hours later.

"It's your own fault," Cassie told him. "After you announced our engagement, your mother insisted on opening half a dozen bottles of champagne, and then everyone wanted to toast to something."

"Maybe I should have waited for a more private venue," he acknowledged. "But seeing you with my family today, how perfectly you fit, I knew there wouldn't be a more perfect moment.

"And Tristyn, in particular, was thrilled about the engagement, because our impending wedding plans ensure that the focus of attention will be shifted away from her, at least until after the ceremony."

"Is she usually the focus of attention?"

"Only since Lauryn and Ryder got married," he told her.

"And her other sister, Jordyn, is the artist married to Marco Palermo and who has the twin boys?"

"You must have been taking notes," he mused.

"A notebook would have come in handy," she told him. "Because not fifteen minutes after meeting Tristyn, I couldn't remember her name."

"Well, I'm impressed," he said. "And the combination of Lauryn's recent wedding with Jordyn's pregnancy has everyone wanting to know when Tristyn's going to settle down."

"But she's with Josh, right?"

Braden scowled. "Where did you ever get that idea?"

"From the fact that he didn't take his eyes off her the whole day."

The furrow in his brow deepened. "Really?"

"Or maybe I just assumed they were together, because

everyone else was paired up," she offered as an alternate explanation, attempting to appease him.

"Well, they're not together," he assured her. "Josh is a friend of Daniel's and his partner in Garrett/Slater Racing."

"So is Tristyn the only one who isn't married?"

"No, Nora is single, too, but her half-sister status provides a little bit of insulation from most of the familial nosiness," he told her.

"They're not nosy," she protested. "They're interested."

"Wait until they all want to help plan the wedding—then you can let me know if they're interested or interfering."

Cassie didn't get a chance to announce her engagement to her coworkers on Monday, because as soon as Stacey saw the ring on her finger, she squealed with excitement—an instinctive reaction that prompted a fierce shushing from Helen. She immediately grabbed Cassie's arm and dragged her into the staff room where they could talk without fear of reprisal.

"Ohmygod," Stacey said, her gaze riveted on the rock. "Is that thing real?"

"I haven't actually tried to cut glass with it, but I assume so," Cassie told her friend.

"Braden?"

"No, Mr. Pasternak," she said dryly, giving the name of one of their oldest patrons, who had a habit of falling asleep in the magazine section.

Stacey rolled her eyes. "Okay—stupid question. But when? Where? How?"

She smiled at the barrage of questions, happy to share the details and some of her own euphoria. "Last night. During a barbecue at his parents' house."

"He proposed to you in front of everyone?"

She shook her head. "No, it was just me and Braden. And Saige—but she was sleeping."

Her friend sighed dreamily. "So...when's the wedding?"

"We haven't set a date yet."

"What are you thinking—summer? Fall?"

"I really haven't had a chance to think about it," Cassie admitted. "Everything has happened so fast. In fact, when I woke up this morning, I had to look at my finger to be sure it wasn't a dream."

"It's a dream come true," Stacey said. "You're going to be Braden Garrett's wife and a mother to his baby girl." She sighed again. "Who would have guessed, the first day he came in here, that you'd be engaged to him less than three months later?"

"Everything did happen fast, didn't it?"

"Love doesn't have any particular timetable," Stacey said. "It's more about the person than the days."

Cassie rolled her eyes. "Are you giving me Pinterest advice now, too?"

"No, that's something I learned from my own experience," her friend said. "I knew that when you met the right man, he would love you as much as you love him."

Cassie smiled at that, but as she glanced at her engagement ring, the usual joy was tempered by doubts and questions.

And when she sat back down at her desk to prepare the schedule for the kids' summer reading club, Stacey's words echoed in the back of Cassie's mind, making her wonder: Did Braden love her as much as she loved him?

Did he love her at all?

Because now that she was thinking about it, she couldn't recall that he'd ever actually spoken those words to her. Not even after they'd made love, when she'd been snuggled in his embrace and whispered the words to him. Instead, he'd kissed her again, and she'd assumed that was proof he felt the same way. Now she wasn't so sure—and she hated the uncertainty.

But she pushed aside her worries and concerns. After all, a lot of men weren't comfortable putting their feelings into words. The fact that he'd asked her to marry him told her everything that she needed to know about his feelings.

Still, she was immensely grateful when a trio of seventh graders came in and asked her to help them find some books for a research project and she was able to focus on something other than the words Braden had never spoken.

It was nearly three weeks after the barbecue at his parents' house before Braden saw Ryan again. Of course, he knew his youngest brother was busy getting his family settled into a new house and transferring his job back to his old office, so he was pleased when Ryan showed up at his door after dinner on Wednesday night.

"There's a Prius in your driveway," Ryan noted.

Braden smiled. "Yeah, it's Cassie's car."

"Has she moved in with you then?"

"No," he admitted. "So far I've only managed to persuade her to bring a few things over, but she's sleeping here most nights."

"Does that mean I've come at a bad time?" his brother wondered.

"It depends on what you want."

"A beer?"

"I've got a few of those," he agreed. "Come on in."

Ryan followed him to the kitchen, where Braden took two bottles from the fridge and twisted off the caps, then handed one to his brother.

"Are you settled into the new house?"

"Mostly," Ryan said, following him out onto the back deck. "Of course, it's a lot bigger than the condo we had in Florida, so some of the rooms are still empty."

"Too bad there isn't a furniture store anywhere in this town," Braden said dryly.

Ryan grinned as he settled back in an Adirondack chair, his legs stretched out in front of him. "Yeah, Harper's already been to the showroom three times."

"She doesn't like anything?"

"She likes *everything*."

"Well, maybe we'll set you up with a friends and family discount."

"Speaking of friends and family—"

"Why do I sense that you're now getting to the true purpose of your visit?"

Ryan tipped his bottle to his lips, drank. "Maybe it's none of my business—Harper told me it's none of my business," he admitted.

"It's generally good advice to listen to your wife," Braden told him.

"It probably is, but I can't deny that I'm a little worried you're rushing into marriage with Cassie."

He frowned at that. "Do you have a problem with my fiancée?"

"No," his brother quickly assured him. "She's great. In fact, she just might be perfect for you."

"Then why the concern?" he asked warily.

"Because I know you haven't known her very long. And because I know you were unhappy in the last few years of your marriage to Dana. And because you told me, after her funeral, that you felt guilty about failing in your promise to Saige's birth mom to give her daughter a real family."

"I'm still not seeing your point," he said, although he was beginning to suspect that he did.

"I can't help wondering—are you marrying Cassie because you want her for your wife? Or because you want her to be Saige's mother?"

"Considering that our marriage will put her in both of those roles, why do the reasons matter?" Braden countered. "And why are you in my face about this when you got married to give Oliver a family?"

"Because Oliver's aunt was suing for custody and we needed to ensure that he stayed with us, because that's what his parents wanted."

"And Saige's birth mother wanted her to have two parents—to grow up in a real family. And just as you would do anything for your son, I will do anything for my daughter."

"The difference being that when Harper and I decided to get married, we both knew why we were doing it."

"I want to marry Cassie," Braden assured his brother. "She's an incredible woman—warm and kind and generous. And Saige absolutely adores her."

"But do you love her?" Ryan pressed.

He tipped his bottle to his lips. "I will honor the vows I make to her on our wedding day," he finally said.

His brother shook his head, clearly unsatisfied with that answer. "She's in love with you, Braden. How long do you think it's going to take her to figure out that her feelings aren't reciprocated? And," he continued without giving Braden an opportunity to respond, "what do you think she'll do when she figures it out?"

"Getting married will give us both what we want," Braden insisted.

"I hope you're right," Ryan said. "Because losing another mother will be a lot harder on your daughter than growing up without one."

* * *

Cassie stood by the open window in Saige's bedroom, frozen by the conversation that drifted up from the deck as she lifted Braden's sleepy daughter into her arms. She'd just finished reading a story to the little girl and intended to take her downstairs to say good-night to her daddy when she heard voices from below and realized that he had company.

She hadn't intended to eavesdrop, but she couldn't avoid overhearing their conversation—and couldn't stop listening when she realized that they were talking about her.

I want to marry Cassie. She's an incredible woman—warm and kind and generous. And Saige absolutely adores her.

But do you love her?

Her breath caught as she waited for Braden to reply.

I will honor the vows I make to her on our wedding day.

The response answered not just his brother's question but her own, and with those few words, the joy leaked from her wounded heart like air from a punctured tire.

How long do you think it's going to take her to figure out that her feelings aren't reciprocated?

Well, Ryan's conversation with his brother had taken care of that for her. While she'd managed to disregard her own niggling doubts for the past few weeks, she could do so no longer.

And what do you think she'll do when she figures it out?

Cassie forced herself to move away from the window, but she couldn't force herself to answer that question. She didn't want to answer that question. She didn't want to do anything except go back ten minutes in time and never overhear Braden and Ryan's conversation.

Because she could live with her own doubts and uncertainties. As long as she had Braden and Saige, she could live with almost anything. But the one thing she could not live with was the absolute knowledge that the man she planned to marry—the man she loved with her whole heart—didn't love her back.

Unshed tears burned the back of her eyes as she rocked Saige to sleep for what she knew might be the very last time. She couldn't blame Braden. There had been so many clues as to his motivation—most notably Lindsay's visit and her threat to have the adoption revoked—but Cassie had refused to see them.

I will do anything for my daughter.

She'd always known he wanted a mother for Saige— he'd made no secret of that fact. But she'd let herself hope and believe that he wanted her, too. That when he took her in his arms and made love to her, it was because he did love her.

I will honor the vows I make to her...

An admirable sentiment but not the words she'd wanted to hear. Not what she needed from him.

Saige exhaled a shuddery sigh as her thumb slipped out of her mouth, a signal that the little girl was truly and deeply asleep. Cassie reluctantly pushed herself out of the chair and touched her lips to the top of the baby's head before she gently laid her in the crib and tucked her sock monkey under her arm.

Then she walked across the hall to Braden's room and the bed that she'd shared with him almost every night for the past several weeks. Peering through the window, she saw that his brother's car was still in the driveway. Though it was much earlier than she usually went to bed, she put on her pajamas, picked up a book and crawled between the covers. And when Braden finally came upstairs, she pretended to be asleep.

She heard his footsteps cross the floor, then he gently removed the book from her hand and set it on "her" bedside table before turning off the lamp. He moved away again, and she heard the quiet click of the bathroom door closing. A few minutes later, he crawled into bed with her, his arm automatically snaking around her waist and drawing her close, nestling their bodies together like spoons.

She'd been surprised to discover that he liked to sleep snuggled up to her. He protested, vehemently, when she accused him of being a cuddler, so she stopped teasing him because it didn't matter what he called it—the simple truth was that she slept so much better when she was in his arms. It was something that had become a habit far too easily and one that she would have to break. But not tonight.

It didn't take long for his breathing to settle into the slow, regular rhythm that told her he'd succumbed to slumber. And only then, when she was certain he was sleeping, did she let her tears fall, confident that they would dry by morning, leaving no evidence of her heartbreak on the pillowcase.

Chapter Sixteen

It was harder than she'd thought it would be to go through the motions the next day. She was distracted and unfocused at work, unable to concentrate on the most menial tasks. Though she hated to do it, she called Stacey to cover the Soc & Study group that night so that she could take some time at home and figure out her life and her future.

Truthfully, she knew what she had to do, but that didn't make the doing any easier. She loved Braden and Saige and she wanted nothing more than to be part of their family. She wanted to marry the man she loved, but she couldn't marry a man who didn't love her.

She needed to talk to Braden about the conversation she'd overheard, and she didn't want to fall apart when she did. So she spent the afternoon at home with her cats, trying to prepare herself for the inevitable confrontation. But whenever she thought about saying goodbye, the tears would spill over again. When she reached for a tissue to wipe her nose, Buttercup jumped up onto the sofa and crawled into Cassie's lap—which only made her cry harder. And Westley, who rarely paid attention to anything that wasn't dinner, eventually took pity on her and crawled into her lap beside his sister, too.

She gave them tinned food for dinner, because she figured they deserved a reward for their unsolicited support and comfort. And as she watched them chow down, she decided that maybe being a crazy cat lady wasn't so bad.

When they were finished eating, she knew that she'd stalled as long as she could. She dried her eyes again, got into her car and drove to Forrest Hill.

"I thought you had the Soc & Study group tonight," Braden said when he responded to the doorbell and found her standing on the porch. "And why didn't you use your key?"

"Stacey agreed to fill in for me," she said, ignoring the second part of his comment.

He stepped away from the door. "Are you hungry? Saige and I ate a while ago, but I can heat up some leftover lasagna for you."

She shook her head. "No, thanks."

"Well, I'm glad you're here," he said, his tone as sincere as the smile that tugged at her heart. "I got official notice from the court today that Lindsay withdrew her application to reverse the adoption."

"Oh, Braden, that is wonderful news," she said, genuinely thrilled that he wouldn't have to battle for custody of his daughter.

"And to celebrate, Saige has been working on something for you."

At that revelation, her carefully rehearsed words stuck in her throat. "For me?"

"Uh-huh." He took her hand and led her into the living

room where the little girl was playing at the train table. "Look who's here, Saige."

The toddler looked up, her lips immediately stretching into a wide smile when she saw Cassie. "Ma-ma."

Cassie instinctively squeezed Braden's hand as her throat constricted and her eyes filled with tears. Then she remembered why she was here, and she extricated her fingers from his.

"P'ay?" Saige asked hopefully.

"Not right now, sweetie."

Braden lifted a hand and gently brushed away the single tear that she hadn't realized had escaped to slide down her cheek. "What's wrong, Cassie?"

She could only shake her head, because her throat was too tight for words.

He took her hand again and led her to the sofa. "Tell me what's going on. Please."

She drew in a slow, deep breath and lifted her gaze to his. "I need to ask you something."

"Anything," he said.

"Do you love me?"

He drew back, instinctively and physically, which she recognized as his answer even before he said anything.

"Where is this coming from?" he asked.

"It's a simple question," she told him.

"It's a ridiculous question," he said, obviously still attempting to dance around it. "I asked you to marry me—doesn't that tell you how I feel about you?"

"Maybe it should," she acknowledged. "But I'd still like to hear it."

"I want to spend my life with you," he told her, and he sounded sincere. But even if it was true, it wasn't a declaration of love.

"Because Saige needs a mother? Because I complete your family?"

"Where is this coming from?" Braden asked again, his uneasiness growing as she tossed out questions he wasn't sure he knew how to answer.

"I heard you talking to your brother last night," she admitted. "When you told him that you were marrying me to give Saige the family you'd promised she would have when you adopted her."

And to think that he'd actually been happy when his brother had moved back to town.

"Why is it wrong to want a family for my daughter?" he said, still hoping to sidestep her concerns and smooth everything over.

"It's not," she said. "In fact, many people would say it's admirable. Especially the lengths to which you're willing to go to give it to her."

"You're losing me," he told her. But even more frustrating was the realization that *he* was in danger of losing *her*.

"Maybe I'm almost thirty years old, maybe I won't ever have a better offer, but I want not just to fall in love, but to be loved in return. I want the fairy tale." She slid her engagement ring off and set it on the table. "And I'm not willing to settle for anything less."

The sadness and resignation in her tone slayed him as much as her removal of the ring he'd put on her finger. "Cassie—"

She shook her head. "Don't."

"Don't what?" he asked, torn between bafflement and panic.

"Don't tell me again that you care or that we're really good together. Don't tell me again that Saige adores me. Don't paint rosy pictures of the future we can have together." She looked at him, the tears in her eyes slicing like knives through his heart. "Please don't tempt me to settle for less than I deserve, because I love you so much I might be willing to do it."

She was right. As much as Braden didn't want to admit it, she was right. When he'd asked her to marry him, he'd been selfish. He'd been thinking only of what he wanted—for himself and his daughter. He'd wanted to give Saige the security of the family that he knew they could be if Cassie agreed to be his wife.

And all the while that he'd been courting her, he'd known that he wasn't going to fall in love with her. It was no defense that he'd warned her against falling in love with him—because he'd then done everything in his power to make her forget that warning.

She did deserve more—so much more than he could give her. Because it was the only thing left to say, he finally said, "I'm sorry."

"So am I," she told him. Then, with tears still shining in her eyes, she turned and walked away.

And he let her go.

"Ma-ma?" Saige said as the door closed behind Cassie.

With a sigh, Braden lifted her into his lap and hugged her tight.

Losing another mother will be a lot harder on your daughter than growing up without one.

"I guess your uncle Ryan is smarter than he looks," he said regretfully.

But he knew the emptiness he felt inside wasn't just for Saige. An hour earlier, he'd been looking toward his future with Cassie and his heart had been filled with hope and joy. Now he was looking at the ring she'd taken off her finger and he felt as cold and empty as the platinum circle on the glass table.

* * *

Megan dropped a pile of bridal magazines on Cassie's desk when she came into the library Friday morning. "I've been planning my wedding for years and since I'm not any closer to finding a groom now than when I started, I thought you might want to look through these to get some ideas for your big day."

"Thanks," Cassie said. "But I'm not going to need them."

"Don't you dare tell me you're planning to elope," Megan warned.

"No, we're not planning to elope."

"You're hiring a wedding planner," was her coworker's second guess.

Cassie shook her head. "We're not getting married."

Her friend stared at her, stunned. "What are you talking about?"

"I gave Braden back his ring last night."

"What?" Megan's gaze dropped to her now-bare left hand. *"Why?"*

"Because I want to be someone's first choice."

Her friend frowned. "Is this because he was married before?"

"No. It's because he doesn't love me," she admitted softly, her heart breaking all over again to admit the truth aloud.

"Why would you say that?" Megan demanded.

"Because it's true."

"The man asked you to marry him," her coworker reminded her.

She nodded. "And fool that I was, it took me almost three weeks to realize that every time he talked about our future, he never once said that he loved me. Even when I said it first, he never said it back."

"A lot of men aren't comfortable with the words," Megan noted.

"A man who claims he's ready to commit himself in marriage should be."

Unable to dispute the truth of that, her friend picked up the pile of magazines again. "I'll put these in the staff room...just in case."

Cassie didn't argue, but she knew there wasn't going to be any "just in case." She also knew that the awkward and difficult conversation with Megan was only the first of many she would have over the next few weeks.

The problem with sharing the happy news of her engagement with so many people was that she had to either pretend she was still happily engaged—albeit not wearing a ring—or admit that the shortest engagement in the history of the world was over.

Okay, she knew that was probably an exaggeration. After all there were plenty of celebrity marriages that hadn't even lasted as long as her engagement. Or at least one, she mentally amended, thinking of Britney Spears's famous fifty-five hour nuptials.

Of course, everyone had words of advice ranging from "give him another chance" to "you'll find someone else." Cassie knew they meant well, but no advice could heal a heart that was cracked wide-open.

Almost as bad as the aching emptiness in her chest was the realization that she dreaded going into work Tuesday morning. When she woke up, she wanted to pull the covers over her head and pretend that she was sick so she could stay home with her cats and avoid seeing Braden's mother and daughter. The apprehension was an uncomfortable weight in her belly, but it also helped her stiffen her spine. Because she loved her job and she wasn't going to let a failed relationship take that joy from her.

Still, she had to force a smile for her Baby Talk class. It was all she could do to hold back the tears when Saige released her grandmother's hand and ran to Cassie, wrapping herself around her legs, but she went through the motions. And because all of the caregivers were focused on their children, no one seemed to realize anything was wrong.

But after class had ended and everyone else was gone, Ellen approached her. Cassie braced herself, not sure what to expect from the woman she'd always liked and respected but who didn't understand the concept of boundaries. So she was surprised when Ellen didn't say anything about the failed engagement. In fact, she didn't say anything at all; she just reached for Cassie's hand as she walked past her on the way out, giving it a gentle but somehow reassuring squeeze.

If she was surprised by Braden's mother's discretion and unexpected show of support, she was even more surprised when Irene defended Braden, insisting that his feelings for Cassie were probably deeper than he was willing to acknowledge.

Cassie appreciated the sentiment but she refused to believe it, refused to let herself hope and have her hopes trampled again.

Braden didn't want to talk about the break-up with Cassie, so he didn't. Whenever anyone asked about her, he said she was doing great. If someone wanted to chat about the wedding, he just said they hadn't figured out any details yet. And while he knew the truth would eventually come out, he was feeling too raw to deal with it right now.

Of course, his mother didn't care about that.

"I'm a little confused," she said, when he picked Saige up after work on Tuesday. "On the weekend, we were talking about potential wedding venues, and then, when I took Saige to the library for Baby Talk today, I discovered that Cassie wasn't wearing her engagement ring."

"Maybe it needs to be sized," he suggested.

"Even if that was true, it doesn't explain why your supposed fiancée looked as if her heart was broken."

"I don't know why her heart would be broken," he grumbled, finally giving up the pretense that everything was status quo. "She was the one who decided to give me back the ring."

"And I've known Cassie long enough to know that she wouldn't have done so without a good reason, so what was it?"

He busied himself sorting through a pile of miscellaneous stuff—junk mail, flyers and the book Cassie had lent to him from her personal library—on the kitchen island. "Because I didn't echo the words back when she told me that she loved me," he finally admitted.

Ellen frowned. "And why didn't you?"

"Because I was trying to be honest about my feelings and I didn't want our marriage to be based on a deception."

His mother stared at him for several long seconds before she let out a weary sigh. "Now I see the problem."

"I'm not going to fall in love again."

She shook her head. "The problem is that you actually believe that's true."

"Because it *is* true," he insisted.

"Honey, you wouldn't be this miserable if you didn't love her."

He set the book on top of the pile so that he could return it to her. Except she might think he was using the book as an excuse to see her again—and maybe he would be. "I'm miserable because I let my daughter down. Again."

"If that's your biggest concern, maybe you should give Heather Turcotte a call," Ellen suggested. "She was asking about you at the library again today."

"Geez, Mom, can you give me five minutes to catch

my breath before you start tossing more potential Mrs. Garretts at me?"

"Why do you need time?" his mother challenged. "If you aren't in love with Cassie—if all you want is a mother for Saige—why aren't you eager to move ahead toward that goal?"

He opened his mouth, closed it again. "I really am an idiot, aren't I?"

"As much as it pains me to admit it—in this situation—I have to answer that question with a resounding yes."

He sighed. "What am I supposed to do now?"

"You figured out how to screw it up all by yourself, I have faith that you can figure out how to fix it."

He sincerely hoped she was right.

Braden knew that after refusing to say the words Cassie had wanted to hear, she would doubt their veracity when he said them to her now. But how was a man supposed to prove his feelings? What kind of grand gesture would convince her how much she meant to him?

It took him a while to come up with a plan—and a lot longer to be able to implement it. So it was almost three weeks after she'd given him back his ring before he was ready to face her again—to put his heart and their future on the line.

The moment Cassie saw him waiting on her porch, her steps faltered. He forced himself to stay where he was, to wait for her to draw nearer, but it wasn't easy. The last few weeks without her had been the emptiest weeks of his life, and he wanted nothing more than to take her in his arms and just hold her for a minute. An hour. Forever.

She came up the stairs slowly, pausing beside the front door. "What are you doing here, Braden?"

"I needed to talk to you and you haven't returned any of my calls."

"Maybe I didn't return your calls because I didn't want to talk to you," she suggested.

"I considered that possibility," he acknowledged. "But it's not in my nature to give up that easily."

"Where's Saige?"

"With my parents. I didn't want this to be about anything but you and me."

"I have things to do," she said. "So please say whatever you need to say and then go."

"I love you, Cassie."

She looked away, but not before he saw the shimmer of tears in her eyes. She didn't say anything for a long moment, and then she shook her head. "It's not enough to say it—you have to mean it."

"But I *do* mean it," he told her. "I meant it even when I couldn't bring myself to say it, but I didn't want to admit the truth of my feelings because I'd promised myself that I wouldn't fall in love again.

"I want you in my life, Cassie. I *need* you in my life. I don't even care if you don't want to put the ring back on your finger—not yet. I want to marry you, I want to spend my life with you, and yes—I do want you to be Saige's mother because you're so great with her and I know how much she loves you. But most importantly, I just want to be with you, because my life is empty without you.

"When I finally realized I loved you, I tried to figure out why—what it was about you that made me fall in love with you. And I discovered that it wasn't any *one* thing— it was *every*thing. And every day I'm with you, I discover something new that makes me love you even more than the day before."

"You're doing it again," she whispered softly. "Saying all of the right things."

"But?" he reluctantly prompted, because he could hear the unspoken word in the tone of her voice.

"But you're a businessman. You know how to close a deal. I don't know if you really mean what you're saying or if you're saying it because you know it's what I want to hear."

"You have every reason to be wary," he acknowledged. "I'm asking you to trust in feelings that I wouldn't even acknowledge a few weeks ago."

She nodded.

"So give me a chance to prove my feelings are real," he suggested.

"How?" she asked, obviously still skeptical.

"Come home with me so that I can show you something."

Home.

The word wrapped around her like a favorite sweater—warm and comforting and oh-so-tempting.

Except that the home he was referring to wasn't her home, only where he lived with his daughter.

"The last time I fell for that line was my first year at college," she said, feigning a casualness she didn't feel.

"It's not a line," he assured her.

Cassie sighed, but her resistance had already crumbled. It wasn't just that she couldn't say no to him but that she didn't want to. She didn't want to shut him out—she wanted him to force open the doors of her heart and prove that he loved her.

She didn't know what, if anything, could make her trust that the feelings he claimed to have for her now were real, but she was willing to give him a chance. The past three weeks without him had been so achingly empty, because she loved him so much she wanted to believe a future for them was possible.

"I need to feed the cats," she said.

"I'll wait."

Cassie noticed the changes as soon as she stepped through the front door and into the wide foyer of Braden's house. The previously bland off-white walls had been painted a warm pale gold. The color was still subtle but it drew out the gold vein in the floor tile and provided a sharper contrast for the white trim.

The living room was a pale moss green and the furniture was all new—the off-white leather sofa and armchairs having been replaced by a dark green sectional with a chaise lounge, and the contemporary glass-and-metal occasional tables replaced by mission-style tables in dark walnut. The only piece of furniture that remained from her last visit was Saige's train table.

"End of season sale at Garrett Furniture?" she asked, her tone deliberately light.

"Something like that," he agreed.

"And the paint?"

"My cousin Jordyn. You seemed to like what she did in Saige's room, so I asked her to pick out the colors."

"She has a good eye," she noted.

As they continued the tour, she discovered that every single room—aside from Saige's—had been redone. Not all of them had new furnishings, but each had at least been repainted with decorative accents added.

"Why did you do all of this?"

"It's partly symbolic," he confessed. "To illustrate the warmth and color you brought back into my life. But it's mostly practical, because I hoped that if you actually liked my house you might want to spend more time here, and maybe reconsider moving in. Of course, if there's anything you don't like, we can change it. We can change everything, if you want."

"I do like your house," she told him. "And everything looks fabulous, but—"

"Hold that thought," he said. "There's still one more room to see."

She'd been so amazed by the changes he'd made throughout the house, she hadn't realized that he'd ushered her past the main floor den until he paused there now. He seemed more nervous about this room than any other, which made her even more curious about what was behind the closed doors.

"The painting was simple and, with a full crew of men working round the clock, pretty quick," he told her. "But I wanted some more significant changes made in this room—which is what took so long. Thankfully, Ryder put me in touch with the right people or I'd still be waiting."

Then he opened the doors.

The room, originally a simple main floor office with a desk and a few bookcases, had been transformed to include floor-to-ceiling bookcases, lots of comfortable seating and a fireplace that was almost an exact replica of the one in Cassie's living room.

She had to clear the lump out of her throat before she could speak. "The bookcases are empty," she finally said.

"Not completely," he said, taking her hand and drawing her over to a shelf between two windows where she could see a single book lying on its side: *The Princess Bride: S. Morgenstern's Classic Tale of True Love and High Adventure* by William Goldman.

"Did you read it?" she asked him.

He nodded. "I'm not sure I agree it was better than the movie, but it was a good book," he acknowledged.

"You did this for me—so that I would have a place in your house for my books?"

"*Our* house," he said. "You only have to say the word and it's our house."

"What word is that?"

He pulled his hand out of his pocket and showed her the ring she'd given back to him three weeks earlier. "Yes," he told her. "When I ask again, 'Will you marry me, Cassie?' you just have to say yes."

Then he dropped to one knee and took her hand in his. "Cassie MacKinnon, I love you with my whole heart, and there's nothing I want more in this world than to spend every day of the rest of my life with you by my side. Will you marry me?"

She held his gaze, her own steady and sure, and finally answered his question, not with a yes but with the words that came straight from her heart. "As you wish."

Epilogue

February 14th

Every morning when she woke up in her husband's arms, Cassie took a moment to bask in the sheer joy of her new life.

In the five months that they'd been married, Braden had given her everything she'd ever wanted: a home, a family, love. He never missed a chance to tell her that he loved her, and though her heart still swelled each time she heard the words, he showed her the truth of those words in even more ways. Every day with Saige brought new joys and experiences, too. After waiting for so long to be a mother, Cassie was loving every minute of it.

On Valentine's Day, Cassie made a pork roast with sweet potatoes and parsnips, which Saige hated, followed by ice-cream sundaes, which Saige loved. After dinner, Braden presented Cassie with two gifts. A diamond-encrusted heart-shaped pendant and a homemade Valentine. The former was stunning, but the latter took her breath away: Braden's handprints—in red paint—were upside down and overlapped at the thumbs to form a big heart inside which Saige's handprints—in pink paint— formed a smaller heart. On the outside, making a border around the edge, he had written:

For Cassie—on our first Valentine's Day together with tons of love and thanks for being such a fabulous wife and mother and making our family complete. We love you more than you will ever know. Braden & Saige xoxoxoxoxo

Cassie's eyes filled as she read the printed words, but she didn't know the tears had spilled over until Saige asked, "Why you cwyin', Mama?"

She wiped at the wet streaks on her cheeks. "Because I love both of you more than you will ever know, too," she said.

Of course, Saige continued to look perplexed. Braden dropped a kiss on the little girl's forehead and told her to go play with her trains. She skipped out of the room, happy to comply with the request.

"Cassie?" he prompted when their daughter had gone.

"Sometimes I can't believe how much my life has changed since I met you."

"But in a good way, right?"

She managed to smile. "In the very best way," she assured him.

He plucked a tissue from the box and gently dabbed at the streaks of moisture on her cheeks. "So these are... happy tears?"

She nodded.

"Okay," he said, obviously relieved.

"But I should warn you," Cassie said, lifting her eyes to his, "I think I'm going to be one of those women who is really emotional in the first trimester."

Braden stared at her for a minute, his hand dropping away from her face as the confusion in his gaze slowly gave way to comprehension and joy. "Are you saying…?"

They'd decided to stop using birth control as soon as they were married, because they didn't know how long it might take for Cassie to get pregnant and they were hoping that Saige would have a little brother or sister sooner rather than later—which was apparently going to happen even sooner than either of them had anticipated.

But she could understand why he'd be hesitant to ask the question. Although she didn't know all the details of everything he and Dana had gone through in their efforts to conceive a child, she knew how disappointed he'd been by their lack of success—and that he would, naturally, be reluctant to hope that it would happen now.

"Yes." She took his hand and laid it on her abdomen. "I'm pregnant."

He whooped and lifted her off the chair and into his arms, spinning her around in circles. Then he stopped abruptly and set her carefully back on her feet and framed her face with his hands. "Are you all right? Have you been to see a doctor? How are you feeling?"

She laughed, a little breathlessly, before she answered each of his questions in turn. "Yes. Not yet. Happy and excited and so incredibly lucky."

The grin that spread across his face assured her that he was feeling happy, too. Even if he still looked a little dazed.

"Wow. That was…fast," he decided.

"Too fast?" she wondered.

He immediately shook his head. "No, it's not too fast," he promised. "And this news is the second best Valentine's Day present ever."

She lifted her brows. "*Second* best?"

"Second best," he confirmed. Then he lowered his head to kiss her. Softly. Deeply. "Second only to you."

* * * * *

Look for Tristyn Garrett's story,
THE LAST SINGLE GARRETT,
the next installment in award-winning
author Brenda Harlen's series for
Mills & Boon Cherish
THOSE ENGAGING GARRETTS!
On sale May 2017, wherever Mills & Boon
books and ebooks are sold.

MILLS & BOON®

Cherish™

EXPERIENCE THE ULTIMATE RUSH OF FALLING IN LOVE

A sneak peek at next month's titles...

In stores from 9th February 2017:

- **Proposal for the Wedding Planner** – Sophie Pembroke *and* **Fortune's Second-Chance Cowboy** – Marie Ferrarella
- **Return of Her Italian Duke** – Rebecca Winters *and* **The Marine Makes His Match** – Victoria Pade

In stores from 23rd February 2017:

- **The Millionaire's Royal Rescue** – Jennifer Faye *and* **Just a Little Bit Married** – Teresa Southwick
- **A Bride for the Brooding Boss** – Bella Bucannon *and* **Kiss Me, Sheriff!** – Wendy Warren

---

Just can't wait?
Buy our books online before they hit the shops!
www.millsandboon.co.uk

Also available as eBooks.

MILLS & BOON®

EXCLUSIVE EXTRACT

Pastry chef Gemma Rizzo never expected
to see Vincenzo Gagliardi again. And now
he's not just the duke who left her
broken-hearted… he's her boss!

Read on for a sneak preview of
RETURN OF HER ITALIAN DUKE

Since he'd returned to Italy, thoughts of Gemma had
come back full force. At times he'd been so preoccupied,
the guys were probably ready to give up on him. To
think that after all this time and searching for her, she
was right here. Bracing himself, he took the few steps
necessary to reach Takis's office.

With the door ajar he could see a polished-looking
woman in a blue-and-white suit with dark honey-blond
hair falling to her shoulders. She stood near the desk
with her head bowed, so he couldn't yet see her profile.

Vincenzo swallowed hard to realize Gemma was no
longer the teenager with short hair he used to spot when
she came bounding up the stone steps of the *castello*
from school wearing her uniform. She'd grown into a
curvaceous woman.

"Gemma." He said her name, but it came out gravelly.

A sharp intake of breath reverberated in the office.
She wheeled around. Those unforgettable brilliant green
eyes with the darker green rims fastened on him. A

stillness seemed to surround her. She grabbed hold of the desk.

"Vincenzo—I—I think I must be hallucinating."

"I'm in the same condition." His gaze fell on the lips he'd kissed that unforgettable night. Their shape hadn't changed, nor the lovely mold of her facial features.

She appeared to have trouble catching her breath. "What's going on? I don't understand."

"Please sit down and I'll tell you."

He could see she was trembling. When she didn't do his bidding, he said, "I have a better idea. Let's go for a ride in my car. It's parked out front. We'll drive to the lake at the back of the estate, where no one will bother us. Maybe by the time we reach it, your shock will have worn off enough to talk to me."

Hectic color spilled into her cheeks. "Surely you're joking. After ten years of silence, you suddenly show up here this morning, honestly thinking I would go anywhere with you?"

Don't miss
RETURN OF HER ITALIAN DUKE
by Rebecca Winters

Available March 2017
www.millsandboon.co.uk

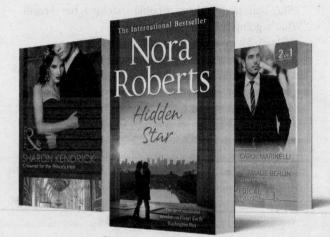

Join Britain's BIGGEST Romance Book Club

50% OFF your first parcel

- **EXCLUSIVE offers** every month

- **FREE delivery direct to your door**

- **NEVER MISS a title**

- **EARN Bonus Book points**

Call Customer Services
0844 844 1358*

or visit
millsandboon.co.uk/subscriptions

* This call will cost you 7 pence per minute plus your phone company's price per minute access charge.

KCB3